MW00780384

AT LAST SIGHT

JULIE JOHNSON

For Massachusetts.

I've been a lot of places, but I always make my way back to you.

"Those who don't believe in magic will never find it."

— ROALD DAHL

PROLOGUE

The Witch Of Salem Wood

A local ghost story

[New England origin, unknown author, late 1900s]

Beware the witch of Salem Wood
The old hag made from stick and vine
She'll steal your soul, drink your blood
But of her sins they'll find no sign

If you hear her creeping near
Moaning, groaning, in the trees
Keep still and quiet through your fear
Or her next victim you will be

For if you make a single sound
Your very voice is hers to keep
Until you're buried in the ground
Another word you'll never speak

CHAPTER ONE

I'm like an ice cube. I seem chill at first but really, I'm just moments away from a total meltdown.
- Imogen Warner, playing it cool

The door creaked open, allowing a shaft of sallow light to spill into the dark bedroom. I kept my eyes shut against it, my breaths steady as a metronome despite the sudden fear that lashed through my chest. My fight-or-flight instincts were screaming at me to do something. Flee into the night, scream like a slasher-movie heroine, clock him over the head with the nearest heavy object… *anything*, really, except lie there, listening to him stumble over the threshold.

I overrode these instincts with sheer force of will.

Stick to the plan, Imogen.

Adrian was drunk. I could smell the scotch rolling off him like cologne. On the upside, his lumbering steps down the hall had given me ample time to feign sleep. Stiller than stone on my side of the king-sized bed, I listened to a set of clumsy hands prying off a pair of shiny loafers that cost more than the junker of a car I'd purchased in secret two weeks before. (All cash, plus some extra thrown in so they'd store it for me on the lot until I was ready to make my escape.)

You're ready, I told myself for the millionth time. *You've been ready for months.*

My heart lurched as his hands fumbled for his designer belt. It hit the floor, as did his immaculately tailored slacks. He slurred a curse as he teetered off balance, catching himself on the wooden bed post. The impact rocked the whole frame.

Eventually, I felt the duvet jerked back. His tall form slid under the sheets and the mattress depressed beneath his weight. I fought the natural urge to tense, keeping my muscles relaxed and my breaths measured. All the while, praying like hell he wouldn't roll my way; praying the amount of alcohol buzzing in his veins would be enough to dampen any misguided romantic inclinations.

Whatever god was listening must've heard my heavenly bargaining because soon enough, his breathing leveled off into rhythmic snoring that reminded me of an old freight train rattling down the tracks. Some of the steel bands of trepidation squeezing my lungs loosened ever-so-slightly.

He was asleep.

Out cold.

I waited a while, until I was certain he was truly unconscious, before I risked cracking open my eyes. The beam of light spilling in from the hall prevented the room from being fully dark, but it still took a few seconds for my vision to adjust. When it did, I examined the man lying two feet away. He was on his side, facing me. His handsome face had gone slack. His perfectly toned physique — painstakingly maintained via daily sessions in the gym with his personal trainer — was hidden by thousand-thread-count sheets. In the space between our bodies, his hands clutched the duvet, balling up the fabric in his fists.

Even unconscious, some part of him was incapable of letting go.

I stared at his hands for a long time. I'd always liked his hands. They were one of the first things I noticed about him. Fine-boned and dexterous. Able to play the piano at any jazz bar with the ease of a professional entertainer, capable of throwing a dart with precision or twirling a poker chip like a magician with a disappearing coin. They packed a serious punch, too, when he put his weight behind them — something I'd learned through painful personal experience.

Believe you me, there was nothing attractive about the holes they smashed in the drywall; nothing elegant about the way they wrapped themselves around your neck and squeezed. And squeezed. And *squeezed*, until the world went black at the edges and you realized, with startling irony, that those beautiful hands could very well wind up the instrument of a particularly ugly end.

Never again, Imogen.

He'll never touch you again.

After tonight, you'll be free.

And he'll be nothing but a bad memory.

I tore my eyes away when I realized they'd drifted up to glare at his slack-mouthed, snoring face. I didn't want to look at his face. I studied his hands again instead, wondering how far I'd have to run to finally be beyond their reach. Across the state? Across the country? Across the world? Nowhere felt far enough.

Still, I had to try.

He'd given me the perfect window of opportunity — one I'd spent weeks waiting impatiently for, biding my time with teeth-grinding determination — and I was not about to waste it. Nights like tonight, after he'd been out on the town, those cunning hands of his were all thumbs, their innate polish rubbed away by an evening of shuffling losing cards and slugging down top-shelf scotch. And, more than likely, shoving fifty-dollar bills into the cleavage of the best exotic dancers Atlantic City had to offer — and there was a *lot* to offer, here in A.C. — if he and his pals decided to swing by the gentlemen's club they favored once their luck at the casino tables turned sour.

It always turned sour.

He didn't think I knew about the clubs. Or maybe he simply didn't care if I knew. Probably the latter, given that half the time he came home reeking of unfamiliar perfume with lipstick stains on his collar. (Talk about a freaking cliché.) As for me, I'd stopped caring where he spent his nights — or his mornings, or his afternoons, or any minute in between — so long ago, I could hardly remember a time before our relationship looked like this. I could hardly remember those evenings in the very beginning when I'd waited up for him to get home, pacing by the door like a little kid, the epitome of excitement.

How far we'd fallen. How low we'd sunken. To this new depth — me, lying in the dark like a petrified corpse, afraid a single hitch of my breathing might alert him to my consciousness. And him, a stranger in the body of the man I used to love.

Love.

Did I ever love him? Truly? Or did I just love the beautiful lies he fed me?

I wasn't sure. All I knew was, last autumn I fell head-over-heels for the man he allowed me to believe he was, those first few weeks. He was careful — so very careful — to hide the monster under his skin. To disguise his true nature with sweet smiles and suave words and promises about how he was going to take me away, far away, from everyone else in my life who wanted a piece of me.

And he did.

He just failed to mention that, in return, he wanted the biggest piece of all.

Unfortunately, by the time I figured that out, it was too late. He'd waited until I got close — moved my meager belongings out of my rent-by-the-week motel room and into his penthouse, let down all my careful defensive perimeters...

Then, he'd sunk his claws in.

Deep.

That's when the dashing facade dropped away, so fast it gave me whiplash. Those chivalrous layers peeled back to reveal the cruelest intentions. The raging beast beneath the smooth-talking gentleman. The insatiable user beneath the generous wine-and-diner. The controlling con-artist in the shape of my fairytale prince.

Honestly, I should've known better.

A prince?

For me?

Fat chance of that. My life was no fairytale. No one in this world was going to save me, except maybe myself. You'd think I would've learned that lesson by now, considering the amount of times I'd been jerked around, ripped off, and screwed over in my twenty-five years on earth.

Alas…

Adrian wasn't going to make all my dreams come true, like he promised he would. He wasn't going to protect me from my past. He wasn't going to be the shield that kept the harsh world at a tolerable distance.

No.

Instead, he wanted to thrust me back into the very spotlight I'd fled. Back into the public eye. Back into the life I'd spent years running from. *All hail the long-awaited return of Imogen Warner, Orlando's own Child Clairvoyant!* She of early-2000s daytime television fame. (Assuming you could call local programming on a limited broadcast network in the suburban wasteland of Florida "fame.")

Adrian didn't realize that I had no intentions of ever stepping back into those sparkly shoes. Or, he realized it, but didn't really care. His greed far outweighed any sort of loyalty to me or my stubborn convictions. In his mind, I was throwing away a golden opportunity to make some cold, hard cash. Wasting my god-given talents when, instead, I should be milking every possible penny out of them.

Don't you see, doll? It'll be great. Your name in lights again, more money than we can count… His voice had been thick with excitement, his dark eyes gleaming like a cartoon villain with dollar signs in place of irises. *I've got it all set up with some guys I know. A six-month residence at The Palace! I'll manage everything, you just have to show up and do what you do best…*

I pressed my eyes closed again, trying not to remember the outcome of that conversation. Even after almost a month, I couldn't forget how he'd advanced on me, backing me into the wall. How his handsome face contorted into a mask of rage I'd never seen before as I adamantly derailed his grand plans for fame and fortune. Those memories were scored into my mind, sharp as the shattered glass from the lamp he chucked clear across the room.

Don't walk away from me, Imogen! I'm talking to you. Why are you shaking your head? No? What do you mean, no? *Do you have any idea how hard I worked, pulling this deal together for us? Do you have any idea how fucked I'll be if you don't agree? This is happening. You'll do this. And you'll thank me when we're sitting on a mountain of millions…*

I'd known, of course. Even before that night, I'd known I had to leave him. We'd been dying for months, a steady decline with a terminal prognosis, but his announcement about the six-month gig he'd arranged for me was the final tug that yanked our life support plug from the wall.

Beep, beep, *beeeeeeeep*

Flat line.

Call it.

Time of death, 2:32AM.

A certifiable goner.

Get the morgue on the phone, pronto.

After that, nothing he did was going to change my mind. Not sweet-talking me, not threatening me, not physically trying to shake some sense into me. Not flipping furniture or smashing light fixtures. Not even a necklace of bruises, courtesy of his fine-boned fingers.

I wasn't going back to that life. It had taken me years to climb out of that pit of despair I'd been raised in. I'd fought hard for my anonymity after show business stripped it away. I'd fought even harder to rediscover my identity after so long letting other people tell me who I was.

No more.

No goddamned more.

His snores were a steady metronome as I slid out of the bed, my feet moving soundlessly across the carpeted floor toward the chair in the corner where a small pile of clothes sat waiting. I put my gloves on first, like always. If I'd had it my way I would've slept in them, but doing so pissed Adrian off even more than usual.

I'm not sleeping next to a fucking freak.

You look like a serial killer with those on.

I didn't — please, Dahmer and Bundy weren't half so stylish — but Adrian never missed an opportunity to take a shot at my confidence, especially when it came to things I was already self-conscious about.

I was fully aware how odd I appeared to outside observers, always wearing gloves, even in the heat of summer. I compensated by purchasing the most beautifully crafted ones I could find. This pair was thin, calfskin leather in a crisp linen color. Buttery smooth against my skin. Once they were on, covering me fingertips to wrists, I felt instantly calmer. More in control of myself and my surroundings.

I let out a long, low exhale.

Breathe, Imogen.

I stripped off my pajamas as quietly as possible, staring out the window as I tugged on the pair of frayed denim cut-off shorts and an oversized Baltimore Ravens sweatshirt. Through the plate glass penthouse windows, I could see the lights of the city spread out far below. It was late, but this place never seemed to shut down completely. The casino names emblazoned on rooftop signs glowed like constellations no matter the hour. The boardwalk was brightly illuminated, a rainbow ribbon of neon threading along the shoreline. The world-famous Steel Pier amusement park jutted proudly out into the Atlantic, its Ferris Wheel flashing a patriotic medley of red, white, and blue.

It was the Fourth of July in just a few days. The city was already in the throes of celebration — but I'd be long gone by the time the fireworks began.

Staring down at the world as I freed my hair from beneath the heavy hood of the sweatshirt, I felt oddly removed from it all. It was like peering into a snow globe; no matter how close I brought my nose to the glass, I'd never be part of that kaleidoscopic tableau of sound and color. I was a perpetual outsider, set ever-so-slightly apart from everyone else on the planet. Always had been, always would be.

It didn't take long to gather my things. I'd packed days ago. There was a duffle of spare clothes stashed in the trunk of the car waiting for me across town. Everything else that mattered — my driver's license, an emergency debit card, a small supply of cash, and the few sentimental items I cared about — were tucked away in a nondescript shoebox in the hallway closet. Ready to go at a moment's notice.

The moment was *now*.

The closet door hinges creaked a bit as I retrieved the box, a flinch-inducing screech in the otherwise silent penthouse. I went still, terrified Adrian might awaken, but all I heard was the distant rumble of his snoring from the bedroom. With the shoebox tucked under my arm, I shoved my feet into a pair of leather flip-flops and headed for the door.

I did not spare a single glance at the framed photograph sitting on the entryway table as I passed by. I didn't have to. I knew the image by heart: the two of us standing in front of the Rockefeller

Center Christmas tree last December, back when we were just starting out. Before Adrian turned cold and cruel, before it all went bad. He was still trying to impress me, then. Sweeping me off my feet, promising me a lifetime of weekend getaways and fancy hotels, room service and nights on the town.

What a laugh.

That was the only trip we ever took. The past seven months, we'd never left the A.C. strip. Adrian didn't like to stray too far from the casinos. (The men he owed money to liked it even less.)

I stepped out into the mellow light of the corridor and let the front door click shut at my back. I pulled the sweatshirt hood up over my head to conceal my bright fall of platinum blonde waves as I waited for the elevator, conscious of the cameras in the ceiling that recorded my every move.

The less attention I drew, the better.

Adrian wasn't friends with the late-night doormen or lobby security guards — he wasn't really friends with anyone, seeing as he was too narcissistic to form genuine relationships — but he knew how to charm information out of people. If he planned to chase after me, I needed as much of a head start as I could get.

Not that he was going to find me.

This wasn't my first time starting over. My life was an endless series of fresh starts. I was the master of reinvention. The queen of new beginnings. I'd lived just about everywhere on the East Coast since I split home a decade ago. Big cities, small towns, medium-sized metropolises, barely-populated backwaters. At this point, I could blend in pretty much anywhere.

For a little while, at least.

Until people got too familiar. Started asking questions I couldn't answer. Pushed for information I wasn't able to give. That's when I knew it was time to disappear again. A ghost in the night with no forwarding address, leaving nothing but curiosity in my wake.

What ever happened to that Imogen girl? With the spooky blue eyes and bright blonde hair? She just up and left, no word, no warning…

Oh well.

Strange bird, that one.

Flighty.

Not a real loss…

I'd worn out my welcome in Atlantic City. Stayed too long. I'd allowed myself to hope, at least at the very start, that things might be different here.

That proved to be a mistake.

One I would not make again.

I didn't quite know where I was headed this time, but wherever I ended up wouldn't be any different than all the others that came before. Not a home. Nothing permanent. Just another stop on the Imogen Warner International Tour of Misery.

I wasn't wallowing in self-pity, or anything. I was just being honest. Speaking from experience. Because, in a quarter-century of life, I'd never felt like I belonged anywhere. Never felt like I truly fit in. It wasn't hard to imagine why.

I mean, really…

What sort of place could a person like *me* ever hope to call home?

CHAPTER TWO

I'm not much of a party girl.
(Pity parties don't count.)
- Imogen Warner, tucked in bed by 9PM

THREE MONTHS LATER...

"WELCOME TO WITCH CITY!" the old-fashioned wooden sign proclaimed in cheerful gold-painted letters. I quirked an eyebrow at it, wondering what sort of place so boldly advertised its occult history. Wasn't that the sort of thing tourism boards and town officials were always trying to sweep under the proverbial rug?

In any case, I was about to find out exactly what Salem, Massachusetts had to offer. I had no choice in the matter. My car had begun to make a scary grinding sound as I crossed the bridge into the city limits — which I pointedly ignored by turning up the radio a bit louder, blasting a Hozier song to ear-splitting decibels.

It was somewhat harder, however, to ignore the smoke that began to pour from beneath the hood several moments later.

Damn and blast.

I pulled over to give the overtaxed radiator some respite. At least, I thought it was the radiator. I wasn't a mechanic — especially when it came to cars that were nearly as old as I was, with over 200,000 miles on the odometer. My car-related expertise came to an abrupt end after the ability to swap a spare tire and refill my windshield wiper fluid. A quick glance beneath the hood was enough to tell me precisely *nothing* about what was wrong with my rust-bucket, besides the fact that it was giving off enough heat to fry an egg.

Frankly, it was something of a miracle I'd made it this far before breaking down. Three months and four whole states north since I left Atlantic City in my rearview. Considering the old clunker only cost me five hundred bucks, I figured I got more than my money's worth. That said, I didn't have another five hundred to my name to fix it.

I'd spent the better half of my summer bartending at a golf course in a podunk corner of Connecticut — *never again,* polo-clad men wielding nine-irons were shockingly bad tippers — followed by a short stint at a beachside cafe in Rhode Island for all of September, where most of the patrons were boozey frat-boy types who left sand on every conceivable surface and pee on the toilet seats.

Serious yuck.

Now, it was late October, and funds were running dangerously low. Morale, somehow, even lower.

"Car trouble?"

I ducked out from beneath the hood where I'd been bent and turned toward the direction of the voice. A woman about my age was standing on the sidewalk, staring at me with unconcealed concern. I returned the favor by staring back with unconcealed confusion — not at her question, at her appearance. She looked fresh off a boat from Middle Earth. (Rivendell, specifically.) Her dark hair was plaited into about a thousand tiny braids. She was wearing a semi-sheer, moss green dress and dainty sandals. A pair of gauzy, gold-dusted fairy wings were hooked over her shoulders, fluttering in the evening breeze. If Legolas had stepped out of the shadows behind her, I wouldn't have batted an eye.

Was it October 31st already?

I thought there was at least another week until the costumed candy-palooza known as Halloween. Then again, I wasn't really in a position to judge anyone's outfit. In my ancient denim cut-offs with the ultra frayed hems, a flowy white peasant blouse I'd purchased secondhand, and pair of platform leather sandals that gave me a much needed lift of two additional inches, I was dressed more for summer than a New England fall night. Not exactly weather appropriate. (But, then, I'd always run warm. I'd been confounding doctors since infancy, reading steadily at 103.1 instead of the typical 98.6 no matter how many thermometers were shoved under my tongue.)

The elf's brows lifted after a moment passed without a reply to her question. I slapped a smile on my face to stop from gaping at her and shrugged helplessly.

"It looks that way." I gestured at my still-steaming engine. "I think it's overheated."

The engine in question coughed up a cloud of acrid black smoke. It smelled a bit like burning hair — sour and stale.

"You *think?*" The girl's nose wrinkled. "It's not going to explode, is it?"

"God, I hope not," I murmured.

"What?"

"I said no, of course not."

"Oh."

We both stared at the engine. It gave an ominous rattle that shook the whole frame and, despite my assurances that it was not about to self-destruct like a set piece in an action movie, I scurried back to stand beside the elf on the sidewalk.

"Maybe we should stand farther away while we wait," she suggested after a moment. "Under that tree."

I glanced over at her. "While *we* wait?"

"I mean... yeah. You're all by yourself, right?"

After a beat of hesitation, I mumbled a soft, "Right..."

"Then I'm waiting with you," she informed me firmly as her eyes darted down the road. "This isn't the best area to hang around in alone after dark."

Great.

Just what I needed to hear.

I looked around properly for the first time and immediately understood what she meant. We were on the outskirts of town, in a semi-industrial area that had either seen better days or not yet succumbed to the sprawl of urban redevelopment. One lone bar appeared to be open a few blocks down, but the rest was mix of strip malls, the occasional fast food drive-through, and vacant businesses with FOR LEASE signs in their boarded-up windows. It wasn't late, but the sun was already setting — this time of year, it was mostly dark by mid-afternoon — and the whole stretch looked rather forlorn in the gathering shadows.

"I'll be fine," I assured the elf. "I'll just have to call a towing company. No big deal."

Except it *was* a big deal. Even as I said it, I was doing mental calculations about the cost of said tow in relation to the dwindling wad of money I had in the shoebox shoved beneath my passenger seat. At my last waitressing gig, I'd barely made enough to cover gas, snacks, my cellphone bill, and the fleabag pay-by-month motel I'd called home. What little remained of my small nest egg from Atlantic City was pretty much used up by the time I crossed the Massachusetts border that morning. If I had more than a thousand bucks to my name, I'd be stunned.

Maybe the elf-girl read the growing panic on my face, because she reached toward me, as if to clasp me on the arm. Instantly, I stepped backward out of range. I didn't want to offend her, but...

People didn't touch me.

Not unless I was prepared for it.

"Sorry, I..." My words trailed off. I didn't know how to explain.

"No worries." Her hands lifted in a placating gesture, the kind you'd use to soothe a skittish horse. "Personal space. Boundaries. Stranger danger. All cool, girl."

I chewed my bottom lip, feeling like a total heel. My reluctance to be touched had nothing to do with *stranger danger,* but it was better for all parties involved if she believed it was.

"You know, my cousin owns a mechanic shop across town," the elf said eventually. As she spoke, she swayed ever-so-slightly in place, shifting her weight from foot to foot like a river reed caught in the current. "Witch City Collision. They're probably already closed for the night, but if you stop in tomorrow, tell them Moonbeam sent you. They'll take care of you and I promise they won't rip you off."

"Moonbeam?"

"That'd be me." She smiled at me. "I'm Moonbeam."

"Your given name is *Moonbeam?*"

She giggled, a frothy sound that bubbled up from somewhere deep in her throat. "No, my given name is Karen. But I go by my Seelie name — Gracious Moonbeam Stardust, Maiden of the Light Court."

I could feel my eyes widening with each word that left her mouth. I racked my brain for an appropriate response. All I could manage was a bewildered, "What's a Seelie name?"

"You know... the Seelie and Unseelie?"

I shook my head.

"Surely you've head of the Faery Courts?"

"Uh..." I eyed her pointed ears a bit more closely. They didn't look like the cheap plastic ones you'd find at a costume shop. They appeared to be genuine prosthetics, blending seamlessly into her skin. I'd never seen anything like them. "No, I can't say that I have."

"The Elden?" the girl prompted, growing impatient with my ignorance. She crossed two willowy arms over her chest. "The Old Ones?"

"I, uh..." I squirmed beneath her disapproving stare. "I'm not sure..."

"What about the Fair Folk?"

"No, I..."

"The Wee People Under the Hill?"

"*Wee* people?"

"It means little," she said rather tersely.

It also meant urine, but I wasn't going to remind her of that. "Right. Of course. Got it."

"You really know nothing of the Tuatha Dé Danann?"

I shrugged helplessly. "Nope."

She stared at me like I was the lowest form of life, a brainless amoeba who'd just crawled from the primordial ooze. "Some people really are completely disconnected from the spiritual world."

I bit my lip to keep from laughing.

Yep, that was me. The celebrity clairvoyant, totally disconnected from the spiritual world.

Inside my gloves, my hands tingled. It had been a few days since I'd had a vision and I was due. Overdue, in fact. I could feel the energy gathering at the tips of my fingers like an electrical charge in the air before a lightning strike, just waiting for an opportunity to release.

"I suppose I shouldn't hold it against you." The elf's eyes scanned me up and down, then flickered over to my out-of-state license plate. "Clearly, you're not from around here. But don't worry — a bit of time in Salem will open your eyes to the possibilities. Did you know it's a mystical epicenter?"

"Like the Hellmouth under Sunnydale?"

My *Buffy the Vampire Slayer* reference sailed right over her head. She narrowed her eyes at me. "The convergence of magic is no joking matter."

"Right. Of course not." I tried to smooth things over, not entirely certain where our conversation had gone astray or why she was looking at me like I'd just admitted I liked to drown kittens for fun. "In any case, I appreciate the mechanic recommendation, Moonbeam. And I really do like your name. Your costume, too... Wow! It's beautiful. Did you make those ears yourself?"

Moonbeam threw her hands up, clearly miffed. "Costume? *Costume?*"

With that, she turned on one dainty gold heel and stalked away. I wasn't sure what I'd done to upset her, but I doubted I'd be getting the family discount at Witch City Collision, now.

Blast.

After Moonbeam's abrupt departure, I figured the situation couldn't get much worse. I, however, was gravely mistaken. Not only was acrid smoke still billowing from beneath my hood, the battery percentage on my cellphone was essentially nil since I hadn't charged it for a while. There wasn't much point. I had no one to call. I only ever used the thing for emergencies.

Emergencies precisely like this one, you unprepared ninny.

I didn't have time to dial a tow — heck, I barely had time to roll my eyes at the 25 MISSED CALLS notification (Adrian really needed to take a chill pill) — before the screen turned black as the phone powered off.

The hits just kept coming...

A quick glance around the rapidly darkening roadway told me what I already knew — this was not the late 1900s and, as such, there were no convenient pay phones anywhere to be found. I was on my own. Literally and figuratively. The street was deserted, the nail salons and tattoos parlors in the strip mall across the way were long since buttoned up for the day. I glanced at the (somewhat seedy looking) bar down the block with great reluctance. Squinting, I could barely make out the black letters scored into the wood on the sign above the door.

THE BANSHEE

A muffled melody of male voices spilled out the open windows, along with the occasional clatter of ceramic balls colliding on a pool table. Even without the row of Harleys parked by the curb, I'd worked enough service industry jobs to spot a dive from a mile away. Desperate though I may be, I wasn't desperate enough to step foot in that joint.

At least, not yet.

I tossed my useless, dead phone on my passenger seat with a frustrated grunt as I contemplated my options. There weren't many.

1. Wait here and hope the car magically regenerated itself

2. Brave The Banshee and beg to use their phone

3. Attempt to diagnose my auto-related woes on my own

4. Hurl myself off the nearby bridge and hope that in my next life, I had better luck

Of the four, the third option seemed like the best place to start. Maybe it was something so simple, even a car-illiterate individual like myself could handle it. Maybe I could just top off the coolant fluid and be on my merry way.

Or maybe you're deeply delusional.

Ignoring the defeatist voice in the back of my head, I yanked off my gloves and threw them down to join the phone on my seat before I returned to face the horror beneath the hood. I'd only just begun fiddling with the greasy cap of the translucent coolant tank when the unmistakable sound of tires rolled to a stop behind my clunker.

God, who was it this time?

Another elf?

A centaur?

A unicorn, perhaps?

By the time I'd stepped around to the side of my car, the stranger's vehicle — a large, black SUV with deeply tinted windows — was parked by the curb and its driver — a tall, broad-shouldered stranger with dark hair, wearing a pair of wickedly cool aviator sunglasses — had alighted from the front seat.

I sucked in a sharp breath the second I clapped eyes on him. The man looked like Superman, for god's sake. (If Superman wore crisp white button-down shirts instead of red lycra and a cape.) He headed straight for me, no hesitation in his stride. As he did so, I couldn't help noticing that he walked from the hips, an undeniable swagger that made my throat lump as the distance between us shrank from fifteen feet to five.

There was authority in that walk. An innate confidence that commanded every bit of my attention without even trying. It didn't take a genius to figure out why — at aforementioned swaggering hips, there was a shiny gold badge clipped to his belt beside a holstered handgun.

Seriously?

Could this night get any worse?

CHAPTER THREE

Why would I choose to "go big" when the other option is to go home?
- Imogen Warner, attempting to get out of plans

A cop.

Of course he was a cop.

Just my ever-flipping luck. I'd been in town for point-two seconds and already my plan to fly under the radar was completely off the rails. I swear, I was a goddamned magnet for worst-case-scenarios. The lump in my throat turned to a ball of nerves, which I attempted (unsuccessfully) to swallow down with a series of rapid gulps. It was nearly impossible not to skitter like a bug beneath a flashlight beam as he came toward me, looking me up and down in a laser-like fashion that seemed to leave not a single detail unaccounted for. I watched his lips part, the beginning of a question forming on them, and I braced myself for the inevitable inquiries.

Who are you?

What are you doing here?

Where are you coming from, tonight?

Can I see your license and registration?

Only… the inquisition never came. As his gaze swept back up to my face and he got his first glimpse at close proximity, his mouth clicked shut, the sharp line of his jaw tightening. It was barely perceptible, but I'd swear his confident stride faltered a bit; he rocked ever-so-slightly back on his heels, as though I'd startled him. Which, in itself, was odd. (In my experience, people were rarely startled by petite blonde women in cheap platform sandals and vintage short-shorts.)

For one blinding moment of panic, I thought he might recognize me — but that was impossible. I'd been out of the public eye for ten years. No way would a random cop in Massachusetts pick me out of a lineup.

He recovered his composure almost instantly, smoothing his expression clear as he came to a halt a handful of paces away. I couldn't see his eyes behind the mirrored lenses of his aviators, but I could tell that they were taking my measure with a sharpness that made every hair on the back of my neck stand on end. After a few moments, when he still hadn't said anything — merely stood there staring at me — I couldn't take the strange silence anymore.

"Uh… *Hi.* Can I help you with something, officer?"

"Detective," he corrected automatically, still seeming distracted. Still staring at me like… like… Well, frankly, I wasn't quite sure how he was staring at me. I just knew I wanted him to stop. In my experience, attention from law enforcement never led anywhere good.

"Right. Of course." I forced a smile through clenched teeth, eager to get this over with. "Can I help you with something, *Detective?*"

He jolted at my question, as though it had snapped him out of a daze. "That's what I'm meant to be asking you."

"Sorry?"

"If you need help. That's what I'm meant to be asking you."

"Except… you didn't." I swallowed hard, still fighting the lump in my throat. It had only gotten larger since he started speaking in that soft, deep timbre. "*Ask*, that is."

"Right." His chest expanded as he took a deep inhale. He seemed to realize he was acting strangely and recovered his manners through sheer force of will. Reaching out a hand for me to shake, he offered a belatedly introduction. "Detective Caden Hightower, Salem PD, at your service."

I ignored his outstretched hand. My gloves were, lamentably, sitting on my passenger seat. No way in hell was I risking skin-to-skin contact with this guy. If he triggered a vision, I'd probably spend the night in a padded cell waiting for a psych consult.

"Germaphobe," I said by way of explanation, looking pointedly at his proffered hand.

His lips twitched. "Is that a fact?"

Why did he sound like he thought I was full of shit? He didn't even know me! I felt myself getting irritated. Or, perhaps I should say even *more* irritated. Between the breakdown, the Lord of the Rings character cameo, and now a freaking cop butting into my business, this particular evening was not going to make the list of '*Imogen's Best Nights Ever*' in my memoirs, that was for sure.

"Yes," I replied in a rather snippy tone. "It's a fact."

He stared me down. Once again, I got the distinct impression he thought I was a total bullshitter. Which, to be fair, I was — but he didn't know that.

"Look," I continued, striving for a level tone. (Only partially succeeding.) "I'm already having a bit of a shitty night, seeing as it's getting dark, my cellphone battery is dead, and my car has decided to melt down in a way that would impress an overstimulated toddler—" This statement prompted a chuckle from him. It was a good chuckle, low and genuine, the kind that came straight from his gut — and set off a flurry of butterflies in my own. I ignored them and barreled on valiantly. "—So, if you're going to give me a ticket for parking in a tow zone or a citation for spewing exhaust dust all over your city streets, just do it already." I swallowed hard and tacked on a belated, "With all due respect. *Sir*. I mean… *Officer*. Er… *Detective*."

He stared at me for another long, unsettling beat. Then, he did something that made all the air evacuate my lungs in one great gust. He reached up and pulled off his aviators, revealing the most stunningly blue set of eyes I'd ever seen in my life.

Christ.

A girl could drown in those eyes.

I'd barely had a chance to recover when he did yet another breath-snatching thing. Looping the arm of his sunglasses in the front pocket of his white button-down shirt, he took another step toward me, so we were standing close — way closer than two strangers had any reason to stand. I normally would've backpedaled to maintain some breathing room, but with the clunker directly behind me, there was nowhere to retreat.

"I'm not going to ticket you," he said softly. "The detective badge—" He tapped the gold shield in question. "—means I stopped doing traffic cop duties a long while back."

"Oh." Some of my panic ebbed.

His lips twitched again. "Yeah."

"Then… what gives?"

"I'm not sure I understand your question."

"Are you investigating me for a crime?"

"Why?" he countered without missing a beat. "Have you committed one I should be aware of?"

"I… What… You…" I swallowed down my stammers when I realized there was a humorous light dancing in his eyes.

He was… *teasing* me?

He was teasing me!

That was definitely not standard police protocol.

Sucking in a deep breath, I tried my best to appear blasé in the face of his ridicule, but my voice still came out strangled with barely-leashed irritation. "No, Detective. I have not committed a crime. Obviously."

"Shame," he murmured. "I bet you'd look good in my cuffs."

My eyes bugged out of my head. Was he threatening me? Was he... *hitting on me*? I wasn't sure which alternative was more ludicrous. Before I could ask, he took another step in my direction. We were only a foot apart, now. My spine was pressed so tight to my car door, I was pretty sure I'd have a handle shape imprinted on the small of my back for the foreseeable future.

"Uh..." I tilted my head all the way back to keep my eyes locked on his. He was tall — way taller than me, at least six-foot-two. "What are you doing?"

"Well, I was planning on heading home, taking my dog for a run..." His head tipped to the side. "But now I'm standing here with you."

"You... Wha... *What*?"

"Which part was confusing? That I run or that I have a dog? Careful how you answer, you might wound my fragile self-confidence."

If this guy had even one self-conscious bone in his body, I'd be flabbergasted. He held himself with such calm, cool, collected energy it was borderline intimidating. I sucked in another gulp of air and repeated, "*What?*"

"We do about four miles every night," he confided, still eerily calm. "Six if it's been a shit day, but in that case I don't bring the dog. He's actually more of a puppy. — still weaves like a drunken sailor half the time and pees every twenty steps, which sort of fucks with my cardio routine. We're working on it."

I stared at him, stunned totally silent, mouth gaping like a fish on dry land.

The cop evidently had no trouble at all holding up a one-sided conversation. "I rescued him about five months ago. He was supposed to be mid-size, but I'm guessing the shelter's assumption he was mostly Labrador Retriever was wrong, seeing as he's already the size of a small horse. I'd stake my badge he's at least half Newfoundland." He paused in thought. "Though, I'm not one for gambling and, let's be honest, I can't afford to lose the badge. I'm going to need every cent of my paycheck to keep him in kibble. Eating me out of house and home, the monster."

"Uh, sorry, but..." I shook my head, utterly baffled. "Why are you telling me all this?"

"You asked."

"I most certainly did not!"

"You asked what I was doing tonight," he retorted, voice infuriatingly level. "Since my plans include Socks—"

"*Socks?*"

"My puppy. That's his name."

"You named your puppy *Socks?*"

"It's his favorite snack, I thought it was fitting."

I stared at him some more. I genuinely couldn't tell if he was messing with me or not. For the first time in recent memory — hell, for the first time maybe *ever* — I had the most bizarre urge to grab his hand and trigger a vision, if only to get a little insight into the inner workings of his brain. (Obviously, it was an urge I suppressed.)

"Of course, most people around here assume it's short for the baseball team," the cop said, scoffing lightly. "As if I'd ever root for the Red Sox. My cousin is an assistant coach for the Orioles. I'd be excommunicated from the family, using Boston as a namesake."

Somehow, our conversation had gone remarkably off course. I desperately needed to bring our focus back to the matter at hand (i.e. my car) and then get the heck out of this odd little town, away from its even odder inhabitants. "Look, Highheeler—"

"Hightower."

"Right. Whatever." I took a calming breath. "I think it's great you rescued a Newfie puppy named Socks—"

"Funny, you can get my dog's name right but not mine."

I pointedly ignored his muttered remark and continued, "I just really don't know why you felt the need to tell me, of all people, about it."

"You asked," he claimed. (Again!)

"I did *not*!" I retorted. (Again!)

"You asked what I was doing, didn't you?" His eyes were all crinkly at the corners. It might've been cute if it weren't so maddening.

"Technically, I guess I did ask. But I certainly didn't mean—"

He cut me off. "You asked, I answered. That's it. End of story."

"I— You— That—" I wasn't sure whether to be annoyed, amused, or astounded by his willful misinterpretations. Choosing annoyance, I narrowed my gaze. "That's not what I meant and you know it!"

"Oh?" Those bright blue eyes of his were dancing with humor. "What did you mean?"

"What are you doing *here*?" I exploded. I wasn't entirely sure why I was so worked up — usually, my feathers weren't so easy to ruffle. But something about this guy was... *ruffling*. Ruffling in a big way. "Why did you pull over at all if you aren't planning to ticket me?"

"Do you want me to ticket you?"

I scowled up at him. "Definitely not!"

"Is there a reason you're yelling at me?"

"I am not yelling!" (Okay, I was very possibly yelling.) "I'm just confused as to what you need from me, Detective."

"I don't need anything from you. You're not in any sort of trouble."

"Oh." That was a relief. "Then what are you doing here?"

"Generally, when I see a woman stranded on the side of the road, I like to offer assistance."

"You just said you were headed home," I felt the need to point out. "To Socks."

"And?"

"You're clocked out for the day. This—" I gestured at the car behind me. "—isn't your problem."

"Then you don't need any help?"

My teeth ground together in frustration at his rather baiting question. "I..."

"Need help," he finished for me. "Hence, me pulling over."

"Did you just say *hence*?"

"Are you deflecting from the issue at hand?"

"It's not *your* issue," I said, even more irritated than before. "I was managing just fine before you came along, thank you very much!"

"Stranded in the dark with a dead cellphone battery and a car that belongs in the junkyard?" His skepticism was thick. "Yeah. You're right as rain."

Shit.

I was so worked up, I'd momentarily forgotten about the dead cellphone situation. My cheeks heated as an embarrassed blush stole across them. Stoic as Superman, he watched it happen without saying a word. Then again, he didn't need to — he had a way of making me feel flustered and foolish, just standing there looking at me.

Through sheer force of will, I adopted a bitchy tone instead of a mortified one. "Are the insults part of your chivalrous plans to save me?"

"Is the defensiveness part of your issue accepting assistance even when you clearly need it?"

This.

Freaking.

Guy.

I (begrudgingly) swallowed down my pride. The truth was, I did need help. And much as it pained me to admit... I figured I was better off accepting it from a cop than the bikers at The Banshee.

"Look, Highwater—"

"Hightower."

"I think we got off on the wrong foot."

"Maybe that's 'cause you're wearing sandals in October."

God, he was annoying. "And I do appreciate your offer to help—"

"Oh, clearly."

Ignoring his sarcasm, I forced myself to sally forth. "I was merely pointing out that you're not on duty."

"Why does that matter?"

"You don't have any obligation to help me, that's all."

"I like to think I'm the sort of guy who'd help anyone who needs it, assuming it's in my power to do so. On or off the clock. Badge or no badge."

He was either a bonafide saint or deeply sanctimonious. Seeing as I had about as much faith in men as I had in the almighty — which was to say: *not very much at all* — I was going with the latter.

"Fine. Have it your way." I threw my hands up in a gesture of surrender. "I just need to borrow your phone so I can call a tow. After that, you can be on your merry way. I'm good on my own."

He was already shaking his head, rejecting my words before they'd left my lips. "No."

"No I can't borrow your phone? Or no you aren't leaving?"

"No to both." He stared at me unflinchingly, those blue eyes intent. "I'll handle the tow. I know someone who can bring it to a local shop, get it checked out for you first thing tomorrow. If it's fixable, he'll fix it."

I must've made some sort of face — one that looked, if I had to guess, like Edvard Munch's famously horrified painting *The Scream* — because his own expression softened and the humor bled right out of his stare.

"Diagnostic is free of charge," he said with a casual shrug, like it was no big deal. "The guy at the shop owes me a favor."

Pulling in a breath through my nostrils, I tried not to stomp my foot on the ground like a melodramatic teen. What was *wrong* with this guy? Why was he so damn determined to help a girl he'd just met? Surely, not out of the goodness of his heart.

No one's heart was that good.

"Forget it," I said stiffly. "I'm not looking for a handout."

"Never said you were."

"Then what is this?"

He contemplated that for a long moment. Then he murmured quietly, "There's a difference between asking for a handout and accepting a hand *up* when you've taken a little stumble."

I suppressed a shriek. "Do you have some sort of hero-complex I should be aware of?"

"If by hero-complex you mean basic human dignity... Sure, we can call it that." His dark brows arched upward. "What's your problem with heroes, anyway?"

"I don't have a problem. I just don't buy into the whole...." I gestured vaguely in his general direction. "...thing."

"And what *whole thing* might that be?"

"The whole thing where people are good to one another for no reason at all, without any ulterior motives."

He scoffed. "Let me get this straight. You'd be more willing to accept my help if I had some devious hidden agenda than if I was just a good samaritan, looking out for the greater good? Keeping my karma balanced?"

"I don't give a crap about your karma. I just want to get my car fixed so I can get the hell out of this cursed town."

"Cursed is a strong word."

"According to a very reliable source—" Okay, so, Moonbeam wasn't exactly *reliable*, but... whatever. "—this place is a center of mystical convergence."

His eyes crinkled up at the corners again. "I'm sure it is. But I'm hoping you won't hold that against us as a community."

"Why's that?"

"Because I'm hoping you're going to stick around for a bit."

He was?

Why?

I was instantly suspicious and made sure he knew it, glowering up at him as I snapped, "Have you seen my car? Have you *smelled* my car? I'm not going anywhere until I get a mechanic to fix whatever's causing it to implode before our very eyes. Preferably one who won't charge me an arm and a leg."

"I know it's called a body shop, but I doubt they actually charge you in body parts."

"Are you making fun of me, Highpower?"

"*Hightower,*" he corrected, sounding more amused than insulted by my jab. "Which reminds me — you haven't told me your name."

My mouth suddenly felt somewhat dry. "Why do you need my name? I thought I wasn't in trouble."

"Are you always this jumpy?"

"I'm not jumpy!" I insisted, even though I was so jumpy, the pole vaulters at the Olympic Games would probably find me impressive. To cover said jumpiness, I tore my eyes away from his piercing blue ones and looked around the — now fully dark — street in despair.

I totally should've tried my luck at the biker bar.

CHAPTER FOUR

Judging by most dating profiles I've seen, we as a society really took that "teach a man to fish" proverb to heart...
- Imogen Warner, swiping left on yet another fish photo

Taking advantage of my momentary distraction, the detective stepped around me and made his way to the front of my car. He ducked his tall frame under the hood to examine the engine without preamble. I trailed helplessly behind him, studying the broad planes of his back as he bent forward to tinker with something out of view.

"What are you doing?"

"Knitting," he replied drolly, not bothering to look away from the engine. "What does it look like I'm doing?"

It looked like he was messing with my (already thoroughly messed-up) engine.

I sighed. "Do you even know what you're looking for?"

He grunted noncommittally in response. A lock of his thick, dark hair fell over his brow as he fiddled with the steaming crap-heap I called a car. Each time he moved, the muscles rippled beneath the fabric of his button-down shirt in a way that was so unconsciously attractive, I forced my eyes to the sidewalk until he finished doing… whatever it was he was doing under there.

"Well?" I asked the pavement once his shoes stepped back into view. "What's the diagnosis, doc?"

There was a distinct pause — after which, he reached into his pocket, retrieved his cellphone, and proceeded to make a phone call.

"Puck? Yeah. It's Cade Hightower. How the hell are you, buddy?" He paused briefly to listen. When he spoke again, his voice had warmed a few degrees. "That's great news. Long time coming, too. I'm thrilled for the two of you." Another pause. "Listen, the reason I'm calling…" His eyes found mine again. "A friend of mine is in a bit of a jam."

My brows soared upward.

Friend? I mouthed.

He winked. "Her car — liberal use of the term — broke down. I gave it a once-over, but this is beyond my capabilities. More miles on this thing than on Forrest Gump's sneakers. Radiator looks totally shot, the water pump has seen better days. God only knows what else. Can you send one of your guys around tomorrow morning, tow it into the shop for a look? See if it's salvageable or better off in the scrap heap?" He listened for a long moment. "Yeah. Full run-down. Thanks, bud. I appreciate you making the time. I'll text you the address in a few. Mhm. You too." He hung up, slid the phone back into his pocket, and announced, "The car's handled."

I was still processing his rather alarming description of my vehicle. "*Better off in the scrap heap?*"

He shrugged.

"The *scrap heap?!*" I repeated, voice pitching up an octave.

"Look, Puck could probably get this shitbox souped-up and ready for the Indy 500 if you gave him enough time. But there's no point throwing good money after bad. He'll be straight with you about what's wrong and whether the repairs are worth it. That's why I called him."

I shook my head in disbelief. "I didn't ask you to do that."

"You didn't ask for it, but you needed it all the same."

"That simple?"

Ignoring my sarcasm, he nodded as he stepped toward me, closing some of the distance between us again. "Yeah. That simple. Like I said before — basic human dignity."

"Did you grow up Amish or something?"

One dark brow arched. "Excuse me?"

"It's just… in my experience, people don't treat one another with your so called—" In the narrow span between our bodies, I did finger quotes. "*—basic human dignity—*" My hands dropped down to plant on my hips. "—all that often. In fact, most of the time, people do the exact opposite."

He digested this information in silence for a long stretch. A small indent appeared in the space between his eyebrows as they furrowed together. "I'm sorry."

I started, surprised by the out-of-left-field apology. "Why are you sorry?"

"Because, clearly, wherever you were before this… whoever you were with before this… you weren't treated very well, if your first instinct when meeting someone new is to assume you're about to be screwed over."

Okay, now, that was *it*.

I was officially ticked the hell off. Where did this guy — this total *stranger* — get the nerve, saying something like that to me? He didn't know the first thing about me. He didn't know where I came from, who I was, what I'd done. I could be a terrible person, so far as he knew, and he was treating us like long lost pals.

My teeth ground together. "Listen, Hero-Hair—"

"*Hero-Hair*?" he echoed, amusement evident.

"Oh, don't sound so shocked. You've got that perfect, Clark Kent messy-but-somehow-perfectly-styled hair going on. Those little distinguished streaks of silver at the temples that say, *'Of course you can trust me. I'm one of the good guys.'*" I eyed the offending hair in question with ill-concealed disgust. "It's hero-hair, dude. And I see right through it."

"Did you just call me dude?"

"No," I lied.

"You did. You called me dude."

"I said *detective*."

"Are you lying to an officer of the law?"

"Of course not," I lied again. "Maybe you should get your hearing checked. It's dangerous to be running around after criminals if you can't hear them coming."

"Your concern for my welfare is touching." He paused, mouth twitching when he caught me leveling another scathing look at his perfect hair. "Would it make you more or less angry to know that I rolled out of bed this morning and didn't even touch a comb?"

"More."

"I surmised as much," he murmured. "You have somewhere to stay tonight?"

My wide eyes jerked back to his. "I'm not staying with you."

"Did I invite you to stay with me?"

"No." I flushed in embarrassment. "Of course not. I meant I'm not staying in this town."

"What's wrong with my town?"

"*Witch City?*" I shook my head rapidly, wishing my cheeks weren't flaming red as I desperately sought a change of topic. "I think not. What kind of nickname is that, anyway?"

"You've never heard of Salem?" He looked genuinely bewildered by the concept.

"Should I have?"

"1600s... Mass hysteria... Innocent civilians prosecuted for witchcraft... Lots of hangings and other unpleasant shit..." His head canted to one side. "Any of this ringing a bell in that beautiful head of yours?"

I decided — for my own mental health — to bury the fact that he'd just called me beautiful somewhere deep in my psyche, where it could not haunt me for the rest of time. Instead, I focused on what else he'd said. Truth be told, his words were ringing several bells in my cerebral cortex — a portion of my brain left vastly underutilized since I got my GED at age sixteen.

I'd heard of the Salem Witch Trials. Hell, everyone in the continental United States had heard of the Salem Witch Trials. They were famous. Notorious, even. A dark chapter in American history that, for whatever reason, historians and teachers seemed all too jazzed to revisit every term when discussing the Colonial Era.

"So you *have* heard of Salem," he said, reading the recognition on my face. "Let me be the first to officially welcome you. Don't let the wand-waving locals scare you off. They're harmless. Mostly."

Mostly!?

"If you need somewhere to stay, the Hawthorne Hotel downtown is nice," he said. "Reputedly haunted, but the ghosts are of the friendly variety. So I hear, anyway."

I glared at him.

He ignored my glare and carried on. "It's a ways from here, though… and now that I think about it, I doubt they have any vacancy. October is high season in Salem. Pretty much everywhere is booked solid for the next few days, until the Halloween madness subsides and the tourists head home."

Fantastic.

I really couldn't catch a break, tonight.

(Or ever. But especially tonight.)

"Do any of your recommendations have vacancy?" I asked. "Preferably ones in walking distance, without any friendly ghosts floating the halls?"

His eyes flickered over my shoulder, down the dark road. His full lips went flat with either reluctance or displeasure (I didn't know him well enough to tell) as he crossed his arms over his chest. "There's an inn a short ways down the block. The Sea Witch. No frills, no amenities to speak of… but not a bad spot to spend the night if you're in a jam. And almost guaranteed they're not at capacity. It's… not the kind of place people stick around long."

"Perfect. Like I said, I'm not sticking around."

"We'll see."

That sounded rather ominous. "What do you mean, *we'll see*? Are you planning to detain me?"

He laughed — a warm, unbridled sound. "Salem has a way of pulling people in. Sort of its own gravitational force, so to speak."

"Moonbeam was right, then? It *is* a center of mystical convergence?"

"I'm reluctant to throw in my hat with someone named Moonbeam."

"You aren't wearing a hat," I pointed out.

"It's an expression." His eyes did the crinkly-amused thing again. "All I know is, when people get here… even the ones who don't plan to stay for more than a night or two tend to… *linger*."

"You sound like you're speaking from personal experience."

"Probably because I am. Just over a year ago, I came up this way for a federal outreach training in Boston. I had a day off before my flight back to Baltimore, thought I'd use it to check out some of the local towns. I stumbled across Salem and the rest is history. I applied for an open position on the force the very next day. Within six weeks, I was here."

I stared at him, baffled he'd revealed so much about himself with minimal prompting. Who *was* this guy? Why was he so straightforward? It wasn't normal. Most people were cagey, always keeping their cards close to the chest. Yet he put all his cards right down on the table without my ever asking to see them, let alone demanding to see mine in return.

Again, I found myself battling the insane urge to touch him, if only to get a glimpse inside his head. Surely, the Clark Kent facade harbored dark, sinister motives. Surely, the Hero-Hair was a carefully styled ruse…

"You still with me, Goldie?"

"Goldie?"

He looked at my hair, which was cascading around my shoulders in a platinum halo of untamed waves. "You gave me a hair-related nickname. I figure fair's fair."

"Hero-Hair is an insult. Not a nickname."

"Potato, po-tah-to…"

I rolled my eyes. "Look, just because Salem exerted its weird gravitational force on you doesn't mean I'm sticking around. I wasn't even supposed to be here. I wouldn't have stopped at all if not for…" I glanced at my clunker. It was a rather unimpressive sight, sitting there in all its rusty glory. "Let's just say I didn't have much say in this particular detour."

"Where were you headed originally?"

I dropped my gaze back to the pavement, avoiding his eyes as I scrambled for an answer to his question that wouldn't make me sound certifiably insane. I couldn't tell him the truth — that I didn't even have a destination when I set off this morning. I'd just known I couldn't spend another freaking second in that god-awful Providence motel with its mildewed bathroom tiles and wallpaper that reeked of secondhand smoke from whatever poor unfortunate soul stayed there before I checked in.

"Hey."

My eyes jerked back to the detective's face at his soft word. His chiseled features were illuminated by the streetlight that had just flickered on overhead, and his expression was oddly gentle. "Are you all right?"

"Of course I'm all right," I said automatically. "Do I not seem all right?"

To this, he had no reply.

I blew out a sharp breath. "Stop that."

"Stop what?"

"Looking at me like I'm some wounded bird with a broken wing you found on the side of the road."

He glanced down at my arms, which I'd crossed over my chest in order to glare at him more effectively. "Your wings look perfectly fine to me."

"Are you trying to piss me off?"

"No. I guess it comes naturally."

My glower intensified.

He carried on, "You, however, seem naturally inclined toward violence."

"I am not!"

"So much wrath in such a petite package."

"You just met me. You don't know anything about me."

"I'm a good judge of character. Reading people is kind of my whole job." His lips twitched as he suppressed a smile. "Detective, remember?"

I blew out a breath. "For your information, I am not full of violence or wrath. I'm just... *annoyed*. Okay?"

"At your shitbox car? Or at me?"

"Must I choose?"

"Are you always this belligerent toward people who are trying to help you?"

"I'm not being belligerent!" I insisted. (Belligerently.) "I'm just... I'm having a bad night, as I've already informed you." I paused. "I'm having a bad week, actually. A bad month. A bad year."

"If you're about to break into the theme song from F.R.I.E.N.D.S. I'm going to have to arrest you."

"*Arrest me?* For what?"

"Noise violation, disrupting the peace, take your pick. I'm a pretty understanding guy, but I draw the line at sitcoms with laugh tracks."

He was teasing me.

Again!

"Stop joking around. You're a cop. You're meant to be taciturn and stern." My gaze dropped to his stomach which, beneath the fitted button down, appeared to be washboard-flat. "You're also supposed to have a beer gut."

"Yeah... Turns out, chasing the bad guys is a lot harder with a gut."

"Do you do a lot of bad-guy-chasing?" I couldn't help myself from asking. "In this little town?"

"You might be surprised."

I glanced around. "Seems like any other quiet corner of suburbia to me."

"Looks can be deceiving." He paused and crossed both his arms — which, by the way, were so ridiculously muscular they tested the structural integrity of his shirt sleeves — over his chest to mirror my pose. "You never answered my question."

"Which one?"

"Where is it you're coming from?"

Once again, I fought the urge to squirm. "Oh, here and there. You know."

"I don't know, actually. That's why I asked."

"Are you asking in the official capacity of the law or out of personal curiosity?"

"Must I choose?" he echoed my earlier taunt, mimicking my voice.

"Look, Highballer—"

"*Hightower*. Though, you might as well call me Caden. Or Cade, if you like."

I blinked at him. "What? Why?"

"Detective seems a bit formal, given the circumstances."

"And what circumstances might those be?"

"The circumstances in which I ask you out to dinner, and you accept."

My mouth dropped open. "Excuse me?"

"You like Mexican food?"

"Mexican food?"

"Beef, beans, cheese, usually combined in some form of hand-held corn-based vessel," he said slowly. "Tacos, burritos, tortillas… Chimichangas, quesadillas, enchiladas…"

"I know what Mexican food is!"

"Apologies. You seemed confused by the concept." He appeared to be fighting a grin — a battle he was dangerously close to losing, I might add. (I, for one, had no idea what he found so amusing about all this.)

"I am not *confused by the concept*." My eyes narrowed scarily. "You do not have to man-splain Mexican food to me."

He lost the battle against his grin with a flash of straight white teeth that did something to my stomach. Something that brought to mind the floor routine of an accomplished gymnast. (Read: *somersaults*.)

"I'd broach the alternative of Thai food," he said, still grinning. "But I'm concerned you might react poorly."

This freaking guy!

Shoving down my bizarre urge to laugh, I forced an icy tone. "You must think you're pretty charming, huh? Using that detective badge like some kind of pickup line at a happy hour bar to lure in unsuspecting women?"

"You? *Unsuspecting*? You're about the most suspicious person I've ever encountered — and I've been on the force nearly a decade."

"Oh, spare me the knight in shining armor act. I'm not buying it, Hero-Hair," I half-snarled, doubling down on my anger so it wouldn't slip away entirely. "Nor am I impressed by you appearing out of the shadows like some guardian angel, descending from the heavens to save me from my shitty life. I don't need saving. And I definitely don't need you."

"Noted."

My whole body jerked backwards at his easy agreement to my — rather acerbic — declaration. "*Noted*? Just like that?"

"Sure." He paused again, his brows doing the little furrowed thing that was annoyingly endearing. "Too bad, though. There's a great food truck not that far from here. And don't even try telling me you aren't hungry. Your stomach has growled at least three times in the ten minutes we've been here talking."

I processed this statement for approximately two-point-three seconds before exploding, "Are you *kidding* me?"

"Do I seem like I'm kidding?"

He did not.

In fact, he seemed alarmingly serious.

My chin jerked up. "I don't know you well enough to answer that question."

"You would if you went out to dinner with me."

"I don't want to go to dinner with you!" I exclaimed. "I don't even know you."

"That's sort of the whole point of dinner."

I made an incoherent screeching sound, which brought to mind a baby pterodactyl.

"If there's something you want to know about me, just ask," he said, unbothered by my outburst. "I'm an open book."

He honestly was.

And it was *annoying*.

Not refreshing.

(At least, that was what I told myself.)

"Detective Hightower," I forced myself to say, smiling through clenched teeth. "You may be an open book, but I don't like to read."

This was a blatant lie. I loved to read. I was the little kid who rode her bike to the library twice a week, filling her backpack up with hardcovers each visit because she didn't have any friends that weren't fictional growing up. But he didn't need to know that rather embarrassing factoid about me. In fact, he didn't need to know any factoids about me.

We weren't going to be friends.

I didn't *do* friends.

The sad truth was, not all that much had changed in the companionship department since my youth. Fictional friends were still the only kind I was willing to risk.

Cade — *Detective Hightower* — folded his arms over his chest and resumed staring at me. "So that's a no on tacos, then?"

"It's a no on tacos, Detective."

"Cade."

"Detective," I countered firmly.

His eyes crinkled. "Better than Hero-Hair, I suppose."

"I could think up a worse nickname. Trust me."

"Oh, I don't doubt it." He paused. "And it's okay if you can't do dinner tonight. We'll raincheck."

"No, we won't. Are you hard of hearing? I'm not going to be in town long. I wouldn't be in town at all if I hadn't broken down against my will. And once my car is back in action, I'm out of here."

At that, Cade — *De. Tec. Tive. High. Tower.* — stepped alarmingly close to me again. His bright blue eyes locked on mine, and there was no escaping them. "Come on, Goldie. I'll give you a ride to The Sea Witch. Get you settled in."

"That's not necessary."

"It is."

"You said it's just down the block!"

"I also said I'd give you a ride."

"You've already taken care of my car. There's no need for more meddling."

"If you think I'm leaving you here in the dark with no phone, no idea where you're going, and nothing but your own pigheadedness to keep you company… you have vastly underestimated my meddling capabilities."

I scowled at him — my best one, the one I reserved for sandy-footed frat bros who'd had one too many spiked seltzers on a Saturday afternoon and were seconds away from puking on my freshly cleaned bar-top.

"Scowl all you like," he said amiably. "But do it while you pop the trunk, will you?"

When I didn't move fast enough for his liking, he turned on a heel and stalked over — with that damn authoritative swagger! — to my driver's side door. In a flash, he'd retrieved my keys from the ignition and hit the button to unlatch the trunk.

"What are you doing?" I hissed, trailing in his wake as he made his way to the back of the vehicle. "Did you just pocket my car keys?!"

"I'll pass them along to the mechanics."

"You can't just take—" My eyes widened as I watched him reach into the depths of my trunk. "*Hey*! That's my stuff!"

My hisses fell on deaf ears as he slung the strap of my leather backpack over his shoulder, swiped my full-to-bursting duffle bag with a one-handed grip, turned his back to me, and ambled toward his SUV like he had all the time in the world.

"I'll be in the car whenever you're ready."

"Stop!" I called. "Stop right there!"

He didn't.

"You— This—" I was spluttering again. "This is illegal! You're committing a crime!"

"Which one?" He sounded unconcerned.

Shit. *Which one?* Good question. I wasn't a legal expert — despite the embarrassing volume of *Law & Order* episodes I'd consumed in my lifetime. I had no idea which law he was currently breaking. Thus, I latched on to the first charge that popped into my head.

"It's police brutality!"

He laughed — full on *laughed* — at that. "Brutality? Really?"

Damn and blast.

"Then, it's police *coercion!*"

"Coercion implies a threat," he countered breezily, without so much as breaking stride. "Have you been threatened?"

Well… no. Not exactly.

But…

"Unlawful search and seizure!" I cried with a lightning bolt of recollection, thankful that all my hours clocked with Benson and Stabler paid off at last. "A police officer needs probable cause to confiscate possessions without a warrant!"

He kept right on walking. "Good thing I'm off the clock."

This!

Freaking!

Guy!

"Fine!" I called after him as he reached his SUV. "But I'm pretty sure it will still be considered kidnapping, on or off the clock!"

Pausing with his grip on the door handle, he glanced back at me and grinned. The sight of that grin made my stomach somersault all over again.

"Maybe you should report it to the station," he suggested. "There's a local detective on the force who'd be more than willing to help you sort it out. Handsome. Great hair. Fantastic taste in women. You didn't get it from me, but I hear he can easily be bribed with a beef burrito from the food truck on Canal Street."

With that, he got into his SUV and shut the door… leaving me alone with my clunker, a dead cellphone, and very few choices. After about twenty seconds — during which I contemplated a variety of ways I might commit homicide against a member of law enforcement without being caught and thrown in the slammer for the rest of my life — I dragged my heels over to my car, shut the hood with a slam, retrieved the battered shoebox from beneath my passenger seat, pulled on my gloves, and shoved my useless phone into my back pocket.

Detective Hightower had the good grace not to look smug as I climbed up into his SUV. But his eyes were doing that crinkly thing again as he spun the wheel, pulled away from the curb, and drove me down the block to The Sea Witch.

CHAPTER FIVE

I'm just saying... there's a reason the worst week of the month is called MEN-struation, not WOMEN-struation.
- Imogen Warner, linguistic expert

The Sea Witch was not a five-star hotel. It wasn't a hotel at all. The annoyingly persistent Caden Hightower had called it an inn, but it was really more of a bed and breakfast.

Once a grand estate overlooking the sea, the B&B was now a mere echo of its former glory. Beneath the intricate Victorian architecture, it was rather rundown — chipping paint and a sagging front porch that did not seem entirely structurally sound. The old mansion had numerous additions that were obviously not part of the original construction, all of which appeared to have been tacked on at different time periods, with little consideration of overall aesthetic cohesiveness. The result was a strange Frankenstein of a place, its ornate, gothic central structure supplemented by an oddly modern wing on the left side, an in-ground pool at the rear surrounded by chain link, and an angular mid-century sunroom sagging beside the parking lot.

I'd stayed worse places. (Occasionally)

I'd also stayed better. (Even more occasionally.)

But, hey, I could survive just about anywhere for a night. I figured it was as good a place to crash as any. Better than the cold backseat of my car, that was certain. Though, it was clear from the moment he drove into the lot, the handsome detective who'd commandeered my entire life without consent was of a differing opinion. He did not look enchanted by the crumbling facade, or charmed by the splintered wooden steps that led up onto the front porch.

One of the lights flanking the entry was out, but the interior was illuminated. A warm glow spilled through the front windows onto the porch and into the parking lot. And the sign by the street — a weather-beaten wooden monstrosity in the shape of a ship bust, with the words THE SEA WITCH INN embossed in old fashioned lettering — was accompanied by a glowing, neon VACANCY message.

Good enough for me.

"I'm not sure about this," Cade muttered, eyeing the inn through the windshield.

I rolled my eyes as I slung my backpack over my shoulders and lugged my duffle from the floor. "Well, I am. Thanks for the entirely unnecessary escort down the block, Detective. I don't know how my tiny womanly brain would've located this place without your expert guidance."

"You're welcome."

He was grinning at me. Before I could do something ludicrous — like grin back at him — I turned away, yanked on the handle, and practically vaulted from the SUV with the duffle strap slung over my shoulder and my pathetic shoebox tucked under one arm. I didn't even bother to say goodbye as I slammed the door shut and scurried toward the front door without looking back.

I knew I was being rude. I also knew it was better for all parties involved if I got away from the too-charming-for-his-own-good Caden Hightower as soon as humanly possible. Nothing positive could come from an entanglement with someone like him. He asked too many questions — not to mention pushed all my buttons. (And, frankly, seemed to enjoy doing it.)

Unfortunately, in my haste to escape, I overlooked one crucial detail. Namely: his willingness to meddle in affairs that did not concern him. I'd made it only a few strides across the parking lot when the engine shut off, the driver's door slammed, and the foreboding sound of boots began crunching on the gravel in my wake. I picked up my pace but by the time I hit the creaky front steps, Cade was striding along at my side, his long legs easily matching my hurried ones.

"What do you think you're doing?" I hissed, stopping on the creaky porch. Two moths were fluttering by the single working lightbulb, their papery white wings casting eerie shadows.

"Making sure you get settled," he said patiently.

I gripped the strap of my duffle so hard, my knuckles went white. "That's entirely unnecess— *Wait!*"

Cade did not wait. He had, in fact, already reached around me and pulled open the front door. He held it wide, boots planted firmly on the porch, looking for all the world like he had no intention of moving until I did.

"After you," he said, eyes crinkled in amusement.

I didn't move a muscle. "You're letting in the moths."

"Then you'd better go in."

I scowled at him. And then, jerking my chin in a haughty manner in an attempt to summon my small slice of remaining dignity, I stormed past him into The Sea Witch.

His amused chuckle chased me over the threshold.

The lobby area was small but surprisingly cozy, with a mishmash of antique furniture and a vaguely nautical theme. It smelled of wood polish and old books — probably due to the stuffed shelves that lined the wall beside a curving grand staircase that led to the upstairs rooms. A crystal chandelier cast the whole space in soft, suffused light. Almost directly beneath it, a chest-height reception desk faced the door. An ancient computer monitor sat atop it along with a large ledger book. A woman — presumably the receptionist — stood behind it.

She was youngish, probably in her mid-thirties, with light brown hair and delicate features that were, at this precise moment in time, screwed up in an expression of frustration. She did not greet us immediately; her focus was entirely consumed by the needle she was attempting to thread in the dim glow of her desk lamp.

"Be right with you," she murmured without looking up. "I've almost got it..."

I stopped in my tracks. Cade stopped directly beside me. In silence, we waited, watching as the receptionist steered the flimsy thread toward the tiny hole at the end of the needle. She let out a sharp wail that made me jump half a foot in the air when the thread missed its mark by several millimeters. Tossing down the spool on her ledger book and shoving the needle into a red pin-cushion shaped like a tomato, she finally glanced up at us. Traces of her scowl were still present as she locked eyes with me.

"Sorry about that. I've been trying to get that damn thing threaded for a half hour. I'm about ready to tear my hair out by the roots."

"Uh... no worries." I set down my duffle on the rug — oriental style, somewhat frayed but still pretty. "You know, it's easier if you lick the end of the thread first."

"I tried that. No luck." She sighed heavily. "If I don't get this costume sewn by Halloween, I'm going to have one very disappointed alien on my hands."

My brows went up.

Seeing my confused expression, she reached beneath the desk and retrieved a shiny, fluorescent swathe of fabric. I'd never seen a shade of green quite so bright.

"My youngest son is in a big Martian phase at the moment. I

promised I'd make him look like a proper space invader. How hard could it be, right?" She grimaced and flung the fabric aside. "Apparently, *really goddamn hard*. I can't even get the needle threaded! How the hell am I supposed to follow a pattern for an entire costume in three days?"

"Hand it over," I said immediately, approaching the desk. I set down my shoebox to accept the spool and pincushion when she passed them to me. Within seconds, I'd doubled the bright green thread over itself to create a sharper end, pulled it taught, and guided it through the eyehole of the needle. "There," I murmured. "All done. You're good to start sewing."

"Hey, thanks!" The receptionist grinned at me as I passed the spool back to her. "You're a lifesaver."

"It's really no big deal."

And it wasn't. I was an old hand at mending, having acquired much of my wardrobe from second-hand shops over the years. I knew how to sew a hem and replace a seam and re-attach a missing button. Most of my clothes looked far more expensive than they were because I'd hand-tailored them to fit my exact measurements.

"It's a big deal to me," the woman said, carefully setting down the pincushion in the corner of her desk, as though terrified any sudden movements would cause the needle to spontaneously un-spool. "And it will be to my son as well. You're saving the entire inn from a full-blown Martian meltdown."

I shrugged, feeling suddenly embarrassed. "Well, we wouldn't want an intergalactic incident on our hands."

She laughed and her whole face lit up in the process. "Any-way... Now that you've solved my problems, what can I do for you? Are you checking in?" For the first time since we'd arrived, she looked past me to the man hovering at my back. Her eyes widened as she took in his tall form. "Oh! Detective Hightower! I didn't even see you there."

Was I mistaken, or were the pretty receptionist's cheeks turning pink at the mere sight of my handsome cop?

Not that he was *mine*.

He was just—

I cut off the train of thought before it could further develop, but there was no shaking the unpleasant feeling that settled in the pit of my stomach as I studied the admiration in the receptionist's eyes — no longer directed my way, but shining like a spotlight directly on Cade Hightower.

"Georgia," he greeted her, stepping up beside me. We were so close, our shoulders were almost brushing. I fought the urge to sidle away. "How are you doing?"

"Oh, me?" Yep, her cheeks were definitely pink — and growing pinker by the second. "I'm fine, just fine."

"And the boys?"

"They're good." She looked back at me. "Or, they will be, thanks to your girl, here."

"I'm not his girl," I said immediately.

"Glad to hear it," Cade said, his words muffling mine.

"So…" Her gaze shifted back and forth between us. "You'll be needing a room for two, then?"

"No!" I practically screamed.

The receptionist flinched, startled by my yell.

"We don't— We aren't together!" I forced myself to speak in a (slightly) more reasonable tone. "We just met, like, twenty minutes ago. He's practically a stranger."

"Okie dokie," the receptionist said slowly, looking at me like I had a few screws loose. "Room for *one* it is…"

Cade seemed to be choking down laughter. "Thanks, Georgia. I'm just here making sure she gets settled in all right."

I turned to face him. "And you've done so. See? I'm settled. Now, you can go."

He planted one hip against the reception desk and leaned against it with his arms crossed over his chest, looking for all the world like he was modeling for some kind of police department fundraising calendar. (October had never been so sexy.)

"Georgia," he said, addressing her even though his eyes never shifted from me. "What's the going rate here at The Sea Witch, these days?"

"Standard rooms start at one-twenty a night."

A chill swept through me.

One-twenty a night? For this crappy old place on the outskirts of town? I'd be flat broke before the week was out! And that wasn't even factoring in whatever my car repairs were going to cost. The tow alone would set me back. Contrary to the detective's assurances that Puck the auto-whiz owed him a favor, I had no intentions of accepting charity. I'd been paying my own way for a decade. No reason to stop, now.

Cade was watching me closely. He seemed to read every bit of anxiety on my face as easily as he would the page of a book. The furrow was back between his brows and thoughts were working in his eyes. His voice went low — so low, I could barely hear it. "Is that good with you?"

He was, by some small mercy, kind enough not to ask his real question. (Which was, *Can you afford this place or should I find you somewhere even more run-down?*) I swallowed my mortification and nodded. "Of course it's good with me."

The furrow between his brows deepened. There was no humor in his eyes. None. Not even a trace of a smile twitched at the corners of his lips. He totally knew I was full of it.

God, this was humiliating.

I'd experienced plenty of embarrassment in my time on this earth, but standing there in that moment, I was hit with a wave of it unlike anything previously endured. I wished he would just go, already.

Why was he so insistent on hanging around?

I really didn't want him to hear me tell the sweet lady at the desk I could only afford one night. And I really, *really*, did not want to crack open my pathetic little shoebox and start counting out my meager stack of cash while the weight of those sharp blue eyes flattened me into a pancake of mortification.

Perhaps sensing the tension, the receptionist interjected. "We do a weekly discount: six hundred if you stay seven nights." She paused, then muttered, "Not that anyone does."

I was still staring — glaring — at Cade. "Just go. Please."

"Goldie—"

"*Go!*"

My voice cracked on the word, and everyone jolted at the sound — even me. Shoving down my embarrassment, I forced myself to hold his eyes and, in a more level tone, repeated, "Go. Please. I've got it from here."

He studied me for another long moment. I thought he wasn't going to listen but, miraculously, he hauled his tall frame off the desk and straightened to full height. Reaching into his back pocket, he pulled out his wallet and extracted what appeared to be a business card. He used one of the desk pens to scrawl a phone number on the back in blocky, masculine writing. When he was finished, he could've simply handed it to me but instead, in a blink, he reached out and tucked the tiny white square of card-stock into the back pocket of my cut-off shorts.

It happened so fast, I didn't even have time to backpedal.

"What—"

"My cell number," he said simply, stepping away. "Call me tomorrow about your car. I should have an update from Puck by mid-afternoon."

"That's not necess—"

"Tomorrow," he said firmly, cutting me off before I could tell him I wouldn't be dragging him into any more of my problems. "Or before that. If you need me for any reason—"

"I won't!"

"Right." His eyes crinkled at the corners. "Sleep well, Goldie."

He crossed to the door with long-legged strides. He was

halfway there when, from the parlor-style room on the right, a small form raced into the reception area, moving so fast he was almost a blur. He skidded abruptly to a halt, nearly tripping on the rug in the process. Cade's large hand settled on the boy's shoulder, steadying him before he could face-plant at his feet.

"Whoa there. Slow down, bud."

"Detective Hightower! Detective Hightower! It's me! Rory! Remember?"

Cade planted his hands on his hips and stared down at the little boy, who was no more than six or seven, by my best guess. He was barefoot, tousle-headed, and dressed in pajamas that were covered in small silver spaceships.

"Rory?" Cade echoed. "Hmm… No, I don't think so…"

The kid looked crushed he'd been so easily forgotten. "Really? You don't remember? We met in the summertime! At home —" He looked quickly at his mother and a note of uncertainty crept into his voice. "I mean, at our old place. At Dad's place."

"No, that can't be." Cade shook his head back and forth. "Rory was a little boy. You look more like an alien to me."

An utterly delighted grin moved over the kid's face. He looked a lot like Georgia — light brown hair, bright hazel eyes, and fine, foxlike features. "That's right! I'm going to be a Martian for Halloween! I wanted the costume with the built-in lasers we saw at the store. It comes with a matching helmet! And a pair of blasters! But Mom said it cost too much." His smile crumpled a little, but he forced a chipper tone. "Now she's making me a costume from scratch! And it's gonna be *awesome*! Right, Mom?"

"Right," Georgia echoed morosely, no doubt thinking of the monumental sewing task ahead of her. She'd come around her desk to face-off with her son. "Bub, what are you doing out of bed? It's way past your bedtime."

"I heard voices," the kid said, like his reasoning should be obvious. He looked abruptly at me, naked curiosity in his eyes. "Who are *you*?"

"She's a guest, Rory," Georgia said patiently. "She's staying here tonight."

"Sweet!" He threw both arms into the air over his head in celebration. "Are you here for Halloween?"

I shook my head. "Just for one night."

"If you stay a week, it's cheaper." He looked at his mother. "Did you tell her, Mom?"

"I told her, Rory."

"Then why's she only here one night?"

"I'm just passing through," I informed him.

He planted his hands at his hips, mirroring Cade's pose in miniature form. "You should stay for Halloween. It's, like, the best holiday ever. The whole town is one big party. And I know from last year which houses hand out the king-size Snickers!"

"Sounds cool," I told him. Mostly because, well, it did sound cool.

He nodded sagely. "It is *wicked* cool. But you'll need a costume."

"If I stay, can I be a Martian, too?"

He frowned as he examined me, perhaps evaluating whether or not I was rad enough to be a member of his alien horde. "I don't know… Do you even like space?"

I tried very hard not to giggle at his solemn question. "Sure do."

"What's your favorite planet?"

"Pluto," I said instantly.

"Pluto isn't even a planet anymore," he countered.

"It was when I was growing up."

"Yeah, but you're, like… old."

Only someone under ten would classify twenty-five as *old*. "Thanks a lot, kid."

"Rory, that's enough." Georgia pinned him with a look. "What have I told you about harassing the guests?"

"Um…" He thought hard. "Don't do it?"

"Exactly." Georgia grabbed him by the hand and yanked him away from Cade, who was standing there watching all of this unfold with an expression of barely-contained mirth. "Off to bed you go, bub. And if you come out again, I'll let your brother pick the kind of candy we pass out this year."

Rory's face contorted in horror. "But Declan likes *Junior Mints*!"

He said *Junior Mints* as though they were lined with cow dung instead of chocolate. And then, in another blur of limbs, he was gone — racing into the parlor room and out of sight.

"Goodnight! Sleep tight!" Georgia called after him. She heaved a sigh as she looked at me. "Sorry about that. We live in the back rooms here on the first floor. Usually, the boys are pretty good about staying in their designated space, but..."

"It's fine. He's adorable."

She looked relieved. "Thanks."

"How old is he?"

"Seven. His big brother is eleven — and currently occupied by a new Nintendo game, otherwise he'd no doubt be out here raising hell as well." She chewed her lip. "They're good boys, I promise. Most of the time. If they bother you at all during your stay, just let me know and I'll handle it." Her eyes drifted over to Cade and, for the first time, I saw the deep sadness in them. "They've had a rough go of it since I split with their dad a few months ago."

"Has Donny been coming around?" Cade sounded more serious than I'd ever heard him. "Or is he abiding by the protection order?"

"Donny is... Donny. You know he doesn't have much respect for police. Or anyone else, for that matter."

"Georgia—"

"It's fine, Detective." Her smile was weak. "I promise."

"It's not fine. A judge ruled he was unfit to be around you. I know you're planning to petition for full custody of your boys. If you keep allowing him to violate the order, you're only making that legal battle tougher."

"I know." Her voice got small. "He hasn't been violent. Not lately."

"Georgia—"

"Don't worry. I know he won't change. I'm not that stupid. You don't have to worry about me going back to him — not ever again. But the boys... they don't understand. Even if Donny is a rotten bastard to me, he's still their dad. They miss him. They still ask all the time when we're going to move back home."

Cade's face was set like stone. "The sooner you're honest with them, the easier it will be for them to accept that they're never going back there."

"I know." Her voice broke. "I know, all right? And I'll tell them. Soon. I swear."

"In the meantime, you'll keep me informed if Donny comes around again. You'll let me know if he escalates in any way," Cade said, and it was not a request — it was an order.

"Of course, Detective."

"He may not respect the law, but he will abide by it," he added. "I'll make sure of that, Georgia."

She blew out a breath. "Okay. Okay. I promise, next time he shows up unannounced, I'll call the station."

"If you can't get me at the station, call me directly. You have the number."

She nodded. "I do."

"It's going to be okay," he said in that deep, authoritative timbre of his. "I'll make sure of it."

"Thanks, Detective."

Cade shot me one last lingering look — a look, I might add, that made the previous somersaults in my gut appear amateur by compare — and murmured, "I'll be seeing you, Goldie. Soon."

Then, he turned on his heel and stalked out the front door, into the night.

For a moment, there was only silence in the reception area. When I mustered the courage to look over at Georgia, I found she was already studying me, her curious eyes moving back and forth the between me and the door. A slow grin moved over her face.

"Are you *sure* you don't want that room for two?"

CHAPTER SIX

Climate change is the ultimate glow-up.
After being mistreated by men, Earth is getting super hot!
- Imogen Warner, doom-scrolling at 3AM

Despite its unimpressive exterior facade, the rooms inside The Sea Witch were surprisingly well appointed. At least, my room was. After checking me in — without batting so much as an eyelash at my shoebox of wrinkled bills when I'd forked over a hundred and twenty precious buckaroos — Georgia had led me up the curved, creaky staircase to the second floor, down a short hallway to a door marked with a tiny gold number 5 nailed above the ornate center knob.

"No fobs or keycards," she said apologetically, lifting up a heavy brass key with a teal tassel on the end. "We keep things old school, here."

She held the door open for me to walk inside, then followed me in like we were old friends, chatting away the entire time about the continental breakfast, which would be served in the parlor room from seven to ten, and lamenting the fact that I hadn't come earlier in the season when the outdoor pool was still open for business.

I half-listened as I studied the nautically-themed room, with its deep blue and green color palette, various oil paintings of ocean scenes, and knickknacks scattered around on practically every surface — featuring, but not limited to, a ship inside a bottle on the table by the window and a painted mermaid statue on the desk. The coat hooks by the door were shaped like seahorses; the twin nightstand lamps like seashells.

"Sorry, I know it's a bit over the top—"

"It's perfect, Georgia."

"Gigi." She smiled at me. "Everyone calls me Gigi."

Except Detective Hightower, I thought.

"I'm Imogen," I told her, even though she'd already seen my ID when I checked in. "No nickname. Everyone calls me Imogen."

Except Detective Hightower, I thought again, then quickly shoved all thoughts of him away.

"It's great to have you with us, Imogen. I'll get out of your hair, now. You must be tired. But if you need anything, just holler!" Gigi chirped at me. "I'm only a floor away and these walls are thin as paper!"

She said this as though it was a selling point.

Shutting the door with a wink and a wave, Gigi disappeared. Calling a weak goodnight after her, I dropped my duffle and shoebox on the floor and promptly collapsed face-first on the bed. It wasn't the most comfortable mattress, but there were no mystery stains anywhere to be seen on the faded blue duvet and the sheets smelled freshly laundered. I laid there for a while, wondering what deity I'd offended in my previous life to find myself here — down on my luck in another cheap hotel room in another random town that I'd have to leave in my rearview ASAP, because the townsfolk were alarmingly friendly and prone to sticking their noses where they didn't belong. I figured I must've done something pretty awful in my previous incarnation.

Car salesman, maybe? Con artist? Person who never returned their cart in the grocery store parking lot? The cruel, wicked stepmother to a girl locked in a tower?

The possibilities were endless.

After about ten minutes, I forced myself to stop wallowing and take a shower. In my experience, if I allowed a pity party to drag on longer than ten minutes, it became something more nefarious. A pity soiree. A pity gala. A pity jamboree, if you will. And I had it on good authority that no one in the history of mankind ever had a good time at a jamboree.

The water pressure was spotty at best and the tap ran cold far too soon for my liking, but I still felt markedly better when I stepped out. A mellow calm had settled in my bones as I reached for the folded towel on the wall-mounted rack. I'd sleep well, tonight. In fact, I was already fantasizing about the moment I'd finally slide into bed, so caught up in my thoughts I didn't see the tiny wooden figurine sitting on the shelf beside the towels until it was too late. My bare fingers collided with the carving and it tumbled toward the floor.

I never heard it hit the tile.

The moment my fingertips grazed the figurine, the vision slammed into me with the force of a sledgehammer. I stumbled back into the water-beaded shower wall. Purple sparks erupted on the peripheral of my visual field, then closed in as striped bathroom wallpaper and porcelain fixtures were swapped for a different scene entirely.

The campground is dark.

The night is cold.

So cold, the man's breath fogs the air as he bends closer over the tiny wood block in his hands. The flick of his knife is rhythmic as he whittles his design one sliver at a time. His focus never shifts except in the brief moment he pauses to throw another log on the campfire, sending a shower of sparks into the shadows.

Tears stream down his face as he works. Tears he does not bother to wipe away, but lets fall from his chin and onto the fabric of his hunting coat.

More purple flashed like a firework display across my eyes as the vision changed, shifting with disorienting speed.

The sun is bright overhead, bleaching the hilltop cemetery of color. In the distance, a harbor is visible. Old wooden schooners bob at moorings and glide down a central channel.

The man's tears are gone. He stands over a fresh grave. The grass has not yet grown in and the tombstone is too pristine to have spent much time in the elements. The name chiseled on the front reads PORTER. *There is a death date* — APRIL 19, 1775 — *along with a series of words.*

BELOVED SON, HONORED SOLDIER, ETERNAL PATRIOT

The man reaches forward and traces three of the chiseled letters with reverence.

SON.

This is his son's grave.

He is stoic in the face of his grief, but his hand shakes a bit as he places a figurine — carved in the shape of a soldier, with a tricorn hat and extended musket — at the base of the tombstone. The man begins to speak, but his words are inaudible. There is only the sound of the wind, a mournful wail off the water. And then—

As quickly as I'd left it, I was back in the bathroom at The Sea Witch, slumped naked against the damp tile wall. My skin was clammy. My lungs were screaming for air. I dragged a shaky breath into them as the last of the purple sparks dissipated from my eyes with a few hard blinks.

It had never seemed fair — how snapping into a vision took less than a heartbeat but coming back to reality took ages. I knew from experience that even after I caught my breath and regained my composure, the effects would linger, the chill of the vision clinging to me like an invisible film for the rest of the evening.

The fluorescent vanity light over the mirror hummed faintly as I stepped out of the tub, wrapped a towel around myself, and tried to shake off the shivery sensation sliding up and down my spine. Only moments before, I'd been warm and relaxed from my shower. Now, I felt as windswept and grief-stricken as that wood-carver in the seaside graveyard.

I eyed the fallen soldier figurine, which had clattered to a stop beside the sink pedestal. It had deteriorated a bit with time, but looked remarkably well preserved given its age. How had it ended up here, of all places, as bathroom decor at a rundown B&B? Had someone picked it up one day, thinking it no more than a lost trinket, and brought it home with them? Had it been passed down through generations, only to be sold at some musty estate sale decades later?

I didn't allow myself to dwell too much on these questions. There was no point. Not when I'd never know the answers. That was the tough thing about the visions: they offered me a snapshot, not a full storyline, rarely lasting long enough to sate my curiosity or give me any true insight. Most of the time they were more frustrating than illuminating — which was one of the reasons I preferred to avoid them whenever possible. My gloves provided a much-needed barrier of protection against unwanted triggers and allowed me to live a (relatively) normal life.

Of course, not every object I touched sparked a vision. Most things were just that: things. Only the rarest of objects were imbued with enough emotion to send me spiraling into someone's memories. Take the soldier figurine, for instance. With each flick of his knife, that father had embedded a bit more of his grief into the wood, until his devastation was as much a part of the design as the shape of the hat or the slope of the musket barrel. Until the trace of his sadness was so strong, it persisted even after all this time. An eerie emotional echo.

It was just rotten luck that I'd happened to touch it; that it happened to be in this room in the first place. For every thousand objects I took into my palms, perhaps only one would result in that dreaded starburst of purple sparks. The problem was, there was no way to tell a harmless knickknack from something that would catapult me into the past without warning.

Not until it was too late.

There was no rhyme or reason when it came to the type or shape or location of triggering objects. I'd once been thrown into a vision while picking up a few loose coins from the floor during a bartending shift, not realizing there was a hole in the tip of my glove until the sticky linoleum was swapped for the cold marble floor of a vault, and the bottles of liquor at my back were replaced by a trio of bank robbers in black balaclavas, pointing guns at the teller who was emptying the contents of her register into a bag with trembling hands. (I'd needed a shot of tequila, after that one.)

I used a tissue to pick up the figurine and stashed it away in the medicine cabinet, where there would be no more accidental encounters. Usually, triggering objects — even extremely old ones — only had enough instilled memory to spark a single vision. But some emotional echoes were stronger than others. I wasn't taking any chances during the rest of my stay here.

After changing into pajamas, I slathered on moisturizer and combed out my long tangle of damp curls. I didn't have the energy to blow it dry, even if it meant waking up with volume to rival Dolly Parton. It had been a long day even before the vision, and traces of exhaustion were etched all over my face. I studied my reflection in the mirror as I brushed my teeth. The contrast between my pale blue eyes and the dark bags beneath them was starkly unattractive.

Flipping off the lights, I made my way to bed in near total darkness. As I crossed the room, my bare feet tangled on my discarded clothing, nearly sending me sprawling. When I crouched down to pick them up, my gaze snagged on a small white card sticking out of the pocket of my shorts. Detective Hightower's business card. Before I could stop myself, I was reaching for it with my bare hands.

I sucked in a sharp breath, bracing for another vision, but my fingers gripped the cardstock and...

Nothing.

No violet sparks, no rippling visual field.

I didn't allow myself to question why I'd been willing to risk touching *this* particular object. Nor did I allow myself to wonder why, instead of relief, I felt something more akin to disappointment when no vision overtook me. And I definitely, absolutely, positively did not allow myself to psychoanalyze why I felt the urge to carry the card with me into bed, beneath the covers, where I traced the faintly embossed letters that spelled out DETECTIVE CADEN HIGHTOWER, SALEM POLICE DEPARTMENT over and over with my fingertip until, finally, my eyes drifted shut and I fell asleep.

"The waffle machine is broken again," Rory announced morosely, slamming his plate down beside mine on the long oak table that stretched across the first floor parlor. Seeds from his everything bagel flew in all directions. "This totally *sucks*."

"Rory! Don't say *sucks*."

The kid rolled his eyes at his mother's chastisement, which she delivered without even turning from the coffee machine where she was filling up her mug. The parlor was drenched with early morning sunshine, which slanted through the bay windows that faced the side lawn. It was spacious enough to feed at least twenty, but at the moment only one other guest was present — an elderly man who'd seated himself at a tiny table in the far corner and never once looked up from his newspaper in the twenty minutes since I'd arrived downstairs.

Gigi's sons more than made up for the sparse attendance in both energy and appetite. If they weren't actively chewing, they were chattering. I'd barely gotten two words in as I fixed myself a mug of coffee, as I sent my sliced croissant around the toaster conveyer belt, as I dolloped jam onto my plate and carried it back to the table.

Rory settled in on the seat beside mine with a low grunt. "Declan says sucks all the time, Mom."

"Don't be a narc!" Declan hissed, plunking himself into the chair across from his brother. His bowl looked like it contained at least three different varieties of cereal and was so full, milk sloshed over the edges and began pooling on the placemat. It was his second helping.

"What's a narc?" Rory asked.

Declan ignored his little brother, shoving a heaping spoonful into his mouth and chewing at superhuman speed. He looked a lot like his younger sibling, though his hair was nearly brushing his shoulders instead of close-cropped and his eyes were a dark brown instead of hazel.

Rory turned to me. "What's a narc?"

I choked on my croissant. "Um..."

"Boys! Leave Imogen alone." Gigi winked at me as she exited the parlor, hurrying back to the front lobby where the desk phone was ringing off the hook.

"We aren't bothering her!" Rory called after her. He turned to me, brows high on his forehead. "We aren't, right?"

Shaking my head, I took another large bite of my croissant and washed it down with a sip of coffee. "Not at all."

"Cool." Rory took a bite of his bagel, made a disgusted face, and promptly discarded it back on his plate. "Yuck! This tastes like dirt."

"Cereal's good," Declan declared without looking up, still wolfing down spoonfuls.

"I don't want cereal." Rory was adamant. "I want *waffles*."

"Don't be such a crybaby," Declan grumbled around a mouthful. "We're lucky Mr. Monteith lets us eat here for free."

Mr. Monteith, I had learned from the boys only moments before, was the proprietor of the illustrious Sea Witch Inn. He didn't seem to have much interest actually proproieting, though, seeing as he spent most of the year living in Florida and only occasionally swept back into town to make sure things were running smoothly under Georgia's management.

"What's with the gloves?"

I nearly spat out my coffee at Rory's sudden question. I turned to look at him and found he was studying my white, lace-detailed gloves with naked curiosity.

"Um… it's fall," I hedged. "Everyone wears gloves in the fall."

"Yeah, when they're outside. Not inside." His huge hazel eyes narrowed a shade. "Definitely not during breakfast."

I merely shrugged. "Maybe I just like them. They're fashionable."

His eyes narrowed further; he wasn't buying it.

"Or," I said conspiratorially, lowering my voice to a whisper. "Maybe I have superpowers. Maybe, when I touch things, I have psychic visions I can't control." I waggled my fingers at him. "Maybe I'm a totally cool clairvoyant with magic you can hardly fathom."

There was a long beat of silence.

Then, from both boys in perfect unison, "Yeah, *right*!"

I shrugged and sipped my coffee, unbothered.

"Mom says it's bad to fib," Rory informed me.

"Who says I'm fibbing?"

"Me!"

"And I'm supposed to trust *you*? A self-proclaimed alien?" I shook my head at the kid. "I don't think so, E.T."

"What's E.T.?"

I stared up at the ceiling and wailed, "God, what's happening to the youth of America? To cinema? Classic films have fallen by the wayside! It's a travesty, I tell you! A travesty!"

Another silence descended.

When I glanced back at the boys, they were both staring at me like I was more than a little insane. Across the table, Declan pushed his — now empty — bowl away. He leveled me with a wholly unimpressed gaze and remarked, "You're kinda weird, you know."

Sighing, I muttered, "I do, in fact, know that."

"Don't be a dick, Dec!"

"Don't say dick, dick!" Declan shot back at his younger brother.

"*MOM*!" Rory was abruptly on his feet. "Declan called me a dick!"

"Only 'cause he called me a dick first!"

"Stop saying dick!"

"*You* stop!"

Suddenly, I was alone at the table. Alone in the room, in fact, seeing as the elderly gentlemen had fled with his newspaper sometime around the second *dick*. Pushing and shoving the entire way, both boys raced out of the parlor into the front lobby, leaving their breakfast plates behind. I quietly stacked them beneath my own and carried them over to the kitchenette area by the far wall, disposing of the scraps in the trash and rinsing them under the tap.

I did my best not to eavesdrop, but I could hear the muffled strains of conversation as Gigi soothed the fraternal squabble, her measured tones an underscore for the rapid-fire volley of her boys. By the time I'd washed the dishes and placed them on the rack to dry, a subdued Rory and Declan were marching through the parlor, headed for their apartment at the back of the first floor. They wore matching expressions of chastisement.

"I was just about to do those dishes!" Gigi announced, appearing suddenly beside me. "Thanks. Rory and Declan usually know better than to leave their mess lying around."

"No trouble at all."

"I'm sorry if they disturbed your breakfast. They're off to get ready for school now, so you can enjoy your coffee in peace without any more roughhousing. Assuming they don't miss their bus, that is..." Her smile was apologetic. "I'd promise that it isn't always so chaotic around here, but... I've never been a good liar."

I laughed. "I don't mind. Honestly. They're just kids being kids."

"Most days, I feel like I'm raising two hellions." She blew out a sharp breath. "And failing majorly as a mother."

"You're not. Trust me. I..." I hesitated for a beat, then plowed on. "I know what bad parenting looks like. This isn't it."

"You're sweet."

"Not really. I just call it like I see it."

Her smile lost its apologetic bent and turned full-fledged, transforming her face from quietly pretty to truly stunning. "I have to get back to the front desk. But if you have a few minutes, I'd love the company of someone over the age of eleven. The night manager, Rhonda, isn't much for conversation. Same goes for our handful of other guests. Top off your coffee, then come have a chat."

I did exactly that, following her out to the reception area. In the light of day, the space was actually quite pleasant. I eyed the overflowing bookshelves as I settled in on the plush bench seat beneath the window, wishing I had the luxury of curling up in the sunshine with a new novel and ignoring all my problems for the rest of the day.

"You're welcome to borrow any of them," Gigi said, noticing the direction of my gaze.

"Oh. I doubt I'll be here long enough…"

She frowned. "It's a shame you can't stay a few more nights. I just finished this series about sexy fairies. I know what you're thinking. *Fairies? Sexy?* But they aren't the Tinker Bell sort of fairy. They're super powerful, badass, *dude* fairies. They all have dark hair and really big—"

My brows arched.

"—wingspans," she finished, giggling. "Look, just trust me. Read it. You'll be obsessed. All human males will forever pale in comparison to these fictional fae hotties."

"That's a low bar to jump. Human males aren't all that impressive."

"Girl, you are preaching to the freaking choir." She tucked a lock of hair behind her ear. "My ex, Donny, is a real piece of work."

I'd gathered as much last night. "How long have you been divorced?"

"Technically, we aren't yet. He refuses to sign the damn papers, no matter how many times I send them. I have a temporary restraining order to keep him away from me and the boys, but it's going to be a long legal battle to permanently untangle him from our lives. Not to mention a heck of a lot of cash. And even then, there are no guarantees. A judge might *still* side with him. He's an utter asshole at the core, but he can be pretty charming when he needs to be — just ask my twenty-two-year-old self, who fell head over heels for the charade."

"He sounds like he's related to my ex, Adrian," I muttered. "There must be some way to get him to sign without dragging it into court…"

"You haven't met Donny. My old pit bull had an easier time letting go of things."

I took a sip of my coffee, scorching my tongue in the process. "You could always try whacking him on the nose with a newspaper."

"I might, if I knew the bastard wouldn't hit back — and he'd use his fists, for the record. He broke my arm in two places the last time I stood up to him. That's when I decided enough was enough. I got my boys, then I got the hell out."

Any trace of levity fled my voice. "God, Gigi, I'm so sorry. I didn't mean to make a joke of your situation—"

She waved away my words. "Don't apologize. It's better to laugh than cry about it all day. And if I can't find the humor in the tragedy… Somehow it feels like he's already won."

"I understand," I said softly. "Believe me, I understand."

And I did. I understood all too well what it was like to live under the same roof with a man who made your stomach churn with the sour taste of fear. I knew, even after you left, that sour taste took a long, long while to fade.

Maybe it *never* really faded — not entirely. Maybe you just got used to it. Hell, it had been months since I left Adrian and, sometimes, I could still hear his voice screaming at me in the dark; still feel his hands wrapped around my neck, squeezing the life out of me.

I didn't tell Gigi this. I didn't have to. She looked at me, I looked at her, and there was a moment. A moment of pure, feminine understanding. Whatever empathy she read in my expression, whatever shared experience she saw in my eyes, told her all she needed to know, without my ever needing to say the words aloud.

There was something so tragically sad about that — the instant bond between two women who'd endured the same trauma — but there was something inherently beautiful about it, too. Kinship and connection born from the worst sort of horror. A little light coming out of all that darkness.

We were silent for a short stretch, sipping our coffee. It wasn't an awkward silence, it was a companionable one. The kind I hadn't experienced in far too long.

"At least I have the restraining order," she said finally. "The police will protect me if Donny escalates. Theoretically."

"Cade said—"

"Ah yes, refresh my memory... What did *Cade* say?"

My cheeks flushed at the blatant suggestion in her tone. I immediately amended, "Detective Hightower—"

"*Sexy* Detective Hightower." Her brows waggled.

"Gigi!"

"Okay, then... *Silver Fox* Detective Hightower..."

"Georgia!"

"Imogen!"

"I don't know what you're implying, but—"

"Oh, come off it." She set down her mug. "Don't even try to pretend you haven't noticed how hot that man is. I sensed the tension between you two last night."

"There was no tension!"

"Honey, it was so thick I could've cut it with a knife, slathered it on toast, and still had leftovers for breakfast tomorrow."

Damn and blast.

"Look, if there was tension, it wasn't the kind you're thinking of."

"You mean the *rip his clothes off with your-teeth* kind? Because I'm pretty sure that's what I was sensing..."

"No, definitely not. It was the *grind-my-teeth-in-utter-frustration* variety."

"Sexual frustration?"

"Gigi," I said warningly. "My car broke down. He was being nice to a stranger in need. That's all."

"Keep telling yourself that, Imogen."

"He was just doing his job!"

"His job is catching criminals, not personally escorting women to a local inn, making sure they're settled, then calling first thing in the morning with updates about their cars."

I sat up straighter. "Hang on. Rewind. He called?"

"Twenty minutes ago."

"And?" The word nearly exploded out of my mouth, such was its velocity.

"Oh, *now* you're interested in chatting about the handsome detective?"

"Gigi, I swear—"

Her giggles might've been infectious if they weren't at my expense. "Take a breath! He only wanted me to pass along a message that your car is at the auto-body shop being checked out as we speak. He said he'll have an update on the extent of the repairs by this afternoon but, from the initial diagnostic, you're not going to be driving anywhere for a while."

That didn't sound good. "Define *a while*."

"Seemed like a few days at least. A week at most."

"A week?!"

"Hey, don't shoot the messenger!" She held up her hands defensively. "Apparently, your car isn't exactly fresh off the lot. They have to order a replacement part from somewhere else..."

Of course they didn't have the parts in stock for my shitbox. That would be too easy.

"He wants you to call him." Gigi was grinning like this was the best day of her life. "Please tell me I can be in the room, and that you'll put it on speakerphone so I can listen in."

"Absolutely not. I met you, like, twelve hours ago and I already know there's a zero percent chance you will be able to contain your background giggles."

As if to prove my point, she burst out laughing. "Point taken. But you cannot deprive me of all that simmering sexual tension forever. I'll expect a full report afterward."

"Splendid," I groused sarcastically. "More joys to look forward to, along with car trouble and an overbearing cop meddling in my affairs."

And spontaneous visions triggered by Revolutionary War Era knickknacks.

And a rapidly dwindling bank account.

And...

"Look on the bright side!" Gigi interrupted my slow spiral into panic. "This means you'll be staying with us for a few more days."

I glanced at her and attempted a smile. "Yeah, and going broke in the process."

Her own smile fell away. "Sorry. I wish there was something I could do about the rate, but when it comes to the books, Mr. Monteith is kind of a stickler—"

"Stop. This isn't your problem." I squared my shoulders and took a deep breath. "It's six hundred for the week, right?"

Gigi nodded. "You don't have to pay me right this second, though—"

"Might as well bite the bullet." I rose to my feet and began to cross the room. Before I reached the parlor threshold, I paused and glanced back at her. "Hey, you don't happen to know of any places around here that are hiring part-timers? Maybe somewhere I could pick up a few shifts this week, before I leave town? Enough to cover my car repairs?"

And my cellphone bill.

And gas.

And snacks.

And possibly a bottle of tequila to drown my sorrows.

"Hmm..." Her lips pursed as she mulled over my question for a moment. "I mean, you're welcome to use this old thing to search for listings online..." She gestured toward the ancient-looking computer monitor on her desk. It had to be older than Declan. "Fair warning, the internet is spotty at best and it shuts itself down every twenty minutes."

I snorted. "Efficient."

"You could always check the job board downtown. A lot of local businesses post flyers there. Then there's always the Salem Gazette want-ads section..." Her face lit up. "Oh, you know what? You should try The Gallows!"

"The Gallows? I'm looking for gainful employment, not grisly execution."

She rolled her eyes. "No, no. It's this cute coffee-slash-occult-slash-book store smack in the center of the city. Great vibes, ah-freaking-mazing decor. They make a killer pumpkin spice latte and sell all sorts of spooky trinkets. Not just touristy stuff, either — we're talking real witchy-woo-woo shit. Iron cauldrons and pre-bottled curses and crystals of mystical origin."

"Sounds... unique?"

"It totally is!" Gigi exclaimed, missing my skepticism entirely. "They do tarot readings and everything, right in the back of the shop! Or... they did. I heard through the grapevine that their resident psychic recently fled the state." She shrugged. "I'm sure Gwen will find someone new ASAP."

"Gwen?"

"The owner, Gwendolyn Goode. She's this slightly kooky, ultra fashionable redhead. Big temper, bigger heart. You can't miss her, she's always there. Last time I went in, she told me she was looking for some part-time help since the place has gotten so popular... If you stop by, tell her Gigi says hello!"

"Sure," I agreed in an absent murmur.

My brain was still stuck on what she'd said before — about the vacant psychic position. Over the years, I'd racked up plenty of experience with tarot cards, palm lines, tea leaves...

You name it, I read it.

I could easily rake in a few hundred bucks in a week doing private readings. More than enough to cover my car repairs and get the heck out of dodge. If I did a little advertising, broadcast my reputation as a once-famous clairvoyant with B-list celebrity status around town...

I'd be turning clients away.

I shook my head, banishing that train of thought almost as soon as it arose. Dipping my toes back into that world, where I used my powers for profit, was something I had no intentions of doing.

Not unless it was a last resort.

Gwendolyn Goode — *what sort of name was that, anyway?* — and her witchy little shop would simply have to find someone else.

CHAPTER SEVEN

I like my emotions how I like my water.
All bottled up.
- Imogen Warner, getting in touch with her feelings

Fallen leaves crunched beneath the bicycle tires, flying up behind me in a vortex as I rode. At Gigi's insistence, I'd borrowed Declan's bright green two-wheeler for my day of job hunting. (Sometimes, being so short-statured came in handy.)

The air on my cheeks was crisp and cold, but I didn't mind. My body temperature was even more elevated than usual from the rapid pedaling that carried me down one of paths that crisscrossed Salem Common, into the heart of the city.

So far, Salem wasn't like the other stops I'd made on the Imogen Warner International Tour of Misery. Mostly because it was absolutely adorable. Small town charm practically oozed from the cobblestones, which were strewn with crunchy leaves of various red, yellow, and brown hues. The houses I passed by were old and historical — ornate Victorians and stately Colonials lined the square, which looked like something out of a *Gilmore Girls* episode with its round stone bandstand and lush grass lawn. Every bench was occupied by people chatting, drinking coffee, snapping photographs, reading books. I wished more than anything that I had time to hop off my bike and waste away the day in the park alongside them. But I was a woman on a mission.

First stop: the job board.

Gigi had warned me the area would be busy — *'Two days till Halloween… The entire town is mobbed with tourists looking to get their freak on! And I do mean that literally!'* — but even with the warning, I was unprepared for the sight that greeted me when I hit downtown.

I braked hard, screeching to a stop and staring, mouth agape, at the dense crowd. There were people everywhere, filling the entire street from end to end, spilling off the sidewalks onto the road — which, thankfully, was currently closed to car traffic. Practically everyone was dressed in full costume even though it was mid-morning. I saw vampires with fake plastic teeth, alien invaders with green face paint, monsters with horns jutting from their heads, and characters from every pop-culture phenomenon over the past twenty years. Marvel Avengers, Star Wars Jedi knights… Zombies, scarecrows, devils… Above all, though…

Witches.

So many witches of every possible variety. It was a veritable sea of pointy hats and striped tights, black cloaks and swirling skirts. Some were historical, in corsets and petticoats, holding baskets of herbs or gnarled walking staffs. Others were chic and cool, with heavy eyeliner, artfully torn fishnets, and sexy leather bustiers.

My eyes were saucer-wide trying to take it all in as I parked Declan's bike in one of the racks across the street from the imposing stone facade of the Witch Museum. Clearly, it was a popular tourist destination. A long line of people snaked around the corner, waiting for their chance to enter. A little girl dressed like Elsa from *Frozen* waved at me from where she stood sandwiched between her parents.

I waved back, wondering if they made those sparkly princess gloves in my size. For obvious reasons, Elsa was my favorite of the Disney Princess brigade. (I mean...*Conceal, don't feel?* Talk about relatable.) My own gloves today were lace, with dainty buttons at the wrists. They matched my dress — a white, boho-style number I'd thrifted ages ago, with drapey sleeves and lacing at the bodice. Not exactly bike riding attire, but I wanted to look nice for my job hunt.

Adjusting my skirt, which had ridden up slightly as I pedaled, I ran my fingers through my windswept waves to tame them as I best I could without a brush, pointed my low, snip-heel booties in the direction of the mob scene, and started walking. I passed by the busy Hawthorne Hotel, with its (supposedly) friendly poltergeists, then meandered down Essex Street, which seemed to be the main hub of activity.

It wasn't much of a street, seeing as cars couldn't drive down it. But there sure were a lot of people. I passed by a guy dressed like Freddy Kreuger, giving him wide berth, and in the process almost smacked straight into Dracula. His white face paint was nearly an inch thick, his collar was up around his ears, and his plastic fangs were lopsided when he grinned.

"I vant to suck your bloooood!" he informed me in a terrible fake Eastern-European accent.

"Sucks for you." I darted around him, calling back over my shoulder, "You can't always get what you vant!"

He was crestfallen.

Leaving Dracula in my dust, I wove slowly through the throngs, coughing on fake fog that poured from shop entryways, ducking to avoid ruining photographs. Everywhere I looked, people were posing with scary costumed movie villains, sticking their heads into fake stocks and pillories, snapping selfies in front of the fountain, buying snacks from the various food vendors, sitting for outlandish caricatures, and pausing to listen to the busking musical artists who'd set up to perform. Massive orange banners were strung overhead, proclaiming SALEM'S HAUNTED HAPPENINGS in spooky black font.

A man dressed as a knockoff Jack Sparrow shoved a glossy pamphlet into my hands, which advertised half-off admission at the local Pirate Museum. As I walked away, he complimented my 'fine sea legs' which may or may not have been a misguided attempt at flirting.

In any case, by the time I made my way to Derby Square — the small plaza home to the Old Town Hall — I had three other pamphlets from different street hustlers advertising ghost tours, witch history walks, and psychic readings. I slipped them into my backpack as I fished out my small leather-bound journal and a pen to take notes.

The community bulletin board was right where Gigi said it would be, smack in the center of the plaza. Every square inch of it was plastered with flyers. There was the typical fodder — yard sale announcements, shop advertisements, car wash services, missing pet reward posters, a schedule of events for an 'Autumn in the Park' concert series... I scanned for potential job listings amongst the multicolored mishmash, lifting the top layer to reveal even more papers tacked underneath.

After a decade of practice finding part-time gigs, I knew what to look for and what to ignore. In under five minutes, I'd amassed a series of potential leads — a dog-sitting service was looking for new walkers, a family-owned sailboat charter needed crew, a home renovation company was seeking commercial painters, and several local bars and restaurants were in desperate need of staff to get through the high season. Nothing exceptional... but I'd done worse things for money. (Don't even get me started on my short-lived stint as a stall-mucker at a horse farm in a podunk corner of Pennsylvania three years ago.)

After jotting down the necessary phone numbers and information, I left the Halloween hullabaloo behind and sought out a quiet spot to make my calls. This took a fair bit of walking, but eventually I found an empty bench on the outskirts of town, overlooking Salem Harbor.

First up?

A place called Mercy Tavern was looking for a new bar-back. I summoned my most pleasing phone voice and began to dial…

"Sorry! We only hire with a firm commitment of at least three months."

"Even for seasonal employees?"

"That's our policy. Honestly, it's not even worth the time it takes to train someone if they leave before that."

"Okay. I understand." I blew out a frustrated breath. "Thanks anyway."

I scratched out the last lead on my list with an aggressive line, digging the tip of my pen so hard into the paper it threatened to tear. I'd spent the past hour utterly striking out in my hunt for employment. Every position I called about was either already filled or looking for someone who had more than a few measly shifts to offer. The only promising one — the local dog-walking business — didn't answer the first time I called. On my second attempt, someone *did* answer but the barking in the background was so loud, I couldn't hear whatever they were saying.

I'd try again tomorrow.

I stared at my phone for a moment, hesitating before I put it into my bag. There were three missed call notifications from an unlisted number — Adrian really needed to get a day job, he had way too much time on his hands — but that wasn't why I hesitated. I was due to phone a certain detective for an update on my automotive woes. Past due, in fact. I'd programmed his number into my phone this morning when I woke up in preparation. (As if I hadn't memorized it already, staring at his business card all night like a creepy stalker.) Yet… I couldn't bring myself to actually make the damn call.

Maybe I was terrified he'd tell me bad news. That my car had self-destructed in the auto-body shop, and the only way I'd be leaving town for the foreseeable future was on the stolen bicycle of a sixth grader. Or… maybe I was afraid he'd ask me out again. Maybe I was afraid, if he did, I'd do something insane. (Like say *yes*.)

Better to put him off for a while. What was that famous saying about procrastination? *'Why do today that which you can avoid until tomorrow?'*

Yep. I was pretty sure that's how it went.

Zipping my notebook and phone away in my small leather backpack, I headed back toward the heart of town where I'd left my bike. I didn't rush. I strolled. I meandered. Hell, I even moseyed, choosing streets at random, letting my feet pick the path as they saw fit. It was a picture-perfect fall day — sunny and slightly breezy, the warm wind off the water stirring the fallen leaves that crunched beneath my boots. Everything was bathed in that distinctly golden light only autumn could conjure, like the whole world had been dipped in a vat of caramel.

Countless restaurants and cafes lined the sidewalks, with outdoor patio sections brimming with patrons. The aroma of fresh seafood was mouth-watering as waiters carried towering plates of steaming red lobsters, lemony-garlic mussels, french fries, and battered haddock filets from the kitchens in a near-constant parade.

My stomach rumbled loudly. Lunchtime had come and gone and my measly croissant had long since digested. It took iron-clad self control to keep my boots from turning of their own accord toward the door of Broomsticks Bakery, which was emitting a scent delicious enough to stop even a gluten-hater dead in their tracks.

You have car repairs to consider, Imogen, I reminded myself, ignoring the mouthwatering display of baked goods. *Step away from the baguettes!*

There were many different businesses on the main drag, but one in particular caught my eye as I passed by. It had the look of an ancient apothecary shop. The front was all glass and wood, with a gorgeous witch-themed window display that featured a metric ton of books and baubles. Some of the books actually appeared to be flying through the air, no doubt strung up with invisible fishing line. I was instantly enchanted, and found myself grinning like an idiot at the sight — at least, until my eyes drifted up to the wooden sign hanging over the door, which proclaimed:

THE GALLOWS

The 'O' was in the shape of a noose.

I felt my stomach pitch, all traces of hunger vanishing in an instant. I could practically still hear Gigi's voice ringing in my head.

The owner, Gwendolyn Goode, told me she was looking for some part-time help since the place has gotten so popular…

Cute facade notwithstanding, the place didn't exactly scream popular. In fact, it looked empty. The hanging placard on the door announced CLOSED. Beneath it, though, in feminine handwriting, someone had tacked up a sheet of paper, upon which was scrawled an additional message.

HELP WANTED!
INQUIRE WITHIN.
(SERIOUSLY. I'M DESPERATE.)

I told myself to keep walking. And yet… for whatever reason, despite all attempts to avoid this place, fate had brought me here. I'd never been one to ignore fate. (In fact, I felt strongly that doing so was often a recipe for disaster.) Besides, my other employment-hunt efforts had been a total bust thus far.

Desperate times, desperate measures.

Bracing my shoulders, I ignored all my instincts that were screaming at me to run the opposite direction and, before I knew it, I'd closed the gap between me and the door, grabbed the knob, and pushed. It wasn't locked — the hinges creaked faintly as it swung inward with a tinkle of bells overhead.

I sucked in a breath as I stepped over the threshold, my eyes sweeping the cavernous interior. Painted in shades of green and gold, it was part cafe, part bookshop, part apothecary. *All* stunning. The first thing I saw were the books. Books everywhere, as far as the eye could see. They dominated the left side of the room, stacked on tables and shoved onto long shelves that stretched deep into the space in a cozy maze of polished mahogany. The right side was less *literature,* more *latte* — a gleaming emerald bar housed a cool-as-hell gold espresso machine. The floors beneath my boots were heavy, historical hardwood. The lofty ceilings overhead were an insanely beautiful gold patina. Deeper into the shop, where the bookshelves became curiosity cabinets, bundles of herbs hung from aforementioned ceiling, infusing the air with an earthy, herbal smell that made my toes curl.

It was an inviting space — one that encouraged you to sip a coffee for an hour or three as you flipped the pages of the glossy hardcovers on the bestseller table, to lose yourself in the oddities that seemed to be stuffed in every nook and cranny. But there was no time to peruse. Not today. Because the shop wasn't empty, as I'd expected.

There were a handful of people around my age inside. And all of them, every last one, was staring at me. Not in a *"How can I help you today?"* sort of way, either. No, they were staring at me like I was a villain busting into the saloon in an old Western movie, about to whip out a set of dueling pistols and start firing them into the air, then taking trollops hostage unless someone emptied the gosh dang safe before the sheriff showed up.

(What can I say? I had a big thing for cowboy romances in my early twenties. Don't judge me.)

The mixture of hostility and suspicion hit me like a sucker punch. I stopped short after only a handful of steps, trying to decide where to look first; who to look at first. It didn't help matters that, in addition to being rather inhospitable, they were also all absurdly attractive.

Had I walked in on some sort of modeling convention?

First, there was Mr. Man Bun by the New Age bookshelf, who had wicked facial hair and eyes so bright hazel they were nearly gold. If he wasn't enough to give me heart palpitations, there were two identical twins — yes, I said *twins* — with lush dark hair and inky, intense eyes lounging on a green velvet sofa by the window display, whose handsome faces were contorted into such menacing expressions I nearly piddled like a nervous chihuahua confronted with a set of dobermans.

Moving on!

My eyes skimmed quickly over the broad frame of a guy standing with his back to me (who appeared to be sipping from a giant coffee mug), and did not stop until they reached the espresso bar, where two couples were clustered. The pair on the stools — a girl with dark glossy hair and a bookish, blond guy with spectacles — seemed friendly enough, smiling faintly in welcome.

The pair behind the vintage cash register — a drop-dead-gorgeous redhead, plus a freakishly hot brunet brute who looked suspiciously similar to the scary-intense twins, only his eyes were so bright green I could make out the shade at a dozen paces — wore mismatched expressions. (Hers, welcoming; his, decidedly less so.)

From Georgia's description, I figured this must be the infamous Gwendolyn Goode.

"Um…" I swallowed hard. "Hello…"

The room full of hotties all stared at me in silence, clearly waiting for me to explain myself.

Shit.

I tried (and failed) to cover the uncertainty in my tone. "I'm looking for the owner of this shop…"

The air grew even more tense as I trailed off. Everyone glanced at the redhead. (Myself included.)

"That would be me," she said, walking out from behind the counter to greet me, breezing by the man who'd been sipping from his mug when I first walked in. I finally got a glimpse of his face… and was instantly flooded with panic as I realized it was a face I recognized.

Chiseled jaw.

Full mouth.

Dark brows.

Aristocratic nose.

Insanely blue eyes.

Shit, shit, *shit!*

Of all the cafe-slash-apothecary-slash-bookstores in the world…

The man leaning casually against the counter was none other than Detective Cade Hightower. Our gazes locked for a supercharged moment. His coffee mug was frozen halfway to his mouth. He looked just as stunned to see me as I was to see him. Which was, perhaps, why he didn't say a single word as he stared at me, those magnetic ocean eyes scanning me up and down with a mixture of surprise and… something else. Something I was way too chickenshit to identify.

As for me, I didn't allow myself more than a second of gazing at that head of glorious Clark Kent hair, nor the muscular body that filled out that crisp white button down in a way that should be considered entrapment… but, hell, a single second was enough.

More than enough.

By the time I peeled my gaze away from him and directed it back at Gwen, she'd come to a stop a handful of feet in front of me. The green-eyed hunk, for the record, had shadowed her every step across the shop and, as I watched, not-so-subtly positioned his towering frame in front of hers. As though he was protecting her.

From *me!*

I tried not to take this personally. I was a stranger, after all. From the "touch her and die" vibes rolling off this guy, I got the immediate sense he would protect the woman at his side from any potential threat, no matter how small. That he'd lay down his life for her, even kill for her, without blinking.

I didn't know whether to be intimidated or insanely jealous that no one had ever, not once, looked at me the way he was looking at her. Though, it must be said, he did not seem exceptionally pleased when she stuck out her hand for me to shake, grinning at me like we were long lost friends.

"Gwendolyn Goode," she introduced herself. "And you are…?"

I hesitated a short beat — during which my eyes darted to Cade. He was still frozen, mug mid-air, watching me. I jerked my eyes back to Gwen's as I forced my hand to lift from my side and clasp hers for a (very) brief shake. I was wearing my gloves, but… still.

I wasn't taking any chances.

"Imogen Warner."

"Imogen," she repeated, still smiling. "Nice to meet you. Is there something I can help you with?"

I couldn't stop my eyes from darting to Cade again. He'd finally set down his mug. His arms were crossed over his broad chest and his head was tipped slightly to one side, evaluating me with the razor-sharp perception of a trained detective.

That did not bode well for me.

"Uh…" I swallowed hard and refocused on Gwen. Her warm, welcoming smile had not faded, but her eyes were plainly curious as they shifted from me to Cade and back. She'd noticed my wandering gaze.

Damn and blast.

I needed to stop looking at him.

"I'm…" I bit the inside of my cheek, hoping the pain would focus me. "Well, actually, I'm here about the job posting."

"Oh!" Gwen exclaimed, brightening instantly. "The backup barista job? That's fabulous!"

My mouth opened to retort, but she barreled on.

"We're closed today but I assure you, usually it's wall to wall customers in here. Especially this time of year." She leaned forward a shade, like she was confiding a secret to a gal-pal, and the man at her side stiffened even further. "As it turns out, I'm looking for more than part-time if you're in need of a full-time gig—"

"No," I cut her off before she could start rattling off job benefits. "Actually... I'm here about… the psychic position?"

I'd thought the air in the shop was tense before but, when I said that, the tension ratcheted up tenfold. Everyone shifted slightly, straightening in their seats, positioning themselves to get a better look at me.

I could feel the weight of their scrutiny from all sides — the twins' inky eyes burning holes in the back of my head, Mr. Man Bun's hazel stare heating my left side, the couple on the stools staring intently at my right. Somewhere behind Gwen, a certain detective was cataloguing my every blink.

Gwen, however, seemed impervious to the apprehension radiating around her shop like a shockwave. She was grinning at me so wide, it made me momentarily forget to be anxious.

"You're a psychic?"

I shrugged. "Sometimes."

"That's so freaking cool!"

"Uh… thanks?"

"Don't thank me! I should thank *you*! You are the answer to my prayers!"

I blinked at her, startled. "Um..."

"Honest to goddess, I thought my customers might stage a full-on coup if I opened back up for business tomorrow without filling Madame Zelda's position." She glanced around her vacant shop. "Obviously it's like *Night of the Living Dead* around here this afternoon. But, trust me, it's never like this. Most of the time, we have a line out the door. There've been so many requests for readings, especially with Halloween so soon... Everyone is going to be so flipping excited I've hired someone."

"The thing is—" I started.

She cut me off before I could explain I was only looking for a week or so of work, not opening a 401k and taking advantage of her healthcare plan. "Can you start right away?"

"Gwen," her green-eyed hunk said warningly.

She ignored him, still grinning at me. "There's this little private room in the back where you can do your readings—"

"Gwen," the hunk repeated, even more warningly.

"Come on," Gwen reached out, as if to grab my hand. "I'll show you!"

Thankfully, before the vivacious redhead could get her grip on me, the green-eyed hunk intervened. His patience had definitely expired — a fact he conveyed by tagging her around the shoulders and turning her to face him instead of me.

"Gwendolyn—"

"Oh, don't you dare *Gwendolyn* me, Graham Graves!"

"We've talked about this."

"We talk about lots of things," she fired back. "You'll have to be more specific."

"*Specifically,*" Graham Graves — *of course* the cool-as-hell dude had a cool-as-hell name — growled. "We talked about you not hiring any random person off the street without letting me do a background check first. Full profile, no stones unturned, no skeletons hiding in closets. Remember?" His intense eyes cut to me. From the icy frost they were blasting my way, it didn't take a rocket scientist to realize he did *not* like what he saw. "This girl could be another Zelda. A quack at best, a grifter at worst. I'm not willing to risk your safety before we find out where she falls on the criminal enterprise scale."

I flinched slightly at his caustic evaluation of me. I didn't know what this Madame Zelda had done, but she certainly had not left The Gallows on good terms — or left a good impression about those of us in the mystic biz. What I did know, however, was that I didn't want this guy, who radiated very unsettling energy, digging into my past.

Background check?

Full profile?

No stones unturned?

No skeletons in closets?

No freaking way.

I liked my stones just the way they were. Not only turned over — buried six feet beneath the earth. Along with my skeletons.

(Who was dumb enough to keep their skeletons in their closet, anyway? Hello!? Buy a shovel, lazybones.)

"Graham!" Gwen snapped, her temper rising like a summer storm. "You cannot just call people names! You're being insulting!"

"I'm being honest," he countered.

"Well... stop it!" She swatted him on the arm, but there was no real anger behind her strike. "Imogen hasn't done anything to deserve your rudeness!"

"I don't know the first fucking thing about *Imogen*," he said flatly. Though, his tone gentled somewhat as he stared at her for a beat, then added, "And neither do you, baby."

"Graham—"

"You nearly died on me a week ago. If you think I'm putting you at risk ever again—"

"You're overreacting, per usual!"

"And you're *under*reacting, per fucking usual."

"This seems sort of like a bad time," I interjected softly, beginning to backpedal toward the door. "I'll just… get out of your hair…"

Gwen and Graham both ignored me. They were too busy glaring at each other to notice I'd even spoken. Beneath their anger, however, their attraction to one another was so palpable, it was borderline voyeuristic to witness.

Normally, I would've felt guilty for starting an argument, but I got the sense all this fighting would merely serve as fuel for the next opportunity they got to rip each other's clothes off. I'd bet the last few benjamins in my shoebox that their sex life was off-the-charts hot.

Not that it was any of my business.

"Sorry to have bothered you," I murmured, taking a few more steps backward. "I'll just… uh… come back… another day…"

As in, *never*.

"Stay put," Graham barked without looking at me.

Like I was a dog!

"*Me*?" I squeaked, certain I was mistaken.

"You," he countered, still not looking at me.

What the fuck?!

Who did this guy think he was?

"No, I don't think so," I said, picking up my pace. "Coming here was a mistake—"

"Welles," Graham clipped.

Welles?

"So, I'll just be going—"

My retreat was halted by a solid wall.

At least, I thought it was a wall — until I felt it shift against my spine, warm and muscular and most definitely *alive*. Sucking in a startled breath, I whirled around to see Mr. Man Bun had come unstuck from his spot by the bookshelves and was now standing directly between me and my escape route. His boots were firmly planted on the hardwood and his frame completely blocked the door. He was so tall, I was pretty sure I strained a muscle in my neck when I craned my head to meet his hazel-gold eyes.

"Excuse me..." I fell back on my manners, for lack of any idea what one was supposed to say in a scenario like this. "Would you mind moving?"

"Yep."

"Yep as in, *you'll move?*" My brows went up. "Or yep as in, *you mind?*"

He just grinned at me, the handsome bastard.

God!

What was wrong with the people in this city? Were they putting something in the water that made them all so alarmingly meddlesome? Was that crisp fall air critically low on oxygen, cutting off vital brain functions such as *reason* and *logic* and *common sense?*

Coming to The Gallows was a colossal miscalculation on my part. I didn't care if Gigi swore backwards and forwards that it was cool. I didn't care that the interior was so aesthetically pleasing, just being there was a certified mood booster. I didn't even care that fate herself had steered me straight through the front door. All I cared about, in that moment, was getting the heck out of there.

Behind me, I could hear Gwen and Graham going back and forth, bickering. The couple on the stools seemed to have joined the fray, taking sides in the argument, adding their voices to the discourse. But I was too worked up to listen. My only concern was getting away from these nutcases. Eyeing the doorknob, I attempted to dart around Mr. Man Bun while he was momentarily distracted by the argument unfolding behind me. My plan was foiled in less than a second. He shifted his mammoth body directly in front of the knob, so it was impossible to grab.

"Get out of my way!" I hissed through clenched teeth. "Now!"

"No."

"Are you serious right now?"

"As a heart attack."

"Oh, as if *you're* going to have a heart attack," I snapped. "What's your body fat percentage? Negative one? I bet your valves are just *pristine*. I bet your cholesterol is *impeccable*. I bet you are the *picture* of cardiovascular health!"

There was a distinct pause. Then, in an amused tone, he said, "You need to work on your insults."

"Okay. Sure. I'll do that. I pinky swear, I'll march straight out of here and spend the next seventeen consecutive hours practicing all the ways I can more effectively eviscerate you in our next verbal sparring match… so long as you stop *blocking the freaking door* and *move out of my way*!"

"Can't do that," he said flatly.

"Why the hell not?"

"Graham says you stay, you're staying."

I repeat…

What.

The.

FUCK?!

"I don't care what Graham says. I'm going now and you can't— *Stop shaking your head at me!*"

Mr. Man Bun stopped shaking his head.

But he did not move.

"You're pissing me off," I informed him.

"I see that."

"Move!"

"Nope."

"This is insane! You don't even know me!"

"Precisely the point. We need to make sure you are who you say you are. Not some psychopathic pagan planning on butchering any livestock, leaving bloody pentacles, attempting to sacrifice Gwen during the next full moon… Any of that shit."

I stared at him some more. Then, weakly, whispered, "Are you joking?"

He shook his head.

I was afraid of that.

"You're nuts," I announced, whirling around to scowl at the entire store as a collective unit. "All of you. Everyone in this city. Totally, completely, *nuts*. The whole can!" I pointed a finger at the twins, who were still lounging on the emerald sofa by the window display like they hadn't a care in the world. "The fancy mixed kind, not just peanuts. We're talking cashews, we're talking almonds, we're talking maca-freaking-damia!" My voice pitched upward, to a yell, as I turned back to Welles. "*NUTS*!"

Sometime during my tirade, the shop had fallen silent. I heard no more voices behind me. I did, however, hear the sound of measured footsteps slowly crossing the hardwood, getting closer and closer before finally coming to a stop directly behind me.

A tingle shot straight down my spine.

I was pretty sure I knew who was standing there, but I was far too cowardly to turn around and confirm my suspicions.

Mr. Man Bun didn't move a millimeter, either. But his eyes shifted over my shoulder, locking on something — someone — that made his mouth tighten ever-so-slightly. And when that mouth muttered, "You have a claim, here?" I got the craziest sense he wasn't talking to me.

This suspicion was confirmed when another voice — one I recognized instantly — responded with a deep, "Back off her, Welles. I'm not going to say it twice."

CHAPTER EIGHT

Time is Irish. With a last name like O'Clock, how could it not be?
- Imogen Warner, taking an interest in genealogy

Cade's shoulder brushed mine as he stepped up beside me. His eyes were locked on Welles and his face was set in a stone-cold expression I'd never seen him wear before. Probably because, despite his suggestion to "back off," the man blocking the door had not moved even one of his (many, *many*) muscles.

"Guessing that's a *yes* on the claim," Welles said, cracking another grin.

Cade did not return said grin. "We've never had problems before, Welles. Let's not start now."

Welles lifted his hands in a conciliatory gesture. "Just following orders, Detective. Take it up with Graves."

As if he'd been summoned, Graham joined the fray — trailed closely by Gwen, who was periodically smacking him on the arm as they crossed the room.

"See what you've done!" *Smack*. "Now Cade and Welles are in a standoff!" *Smack*. "And Imogen looks scared out of her ever-loving mind!" *Smack*. "Are you happy now, Graham Crackers? Huh? Are you?"

Graham was completely unaffected by the continual assault. He looked down into Gwen's glaring face, mouth tugged up at one side in amusement. "If you're trying to pick a fight with me just so we can have makeup sex later… It's working."

Smack! "You are so annoying!"

"I also happen to be right." He glanced at me, then at Cade, then back at me. "I realize we haven't exactly thrown down the welcome mat for you. We have reason to be a bit wary of strangers around here, these days."

"Sure. Fine. Whatever," I said, crossing my arms over my chest. "I didn't mean to stir up any trouble. If you'll have your bulldog here—" I shot Welles a glare; he grinned back at me. "—move, I'll never darken your doorstep again. You have my word."

"No! Please, don't go!" Gwen pleaded with me, her light green eyes round with desperation. "Don't let the Gravewatch boys scare you off! They're just overprotective, after last week. See, there was this whole witchy drama where I almost bit the dust—"

"Gwendolyn," Graham interjected. "For the last fucking time, *she is a stranger*. You've already told her your full name. She does not need any more details about your personal life."

Gwen rolled her eyes. "So what if she knows my name? This is the age of the internet. I'm Google-able. In fact, I Googled myself just yesterday." She glanced at me. "I'm thinking of setting up a website for the store. Doing online orders, expanding our reach… Online bookings for your readings, too!"

I blinked at her, at a loss for a proper response.

Undeterred, she panned a hand through the air like a gameshow host revealing a prize. "I can see it now: The Gallows goes global!"

Graham did not look pleased by the thought of worldwide attention aimed at his girl. "Firecracker, can you please — for my sanity — at least *attempt* to resist the urge to turn everyone you meet into your new best friend?"

"I do not turn everyone into my new best friend!"

"You do," he countered, eyes flashing over to me for a beat. "Looking trustworthy does not mean they *are* trustworthy. I thought you'd learned that lesson already — the hard way: lying on a fucking crypt, a blade at your throat." His jaw tightened, a muscle leaping in it as he tried to lock down his emotions. "Just because you like someone's goddamn outfit doesn't mean you should spill your whole life story—"

"I am not spilling my entire life story!" Gwen scoffed. She glanced at me, scanning me up and down. "I do like your dress, though. Where'd you get it?"

"Thrifted."

She nodded appreciatively. "Sweet. There's a great little secondhand shop around the corner, I'll take you—"

"Can we possibly focus on the actually important shit here," Graham interrupted. "Instead of your ridiculous penchant for fashion?"

An outraged feminine gasp came from the espresso bar area.

Welles looked up at the ceiling and loosed a low whistle, as if to say, *You've done it now, boss.*

Cade shook his head, like he knew all hell was about to break loose.

I, wisely, chose to remain silent.

"I'm sorry," Gwen snapped, not sounding sorry in the slightest. "Did you just say my penchant for fashion is *ridiculous?*"

"Gwen's fashion is iconic!" A female voice chimed in from behind us. It was the glossy-haired girl on the stool. "We can't all rock leather jackets and motorcycle boots every day like your little legion of badasses. Unless you plan on putting us on the Gravewatch payroll and giving us flack jackets, you mind your own business about what a woman wears, Graham Graves!"

Gwen ducked around her boyfriend's back to grin at her friend.

"Thanks, Florence. You know, now that you mention it, matching flack jackets might be cool."

"Totally." The girl — Florence — nodded in agreement. "Do they come in different colors? Or are they all just black?"

"I don't know." Gwen looked back at Graham. "Do your bulletproof vests come in others colors? Maybe something in a pastel?"

Graham was pinching the furrow between his brows, as if he had a headache brewing. Rather than risk the two of them descending into yet another squabble, I decided to wade in. My timely escape depended on it.

"For the record, I'm not a psychopathic pagan out for your blood," I informed Gwen. "I'm just passing through town and need to pick up a little part time work while my car is being repaired." I resisted the urge to glance over at Cade when he let out a low scoff. "This morning, I was talking to Georgia — the manager of The Sea Witch Inn, where I'm staying — and she suggested I try The Gallows. She also says to say hi."

"Oh! Gigi! She's the best." Gwen grinned. "And her boys are adorable. Last time they came in, they upended the entire essential oils display while play-wrestling over one of the voodoo dolls. The whole place smelled like lemongrass for weeks."

I didn't see how this could possibly be viewed as 'adorable' but I wasn't about to argue. I'd seen how Gwen reacted when people disagreed with her — and I did *not* want my arm smacked to black and blue, thank you very much.

"You should see them in the mornings." My lips twisted in a half-smile. "Continental breakfast has never been quite so... lively."

She laughed. "I'll take your word for it."

"Anyway, I'm only in town temporarily—" Another scoff from Cade. It took monumental effort to continue ignoring him, but I managed. "So, I was hoping to make some quick cash doing readings. Now that I know you're in the market for someone more permanent..." *And that your boyfriend is planning to do a deep dive into my past.* "...I'll find something else."

"Oh..." Gwen's grin vanished. "But—"

"I really should get going," I cut her off before she could try to convince me to stay. "It's already late afternoon, I have a few more places to check with before businesses close for the day."

Okay, so that last part was a lie.

I didn't particularly like lying to Gwen, who seemed like a nice person... but I really needed to get out of there.

For a minute after I trailed off, there was only silence. Graham stared at me in that cutting way of his, perhaps weighing the truth behind my words. Welles was leaning back against the door, arms crossed over his chest, boots crossed at the ankles, a faint smile playing at his lips. Cade... actually, I didn't know *what* Cade was doing, since I adamantly refused to look his way for fear of what would happen once I found myself ensnared by those bottomless blue eyes. Gwen looked distressed, teeth worrying her bottom lip.

"It's a bummer you're only in town such a short time," she said finally, a newly determined set to her shoulders. "But I'm sure we can work something out. Everything around here is pretty flexible. And I'm the boss, I make the rules, so—"

Graham made a growly sound of frustration. "Gwen, again, I need to point out this girl could be dangerous—"

"I'll vouch for her."

Everyone's heads whipped toward Cade. It was the first time he'd spoken in several minutes and the deep timbre of his voice cut through the air like a guillotine.

"*What?*" I breathed.

"You'll vouch for her," Graham repeated, eyes locked on Cade's.

Cade nodded. "Imogen's clear."

"You sure about that, Hightower?"

"I don't waste my breath on shit I'm not sure about, Graves. You should know that by now."

I stared up at Cade's profile, studying the sharp line of his jaw as he and Graham engaged in some sort of non-verbal conversation. I didn't know what to feel. What did he mean, he could vouch for me? What did he mean, I was clear?

Clear of what?

Had *he* been digging into my past?

The thought made my lungs seize and my stomach drop.

"I don't need you intervening, Hero-Hair," I whisper-yelled at him.

Gwen snorted softly. "*Hero-Hair?* That's hilarious."

I didn't look at her. I couldn't look away from Cade as his head tilted down to mine and those eyes — those damn eyes — captured mine in a way that made all the air evacuate my lungs.

"Is there something wrong with your phone?"

I blinked, thrown off by the out-of-left-field question. "What? No."

"Your charger, then?"

"My charger works fine. I don't understand—"

"Then the reason you didn't call me back," he spoke over me. "Would be what, exactly?"

Shit.

He was pissed.

My mouth clicked shut as I tried to formulate a proper excuse. I couldn't tell him the truth — *i.e.* that I was too chickenshit to dial him back — so I decided it was best to keep silent.

He leaned a shade closer, eyes narrowing. "Goldie. I'm waiting. In fact, I've been waiting all damn day. Guess what? My phone never rang."

"Georgia passed along your message!" I blurted, feeling defensive.

"The message was *to call me back*."

"Yes. Call you back. Not call you back by *noon*. Not call you back *immediately*." My hands were balled into fists at my sides. "There was no deadline!"

He stared me down.

My fists curled tighter. "I've been a bit busy with the job hunt, okay? I was going to call you once I finished up here."

That was yet another lie.

And he knew it, given the way his eyes narrowed even further.

"How was I supposed to know you'd be here when I walked in?" I prattled on somewhat nervously. "I mean, what are the odds?"

"I told you last night, this place is more like a small town than a city."

"Last night?" Gwen whispered, curiosity practically seeping from each syllable. "What were you two doing last night?"

I'd been so caught up in Cade, I'd totally forgotten we had an audience. Jerking my eyes away, I glanced around the circle — which had widened to include the twins and the couple from the bar stools.

Fantastic.

More witnesses to my humiliating exit.

"As fun as this has been..." I hiked the thin leather strap of my backpack more firmly up my shoulder and took a step toward the door. Toward Welles, who was still serving as a human wall. "I need to get going. *Now*. So, if you don't mind..."

A strand of chestnut brown hair had escaped from the man-bun. Welles reached up and tucked it behind one ear as he side-stepped out of my path. His hazel-gold eyes were sparkling with good humor as he bent slightly at the waist and ushered me toward the door with a mocking flourish.

"Gee, thanks," I snapped as I practically bolted past him, yanking the knob before any more of these lunatics could deter me.

"Wait!" Gwen cried out. "We never talked about your hours!"

I was already halfway out the door, but I hesitated on the threshold long enough to shoot her an apologetic look over my shoulder. "Sorry." I tried to swallow down the rest of my words, but they spilled out anyway. "Your shop seems like an amazing place to work."

"Then stick around!"

"I can't. I..." My eyes moved to Graham, who was still glaring at me like I was a criminal mastermind, then returned to Gwen. "It was nice meeting you."

Tearing my eyes from hers, I stepped out the door and allowed it to swing shut behind me — only, it didn't. Cade, close on my heels, planted a foot in the jamb to stop its swing. At the same time, his hand shot out and grabbed mine, effectively halting my escape.

What the..?

I froze, momentarily stupefied by the sight of my delicate, lace-covered fingers intertwined with his strong, tanned ones. I was so rattled, it didn't even occur to me to try and pull away — at least, not for a few seconds. When I did try, it didn't matter. His grip was like iron. Inescapable.

"Cade!"

He ignored my hiss of protest. He wasn't even looking at me. He was half-turned to face Gwen. "What time do you open tomorrow?"

"Nine," Gwen answered, staring wide-eyed at our interlocked hands. I was still yanking intermittently — and getting precisely nowhere with my efforts.

There was a short pause from Cade. Then, "She'll be here."

Before I could even object — I so would *not* be there! — he removed his foot from the doorjamb, allowing it to swing closed behind us, and used his grip to steer me out onto the brick pedestrian mall.

"Hank, my man, how's business?"

"So fuckin' busy. Sausage and peppers are gonezo. Almost sold outta dogs, too," the burly vendor standing behind the food cart replied in a thick Boston accent. *Peppers* came out *pep-pahs*. *Fuckin'* was *fah-kin*. *Dogs* sounded like *dahgs*. "But I've got plenty of brats and footlongs left. You want your usual?"

Cade nodded, then glanced down at me. The sunlight streamed all around him, a golden halo. He was still holding my hand. I'd stopped trying to yank it out of his grip several minutes ago when I realized I stood exactly zero chance of success. And then there was the fact that, without his hold, I'd almost certainly have lost him in the dense crowd.

The throngs of people thickened with each passing hour. As sunset approached, more and more costumed revelers flooded into the city, eager to partake in the Haunted Happenings. By the time we cleared Essex Street, turning onto a narrow side-way, I was clinging to Cade's hand like a life-ring in a riptide, trying not to be trampled by ghosts, ghouls, monsters, and mummies.

"What do you want?"

"Nothing," I said immediately. "I'm not hungry."

"Liar."

I narrowed my eyes at him, annoyed. Mostly because I *was* hungry. The hot dogs smelled delicious. Plus, they were sold with those deep-fried braided pretzel buns that elevated the experience from street grub to gourmet dining.

"Fine. I'll just take a regular hot dog with mustard."

Cade's eyes did the crinkly-amused thing as he turned to face Hank. "She'll have a footlong."

"Just a regular is fine," I protested.

Hank's eyes shifted from me to Cade, brows high on his head.

"Footlong," Cade repeated firmly. "Mustard."

With a nod, Hank got to work.

I sighed.

Deeply.

Cade chuckled at the sound. "Oh, come on, Goldie. You can't

blame me for trying to put a little meat on those bones. You look like you're about to blow away in the next gust of wind."

"Don't worry. Even if I do, you're holding my hand so tight, I'll just fly around your head like some weird human-shaped kite."

Chuckling again, he finally released my hand in order to accept his food — a truly ginormous bratwurst loaded with all the fixings. Relish, sauerkraut, onions, mustard, and ketchup. It was piled so high, it tested the structural integrity of its small cardboard container. While Hank got to work on my foot long, I unzipped my backpack and began rooting around the bottom.

"What are you looking for?" Cade asked, grabbing about a million napkins from the silver dispenser.

"My wallet."

"Don't bother."

I glanced up at him. "You aren't paying for me."

"Goldie, it's a hot dog."

"Technically, it's a footlong."

"I can still afford it," he said wryly. "You want five courses at a Michelin starred steakhouse… We'll have to dip into Socks' tennis ball budget, but I can probably still swing it."

The look in his eyes told me I was not going to win this particular battle. I held up my hands in surrender and he grinned as I re-zipped my bag.

It was a good grin.

"Here you go, little lady."

I might've objected to Hank calling me *little lady* if he weren't currently handing me the most delicious culinary creation I'd ever seen in my life. It was longer than my arm and, with the braided pretzel bun, nearly as thick. My mouth instantly filled with saliva as I took it from him, resisting the urge to sink my teeth in like a total street urchin.

"Thanks, Hank." Cade held out some cash, but the vendor waved him off.

"You know your money's no good here, Hightower."

"How many times are we going to have this argument?"

"As long as you keep coming by my stand for lunch." His eyes moved to me. "Your girl is hungry. Don't make her wait. Nothing worse than a cold dog."

I'm not his girl.

The words were on the tip of my tongue, but I swallowed them. I didn't want to insult the man. Plus, he happened to be right. There really was nothing worse than a cold dog.

Cade gave the vendor his sternest look. "Hank—"

"Get outta here already, would you?" Hank waved us off. "I've got a line forming."

The detective shook his head in disapproval, but allowed the vendor to greet his next customers. The moment Hank's back turned, however, Cade took the opportunity to slip a twenty into his tip jar.

"Come on, Goldie." He jerked his chin toward the sidewalk. "I know a sunny spot nearby where we can eat these."

I said nothing, merely turned and started walking the direction he'd indicated. He fell easily into step beside me, instinctively guiding me through the dense crowd like my own personal bodyguard.

"See you tomorrow, detective!" Hank called after us.

"Later, Hank!"

People parted before us like the Red Sea — perhaps noting the shiny gold badge at Cade's belt or the gun clipped beside it. We took a few more steps down the sidewalk before I summoned the nerve to ask, "You eat there every day?"

Cade scoffed. "Hell no. I'm not trying to have a heart attack by thirty-five."

"But—"

"This is my town," he explained, shrugging. "Comes with the job."

"Your job is to befriend Hank the Hot Dog Man?"

"No, my job is to keep people safe. To do that, you have to talk to them. I don't have a beat to patrol anymore, not in an official capacity, but most days, I still walk every street downtown at least once. There's no better way to take the pulse of the city than chatting up the locals. They always know the comings and goings before anyone else."

His words proved to be more than bluster. As we walked down the street, we passed several more vendors in food trucks, rolling carts, and pop-up stands, all of whom offered a wave or a smile or a "Hey, Hightower!" Their friendly gazes turned curious when they spotted me strolling at his side, but there were more than enough smiles to go around for me, too.

There's definitely something unnatural in the Salem air...

It was an odd little city — and I wasn't just talking about its residents. It seemed intrinsically at odds with itself. Half historical, half modern; half serious about its dark history, half embracing the kitschy tourist boom that history inspired.

From the businesses to the architecture, it was split between past and present in a way that should've been jarring... but, somehow, really worked. Ancient graveyards sat squarely beside modern art museums. Musty antique shops were squished in next door to neon-lit BDSM stores. Handcrafted Amish soaps and vintage jewelry were sold from pop-up stands directly outside a tattoo parlor with thumping death metal pouring from the front door.

A total enigma.

To my own great surprise, I loved every square inch of it. Maybe because... well, I was a bit of an enigma myself.

Cade's "spot" turned out to be a bench on Salem Common, not far from where I'd left my bike. Situated beneath two graceful willow trees that had turned to a riot of gold and yellow, it was partially shaded from the sun and offered a perfect view of the bandstand. We ate in silence for several moments, mouths too full to speak. There was plenty of people-watching to do, with the constant parade of walking tours, amateur photographers, and couples strolling hand in hand down the crisscrossed paths, enjoying an idyllic autumn afternoon.

Cade polished his brat off before I'd even made a real dent in my foot-long. My stomach was already approaching max capacity and I had several inches to go.

"I told you I couldn't eat this much," I muttered, pressing my free hand against my abdomen. The lacing of my dress felt tighter than it had this morning. "I'll never finish it."

He shrugged, leaning back to wind his long arms along the top of the bench. He closed his eyes as he tilted his head back to the sun, the picture of relaxation. He seemed perfectly content to sit in the quiet of the moment rather than fill it with aimless chatter or check his phone messages or, worse, talk about himself nonstop — something Adrian did whenever given the opportunity.

It was, quite frankly, a novel concept: a man who was simply *at peace* — and in whose presence, that same peace extended to you, like an invisible forcefield of protection from the chaos of the rest of the world. My throat lumped as I studied him from the corner of my eye.

Damn if that wasn't an attractive quality.

I'd not experienced much of it myself. Peace, that is. I'd been a lot of things throughout my life — adaptive, mainly, but also anxious, paranoid, detached… and unsettled. I hated that last one.

Unsettled.

Uncomfortable.

Unable to relax.

Take your pick, they all applied.

Most people thought the opposite of peace was war. (Looking at you, Tolstoy.) It wasn't. It was *paranoia*. Constant vigilance. The perpetual brace for the hurt you knew was coming, the moment you dared let your guard down.

So you simply never did.

You walked through life with your dukes up, ready to punch.

No sudden moves, buster. I know you're coming. That betrayal you're planning? I'm expecting it. That lie you told me? I already considered it, along with twelve other possible cock-and-bull fabrications you might come up with. That knife you're ready to plunge into my back? Honey, it's already in my hand. I've been holding it for weeks.

I expected the hits before they even manifested as possibilities in the minds of my opponents, let alone landed on me. But that hyper-vigilance came at a cost. And that cost was my peace.

I envied Cade Hightower in that moment for finding his. I also wanted to wrap all my limbs around him and soak it in like a sponge, as if such tranquility could be transfused by osmosis. Before I could act on such a ridiculous notion, I forced myself to look away from his reposed profile.

Several college kids were LARPing on the grass not far from us, their fake swords swinging through air, chain metal clanking, medieval chatter an oddly incongruous background track to the modern setting.

"You planning on finishing that?"

I glanced over at Cade when he spoke. He hadn't moved a muscle, but his eyes were slivered open, staring into mine. The way the dappled light played across his chiseled features was so gorgeous, it made my heart ache.

"All yours." I handed him the remaining quarter of my lunch, which he promptly devoured in a single bite. My lips twisted as I watched him chew. "Now I know why you insisted on the footlong."

He grinned. "Ever considered a career as a detective?"

"Apparently, I already have a new career as a part time psychic. Thanks to you."

"What's with the tone? You were searching for a job. Now you've got one. I figured you'd be happy."

"*Happy?*" I blinked, mystified — which, it must be said, had been my primary cognitive state since arriving in Salem, Massachusetts. The idea of ever being happy was so far out of my reach, I couldn't even process it. "Relieved might be more accurate. I have car repairs to pay for, after all."

"I told you—"

"So help me god, Detective, if you say something ridiculous about it being *covered* or the mechanic *owing you a favor* I will ask those LARPers to come over here and stab you with their fake swords." I paused. "You might not die, but you will definitely be embarrassed in front of all these lovely people in the park."

He laughed — a full-out, no-holds-barred laugh that made a shot of heat furl from my stomach downward to... places better left unspoken.

"You know, it's probably not wise to threaten the life of a police officer. Especially not to his face."

I thought about that for a beat, then shrugged. "I'll risk it."

He chuckled again, then closed his eyes. His posture was entirely relaxed as the sun beat down. The breeze tousled his thick hair like errant fingers. I stared at the silver streaks by his temples, thinking another man might not be able to pull off the silver fox look quite so well.

"Can I ask you something?"

His reply was instant. "You can ask me anything. Open book, remember?"

Oh, I remembered. "What's Gravewatch?"

"Graham Graves is a private investigator. A damn good one, too. He has his own consultancy firm, contracts out with all sorts of law enforcement up and down the eastern seaboard. Local departments, federal cases, private gigs... You name it, his boys do it."

"His... boys?"

"He's got a whole team at his disposal. All highly trained in lethal weaponry, personal security, and investigative work. Some of them have... other skills."

Somehow, I didn't think he meant crocheting. "Such as..?"

"Crisis negotiation. Hostage recovery." He paused, eyes slivering open again. "Interrogation tactics."

"Is that some kind of euphemism for torture?"

"They're good men to know if you're ever in a jam," he said, not answering my question. "Professional. Discrete. You met a few of them today."

I jolted back against the bench, so startled I didn't even realize that doing so brought me directly beneath the span of Cade's outstretched arm. "Who?"

"Hunter and Holden. Plus, Welles."

"The twins and Mr. Man Bun are part of the legion of badassery?" I could hear the skepticism in my own voice.

"What is it with you and hair-related nicknames?"

I didn't answer his question. Mostly because a thought had just occurred to me — a distinctly unpleasant one.

"Hang on a minute... You vouched for me earlier in front of not only Graham 'If Looks Could Kill' Graves... but more than one of his goon squad? All of whom now have me in their sights?" My voice pitched up an octave. "And by '*sights*' I quite literally mean *gun-sights* because apparently they're all highly trained assassins?"

"Assassins might be a stretch. Think of them more like... freelance assets with a variety of employable skills."

I scowled at him, not at all amused by his flippant tone in the face of my growing panic. "Why did you do it?"

"Do what?"

"Vouch for me!" I half screeched. "You don't even know me."

"What do you mean? We go way back."

I leaned harder against the bench. "Don't joke around. I'm serious. You told that asshole—"

"Graham isn't an asshole."

I stared at him, dubious.

"Okay, he's an asshole," Cade amended. "But in this particular scenario, he has a pretty damn solid reason for being one."

"You mean last week when Gwen nearly—" I lifted my hands to do finger quotes. "*—bit the dust?*"

He nodded. "It all turned out okay in the end, thank Christ, but things easily could've gone the other way. Graves is a man who thrives on control above all else. For a few hours, he lost it. Didn't know if she was alive or dead. I've never seen him so shaken up. If something had happened to her…" He shook his head slowly, all traces of humor fading. "Let's just say, I'm glad everything worked out the way it did. Not only for Gwen. For the whole damn city."

"What do you mean?"

"The Gravewatch boys would've carved a swathe of destruction no amount of paperwork could justify."

My hands knotted together in my lap. "Do you think… I mean, would he really…"

"What is it, Goldie?"

"Graham. Is he really going to dig into my past?"

"Honestly? Yeah, he probably will."

"But— that's not—" I was spluttering. "There's no need for him to do that! Who I am, where I come from… That's none of his business!"

Again, he didn't move, but a stillness settled over him. The sense of utter peace vanished in an instant. Relaxed Cade was no longer sitting next to me; Detective Hightower was. And his eyes were suddenly as serious as his tone. "Why are you so freaked?"

"Besides the fact that some super-spy PI is digging through my personal affairs?"

"Everyone has shit in their history they don't want dug up."

"Not like mine," I muttered under my breath.

"Hey. Look at me."

I did. My teeth dug into my lip at the look in his eyes. Gentle. Almost protective. No one had ever looked at me like I was worth protecting. Usually, it was the other way around. People treated me like I was the thing they needed protection *from*. Like I was something to be exploited, manipulated, or, more often than not, avoided.

But Cade…

God, I could barely breathe when he was looking at me like that.

"No matter what Graves digs up, it won't matter," he told me in that deep, matter-of-fact tone. His arm shifted off the top of bench to curl around my shoulders, squeezing reassuringly. "He's not going to bring that shit anywhere near you."

I sucked in a surprised grasp as the steady weight of his arm settled around me. I hadn't been held in a long time. A long, *long* time. There was no denying how good it felt. Too good to shake off, even though I knew I should.

Fighting the urge to relax into his warmth, my whole frame was stiff with tension as I asked, "How do you know?"

"Because I'll be standing between you two, blocking him when he tries."

Shit.

That was a nice thing to say.

I swallowed hard against the lump in my throat. "Aren't you curious?"

"About?"

"The things he's going to dig up."

"No."

"*No?*"

He shook his head. His eyes never left mine, but his arm tightened around my shoulders. As though he knew what he said next was going to make me run for the hills.

"I don't need to look into your history. I know exactly who you are, Imogen Warner."

CHAPTER NINE

Everyone compliments the cute romper when you wear it. But when you get inside the bathroom stall, it's just you and your choices.

- Imogen Warner, fully nude on a public toilet

My breath caught.

This was it.

He knew me — *recognized* me — either from my childhood days of daytime television fame, or the drama that unfolded after I fled Florida as fast as I could. Unless he'd beaten Graham to the punch and run a background check of his own last night.

I supposed that was possible. Probable, even. He was a detective. He had the resources to pull up my records. They were supposed to be sealed, since I was a minor when everything with my uncle went down. But there was more — a lot more — to find if you knew where to look.

Baltimore, to be specific.

I'd been nineteen when the Crawford case exploded all over the headlines. A legal adult. A causal internet search would expose that dark chapter of my past — one I'd done my damndest to forget. I could only imagine what the internal police records said about me.

God, I had to get out of here.

I bit the inside of my cheek so hard I was surprised I didn't taste blood. My voice was as stiff as my shoulders when I said, "Look, I don't know what you think you know—"

"You're a good person. That's what I know."

I jolted in surprise.

What?

A good person?

Maybe he didn't know about my past, after all.

His eyes were crinkled up in amusement. "Why? What did you think I meant?"

Realizing my mouth was agape, I clicked it shut and swallowed hard. "Nothing. I just... I wasn't..." I shook my head and told myself to stop talking before I gave him even more reasons to be suspicious of me.

He stood up abruptly, apparently done with this conversation. Tossing our trash in the bin beside the bench, he reached out a hand for mine. "Come on, Goldie."

"Where are we going?"

"The auto shop." He paused, waggling his fingers impatiently when I didn't grab them. "I told Puck I'd bring you by sometime today so we could talk about your car."

"But..." I shook my head rapidly. "You didn't even know you'd see me today."

He grinned, like that was an adorably misguided thought. Then, patience expiring, he bent forward, swiped my hand from my lap, and pulled me to my feet. He tugged me along behind him, large strides eating up the path back toward where we'd come from.

"Hang on!" I dug in my heels. "We're going the wrong way!"

"My cruiser is parked behind the Hawthorne."

"Well, my bike is parked by the Witch Museum!"

He arched a single dark brow. "Where'd you get a motorcycle?"

My cheeks flooded with heat. "It's... uh... more of a two-wheeler."

"Ah. A bicycle. That makes more sense." His other brow arched to join its mate. "Georgia's?"

"Declan's."

There was a short pause. "You borrowed a ten-year-old's bicycle?"

"He's eleven!"

"Goldie..." Cade shook his head. His shoulders were shaking too — from suppressed laughter. "That's not really the point."

"Oh, whatever!" God, my cheeks were on fire. "Just tell me where the auto-shop is and I'll meet you there."

He shook his head, tightened his grip on my hand, and began marching in the opposite direction, toward the Witch Museum. I had no choice but to scurry along after him or else be dragged.

"Cade! Where do you think you're going now?"

"To get your bike," he said without breaking stride.

"It's not a tandem."

He looked over his shoulder to grin at me. "I'm not planning to ride with you. This isn't a chick flick."

"Who said anything about—"

"We'll wheel it to my SUV," he cut me off. "It should fit just fine in the trunk of my cruiser."

"You are the pushiest, most irritating, meddlesome—"

"Goldie."

"What?!"

"The auto-shop is a five mile ride, total opposite side of town from The Sea Witch. You can call me whatever names you want, all the worst adjectives you can come up with... I don't give a shit. I'm still not about to let you ride there alone. Not when it's getting dark out. Not looking like you do. Not ever. But especially not two nights before Halloween, when the whole damn city is flooded with all kinds of people looking for trouble."

I digested this for a moment and, eventually, was forced to deem it a reasonable statement. To cover my annoyance, I narrowed my eyes and echoed, "*Looking like I do?* What does that mean?"

He stopped short. His gaze flickered up and down my body for a moment, lingering briefly on my bare legs, then drifting up to catch on the lacing at my bodice for another fraction of a second, before finally making its way back to my face. The banked heat in his eyes was undeniable. Seeing it there sent another delicious furl of attraction through every one of my nerve endings.

Shit.

"Looking like you do," he repeated, voice rougher than usual. "That hair. Those eyes. And that smile — on the rare occasion you've actually let me see it — is like a gift. Fucking breathtaking."

This.

Freaking.

Guy.

!!!!!

My lips were parted, mouth gaping like a fish on dry land, unable to draw in air let alone form a suitable response. Luckily, Cade didn't seem to require one. He reached out with his free hand, placed a single finger beneath my chin, then gently pushed upward until my teeth met with a soft click.

"You gonna make it?" he asked, voice playful — though his eyes were still simmering with heat.

I nodded. (Even though, frankly, I was not completely certain I wasn't about to keel over from lack of air.)

"Good," he said.

And, with that, he turned and led me across the Common to retrieve my bicycle.

Goodfellow Custom Cars sat smack in the middle of a street peppered by tire shops, tool rentals services, and self-storage warehouses. It looked pretty much how I'd expected it to look, with a large forecourt, three big bay doors, and a sign declaring it an authorized state inspection site. One of the bay doors was open, and I could see there was a car up on the lift inside. The mechanic working on it swung his head in our direction the minute Cade pulled his SUV into the lot.

Before we'd even parked, the man was moving out to meet us, wiping grease-stained hands on a white rag. His coveralls were folded down around his hips and he was grinning wide in welcome.

"Cade, my man! Been too long. Was beginning to worry you'd found a new mechanic before you called."

"Oh, come on Puck. You know I'm not the type to stray." Cade lifted his fist and bumped it against the man's. "Thanks for getting me in so fast, I know you're always busy."

"For you, I'm not busy. Anytime you need me, you got me. You know that." He scratched the side of his head, which was shaved nearly to the skin. The full beard he was sporting made up for the lack of hair up top. "Just wish there was more I could do for you with this one. Like I told you on the phone, the car is on its last legs. Suspension is shot to shit. Brakes are going, transmission isn't far behind. I can replace the tires, tune up the engine, but it's like putting lipstick on a pig. The water pump part I ordered—" He shook his head. "Patch job. Might buy you another few thousand miles of road, but put aside those dreams of a cross-country voyage. You get me?"

Cade grunted. "I get you."

I, it must be said, did *not* get him, seeing as I didn't speak mechanic. I didn't know much about what he'd just said, all I knew was it sounded expensive. As in *way flipping expensive*.

My expression must've conveyed my gathering anxiety, because when Puck's light brown eyes slid to mine, they went a bit soft. That softness disappeared, however, as they did a quick up-and-down scan of my body. A smile was still playing at his lips as he spoke.

"So, Cade, this must be your new… friend."

My smile faltered a smidge at his well-timed pause. I powered through my discomfort, giving a little wave of my gloved fingers. "Um. Hi. I'm Imogen Warner. Owner of the rust bucket currently occupying your bay. It's nice to meet you."

His smile widened. He looked back at Cade. "Gotta say, man, I had friends like yours, I might not be so happily married."

Cade chuckled, low and amused.

My brows went up. *Huh?*

But Puck did not explain himself. He merely cocked his head toward the open bay and started walking. "I've got her in the back. If you want to follow me, I'll walk you through the worst of it. Tell you what I can do and what's beyond even my powers. My honest opinion? Might not be worth the cake it'll take to fix her, but that's your call."

Damn and blast.

That was *so* not the news I needed to hear, tonight. I needed to get on the road. The longer I was stuck here, the harder it would be to move on. And I had to move on. It was the only way to stay safe, the only way to stay ahead of everything chasing me.

I might not like my fate, but I was resigned to it. Constant motion. Eternally uprooted. For months — for years — I'd been living on a tightrope. Afraid to lean one way or another, knowing if I did I'd fall off. Afraid to look back, to see if my nightmare was gaining on me.

I knew better than to think I could outrun it forever. And I also knew, when that day came…

My eyes pressed closed, fear churning in my gut.

Adrian may've been the most recent, but he was also the least of my worries. The demons farther back in my past were infinitely more deadly — and more persistent. Even after a decade, I wasn't fool enough to think myself free. One day it would all catch up to me. One day…

He would catch up to me.

In the meantime, I was going to enjoy my freedom the only way I knew how: adding more stops on the Imogen Warner International Tour of Misery. Keeping that tightrope beneath my feet. Keeping my eyes fixed forward and my feet in motion.

The weight of a large hand settled on my arm. I cracked open my eyes to find Cade had moved close. His head was tipped down to mine and his eyes were intense as they moved over my face. I didn't know him well enough to decipher the look he was giving me, but it lasted a long time and it was heavy enough to make me shiver.

He saw the shiver — hell, he *felt* the shiver — and did not seem to like it much. His eyes flashed and his voice came out low. "What's wrong?"

"N-nothing," I stammered, wiping my expression clear, burying my nightmare back where it belonged — deep, deep down in my head. "I'm okay."

"You're not."

"I just said I am!"

His jaw tightened. So did the hand on my arm — not painfully, just enough to remind me it was there. "You lied."

"I didn't!"

"Goldie, you did."

Now, my hackles were going up. "Let's get something straight. You seem to think you know me. Why you think this, seeing as we've been acquainted for approximately *a day*," I snapped, full of attitude, "will go down as a mystery for the ages. But the fact is, you don't know me well enough to know when I'm lying. And you definitely don't know me well enough to demand I share my every thought and feeling with you."

"You do get that I'm a detective, don't you?"

I narrowed my eyes. "Yes."

"So you get that I'm pretty fucking good at knowing when someone is being evasive."

"I'm not being evasive! I'm perfectly o—" My lips clamped shut when his expression darkened.

"You tell me you're okay one more goddamned time, I swear…" Eyes flashing with frustration, he leaned in another few inches, so his face was right in mine. A few inches closer, his lips would be *on* mine. All the oxygen seemed to vanish from the air. "You're not okay. And it's not just about the car repairs. It's not just about today, or last night. Something's eating at you. Something a fuck of a lot bigger than a failing transmission."

What was this guy, a mind reader? I was supposed to be the clairvoyant one here!

"Fair warning, Goldie, I'm a patient guy," he continued, face getting even closer. So close, I could see each individual curl of his thick lashes; the rings of deeper indigo around the edges of his irises. So close, I could almost feel his words as he spoke them against my mouth. "I'll wait. But you're going to tell me what's got you going pale and shaky and quiet, chewing your lip and fighting back tears. And you're going to do it before whatever that is catches up to you, so I can do something about it. If you don't…" His eyes flared with determination. "I'll dig and find it on my own."

My mouth dropped open at his audacity. "You have no right to dig into my past!"

"Second reminder of the evening," he growled. "*I'm a detective.*"

"And that badge gives you the right to swoop in uninvited and stick your nose in my private business?"

This was the wrong thing to say.

I knew it because, very suddenly, I was staring at a Caden Hightower I'd never seen before. One that did not chuckle low in his throat, one whose eyes did not dance with humor. The jovial surface I'd become accustomed to stripped away and, beneath it, there was a different man entirely. One that radiated an intimidating amount of intensity, enough to rival the Gravewatch boys. One that, if I was being honest, scared me far more than the prospect of a massive auto-repair bill.

And, in that moment, I couldn't help it.

I reacted.

My flinch was blatant, lashing through me in an involuntary reflex. Too many times in the past, men had put their hands on me with the intent to do violence. Too many times in the past, I'd seen the switch flip from reassurance to rage. I jerked against Cade's grip, unable to suppress the panic that moved through my gut, that made my breath catch.

To his credit, his hands dropped away instantly. He stepped back two paces out of my space, like I'd doused him with a vat of cold water. His angry expression shuttered in the space between two heartbeats.

I did my best to clear my own face of any lingering fear, but it was too late. Far, far too late. He'd seen my reaction; he knew what it meant. And though his temper was locked down through what seemed to be sheer force of will, I could still see the rage brimming in his eyes. Only this time, it wasn't directed at me.

It was on my behalf.

And that was its own brand of terrifying, for a whole other brand of reasons.

"Someone put his hands on you?" he asked with deceptive softness. His voice was eerily calm, but his eyes — god, they were haunted. "Someone hurt you?"

I shifted my weight from foot to foot, nervously chewing my bottom lip. I didn't know what to say. I'd tried lying to him already, several times, and each time he'd seen straight through it. Still, I wanted to lie. I *badly* wanted to lie, because I had a feeling he would not be best pleased to learn that yes, someone had put his hands on me, and yes, someone had hurt me. More than one someone, on more than one occasion.

My teeth released my lip. "Cade—"

"Answer me, Imogen."

I looked at him across the buffer of distance he'd created between us, feeling the oddest urge to close it. Despite my attempts to sound steady, there was a faint tremor in my voice. "Please... I don't want to talk about this."

His eyes pressed closed and his jaw clenched tight. "Someone hurt you," he said again — this time not a question. "Who?"

"Cade—"

"You tell me who or I take the time to find out who. Either way, he's got a lesson coming. One I plan to deliver personally."

I shivered again. He was not fucking around, I could see that plain as day. I watched the rhythmic tick of his cheek muscle. He looked like he was struggling to get a lock on his rage.

"You're scaring me," I admitted after a long moment, my voice a whisper.

His body stilled. He took a deep breath, his whole frame broadening with the force of it. His eyes pressed closed for a beat. When they opened again, they were the eyes I'd come to know. Not haunted. Not angry. Clear and blue as an October sky.

"You don't have to be afraid of me," he said softly.

Not soft like before — soft in a new way I'd never heard from him. A way that made a lump form in my throat.

"I'd never hurt you," he went on, and it sounded like a vow. "Swear to whatever god is up there, I'd never, ever hurt you. You may not trust me yet, but you can trust me on that."

I nodded, unable to speak without it coming out in an emotional croak.

After another long beat of silence, he canted his head toward the garage. "Come on. Puck's waiting in the back. We'll get you sorted out, then I'll get you back to The Sea Witch."

My throat felt oddly thick. I still couldn't speak, so I just nodded again. He took another deep breath, then started walking. For the first time since we'd crossed paths, he did not fall into step beside me, matching his long legs to mine. His hand did not find the small of my back to steer me gently through the open bay doors. He kept a careful distance as we moved inside, then gave me even more of it as I stood beside my car, listening to Puck rattle off the myriad issues that required fixing in order to get me back on the road.

Back on my tightrope.

Out of Salem.

Out of Cade's life.

I tried to listen to Puck, but my attention kept drifting from the man talking to me to the one leaning in silence against the wall. I couldn't forget the sharp look on his face when he'd seen my flinch, the haunted look in his eyes when he'd gotten the tiniest glimpse into my dark past. And I couldn't help wondering what his reaction would be if he followed through on his promise to dig deeper.

The demons he'd find there weren't just dark.

They were dangerous.

"How do you know Puck?" I asked thirty minutes later, unable to stand the thick silence for another moment. Cade was driving me back to The Sea Witch, and he was not in the mood for chit-chat. He'd said not a word since we left the Goodfellow garage, bidding his friend farewell with a fist-bump, then walking back to his SUV with such long strides, I had to jog to keep up.

He blew out a breath. "I met him on my first case in town. String of thefts targeting the cars in his lot, along with some of the others in that area. I caught the thieving fuck and got him locked up for a dime on felony GTA charges. The rest is history."

"Ten years in prison for stealing cars?"

He nodded. "We aren't talking about your standard Camrys and Hondas, here. Puck is one of the best in the business when it comes to restoring classic cars, repairing luxury models. Did you notice the Aston Martin in the bay next to yours?"

I had, in fact. I'd also not missed the black-on-black Lamborghini parked beside it. It looked like the freaking Batmobile.

"My car doesn't exactly scream *classic* or *luxury*," I felt the need to point out.

"No." A smile twitched at Cade's mouth. "Puck is making an exception for us."

I processed this for a moment, not sure how I felt about being an exception. Or an *us*.

"Anyway, after the case wrapped up, I started bringing my bike to Goodfellow for service."

"Bike as in motorcycle?"

His mouth twitched again. "Puck doesn't handle two-wheelers, Goldie. But he's top-notch when it comes to Harleys."

"You drive a Harley?"

"Is that a surprise?"

"Um… sort of. I mean, you're a cop. Cops are all about following the rules, driving the speed limit, et cetera."

His eyes cut to mine when we stopped at a red light. His wrist was slung over the wheel as he leaned back in his seat. "You make the acquaintance of a lot of cops in your lifetime?"

Damn and blast!

I'd walked right into that one.

"No," I lied. "I'm just… speculating."

"Mhm." He looked like he knew I was lying, but he didn't push me on it. "Turns out, I'm not that big on rules, Goldie. I'm also not a big fan of taking beautiful women out to dinner in the same squad car I use for criminals and degenerates."

"Oh," I murmured, pressing my hands into my thighs. I was trying very hard not to think about what it would be like to climb on the back of a motorcycle, wrap my arms around Cade's middle, and ride off into the sunset. Or, at least, to a nice dinner somewhere. Something about the look on his face told me he was thinking about it too, which should've freaked me out but, instead, made a warm, fuzzy, unfamiliar sort of feeling bloom in the pit of my stomach.

I was staring at him again, and I couldn't look away. The longer my eyes lingered on his face, the heavier the air in the SUV grew. I swallowed hard, trying to get my faculties in order, and Cade's eyes flickered down to watch the bob of my throat. When they moved back up to mine, the heat in them made that warm, fuzzy feeling in my gut ratchet up by several degrees, then spread unmistakably southward.

Oh boy.

I shifted on the seat, pressing my thighs together, hoping it might stop the spreading heat. I thought I was subtle about it, but Cade did not miss the infinitesimal movement. His eyes flared with an attraction that matched mine and he leaned across the center console, eyes locked on my mouth as the gap between us shrank in slow degrees. I kept perfectly still as he came at me.

Was he going to kiss me?

Did I want him to kiss me?

The very thought of his lips on mine was enough to inspire paralysis. I couldn't move. Couldn't breathe. My bloodstream was on fire, the heat between my legs—

Beeeeeep.

The car behind us laid on their horn, alerting us to the light change. (Clearly, they didn't realize they were honking at an unmarked police cruiser.) Cade's jaw clenched tighter as he turned back to the windshield.

The spell was broken.

I sat back in my seat, heart pounding twice as fast as it should be. He hadn't even touched me, but every inch of my skin was tingling. I knit my gloved hands together in my lap to keep still.

The silence was even heavier, now. Full of things I was far too scared to address.

"Do you have a sidecar for Socks?" I asked, desperate to shift this conversation into safer waters. "On your Harley?"

Cade was silent.

"If not, you should get one. Maybe a little pair of doggy goggles, so his eyes don't tear up when you ride."

There was another beat of silence. Then, without warning, Cade threw his head back and laughed — a deep, lush, full body laugh that vibrated through me in a shockwave.

I'd heard him chuckle before, I'd heard him scoff. But I'd never heard him *laugh*. Not like this, anyway. And, god, it was a great laugh. The best I'd ever heard by a mile.

My toes curled inside my boots as I listened to it fade. My eyes were stuck on his face, transfixed by the sight of his strong white teeth flashing in a grin, his eyes crinkling up at the corners. I was so mesmerized, in fact, I didn't even realize he'd turned into The Sea Witch lot and pulled up to the porch. Not until he reached over and shifted into park.

"A sidecar for Socks," he muttered, traces of his grin still evident on his face. "Doggy goggles. Fuck, Goldie. That was funny."

"It was a serious suggestion," I said, trying to keep a straight face.

"I'll take it under advisement."

"You do that."

And then, I smiled at him. I couldn't help it. Watching him smile, watching him laugh… his joy was infectious. But as he watched my lips turn up into a grin, his own disappeared. The humor drained out of his eyes, replaced by that simmering heat I'd seen moments before, at the stoplight. Only this time, it was even hotter.

I thought surely he was going to lean forward, close the gap between us, and kiss me. Instead, he tore his eyes away, took a visible breath, and shoved open his door.

"Come on. I'll walk you to the porch."

Right.

Right.

What was I thinking? I had no business getting involved with this man. Even setting aside the small fact that I'd be gone in a few days, he was a cop. He'd already informed me he had plans to look into my past. I needed to stop imagining what his arms would feel like wrapped tight around me and start holding him at arm's length.

"You really don't have to do that—" I started to protest, but he slammed his door closed. I took a series of steadying breaths, then got out my side and met him by the back of the SUV. He'd already removed my bike from the trunk and set it on the ground. Hitting the button to close the lift gate, he wheeled the bike one-handed up toward the porch, then stowed it beside Rory's smaller red one in the rack by the base of the front steps.

"Um. Thanks," I said, feeling awkward. "For the bike. For my car. For being so, uh... nice to me."

Cade wasn't feeling awkward. I knew this as soon as he turned to me. There was a determined look on his face that made my stomach somersault even more than the heat in his eyes. When he stepped toward me and took my hand in his big one, the somersaults escalated to full on back-handsprings.

"Imogen."

I sucked in a breath. "Y-yes?"

"Something you should know."

Oh, no.

I wasn't sure I wanted to know. But I still managed a weak, "Yes?"

"I'm not doing this because I'm nice."

"You aren't?"

He stepped closer. His eyes were very serious, and they never shifted from mine. Not for a heartbeat. "Nope."

"Oh." My mouth felt very dry. "Then why are you doing it?"

"You want me to tell you?"

I gave a shallow nod.

"I'd rather show you," he murmured, hand tightening.

"What?" I breathed. "What do you—"

My question slipped away into a surprised gasp (which quickly turned into an altogether *different* sort of gasp) as Cade's head slanted down and his lips claimed mine. All thoughts of keeping him at arm's length vanished instantly. I didn't even think about it, I just kissed him back — leaning into his space until my body brushed against his, the hard planes of his chest pressed firm against my curves.

His heat sank into me as his hands slid up my spine, then delved into my hair, his strong fingers twisting in the weight of it. Gentle, but firm. That felt so unbelievably good, I nearly purred. My hands hit his waist, curling around his belt to keep my balance when my knees threatened to turn to jelly.

Damn, the man could *kiss*.

I'd had my fair share of kisses over the years, but never one like this. Cade's kiss was like a sneak attack. Soft, at first, almost gentle. Unhurried. He took his time, coaxing my lips to open under his, sliding his tongue inside once I granted permission. Not demanding or claiming anything that I didn't offer freely.

I soon realized his strategy. He was slowly building the heat with his lips and his hands and his body, steadily fanning the embers of passion until I was burning up with it. Until *I* was the one pressing closer, pushing up onto my tiptoes, winding my arms around his neck.

Cade felt my eager response and returned it without hesitation, growling low in his throat when my fingers threaded into the thick hair at his nape. I desperately wished I weren't wearing my gloves; wished I could feel that silk against my bare skin. I tilted my head to the side, giving him better access to my mouth as he deepened the kiss.

God, that felt good.

Indescribable.

I wanted more and I wasn't afraid to let him know it. My touch grew more urgent as I wound my arms tighter, fingers pressing into his skin to pull him as close as I could get him. A mewl of pure pleasure escaped when he sucked lightly on my tongue, the same instant his hands left my hair to frame my face. I liked the feeling of his big hands cradling my head, his callused palms scraping against my cheeks. I liked it so much, I plastered my body fully against him and surrendered every bit of self-control I still possessed.

Cade made another low, growly sound — one that informed me his own control was slipping. His sneak attack strategy was no more than a memory, now. The kiss had gone wild, and neither of us had the faintest desire to reel it back in.

"Fuck," he muttered against my lips when I was forced to break for a much-needed gulp of air. "That mouth of yours. I thought watching it smile at me was incredible, but feeling it on mine… *Fuck.*"

Did he just say that?

It was safe to say, I was *definitely* smiling as I pushed up onto my tiptoes to kiss him again. No sooner did his lips claim mine than the sudden screech of a door opening made us jolt apart. Cade's arms did not release their grip; he continued to hold me close, even as both our heads whipped toward the porch just in time to see Rory barrel out onto it. He was barefoot, clad in his silver spaceship pajamas. When he saw us, he covered his eyes with his hands and dropped to his knees.

"*EW!* KISSING! GROSS!"

His little-kid voice carried quite well. Well enough to draw his brother outside onto the porch, followed quickly by his mother.

Blast!

I tried to wiggle out of Cade's hold, but his arms turned to steel bands the instant I moved. Gigi's look of stunned disbelief morphed into a shit-eating grin as she took in the sight of me standing there — no doubt flushed and panting — in the circle of a certain silver fox detective's arms. Her hands flew out to snag her youngest around the shoulders.

"Rory, bub, get back inside," she ordered, pivoting him around and giving him a slight push toward the door. "Time to brush your teeth, then get in bed."

"But—"

"No backtalk." Her eyes swung to Declan, who was staring at me and Cade with a mini shit-eating grin of his own. "You too, Dec."

"But it's not my bedtime!" the eleven-year-old protested, indignant. "It's not even seven!"

"You don't have homework?"

"Finished it."

"Fine. One hour of Nintendo," she acquiesced. "*One,* not three. Then pjs and bed."

He heaved a heavy sigh, then followed his brother inside. I flinched at the sound of the screechy screen door swinging shut at his back. Georgia was still standing on the porch, grinning at us like this was the best day of her freaking life. When she caught my pointed glare — the one that clearly said *don't you dare make a comment* — she openly giggled.

"I'll just..." She grinned wider. "Be inside. You guys, um... Take your time. *Really.*"

My glare intensified.

Another giggle drifted out the door as she pulled it shut. As for me, I wasn't laughing. I turned wary eyes back to Cade's broad chest, then up the tanned column of his throat, past his twitching mouth, and eventually to his eyes. There was still a goodly amount of heat burning in their depths, but also an unmistakable edge of humor.

"And what," I said icily, "Are you laughing at, detective?"

"We just got caught making out by a six-year-old, Goldie."

"Rory is seven," I corrected automatically.

"Doesn't make it less funny."

"On the contrary, I don't see anything remotely amusing about this."

"Then you aren't looking hard enough."

With that, he grinned, bent in, and brushed his mouth against mine again. It was a shadow of the kiss we'd shared before, but it was still good. The toe-curling, stomach-somersaulting, heart-fluttering sort of good. When his mouth left mine, I was fighting the urge to squirm. Thankfully, before I could humiliate myself further, his arms dropped away and he stepped back.

"I'll see you tomorrow," he informed me.

My eyes widened. "You will?"

"Goldie." He shook his head. "You think I'm going to stay away after you just kissed me like that?"

"I didn't kiss you. *You* kissed *me*."

"You kissed me back."

I clamped my lips shut because, well, I had.

"Fuck, you're cute." He reached out and tapped my nose with his index finger.

Before I could protest that I wasn't cute, thank you very much, he walked back to his SUV, climbed inside, started the engine, and drove away. I was still standing there like a thunderstruck idiot when I heard the swing of the heavy front door, followed by the telltale screech of the screen.

"So," Gigi called, sounding like she was about two seconds from breaking down into another fit of giggles. "How was your day? Anything interesting happen?"

I dropped my head into my hands and groaned.

CHAPTER TEN

Dating someone new is like getting disconnected from customer service. You have to tell your whole story from the very beginning.
- Imogen Warner, calling tech support

I scowled down at my phone screen, eyes pinned to the ugly message that had popped up as I pedaled to The Gallows.

Getting real tired of this game of cat and mouse you're playing, doll. You don't make it right, I'll make you pay.

The text had come from an unlisted number. No name, no contact info. Still, I knew it was Adrian. It was always Adrian. I mentally scratched 'get a new phone number' onto my to-do list, then shoved my phone into my backpack and promptly put my douchebag ex-boyfriend out of my head.

I had bigger fish to fry, today.

Nervous butterflies fluttered in my gut as I stepped inside the shop. It was 8:35AM. I was officially early, but I'd been pacing by the bike rack for ten full minutes now, and if I didn't stop I figured someone would call the cops on me for suspicious behavior.

(Seeing as, with my luck, the responding cop would probably be one Detective Caden Hightower, I decided I was just fine with being early for my first shift.)

The door swung shut with a tinkle of bells from the old-fashioned chime overhead. This time, there was no greeting party of too-hot-to-handle Gravewatch men leaning against various shelves and surfaces, exuding scary yet strangely enticing energy. Instead, Gwendolyn Goode stood alone by the espresso bar, polishing the steam-wand with a damp rag. She was wearing a super-chic asymmetrical sweater that, even from a distance, looked more expensive than anything in my closet. Her long red hair was swept back from her temples in an elegant twist. Her face broke into a huge smile when she spotted me.

"Imogen!" she squawked, throwing down her rag and rounding the bar. "Oh my god, you're here!"

"Sorry, I'm early."

"Don't be sorry! I'm so glad you showed up. I was worried we'd scared you off yesterday. Graham can be a bit..."

"Protective?"

She rolled her eyes. "Sure. We'll go with that. It's nicer than the word I would've used to describe him."

I glanced beyond her, into the empty shop. "I'm surprised he isn't here now. The way he reacted to my arrival yesterday, I figured he'd be waiting for me with guns blazing."

"My bodyguards have the day off, thank the goddess." A furrow appeared between her auburn brows. "My in-person ones, at least."

"You have *non*-in-person ones?"

"Cameras," she explained, looking sheepish. "The whole shop is wired. The front and back exits are monitored 24/7 by the boys in the Gravewatch surveillance room."

"Seriously?"

"I know it seems like overkill, trust me. But after everything that went down last week..." She shuddered, remembering something unpleasant. "I've learned not to fight Graham on this front. When it comes to taking the proper safety precautions, he does not mess around. Like… *at all.*"

"Clearly."

"It annoyed me when we first got together, but I've decided to see it as charming, not completely overbearing. For my own mental health."

"How long have you been together?"

"Just over a month."

My eyes, which were already bugging out of my head, bugged out even more at this. A month? Graham and Gwen seemed like they'd been together for eons. Since the dawn of time. Maybe even before that.

"Though, we've known one another since we were kids," Gwen added, no doubt seeing my skepticism. "And I've sort of been in love with him since I was eight."

I felt my lips twitch up into a smile. "Ah. That explains it."

"Granted, he was a bit more laidback as the teenage lifeguard heartthrob of my childhood fantasies. I'm hoping now that the dust is settling, he'll calm down a bit with the macho-man antics. My best friend Florence — oh, you met her yesterday, actually!" Her eyes lit up. "Gorgeous, great hair, looks like the lead character of a k-drama?"

I nodded to confirm.

"Right, so, Flo keeps assuring me he's going to mellow out after we've been together a few months," Gwen continued. "I told her Graham's personal dictionary doesn't include the word 'mellow' and that I'd be lucky if he didn't surgically implant a GPS tracker chip in my asscheek while I was sleeping rather than risk me getting almost-murdered again."

My smile vanished at this admission. I wasn't certain if she was joking or not and I didn't know her well enough to ask. For her sake, I prayed she was joking. The thought of anyone having a precise lock on my location was enough to inspire a panic attack.

But Gwen seemed entirely unbothered by the concept of her man monitoring her every move. There was a dreamy, content look on her face as her thoughts drifted; a secretive smile playing at her lips. Her attention only snapped back to me when I shifted from side to side, my booted heels scuffing lightly against the heavy, historical hardwood floors.

"Anywho." She grinned at me. "That's enough about Graham Crackers."

"Are you sure he's cool with me working for you? He wasn't too thrilled by the concept yesterday."

"He's cool."

I must've looked doubtful, because she waved away my worries with a graceful hand-sweep.

"Seriously, Imogen, whatever Detective Hightower told him this morning really seemed to put his mind at ease."

I felt my face drain of blood. "Cade spoke to Graham about me?"

Gwen's eyes widened. "Oh, shoot. I don't think I was supposed to tell you that part."

"What's there to tell?"

She hesitated for a half-second, then blurted, "All I know is, he came over to the house first thing this morning. They disappeared into Graham's office for a chat. A *long* chat. It seemed serious. He left in a hurry afterwards, all business. I couldn't even get him to stay for a cup of coffee!" She blew out a frustrated breath. "I tried to eavesdrop, but Graham just replaced my flimsy old office door with this super heavy oak one when he redid the room, so I couldn't hear much of anything. Whatever your detective said, though, it was enough. Graham didn't make a peep about it when I left for work — even after I mentioned I'd be seeing you."

"He's not *my* detective," I informed her weakly. Semantics were the least of my problems. I was undeniably rattled by the thought of Cade discussing me with Graham 'Badass Extraordinaire' Graves. I supposed I shouldn't be — Cade had warned me last night that he had every intention to dig into my past. I just hadn't anticipated he would share whatever he found with my new boss's boyfriend at the first possible opportunity.

I should have.

This is why you keep away from cops, a snarky inner voice reminded me. *This is why you can't make friends.*

It took all my self-control to keep from bolting toward the door. The long-ingrained urge to pack up my belongings, pile into my car, and head for the hills swept through me in a relentless wave. Unfortunately, with my shitbox still up on blocks and my bank accounts rapidly approaching zero, I wouldn't get far. Not even on Declan's bicycle.

"Don't you worry about Graham," Gwen said gently. Her expression was soft with concern and awareness. I wondered what she'd seen in mine.

Panic, no doubt.

"He's all bark, no bite," she informed me. I must've looked skeptical, because she hurriedly added, "Err… okay, he occasionally bites. But only when he needs to. And I know the Gravewatch boys seem intense, but once you're in, you're *in*. You know?"

No, I didn't know.

I'd never been *in* with anyone. Certainly not a group like Gravewatch.

"Anywho!" She clapped her hands together. "We have more important things to discuss than overprotective macho-men. We open in ten minutes and I have a feeling we're going to be slammed. So. Where to begin?" Her eyes swept around. "Obviously up front here we have the espresso counter where people buy their coffee…" She flourished her hands at an old-fashioned cash register that looked straight out of a historical film. "We're currently down a barista. That means, until I find someone, I'll be on coffee duties. Which, to be perfectly honest, is *not* my forte. Especially when it comes to that beast."

We both stared for a beat at the shiny gold espresso machine.

It was, indeed, a beast. There were more levers and dials than I could count, dual steam wands, and four portafilters. A vat of dark roasted beans towered beside it. I'd been a barista several times in my varied career as a vagabond, but I'd never worked a machine quite that massive.

"I can make a halfway decent latte in a pinch, but I'm no master," Gwen confided, brow furrowing again. "And the locals around here are big fans of foam art, custom flavor creations, and caffeinated concoctions beyond my amateur abilities. *Turmeric-ginger. Pumpkin spice. Dirty chai.*" She groaned. "Shoot me now. If the line starts to pile up, I fear I may crack under the pressure."

"I can do latte art."

Gwen blinked in surprise. "Really?"

"Sure. Nothing fancy, but a maple leaf, a heart, a smiley face... The basics." My shoulders went up and down in a light shrug. "I've worked as a barista a few times."

Suddenly, Gwen was grinning at me so bight, it threatened to blind me. "What are you, like, my personal guardian angel, sent to earth to save my ass?"

I was startled into silence by this question. Gwen didn't seem to notice. She looped her arm through mine and started tugging me deeper into the store. "You're welcome to jump in if you see me drowning in takeaway cups when you're between readings. Lord knows I could use the help. I'll pay you for your hours, of course, on top of whatever you collect from your tarot clients."

I could certainly use the hours — and the cash. "I'm happy to jump in wherever I'm needed, Gwen."

"Perfect!" Her smile went from bright to mega-watt. "Let's finish the tour while we have a quiet minute. I'll show you what I like to call our *Mystical Curiosities* section. There's a second register back there, where people purchase all their books and baubles..."

She dragged me quickly through the maze of shelves. I saw tomes on everything from moon phases to mystical properties to mythological creatures. Some looked fresh from the printers, others were old and clearly well-loved. Gwen pointed out different sections as we passed, chattering aimlessly about the store's varied clientele (*Everyone from tourists to true believers!*) and their unique spiritual needs (*Everything from kitschy knickknacks to authentic athamé blades!*).

Her words, not mine.

My eyes skimmed from the incense stand to the essential oils table to the poppet doll display before we moved down two heavy wood steps, into the middle section of the shop.

Mystical curiosities, indeed.

The walls here were painted a darker green, the air infused by the scent of hanging herb bundles overhead. Several display cases stuffed full of witchy accouterments lined the walls. Cool as hell candles with designs carved in the wax, crystals of every conceivable shade and shape, odd curved ceremonial blades with pentagrams at their bases. There was even a supply of bonafide iron cauldrons.

Tall apothecary cabinets in the center were stuffed full of vials, each of which was labeled with care in elaborate calligraphy. My eyes widened, reading some of the bottled contents: 'Bone Shard' and 'Graveyard Dirt' and 'Eye of Newt' and 'Gaia's Tears.'

"Bathroom is the door to the left, stockroom to the right," Gwen said, pulling my focus back to her. "And, most importantly… here we are! Your space!"

She pointed to the very back of the shop. There, separated by a thick green curtain, was a cozy room painted in the deepest shades of evergreen. Almost black. The curtains were currently pulled wide, held in place by thick gold roping. It looked somehow both spooky and inviting.

"I guess it's technically Zelda's space, seeing as she left all her stuff when she split town in such a hurry," Gwen said from beside me as we both stepped inside. "But as of now, it's yours. Feel free to do whatever you want to make it your own."

The room was barely large enough for both Gwen and I to

stand without bumping elbows. Most of the floorspace was taken up by the round table smack in the center. There was a gorgeous crystal ball resting on it in a gold-gilded stand, plus two comfy-looking armchairs cozied up to either side. The main wall had a floating shelf stacked with thick taper candles. A dimmable pendant light hung from the ceiling. The floor was covered in a thick, patterned rug.

"I'm not sure how you conduct your readings, but Zelda left a bunch of her tarot cards in that corner cabinet—"

"I have my own deck," I murmured, staring at the crystal ball on the table. It was refracting a beam of light that spilled in between the curtains. "You know, you should really keep that covered."

Gwen sucked in a sharp breath. "Why? Can the spirits see me from the other side? Are they watching us now?"

I glanced at her, lips twitching at the look on her face. "No, Gwen. But if the sunlight hits it the right way, it'll start a fire."

"Oh. *Oh*!" She bleated out a startled laugh. "Like a magnifying glass! I never even thought of that. Jeeze, my Aunt Colette will seriously haunt my ass from the Great Beyond if I burn down her shop."

She grabbed me by the hand and squeezed hard. I was wearing my gloves — a pair of camel brown leather that matched my belt and boots — but it still took effort not to shy away. If Gwen noticed my skittishness, she didn't comment on it. Her grin was just as wide and welcoming as it had been the moment I stepped through the front door.

"Thank the goddess you came to Salem, Imogen." Her pale green eyes locked with mine and I could tell she meant every word. "You've been here ten minutes and, already, I can tell you belong with us. I know you said you aren't planning to stick around but, for what it's worth… I really hope you change your mind."

Her words were like a lance to the heart. Not a painful one, but a blow all the same. It moved through me and settled somewhere deep inside before I could even put up a fight.

You belong with us.

I'd never really belonged anywhere. Not for years and years. Which probably explained why quite suddenly (and quite alarmingly) I was blinking back the telltale tingle of tears.

Perhaps sensing I needed a moment to collect myself, Gwen squeezed my hand again, then turned on her kickass spiked stiletto heels and left me to get settled, muttering something about restocking the amethyst before we opened for business. When I was alone, I collapsed into one of the cushioned chairs and looked around at my new 'office' with appreciative eyes.

It really was too bad I had to leave in a few days.

If things were different…

I could get used to belonging in a place like this.

My first day at The Gallows passed by in a blur. I did two readings for walk-in customers before noon. I was a little rusty at first — it had been a while since I had a steady psychic gig — but tarot wasn't really something you forgot how to do. Each card had an official meaning, but it was the way they came together in a spread that made each session unique. A skilled reader could interpret connections and nuances a novice would miss.

My first client was an older woman with steel-gray hair who'd been coming to Madame Zelda for the past few months. Almost immediately, she confessed she hadn't been a big fan of The Gallows' former mystic in residence. She knew exactly what she wanted — a classic Celtic Cross spread — as well as the meanings of just about every card I flipped for her before I could offer my insights. Frankly, I was worried she could've done most of the reading herself, but she paid me more than my standard rate (plus a hefty tip!) and promised she'd be back to see me again next month. The curtain swung shut before I had a chance to inform her I'd be long gone by then.

Oh well.

My second session was with a mother-daughter duo who were in town from Indiana and had never stepped foot in a shop like Gwen's before, let alone done anything as 'kooky crazy' (direct quote) as visit a 'fortune teller.' They wouldn't have known the difference between the Ten of Swords and the Page of Wands if it was written across my forehead in indelible ink. I took the time to walk them through their spreads anyway, trying to make it fun for them as I introduced them to the world of major arcana.

As I shuffled the cards, I realized how much I'd missed this. My deck was a warm, familiar weight in my hands. My fingertips tingled across the thick cards, tracing the faintly embossed words and symbols etched on their faces. The deck had belonged to my mom, before I lost her, and I cherished it. It was one of my few sentimental possessions. One of the few remaining vestiges of a life I could hardly remember, anymore.

Between clients, I helped out Sally in the mystical curiosities section. Sally had shown up just before we opened for the day to serve as "emergency staff" — despite Gwen's insistence that she had things well in hand. (She did *not* have things in hand, well or otherwise, FYI.)

Sally should've been at home playing with her grandkids and collecting Social Security checks, not dealing with crazed customers. However, the octogenarian was not to be deterred. She'd settled in on a stool behind the counter and started toying with the cash register like she'd done it a million times.

"That girl needs all the help she can get, sugar," she said solemnly, though her eyes were twinkling. "Glad she's got you on staff, at least."

I felt so guilty, I didn't have the heart to tell her I was a temporary hire.

Sally looked a bit like Betty White, with the same mischievous grin, slight stature, and curly hair. She was also chatty, conversing with everyone who came through the doors as she rang up their crystal purchases and used books.

In the rare lull between customers, she (regrettably) turned the full force of that chattiness in my direction. Within the first five minutes of our acquaintance, I'd learned she had about a hundred grandchildren, made an award-winning cheesecake with raspberry preserve, and was a practicing Wiccan in a local coven. (The same coven that was somehow tied up in all of Gwen's near-death drama, though she was rather spotty with the details.) She'd been best friends with Gwen's aunt before she passed away and, as such, had been coming to The Gallows since it was just a plain old occult store, long before it was transformed into what she called a 'hipster hotspot.'

In return, she asked me about seventy-five personal questions — everything from my middle name to my astrological sign to my place of birth, which I did my best to dodge. This was tough when we were working elbow to elbow, but grew easier as more customers flooded the shop. There was no time for chatter by the time the lunchtime rush reached full swing.

The door bells chimed constantly with new arrivals. Up front, there was a long line snaking through the maze of bookshelves, awaiting coffees. I could hear the espresso machine hissing away as Gwen tried to stay ahead of the crush of undercaffeinated patrons. It was only slightly less busy in the mystical curiosities section. A cluster of customers huddled around the pre-mixed potions. Several teenage girls were conspiring over a love spell while an older gentleman eyed up a bottle that promised to stop male-pattern baldness in its tracks. I slipped behind the counter as Sally rang them up, then helped bag their purchases.

"You okay back here alone?" I asked her. "I thought I might help Gwen get the lunch crowd under control..."

"Go, go." Sally waved me off. "I'm old, not demented. I've been making both change and conversation since you were no more than a whippersnapper."

I wasn't sure what a whippersnapper was, but I was sure I didn't want to mess with Sally. Leaving her alone, I raced up to the front of the shop. There were ten people in line. Both trash bags were at capacity, ready to overflow with old coffee grounds and disposable cups. Gwen was standing behind the counter, looking frazzled. Beyond frazzled, in fact, she looked like she was about to have a nervous breakdown. Her hair was escaping her elegant chignon, long red tendrils falling down to frame her face. A large espresso stain spread across half her apron. Her hands were shaking as she scribbled an order on the side of the cup.

"Gwen."

"Just a second," she muttered, scribbling faster. "I've got to get this order down. Then, the trash. The milk fridge is almost empty, too." Her eyes flickered up to the woman at the front of the line. "*Hellfire*. That was — what, again? A caramel macchiato?"

"What are you, deaf? I want a dirty chai. Extra hot, extra shot," the waiting woman clipped. She sounded pissed. She looked pissed, too, her face pinched in an unattractive way. "And, as I've told you twice already, use oat milk."

I stepped up beside Gwen, met the bitchy customer's narrowed eyes, and held up a finger in the air. "Just a second."

"Are you freaking kiddi—"

I turned away from the woman before her protest was even out of her mouth and faced my new boss. She'd stopped scribbling, but she was definitely still shaking, top to toe. I gently tugged the sharpie from her grip, set it down, and used my hands on her shoulders to steer her backwards until her butt hit the opposite counter.

"Imogen, the line—"

"Will still be there in five minutes," I finished for her, retrieving a water bottle from the mini-fridge beneath the espresso machine. "Five minutes you are going to take for yourself before you self-destruct."

"I can't—"

"You can. Now, sit. Sip. Breathe. I've got this."

"But—"

I narrowed my eyes at her. "Gwen, I've got it."

With that, I whipped an apron from where it was hanging beneath the menu-board, wrapped it around my waist, and turned to face the crush of customers. The bitchy woman looked even more bitchy than she had twenty seconds before (a remarkable feat), but I didn't really care. I pushed down the urge to tell her to take her snotty self down the block to Starbucks if she was in such a hurry. With a fake smile, I picked up her empty cup and parked myself in front of the espresso bar.

"Double dirty chai, almond milk. Coming right up." I reached for the stainless milk-frothing canister as my eyes moved past the woman to the man behind her. "All right, who's next?"

"You saved my ass today, for the record."

I looked over at Gwen. We were both collapsed on the green sofa at the front of The Gallows, catching our breath. It was six o'clock and we were officially closed for business. Thank the lord for that. The crush never let up until we forced the final customers out the door two minutes ago.

The shop looked like a tornado had ripped through it essential oils out of order, crystals a mess, books askew on the best-seller table — but we were both too tired to move. Cleanup would have to wait for a few minutes.

"I owe you," Gwen added, voice drained. "How do you feel about tequila?"

"Favorably."

"Blended, shaken, or shot?"

"I'm not that picky when it comes to my tequila intake."

Her eyes twinkled. "Good. We'll get a girls' night on the books."

I opened my mouth to respond, but Flo cut in before I could. "I hope that includes me. Or do old friends not get credit for ass-saving, these days?"

Gwen rolled her eyes as Florence dropped down into one of the plush armchairs across from us, planting her feet on the edge of the coffee table.

"You always get ass-saving credit, Flo. Even if you're a pain in said ass about it."

There was no heat in her words. The two women were clearly good friends. I'd known this yesterday, the first time I'd watched them interact about color-coordinated flak jackets, and my understanding of their bond only deepened when Flo blew through the doors at 3PM to lend a hand with the mid-afternoon crowd. She'd already worked a full day as an elementary school teacher — she taught second grade, which I thought was likely to qualify her for sainthood — but jumped right in without hesitation.

Florence moved around The Gallows with the familiarity of someone who'd spent many of her afternoons there — clearing tables, washing dirty mugs, lugging trash to the dumpsters, and seamlessly taking over Sally's spot at the mystical curiosities counter when the octogenarian finally called it quits.

Sally, for the record, possessed an age-defying, bottomless pit of energy. On her way out the door, she'd winked at me, waved to Flo, then wandered close to Gwen, softly cupped her cheek with a wrinkled hand, and murmured something about canasta. (This, for whatever reason, made Gwen's eyes fill with tears but she managed to get them under control before they fell down her cheeks.)

"Was it like that all day?" Florence asked, sounding as dead-tired as I felt inside.

"Yep," Gwen and I said in unison.

"Jeeze. Gwennie, you really need to hire on some more help."

"I know, I know. I'm looking." The redhead blew out a breath. "But it's high season. There aren't a lot of takers. At least, not ones Graham deems employable after his extensive background checks."

A nervous skitter moved down my spine.

"This is a college town," Flo said, undeterred. "Aren't there, like, twenty thousand starving undergrads who'd be happy to spritz tabletops and sweep floors and serve coffee?"

"Like I said, *I'm looking*! I've got interviews lined up for Monday."

"That's days away!"

"Well, it's the only time I can do it!" Gwen glanced at me. "We're closed on Mondays, FYI. I probably should've told you that."

I laughed. "You just did."

"We also open late on Sundays. Noon, not nine."

"Noted."

Her grin widened. "Are you always this go-with-the-flow?"

"I've spent most of my life adrift," I replied without thinking. "Going with the flow is kind of the only option."

Her grin faded slightly. "Adrift?"

Shit.

I really didn't want to share my sad little sob story with Gwen and Florence. I was usually good at keeping my private life separate from my work life. When it came to coworkers, I stuck to smalltalk and steered conversations to their lives, not mine. But there was something about the two of them sitting there staring at me — no bullshit, no judgment, just ready to listen. Something that made me *want* to share. So, before I could talk myself out of it, I did.

"I, uh, sort of left home when I was fifteen." I swallowed hard. "Growing up wasn't so great for me. About a decade ago, it got to a point I couldn't handle it anymore, and I ran. I've been running ever since."

"Jesus," Florence said.

"Oh, Imogen." Gwen's voice had a tremor, but she steadied it. "I'm sorry."

"It's okay. Really. It was a long time ago."

"Maybe," Gwen murmured. "But my own childhood wasn't all rainbows and sunshine, so I know from experience, no matter how long it's been, that darkness can eat at you."

I blinked at her, surprised to hear the stunning woman beside me with the unfailingly sunny disposition came from a dark childhood. Because, well… she wasn't running from her past.

She wasn't running *at all.*

She ran a witchy-cool shop. She dressed in a witchy-cool wardrobe. She had a great group of friends. She owned a home. She was living with a super-sexy private investigator badass who was slowly remodeling said home, room by room — a process which, according to Gwen, started with him building her the custom library of her dreams, complete with a rolling ladder.

No, Gwendolyn Goode was not running. She was planted about as firmly as a girl could be, happily settled in what seemed to be a pretty freaking perfect life. If I hadn't liked her so damn much, I would've envied her.

"The trick is, you can't let it," she added softly.

I jolted out of my thoughts. "What?"

"That darkness. You can't let it eat at you." She paused. "Best way to do that is to fill your life up with light."

I stared at her blankly. I had no response. *Fill my life up with light?* What did that even mean? Where did one even start?

"I think I know a guy who can help you with that," Flo chimed in, easily reading my expression. "Tall? Broad shoulders? Thick, silver-streaked hair? Insane blue eyes? Ass you could bounce quarters off?"

I narrowed my gaze at her. "I have no idea who you're referring to."

Gwen shot Florence an amused look. "Has Desmond heard your prolific descriptions of Detective Hightower's ass?"

Desmond was the bookish blond man I'd seen yesterday, as well as Flo's boyfriend of several years. They lived in a duplex across town and, according to Gwen, were the very definition of a happy couple.

"Des doesn't mind if I look. It's the touching he'd have a problem with." Florence lifted her shoulders in a graceful shrug. Her dark, melted chocolate eyes were on mine. "Can't say I'm not curious about the touching, though… Care to share with the class, Imogen?"

Color flooded my cheeks. "There's nothing to share."

"Oh my god, look at that blush!" Flo pointed at me. "Nothing to share my left foot! *Spill!*"

"Flo, she doesn't have to spill anything she doesn't want to," Gwen interjected. But her eyes moved to me, too. "Though, it must be said, I'm also curious about what's going on between you and Cade."

My mouth opened, then closed without a single word escaping. I wanted to tell them there was nothing going on between me and Cade, but my mind was abruptly full of memories from last night's kiss. His hands cupping my face, his tongue stroking mine, his lips somehow both hard and soft as they moved…

Focus, Imogen!

I swallowed hard. "Honestly? I don't know what's going on."

Flo and Gwen traded a glance.

"He's... confusing," I continued. "He acts like we're together. Which is *insane*. I've known the man two days!"

They traded another glance. Both of them had been witness to my interaction with Cade this afternoon, when he suddenly appeared in the shop. My heart had gone into palpitations when he'd stepped up to the counter, looking gorgeous as ever in a crisp white button down, which was rolled to the elbows to display his powerful forearms.

He didn't stay long, seeing as he was on duty, but the short time he was here, I didn't take a full breath. Not as I took his order for a double-cappuccino, not as I stepped behind the expresso machine to make it, not as I handed it to him. His long fingers had brushed mine as he extracted the cup from my grip. And then, right there in front of an entire store full of customers, not to mention Flo and Gwen, he'd leaned *across* the counter, brushed his mouth against mine, and told me he was taking me out to dinner tonight when we were both off work.

Not asked me.

Told me.

Like dinner was a foregone conclusion.

Like date night was something we'd done a zillion times before.

Like kissing me in front of a whole store full of strangers was no big deal at all.

I was so shellshocked by the kiss and his dinner declaration — okay, I admit, mostly by the kiss — I could barely summon the mental fortitude to inform him I was busy that evening, having dinner with Gigi and her boys at The Sea Witch. This was not a lie. Rory had roped me into it at breakfast, promising that his mom's meatloaf was, and I quote, '*the shit.*'

Unfortunately, his enthusiastic sales pitch led to Declan tattling on him for foul language, which resulted in my quiet morning's descent into another wild display of brother-on-brother violence. I'd hastily agreed, if only to smooth things over. (I didn't even like meatloaf.)

When I'd shared my conflict with Cade, he didn't even blink. He'd just done another delectably soft lip-brush and murmured, "Tomorrow, then."

"Tomorrow is Halloween."

"Yeah." His eyes were smiling. "You can come over to my place. Help me and Socks pass out candy to trick-or-treaters."

A pleasant shiver slid down my spine at that proposition. I had to admit, it sounded nice. To cover my quick-melting resolve, I'd dug deep into my reservoir of bitchy attitude.

"Candy isn't dinner," was my stiff reply.

"I promise to supplement the chocolate intake with something at the base of the food pyramid. I'll order takeout. Or we'll cook."

My brows had gone up. "We'll cook?"

"That a novel concept for you?"

"No," I'd grumbled. "I just don't picture you as a guy who cooks."

"I'm thirty-one, beautiful. Been feeding myself for well over a decade, now."

The *beautiful* took a bit of the bitchy wind out of my sails. I'd tried not to let it show, but that happy, fuzzy warmth was back in the pit of my stomach — and spreading fast. My head got a bit dizzy with thoughts of moving around Cade's kitchen, meeting his puppy, making dinner together... and, admittedly, got even more dizzy with some R-rated thoughts about what might happen *after* dinner...

Cade, being a detective, did not fail to notice my reaction. His eyes were a shade more heated as he leaned in and brushed his lips against mine — yes, a third time! — then muttered "*Tomorrow*" in a way that felt like a promise. Heavy with intent. That happy, fuzzy feeling had multiplied tenfold in my gut.

I could only stand there, frozen like an idiot, as he walked out the door and disappeared, casually sipping his cappuccino as he went. As though he hadn't just effectively rocked my entire world in the span of two minutes. It wasn't until a customer waved a hand in front of my face to get my attention that I jolted back into motion and resumed making coffee drinks.

I'd promptly put the interaction out of my mind for the rest of the afternoon. I knew, if I thought about it, I'd be too distracted to remember the difference between a café au lait and a cortado.

"Earth to Imogen. Come in, Imogen," Florence said now, her voice robotic as she called me back to the present. "This is your captain speaking."

My eyes jerked up as the Cade-daze cleared. "Sorry. What were we talking about?"

Florence and Gwen looked at each other, both trying — and failing — to suppress grins.

"Okay, why do you keep looking at each other like that? It's starting to freak me out."

Gwen's tone was low, soothing. "It's just, in my experience, men like Graham Graves — which is a category that also includes Caden Hightower, for the record — tend to move pretty fast."

I stared at her.

"Like, warp-speed."

"Cheetah-like," Flo added.

"Mach 3," Gwen offered.

"Great." I leaned back against the cushions. "That's just great."

"It *is* great, Imogen." Flo shook her head, like I was insane. "Cade is a solid guy. He's a catch."

"He's *the* catch," Gwen corrected. "Ask any woman with a functioning libido in the Greater Boston area."

I clasped my hands together nervously. "I never said he wasn't."

"Your face did," Flo declared. "You look like someone just suggested you fly transatlantic in the middle seat. And, as far as I can tell, you have no reason to look like that, chickadee. I saw that lip-brush he gave you. That was a good lip-brush."

"That was a *hot* lip-brush," Gwen said.

"Totally," Flo agreed.

They weren't wrong. But... still! They didn't have to say it *out loud*.

"I'm leaving in a few days," I reminded them.

"So?"

I stared at Flo. "*So*, I'm not about to get involved with a man just to blow out of town!"

"You could always stay," Gwen suggested quietly.

"Seems to me you're already involved," Flo barreled on, determined.

Damn and blast.

They weren't wrong on those points, either. I chewed my lip for a few seconds, debating whether or not to unload on them. Then, I blurted, "He kissed me. Last night."

Both of them grinned.

"And he asked me out to dinner."

The grins widened.

"I can't tonight, I'm having dinner with Gigi and her boys," I hurried on. "But he wants me to come over tomorrow instead to pass out Halloween candy and meet his puppy."

"Cade has a puppy?" Gwen practically squealed. "I didn't know that!"

"What are you going to wear?" Flo asked. "You'll need a costume."

Gwen nodded. "Definitely."

"What will I *wear*?! I don't even know if I'm going!"

Flo snorted. "Of course you're going."

"Why?"

"Why? Because, even if you are leaving, you owe it to yourself to enjoy a night with that man before you go. If not for you, for all womankind." Flo's expression was fierce. "This is Caden Fucking Hightower we're talking about. He is fine. He is so fine, he makes me want to dry-hump a pillow."

"Flo, keep it PG-13," Gwen chastised.

"That *was* PG-13. I didn't say I wanted to ride his face until I saw Jesus on the ceiling, did I? No. No, I did not."

A startled giggle shot from my mouth at Flo's adamant declaration. When she heard it, she pivoted her pretty brown eyes my way. "You're going. You're going to find out exactly how firm that ass of his is. And then, after, you're going to *spill*. Preferably over tequila."

"I'm buying," Gwen cut in. "My house. Sunday night."

Flo threw her hands up in the air. "Sweet! Girl's night! I'll bring limes."

They both turned to me expectantly.

Waiting.

And, looking back and forth from one woman to the other, I realized there was approximately a zero percent chance of getting out of any of this. Not tomorrow with Cade, not the debrief to follow. Thus, I settled back against the sofa with a sigh, lifted my limp arms overhead, and said, weakly, "Girl's night."

Flo and Gwen both cheered.

CHAPTER ELEVEN

That girl is so stacked!
(She works at a bookstore.)
- Imogen Warner, willfully misinterpreting

Gigi was hard at work on Rory's costume when I stepped into the reception area. She tossed the flashy neon fabric onto her desk and turned to scan me up and down. "Feel better?"

"I no longer smell like stale espresso beans," I answered, crossing toward the window seat. "Though I'm so tired, I almost fell asleep in the shower."

"Please don't do that. Do you know how much paperwork I have to fill out if a guest conks their head on the tap and dies under my watch?"

I shot her a look as I collapsed onto the cushions, curling my legs up beneath me. They felt like they were made of Jell-O. My eyelids, anvils. My hair was still damp, curling loose around my shoulders. I'd been too exhausted to blow it dry. I was dressed in my most broken-in pair of denim cut-offs, oversized socks, fuzzy wool gloves, and the Baltimore Ravens sweatshirt I'd had for ages. I wouldn't be winning any fashion awards, but Gigi wasn't one to judge.

It was safe to say, my first shift at The Gallows had effectively kicked my ass.

"Thanks again for dinner, Gigi. It was great. The mashed potatoes especially."

"Anytime," she said, lips twitching. "Sorry you got caught in the boys' crossfire. How's your head?"

"It was a dinner roll, not a grenade." I suppressed a smile of my own. "I think I'll recover."

She sighed the distinctly martyred sigh of a single mother doing her best to raise two hellions with a proclivity for food fights at the dinner table. It was late, and the boys were finally asleep — no doubt tuckered out from forty-five straight minutes of bickering over dinner. I'd pedaled Declan's bike back to the inn just in time to join them. The second I stepped through the door, Gigi had plunked the *"Back in a few, ring the bell for service!"* sign onto her desk and ushered me to the table. She hadn't even given me a chance to change out of my latte-splattered jeans.

The back apartments on the first floor weren't spacious, but they were surprisingly cozy. Gigi had taken pains to make the space feel less like a hotel, more like a home. There was little-kid artwork on the fridge — Rory's colorful masterpieces in crayon — and a straight-A report card from Declan's sixth grade classes shoved proudly beneath a plastic magnet.

The kitchen was painted in warm shades of yellow, and decorated with cutesy clutter. Family photographs covered the walls. Most of them showed the boys at various ages, spanning from infancy to now, but a few featured a man I didn't recognize. He was so burly, he looked like a freaking lumberjack, with a thick head of red hair, a bushy beard, and hands the size of hams.

Donny.

I'd watched Gigi as she puttered around her kitchen, setting out placemats and mashing potatoes, corralling her hellions into their seats, and wondered what sort of strength it took to set out photographs of the man who'd done you wrong, for the sake of your sons' innocence. What sort of iron will a woman had to have to stare at that face every day, so her boys wouldn't realize their father was a monster.

A heck of a lot of strength, I decided. More than most people had in all their muscles.

Dinner was, in a word, *loud*. It was so unlike the solitary meals I'd grown accustomed to these past few years, it shocked me mostly silent. The boys were more than capable of carrying the conversation. There was laughter and teasing, ribs being elbowed and tongues being stuck out. I'd forked down my meatloaf and tried to stay out of the fray as they flicked green beans over the centerpiece and kicked one another's shins under the table, much to their mother's chagrin.

After the rolls stopped flying and the boys retreated to their rooms, Gigi had instructed me to get showered, then meet her at her desk for a nightcap. Truthfully, I was tired enough to crawl straight under the covers, but I'd forced myself down the creaky steps to the reception area instead.

"So, how was your first day?" Gigi asked. "Long?"

I blew out a breath. "You have *no* idea. Today was madness. Tomorrow will be worse, according to Gwen, since it's Halloween. She actually used the phrase, 'apocalyptically busy' — whatever that means."

"Welcome to Samhain in Salem."

I grimaced. "I'm not sure I'm cut out for it."

"You'll be fine. Trust me." Gigi sighed heavily. "You want to talk about a long day? I've spent the past twenty minutes glueing tractor beam activators onto the sleeves of this costume. My fingers are all stuck together. I have paddle hands." She held up her hand. Her digits did indeed appear to be fused together.

"What's a tractor beam activator?"

"Beats me." She shrugged. "But Rory says they're vital to his role as an intergalactic planetary patrol officer."

"Sorry, but I still think my day was worse. My favorite jeans reek of espresso, I only did two readings in eight hours, Gwen and Flo forced me into an unsanctioned girl-talk session, and an eighty-year-old Wiccan who looks like a well-endowed Betty White told me I have to come over to her house on Monday morning and learn to bake cheesecake for god only knows what reason."

Gigi stared at me for a long beat. Then, she lifted her fused-appendages into the air and waved them at me. "Paddle hands, Imogen," she repeated severely. "*Paddle hands*."

"Okay, okay! Fine. You win."

"Come on." She waved me closer with her paddle-hand and I snorted at the sight. "Sit your cute butt on that stool and we'll toast to your first day."

"Really?"

"Really." She tilted her chin toward the desk. "Third drawer down. I'd open it myself, but..."

"Paddle hands. Got it." Grinning, I bent and pulled open the drawer she'd indicated. Inside, there was a bottle of limoncello and a set of low-ball glasses. "Aren't you working? I don't want to get you in trouble."

"Oh, relax. We have three guests in the whole dang inn, including you. No one else is going to check in this late. Even if they do, who's going to scold me? *Me*? I'm the manager. And Rhonda will be here at eleven to take over the desk."

"What about Mr. Monteith?

"He's a snowbird."

"Is that slang for someone who does lots of cocaine?"

She giggled. "No, silly. He flies south for the winter. He'll be down in Florida for the next few months. There's no one to get me in trouble. So, pour. We aren't getting any younger."

"We're still young."

"I'm thirty-six!"

"That's young!"

"Spoken like a twenty-five-year-old." She scowled playfully at me. "You just wait. You think it won't happen to you. Then, one day, you're doing deep pore exfoliation in the mirror and *BAM*!" She slammed one of her fused hands down on the desk surface so hard, it made me jump. "There it is. Your first chin hair. Coarse and gray and slightly curly, like it grew from the ass of Father Time himself."

I poured the limoncello. "I think you're being dramatic."

"Talk to me after you start getting targeted ads for Botox."

"I already get those."

"God, the beauty industry is insidious. Being a woman is exhausting. The pressure to be hot twenty-four seven… I can't do it. I don't have the time or the energy to be a 10 full time. My hotness is on a sliding scale. Freelance, if you will."

I nodded. "In my next life, I hope to be reincarnated as a bog witch, who lives at the edge of the woods and strikes fear into the hearts of all men who wander too close."

"Amen to that, sister." Gigi lifted her glass by sandwiching it between both palms, seeing as she still had no individual fingers with which to grip. "Cheers! To chin hairs and peeing a little each time you sneeze! Oh, and to your first day at The Gallows."

"I don't pee when I sneeze."

"That will change once you have kids. Trust me."

A nearly fell off my stool when she said that.

Kids?

For me?

Not likely. Not the way I lived.

What was that saying about a rolling stone collecting no moss…?

Covering my own discomfort, I clinked my glass against Gigi's and took a hasty swallow of limoncello. It was sugary-sweet, a shock to the taste buds. But beneath the syrupy flavor, the burn of alcohol was strong enough to make my eyes water. My expression scrunched as it slid down my throat and I gasped as it hit my stomach.

"Christ, what's in this? Lighter fluid?"

"It's my homemade brew. Secret recipe." She leaned toward me, voice dropping to a whisper. "The secret is grain alcohol."

"No freaking kidding."

Gigi merely shrugged, unbothered, and sipped it like it was the finest scotch. "You'll get used to it."

"Doubtful." I eyed my glass suspiciously before I took another sip. This one went down a bit more easily. "I have a feeling this isn't going to help you finish your sewing project before tomorrow."

She grimaced at the bundle of bright green fabric on her desk. "Don't remind me. I could work all night, I'd still never finish. I don't know how I'm going to break the news to Rory."

"First of all, go wash the glue off your hands. I'll get started on the legs. You'll focus on the arms. Much as I appreciate the need for tractor beam activators, we need to finish sewing the main sections before we move on to the decorative touches." I eyed the yards of unfinished fabric with a grimace. "I'll tell you all about my insane day while we work."

Before I could stop her, she leaned over and threw her arms around me in a bone-crushing hug. I flinched, but she held fast, squeezing me so tight I couldn't get out a single word of protest.

"You're a gem, Imogen Warner. I'm so glad we're friends." Quick as she'd initiated the embrace, she ended it, scurrying around me and into the parlor before I had a chance to blink. "Back in a jiffy!"

I was left standing there in the low light of the dusty chandelier, clutching the unfinished costume so hard my knuckles had turned white. Seriously, what was going on in this town? What were they putting in the water? Between Gigi and Gwen and Florence (and a certain silver fox detective I was *not* going to think about, not now, maybe not ever) I'd made more friends since I stepped over the Salem border two days ago than I had in the two years prior.

It simply wasn't *normal!*

It was, quite frankly, *freaking me out!*

Thankfully, by the time Gigi returned, I'd composed myself. For the next hour, we proceeded to slug down limoncello and slowly piece together the limbs of Rory's space invader costume. Our stitches grew less and less regimented as the clock crept toward ten and the alcohol dulled our dexterity in slow degrees. Still, I thought we were doing well enough. At least, until Gigi broke down in hysterical laughter, face-planting on the desk.

"Oh my god!" She snort-laughed uncontrollably. "I just realized..." Another snort. "I think I've sewn this entire arm on backwards!"

"*Gigi!*"

"I'm sorry! I'm not a professional seamstress!" She paused. "Maybe Rory can be a one-armed space invader."

"How do you expect him to fight off the evil horde of deep-space monsters with one arm?"

"How do you expect me to make rational decisions when I've had four glasses of limoncello?"

"Fair enough." I sighed. "I think this is our sign to stop for the night. The rest is mostly done. We'll fix the arm tomorrow morning during breakfast, before he gets on the bus."

"Just under the wire..." She shot me a lopsided grin. "Would you believe that's the credo on my family crest?"

My answering smile died as the front door to the inn swung open with a violence that made the chandelier rattle. All joy and laughter swept out of the room in a blink as the towering silhouette of a man filled the frame. He was so wide, his arms brushed the jambs to either side. His thickly bearded face was contorted into an expression of such rage, the force of it nearly knocked me off my stool.

"You bitch!" the man boomed.

"Donny," Gigi whispered back, her voice thready.

Suddenly, I was sober as a judge.

"You fuckin' bitch!"

Oh, no.

As the behemoth advanced toward the reception desk, I reached out, grabbed hold of Gigi's arm and attempted to drag her off her stool. I had no plan, just the screaming instinct to put as much distance between us and Donny as humanly possible. But she was frozen like a deer in headlights, not moving even when my fingertips dug into the cotton of her long-sleeved shirt.

The man took two strides closer, his construction boots causing a series of seismic booms across the frayed rug. "You think you can get away with this? Keepin' my boys from me?"

"I'm not keeping them—"

He cut her off. "Shut up!"

Shit, shit, *shit*.

I was not getting a good feeling about this scene. In fact, I was getting a very bad feeling about it. Donny's face was red from fury and, if I had to wager a guess, a fair few rounds at the bar. A volatile combination.

"I'm telling you right now, Georgia, so listen good," he snarled. "You ain't keepin' my boys from me."

Gigi was trembling. I could feel the shakes radiating through her frame as I held her arm. Still, she managed to sound remarkably steady. "Donny, you can't be here right now."

"I'm not goin' fuckin' anywhere!"

Donny's face was mottling redder and redder with every passing moment. He was like a volcano set to blow. And I definitely didn't want me — or Gigi, or her boys — standing in the blast radius when he did.

Doing my best not to call any attention to myself, I reached under the desk with my free hand and slid my cellphone from the front pocket of my sweatshirt. I allowed my eyes to flicker down to the screen for only a brief moment as I scrolled to the most recent addition to my contact list. A number I'd programmed in only yesterday. Before I could talk myself out of it, I jammed my thumb against the screen to dial.

Thankfully, Donny was so busy glaring at his wife, he didn't seem to realize I was in the room, let alone calling reinforcements.

"We have an arrangement," Gigi said, finally sliding off the stool to gain her feet. Even at full height, her husband towered over her. "If you want to see the boys, you need to do it right. Use the proper channels. Talk to your attorney, go through the courts—"

"Fuck that and fuck *you,* bitch!" Donny hissed, clearly not a fan of proper procedure. He took another step, planted his ham-fisted hands on the desk, and leaned over it. Up close, his ruddy skin was marred with several prominent scars — probably souvenirs from a lifetime of bar fights and brawls. "You're not keepin' my family from me. Tomorrow is Halloween. If I wanna take my boys trick-or-treating, I'm takin' my boys trick-or-treating. And there's not a goddamned thing you can say about it."

Gigi's shoulders cowed inward. I saw it. I felt it. Still, she tried to stay strong. "We have to do what the attorneys say—"

"I don't give a fuck about the attorneys! I want to see Dec and Ror. *Now*. It's been weeks."

The only benefit to Donny roaring so loud was that he'd be heard crystal clear through the phone line. I chanced another glance at the screen. The call was connected. I hoped the detective didn't assume it was a butt dial and hang up on me.

"They're sleeping, Donny."

"Then wake them the fuck up!"

Gigi didn't answer. She just stared at him, her expression a mixture of fear and fury.

"Why are you looking at me like that? Don't you fuckin' look at me like that!"

Anger crept into Gigi's voice, bolstering her fear. "How am I looking at you, Donny?"

"Like a ball-busting bitch!"

"Oh, that's lovely. Exactly the kind of language I want around our boys."

"What you want doesn't factor here."

"I'm their mother!"

"And I'm their fuckin' father!"

"Funny, you haven't been so eager to be their father when it comes to child support payments."

Donny's face darkened. "Damn straight. I'm not paying you a goddamned dime to live in a goddamned hotel. Not when we have a perfectly good house three blocks away where those boys belong. Where *you* belong. Just a matter of you remembering it."

"I don't belong there anymore," Gigi said stiffly. "I never belonged there. And neither do Rory or Declan."

Donny's eyes narrowed in a seriously scary way. "Careful how far you push me, G."

God, I hoped Cade was coming. I stole another glance at my phone. The call had been connected for 2 minutes, 21 seconds. I figured even Superman couldn't fly that fast across town.

Damn and blast.

"Go wake them up," Donny barked, crossing his arms over his beefy chest. "I'm done fightin' about this."

"I'm not waking them up! It's a school night, they have to be awake to catch the bus tomorrow—"

"No, they don't. They'll be with me, at home, in their own beds. I'll drive them to school. Or they'll skip. It's fuckin' Halloween."

"It's costume day at school, Donny. They've been excited about it for weeks. They aren't going to skip." Gigi was getting riled up. Her cheeks were red, her eyes flashing. "Rory is going to be a space invader. I made his costume from scratch. Do you know how long that took? And Declan is going as Harry Styles, he's got the boa and everything. I spent weeks searching the racks at thrift stores all over town to find sequined pants in his size." She pulled in a ragged breath. "*They. Are. Going.* That's final."

Her husband's thick, bushy brows pulled in, furrowing his ruddy forehead. "Who the fuck is Harry Styles?"

Gigi's spine went ramrod. "He's a musician."

"Yeah? What kind of music?"

"Pop. He sings that song that's always on the radio, the one about watermelons—"

"No fuckin' way. My son is not going as a pop star in a fucking' feathered boa." Donny said the phrases *pop star* and *boa* like they tasted bad. "He can borrow a Celtics jersey. That's a normal costume for a boy his age. Christ. Sequined pants? Are you shittin' me, woman? You want our boy to grow up gay?"

I thought I hated Donny before I met him. After this conversation, I really, *really* hated him. It took all my strength to keep from physically launching myself across the desk at the asshole, claws-out.

Gigi, I could tell, felt similarly. "Say whatever you want about me," she whispered, every word infused with emotion. "But don't you ever — *ever* — speak about my sons that way. They are free to be whoever they want to be. That applies for costumes and for life in general."

"Fuck me." Donny groaned and looked up at the ceiling. "Were you this much of a wet blanket when I put a ring on your finger?"

"Yes!" Gigi retorted instantly. "Apparently you were too drunk to notice!"

Oh boy.

Donny's head tilted back down to his wife. His eyes had been simmering with rage since he stepped through the door; at that comment, they began to burn.

"Listen, I know this isn't what you want to hear," Gigi strived to calm her tone, perhaps sensing the scary shift in energy. "But the court order says—"

"So help me god, G, you throw that fuckin' piece of paper in my face one more time, I'll shove it so far down your throat you can't breathe."

Gigi flinched.

My lungs spasmed, then ceased working altogether.

"Yeah. That's what I thought." Donny's lip curled; he was pleased with himself, the smug bastard. "Now, go on. I don't have all night."

Gigi didn't move a muscle.

"Thought you cared about the boys getting a good night of sleep."

"Donny, please—"

"Don't you *Donny, please* me. And don't you fuckin' turn those puppy dog eyes my way, Georgia. Spent years lettin' you lead me around by my dick. Not doin' it anymore. You're not gonna tell me where I can be, who I can see, how I can live." He leaned even farther over the desk, his eyes locked on his wife's. The look in their depths sent a chill straight down my spine. "So, you get your fat ass off that stool and go get my boys. They're coming home with me tonight and they're not coming back here. Not ever. I promise you that. I'll make sure they're raised right. Not with feather boas and sequins and a mother who can't afford to put food on the table, or a real roof over their heads."

Gigi quailed. She didn't make a sound, but I felt the lash of his threat move through her like a physical blow. She recoiled as though he'd struck her.

Take her boys.

He was threatening to take her boys.

That's when I finally decided enough was enough. Someone had to jump in here and, seeing as I was the only living soul around, that someone was going to be me.

"Get out."

Donny's eyes moved to me. He seemed surprised to find me standing there, as though he hadn't even noticed they had an audience until I spoke.

"What did you say?" he thundered.

"You heard me." Shoving my phone into my sweatshirt pocket, I took a deep breath and rounded the desk. My socks moved soundlessly across the thick rug as I approached Donny. Miraculously, my hand wasn't shaking as I lifted it to point at the door. "It's time for you to leave, now."

"Who the hell are you to tell me to leave?"

My chin jerked higher. "I'm Gigi's friend."

"Well, *Gigi's friend,* this is none of your fuckin' business, so why don't you just piss off back to wherever it is you came from and let me finish this conversation with my wife?"

"She wouldn't be your wife anymore if you'd sign the divorce papers," I reminded him, perhaps unwisely. "And as far as I can tell, you lost the right to a conversation with her when you started shouting in her face and tossing insults."

His smirk was dark with amusement and anger. "Do you have any idea who the fuck you're talkin' to?"

I didn't, as it turned out. But he didn't need to know that. "Georgia asked you to go, and she did it nicely. I've also asked you nicely. Next up will be the police — and I don't think they'll be asking, so much as telling you to go. And I really doubt they'll do it nicely, seeing as you're in direct violation of the protection order just being here right now."

Two ham sized hands curled into fists with menacing slowness. "You threatenin' me?"

"No. I'm telling you plainly what's going to happen." My heart was pounding hard, but my voice was remarkably calm as I pointed again to the exit. "You're going to walk out that door. You're not going to come back. Not tonight, not any night. If you don't, the only time you'll be seeing your boys will be through a sheet of prison-grade plexiglass when they come for weekend visitation."

My words hung in the air for a few stagnant seconds. No one moved. No one said a word. For a moment, I thought Donny was actually going to see reason. That he would listen to me and leave the premises without any more escalation.

Boy, was I wrong.

He lunged with surprising swiftness for such a large man. His mammoth hands closed over my upper arms so fast, I couldn't even begin to struggle. One minute my feet were planted on the rug, the next they were windmilling the air.

Shit.

Donny carried me across the room like I weighed no more than a feather, then slammed me up against the bookcase beneath the stairs. The impact was hard enough to knock several paperbacks to the ground. Every molecule of air was expelled from my lungs in a single gust. Pain radiated through my spine, fiery hot. It was a miracle he hadn't cracked me in two. I gasped as tears sprang to my eyes.

"Donny, drop her!" Gigi was shouting from somewhere nearby. "Drop her right now!"

I couldn't see her. Donny's scarred face filled my entire visual field as he leaned close — so close, I could see the crumbs caught in his beard, the red-rimmed aftereffects of alcohol in his eyes. He was terrifying. Terrifying in a way Adrian, even in his darkest moods, had never managed to be. His anticipatory expression told me he was more than just comfortable with violence; he actually enjoyed it. Got off on it. Fed from it. And I'd offered myself up on a silver platter.

Not smart, Imogen. Not smart at all, my inner voice chided. *What happened to your survival instincts? You know, the ones that keep you from getting involved in scenarios like this? The ones that keep you alive?*

I didn't know — and didn't have time to ponder it. Donny's grip on my arms was iron-clad. I struggled against it anyway, thrashing for all I was worth, kicking and hissing as soon as I summoned the breath.

"Let me go!"

He didn't. He just shook me again, a bone-rattling move that made my head collide with the wooden shelf. Stars burst inside my eyes on impact.

God, that hurt.

"How's that feel?" Donny snarled, his sour beer breath fanning across my face. "Huh?"

"Feels like—" I managed to gasp, fighting the starbursts with several hard blinks. "—an assault charge."

"Big words from a little bitch," he taunted, his tone dripping with malice. "Not so tough now, are you?"

"Donny, I mean it! Drop her!" Gigi screamed, her voice cracking. I could tell she was crying hysterically. *"Drop her!"*

His hands tightened to the point of agony as he shook me violently, jostling more books.

"I don't know you, but I'm glad I get to be the one to teach you this lesson," he said, grinning as tears slid down my cheeks. "You don't tell me what to do. You don't tell me where to go. You definitely don't stick your snobby nose into O'Banion family business. Get me?"

I glared at him through my tears. I hoped he could read the *fuck you* I was blasting from my eyeballs.

"I said," he roared. *"Do you get me?"*

I managed a nod.

"Good."

Gigi's sharp yell cracked through the air like a whip. "I'm calling the cops! You're out of control!"

Donny dropped me with without warning. My socks slammed against the floor and I nearly face-planted by his beat-up construction boots. I managed to catch myself on the shelf at the last moment. I tried to scramble away, but a beefy arm snaked around my midsection before I made it three feet. I promptly found myself hauled backward against a broad chest in a hold so tight, it was difficult to breathe.

"You call the cops on me, you'll regret it," Donny rumbled at his wife. I felt each word vibrate through his body into mine, low with wrath. "For once in your fuckin' life, be smart. Think it through, G. It'll take the boys in blue ten minutes to get here. You know how much damage I can do in ten minutes."

I swallowed hard against the lump of fear clogging my throat. My eyes moved to Gigi. She looked like she was barely holding it together. Her face was pale and she was leaning against the reception desk like it was the only thing holding her upright. I had no doubt she was remembering, with vivid clarity, exactly how much damage her husband could deliver in that timeframe. Even from across the room, I could see her trembling as her watery eyes shifted from me to Donny and back. The phone in her hand was clutched in white-knuckled fingers, but she didn't move to dial.

"Donny... please." Her voice was a whimper. "Just let her go, then we'll talk."

"Too late for *please*, G. Way too late." His arm tightened as he spoke, spurring a gasp from me. "I'll wait here with your new friend. You go into the back and get my boys."

"Can't we just talk about this before—"

"This ain't up for discussion. *Go*! Get movin'!"

She started moving.

"Gigi, don't," I yelled, stopping her in her tracks. My words came out hoarse. "Don't drag the boys into this."

The arm tightened even more, intensifying the ache in my ribs. "Shut up, bitch!"

Georgia was weeping silently as she stared at me. Her expression was etched with indecision. As for me, I was done with douchebag Donny and his threats. I reached up and pulled at his arm, trying to relieve some of the pressure before he caved in my chest cavity.

Unfortunately, in the bedlam of the past few moments, I'd forgotten one crucial fact.

My gloves.

I'd taken them off to help craft Rory's costume. Which meant, the instant my bare fingers hit Donny O'Banion's beefy arm...

A vision hit me.

Hard.

CHAPTER TWELVE

God, grant me the confidence of a mediocre, medium-ugly man.
- Imogen Warner, psyching herself up

There was no time to prepare for it. Purple sparks showered in my peripherals. My body went limp as a rag doll. And, in the space between two heartbeats—

The pretty young woman stands in the shadowy corner of a dingy bar, her hip braced against the edge of a green felt pool table as she waits for her husband to finish drinking. She wants to go home — she's wanted to go for hours — but he's with his brothers and when those four get together, there's no telling how late the night could go.

She tells herself not to say anything, to keep silent, even though her ankles are swollen and her back is aching. She'd walk the ten blocks if it weren't so cold out, and if it was only her health on the line.

Her hands flutter down to rest against the rounded curve of her stomach. She's due in just a few short weeks. She loves the little life inside her already, so much it almost makes the rest of her marriage worth it.

Almost.

When she finally gets up the courage to call her husband's name and ask for the ride home he promised two hours ago, she knows immediately she's made a mistake. Her light brown eyes never blink as she watches him mutter something to his brothers, then slide off his barstool. He walks to her, grabbing a discarded pool stick as he passes the table, spinning it in slow circles like a baton. It looks flimsy in his gargantuan hands. As though, if he closed his fist even slightly, it would snap like a twig.

She doesn't doubt it would.

She knows how strong those hands are.

The man doesn't stop moving until he's backed her away from the table, farther into his shadows, where no one can see. She takes a breath, holds it in her lungs until they start to burn. There's a grin on his face as he twists the pool stick horizontal, then presses it to her breastbone so she's pinned fully against the wall, one hand to either side of her frame. She tries to smile at him as he does this — like it's a game. Like it's a joke, and she's in on the punchline.

She is fully aware just how fast he can flip from flirtatious to furious.

Her heart is hammering even louder as he leans in to bring his mouth to her ear. So loud, she wonders if his brothers can hear it from across the bar. So loud, she wonders if the baby inside her can hear it, a drumbeat echoing all around his tiny, floating limbs.

"Why is it every time we go out, you gotta embarrass me in front of my brothers?" her husband says in a voice that makes her quake. "Why is it you gotta make me punish you?"

The purple sparks filled my visual field again, and the dark bar disappeared. A new vision moved in on the heels of the first, so fast there was no chance to brace for it.

The man is at the kitchen table, a glass of amber-hued liquor clutched in his large hand. His small sons are moving around on the floor in the next room, steering toy cars down the tracks in the carpet. His wife is standing at the stove with her back to him, stirring spaghetti sauce for dinner. She's still dressed from her day job — a new gig as receptionist at a local accountant's office, answering phones and filing paperwork. His cold eyes move from the sleek coils of her hair to the slender curve of her waist in the fitted cardigan to the low heels on her feet.

"Call your boss." His voice cuts through the kitchen like a knife. "Tell him you're done."

She whirls around so fast, sauce flies off her wooden spoon. It lands on the linoleum with a wet plop, but she does not move to clean it. Her eyes are on the man's, wide with alarm.

"What?"

"You heard me. You're done workin' there."

"Donny," the woman says, her tone placating. "I just started last week. I can't quit. I don't want to quit. The money is great, the hours are great..."

"You think I don't know what's goin' on?" He sucks down the contents of his glass in one gulp. "You think I don't see what's happenin' here?"

The woman holds herself still. Her eyes flash over to the carpet in the living room, but otherwise she does not move a muscle. "What do you mean?"

"I'm not a fool. Look at you, dressed up like a whore," the man spits, pushing to his feet. "That's not for me. That's for him. Your new boss."

The woman flinches. "No, Donny, that's not true."

"Don't you fuckin' lie to me!" The man's bellow echoes off the walls of the tiny kitchen. "I see exactly what's goin' on and I'm not standin' for it. You're done. Call him tomorrow, first thing."

"Okay. Okay, just calm down." There's a tremor in the woman's

voice, but she smooths it. "If you don't like me working there, I can find something else—"

"No."

"No?"

"You'll stay home with the boys from now on. Saves us the hassle of daycare." His voice drops low. "Never liked the idea of you workin' anyway."

The woman takes a shaky breath. "I need to work. I need a paycheck."

"Why? We get by fine with my cut from The Banshee."

"That's your money, not mine. It's only right I contribute—"

"Why? Huh? Why do you need your own money, G? You makin' plans I don't know about?" He rises slowly from his seat, hand still clutching his empty glass. "You planning to fuckin' leave me?"

"No, of course not."

"Don't you fuckin' lie to me!" he roars. "Don't you even try, Georgia. Fuck!"

The boys in the next room are crying now, but the man doesn't seem to notice. He's lost in his rage. His hand lifts and he hurls the glass clear across the kitchen, aiming at the wall behind his wife's head. It shatters into a million pieces, missing her by mere inches, showering the stovetop with razor-sharp shards.

For a moment, there is only the sound of the boys' tearful hiccups. They are in the doorway, watching. The older boy, only six, has an arm looped around the two-year-old's middle, holding him up. Snot streams from his nostrils as he looks at his mother.

"Mommy?"

"It's okay, bub. Go back to your cars. I'll come play in a minute." The woman takes a long breath, then looks at her husband. "I'll call my boss and let him know I won't be back tomorrow."

"Good. Now, clean that up." The man sits back down. "And get me another fuckin' drink when you're done."

The woman moves to get the broom.

To pour the drink.

To make the call.

...but not until she's checked on her boys. Because they come first. They will always, always, always come first.

I slammed back into my own head with a familiar breath-snatching violence. The purple sparks cleared as I blinked, hard. More cleared as I did it again. Then again.

God, of all the inopportune times to have a vision...

I never particularly enjoyed losing control of my faculties. I even less enjoyed doing it when I was at the mercy of someone like Donny O'Banion. It was one of the reasons I did everything I could to avoid human touch.

Touching objects was risky enough. When I touched something inanimate that was infused with emotion, like the soldier figurine, there was always a chance I'd spark a vision. But those spiritual echoes paled in comparison to living, breathing triggers.

Human beings were brimming with emotion, a limitless source of longings and memories and urges and instincts. Sure, not every touch was enough to send me careening into the land of purple-sparks. But more often than I was comfortable with, one errant graze of my fingertips on someone's skin could vault my consciousness into their psyche.

And that was a risk I simply could not take.

The last of the purple sparks cleared, but I still felt weak as a newborn kitten. To everyone else in the room, I'd been unconscious only seconds. To me, it seemed like a year had passed. I was still in Donny's arms, but he was no longer restraining me so much as holding me up. His grip shifted to hold me slightly away from his chest, so he could examine me.

"What the fuck?" he muttered, eyes on my face. He looked (rightfully) confused. I had, after all, just gone from a kicking, fighting hellcat to a limp-legged rag doll.

"Imogen, are you okay?" Gigi flew across the room to us.

"God, you're so pale. Did you pass out? Are you breathing? Please, say something."

"I'm fine," I croaked, sounding the opposite. My eyes locked on Donny's. "Or, I will be when you let me go."

His expression clouded over again, rage replacing his momentary confusion. His grip tightened on my arms. His mouth opened to say something — probably to insist, for the tenth time, that Gigi go wake the boys. Whatever he was going to say, however, never made it past his lips. Because at that exact moment, as I hung there like a dishrag in his ham-sized hands, the life-force effectively wrung out of me...

Detective Caden Hightower crashed through the door.

He moved so fast, I thought he really might be superhuman. One minute he was across the room, staring at the scene with a face like a thundercloud, the next he was right beside us. He ripped me from Donny's grip — which had slackened in surprise at the detective's sudden appearance — and shoved me into Gigi's waiting arms with a sharp, "*Get her out of here.*"

Gigi held me up and, despite her willowy frame, hauled me back toward the reception desk without much effort. I didn't resist. All my focus was on Cade as he ducked Donny's powerful right hook with an agility the drunk man couldn't match. Donny staggered off balance, the momentum of his miscalculation nearly making him topple.

Cade didn't give him a chance to swing again. He dodged two steps to the left, cocked back his arm, and clocked Donny in the face. There was a sickening crack as his fist collided. Donny was a big man, but the power behind the blow was enough to send him to his knees, groaning in pain.

Cade wasn't done. He moved swiftly to execute a tactical chokehold; one arm looped around Donny's neck, the other put precise pressure on the back of his head. His movements were controlled, though his face was still a storm of dark emotion.

"Warned you before, O'Banion," he hissed flatly. "You fuck with the law, it'll fuck back. And harder."

Donny was blinking rapidly, clawing at Cade's arm to free himself, but it was no use.

"Let," he wheezed. "Me." Another wheeze. "Go."

"In a minute," was Cade's rather worrisome reply. "First, I want to make sure you understand what's happening here. Because it seems the last time we spoke, shit didn't sink in."

Donny grunted out a promise. *"Un... der... stand."*

"Do you? Because, see, when I handed you that protection order and told you to stay five hundred feet away from your wife at all times, when I told you not to attempt to see your kids without first clearing it with the custody attorneys, you acted like you heard me. Turns out, you didn't hear me."

Donny's teeth ground together.

"You violate your agreement again before those divorce papers are signed and the judge has his day, I will make it my personal mission to see you behind bars. Permanently. And I won't even have to try very hard. The amount of shady business you and your idiot brothers are into at that dingy hole in the wall you call a bar..." Cade scoffed darkly. "I'll have my pick of charges. And you'll spend the next decade enjoying the many creative uses of community soap."

Gigi sucked in a sharp breath.

Donny was no longer fighting Cade's grip. He looked like he was listening — and not very much liking what he heard, given the newly pallid hue to his ruddy complexion.

"You get me?" Cade barked.

Donny's nod was shallow.

"Good. Then we understand each other." Cade's eyes flashed over to the reception desk. His jaw tightened when he saw neither Georgia or I had left the room, as he'd asked. "What I don't like, O'Banion, is a man who thinks the law doesn't apply to him. A man puts who his hands on a woman to make himself feel like less of a waste of space. So, now, you're going to apologize to your wife for coming here tonight. Then, you and me are going to take a little trip down to the station. Think a night in lockup is exactly what you need to remind you what's at stake here, next time you get a wild hair and want to stir up trouble."

Cade released him and stepped back. The minute Cade's arm fell away, Donny bent double at the waist, gasping for breath, hands planted on the floor to hold himself up. Cade didn't even spare the man a glance. He immediately stepped around the heaving mound of male flesh in the middle of the rug and positioned himself in front of me and Georgia. A human shield. His hand was on his gun holster, allowing him to draw quickly if necessary.

I swallowed thickly.

"Don't have all night, O'Banion," Cade barked. "Apologize."

Donny pushed up to his feet. He looked like his head was about to explode with rage. But he merely bared his teeth in a grimace and hissed, "Nothin' to be sorry for."

Cade tensed.

Beside me, Gigi flinched so hard I felt it. I pressed my shoulder to hers, a nonverbal show of support.

"I said..." Cade leaned forward an inch. "*Apologize.*"

Donny doubled down. "Fuck you! And fuck her."

"O'Banion—"

"I don't want his apology," Gigi cut in.

Cade's shoulders went stiff when he heard her whisper. He did not turn to look at us. All his attention was on Donny as he jerked his chin at the door. "You heard her, then. *Out.*"

It was a small miracle, but Donny went without another word and without any more violence. Cade was on his heels the whole way, but paused for a moment at the threshold. His eyes cut straight to mine and I gaped at the burning fury in them.

He looked pissed. *Beyond* pissed. And not at Donny.

At me.

Shit!

Why was he pissed at me? I hadn't done anything!

...Had I?

"I'm taking him to the station for booking," he clipped. "I'll be back for your statements."

Then, with one last scathing look (again *at me!*) he was gone.

Neither Georgia nor I said a word to one another. There was nothing to say — and, at the same time, far too much. She moved to the window and peered out at the parking lot as Cade loaded Donny into the back of his SUV. I pulled on my gloves, then went to the bookshelf and started returning paperbacks to their proper places.

After a few minutes, I felt her kneel down next to me. I thought she'd come to help me with the books, but instead, she reached out and threw her arms around me in a hug that made my tender ribs spasm.

"I'm sorry," she whispered against my hair, her voice thick with tears. "I'm so sorry you had to witness that."

"It's okay, Gigi. It's not your fault."

"But he grabbed you. He hurt you! God, I—" She swallowed hard. "Are you sure you're all right?"

"I'm fine."

"I'm so, *so* sorry," she repeated. "I don't know how to make it up to you but I swear I will."

I pulled back to meet her eyes. "You have nothing to make up for. Now, help me with the rest of this shelf. Then, we're having another glass of limoncello. My buzz has worn off and I don't know about you, but I could use a little liquid courage before Cade gets back."

Gigi's lips tipped up in a smile — the first I'd seen from her since Donny's arrival — as she reached for a fallen book.

Nearly an hour passed and Cade didn't come back. I took this to mean he wasn't planning on taking our statements tonight, after all. Maybe when he'd said *later* he really meant *tomorrow*.

Or *never*.

Okay, maybe that was wishful thinking. But could you blame me? The idea of my name being listed in an official police report made every bit of my skin erupt in goosebumps.

I didn't stay away from law enforcement because I had authority issues or an objection to navy uniforms or a dislike of shiny gold badges. I had my reasons for being skittish. Very good reasons.

Like Baltimore.

The Crawford case.

Six years ago.

That had been a colossal mess — one the men in charge were all too happy to blame me for when the situation went sideways. Even though I was only nineteen, still just a kid myself in many ways… even though I was only trying to help when no one else could…

In the end, none of that mattered. It was my picture that got splattered all over the papers. It was my name that got dragged through mud. Not the detectives working the case. Not the City Police Commissioner.

Me.

The headlines were still burned into my brain, after all these years.

Former 'Child Clairvoyant' Star Linked to Local Boy's Death

Self-Professed 'Psychic' Leads Police to Grim Discovery

Crawford Hopes Crushed as Rescue Efforts Turn to Recovery

Imogen Warner: Clairvoyant Consultant or Fame-Seeking Fraud?

I could still hear the newscasters' voices on the nightly news, lambasting me with quippy lines and alliterative accusations. I could remember the quotes they read from the 'anonymous sources' they'd interviewed in the aftermath, who insisted they would've brought the boy home alive if not for me butting into their investigation.

"We thought she had a gift. It turned out to be a curse for us, for our investigation, and ultimately for little Joey Crawford..."

I could've defended myself. Given a statement of my own, telling everyone exactly what happened; letting them know the cops had not a single lead when I walked into their precinct and asked to speak to the detective in charge of the case.

I could've told them how I handed Joey to them on a silver platter, safe and sound. How they didn't listen to me when I told them to go in slow. No SWAT team, no guns blazing. Nothing that would make the man who took Joey do exactly what he did, in the end...

But I didn't.

What was the point?

In the court of public opinion, I was already guilty. I wasn't going to stick around and attempt to defend myself to a city full of people who'd already decided I was the villain in that story. So, I packed up my stuff and I did what I do best.

Disappeared.

Started over.

Even after I left Baltimore in my rearview, though, I couldn't shake the lesson I'd learned there. Namely: never get involved with another police investigation. Not even if you think you might help. Better to keep your head down, your connections superficial, your ties easily undone.

I'd lived by that code for six years, and it had kept me out of trouble. (Not to mention my name out of the papers.) Which is why, now, waiting for Cade to come back and take my official statement about the Donny incident... I realized I couldn't do it. I couldn't get involved again. Not even for Gigi. Just the thought of my name on the books made me want to curl up in a protective ball.

"Gigi, I'm heading to bed."

She looked up from Rory's costume, startled by my sudden announcement. There was fabric glue fusing her fingers again. "But Detective Hightower said—"

"He really doesn't need a statement from me. It's not my protective order that was violated."

Her head shook "But—"

"Gigi, please." My voice cracked. "I just can't, okay?"

She stared at me for a while, reading my expression. Whatever she saw there made her eyes fill with understanding as she put two and two together.

"Right. Of course. I'll tell him," she murmured. "You go get some shut-eye, Imogen. You have a long day tomorrow."

"So do you," I pointed out. "Maybe you can call him. Ask him to come back another time to talk to you."

She waved away my words. "I'm way too wired to sleep. Which is good, actually. I can fix Rory's backwards arm and add the activator panels, since I'll be up anyway."

I hugged her goodnight, then made my way up the creaky steps to the second floor, yawning the whole way. I barely managed to brush my teeth, peel off my gloves, and shimmy out of my denim cut-offs before I face-planted on the bed. I'd been exhausted pre-limoncello, pre-Donny drama, and pre-vision. Now, I was closer to post-mortem.

I needed to crash.

Alas, my eyes had been shut for approximately two-point-three seconds when the unmistakable sound of a key turning in my lock made them spring open again.

What the hell?

I sat up in bed as the door swung inward. My mouth dropped open in shock as a man stepped through it. It was dark, but I knew it was Cade just from the way his silhouette moved. The careful way he shut the door. The way his chest expanded as he took a breath. The set of his shoulders as he turned to face the bed, hands planted on his hips.

My whisper was faint. "What are you doing here?"

He didn't answer. He just took a step closer.

"Cade?"

He took another step.

I sat there in the center of the bed, heart pounding out of my chest. His silence was more terrifying than anything he might've said.

"You're scaring me."

Finally, he made a sound. It was a laugh — a twisted, humorless, half-laugh, but still a laugh. The sound snagged in his throat and then, in one great stride, he was at the bed. His hands planted in the duvet as he leaned over me, bringing his face a hairsbreadth from mine. In the dark, I couldn't make out the blue in his eyes, but I could see the anger still simmering there.

"I'm scaring you?" he murmured, voice low. "That's interesting. Glad to know you do possess some sense of self-preservation underneath all that bluster you toss around."

My spine went straight. "Excuse me?"

"You want to explain what the hell you were thinking earlier?"

I blinked, confused by the question. "What do you mean?"

"Are you serious?"

"Cade, you seem angry and I don't understand why—"

The twisted laugh came again. It was worse at close proximity. It seemed somehow wrong, hearing that sound from someone like Cade. Someone good, someone kind, someone steadfast.

"Cade," I repeated. "Please talk to me."

"Doubt you'll like what I have to say. Still, I'm going to say it, even if it doesn't win me any points."

He straightened from the bed and began to pace along the side of it. My eyes tracked him in the dark.

Back and forth.

Forth and back.

Then, he spoke. "Earlier, I get a phone call. It's late, I'm not expecting it. I see the name on the screen. It's a name I'm happy to see. A name I'm fucking beside myself to see, if you want me to be honest, because it's the name of a woman I'm pretty damn interested in speaking to."

I sensed a *but* coming.

Wisely, I chose not to interrupt.

"Except, when I answer, it's not the woman I'm interested in, calling me for a goodnight chat. Instead, I'm listening to that woman wade into the fray of a turbulent domestic situation. I'm listening to that woman put herself smack in between a dangerous man and the object of his obsession."

I bit my lip.

Cade ran a hand through his hair, a frustrated gesture. His exhale was harsh; so was his tone.

"I'm ten miles away, in my car, speeding twice the normal limit. And still, no matter how fast I drive, no matter how many lights I blow through, I know I'm not going to get there in time. I know I'm going to have to listen as that woman loses control of a situation she had no business being in. I'm going to have to listen as she's on the receiving end of violence, be that words or fists."

"Cade—"

"I'm talking now."

My mouth snapped shut.

"You asked why I'm angry? I'm angry because you put yourself in harm's way, and I had no way to protect you. I'm angry because I was on the other line listening, absolutely fucking helpless, when that fuckwad put his hands on you."

"So I shouldn't have called you?"

"Of course you should've called me!" The words exploded out of him in a rush. "But you shouldn't have *had* to call me. That's the point. You shouldn't be anywhere near this shit. You've already dealt with enough of it to last a lifetime."

I stared at him, pulse slowly picking up speed. "How do you know what I've dealt with?"

He just stared at me in the dark, saying nothing.

"Have you been looking into my past?"

Again, he said nothing.

"Cade—"

"You scared me, tonight."

His admission made all thoughts of him digging into my past fly straight out of my head.

I swallowed hard. "*What*?"

A muscle was ticking in his jaw. His voice was a rasp, almost inaudible. "In my line of work, shit can go sideways in a heartbeat. You're trained for that eventuality. You prepare for it every time you step out onto the streets. They teach you how to manage the adrenaline, how to stay in control of your emotions even when they're starting to fray. After a decade, I thought I was used to it. Thought there was nothing that could rattle me. But, fuck, Imogen—" His head shook sharply. "Tonight, when I heard your voice, when I heard you with Donny... When I couldn't protect you— *Fuck*."

I waited, too stunned to say a word.

"I'm not used to feeling that kind of fear," he admitted lowly. His eyes were on mine, burning into me again — only, now, the anger was gone. Now, there was nothing but heat simmering in their depths. "Do you understand what I'm saying to you?"

I did.

At least, I thought I did. He was worried about me. Not as a cop, protecting a citizen. Not as a law enforcement officer, responding to an intense situation.

As a man.

I came unstuck from my spot at the center of the bed. He was stone-still as he watched me move toward him on my knees. I reached the edge of the mattress and, before I could talk myself out of it, my hands flew out and hit his waist. His abs were washboard-flat under my fingertips, the fabric of his button-down shirt as crisp as I'd imagined as I slid them on a slow path upward to his chest. My head craned back to keep our eyes locked.

"You scare me, too," I admitted.

Cade made a sound — half grunt, half growl — and then he was on me. His arm knifed around my midsection and he jerked me up against him, so we were flush together. Eye to eye. His mouth hit mine and I very nearly moaned at the bruising ferocity of it.

This was no lip-brush, no sneak attack. This was a full out assault, a devouring meld of mouths and tongues and teeth. I drank him in with a desperation that dizzied my head, with a need I feared would never be sated. My lips parted for him; his tongue speared inside without pause, tasting me like he was dying for it. I sucked on his tongue, loving the groan that shuddered through him in response.

Desire surged through me in a great flood. It had been gathering strength for a while — for hours, for days — and now, it was unleashed. It commandeered all my senses, swept away any sense of trepidation about getting involved with a man I was planning to walk away from in less than a week.

Even if you are leaving, you owe it to yourself to enjoy a night with that man before you go, Flo had told me only hours ago.

I decided she was right. To hell with the repercussions, to hell with the emotional fallout. I was going to enjoy every moment I could get with Cade. Because somewhere deep down — not quite my gut but somewhere else, slightly to the left, under the ribs — I knew I could travel to a hundred more towns in my lifetime, make a thousand more stops on the Imogen Warner International Tour of Misery, and never *ever* find another man like him.

I might as well enjoy it while it lasted.

The kiss had quickly gone from heated to scalding, then shot straight off-the-charts to searing hot. I couldn't catch my breath, and didn't care to. My knees were threatening to buckle as my bones turned to water. It didn't matter — Cade was holding me up, holding me steady, his strong arms more than capable of taking my weight.

Our mouths never broke apart as he shifted forward to plant one knee on the mattress, then placed me back in the center of the bed. I'd hardly settled when his weight came down on top of me, deliciously heavy, easing some of the hollow ache that was gathering between my legs.

My hands slid up and down the fabric of his shirt as his own shoved their way beneath my baggy sweatshirt. I wasn't wearing anything under it — no bra, just a flimsy pair of cotton panties. His hands stilled for a second when he felt nothing but skin.

"Fuck."

I smiled against his mouth when I heard his low oath. I loved that I could do that to him. But all my humor evaporated as his hands slid suddenly upward. His calluses ghosted over my hardened nipples as he palmed my breasts, his fingers kneading in a way that felt so magical, I nearly bowed off the bed.

"Oh my god," I whispered. "That feels so good."

Then, *he* was the one grinning against *my* mouth. Clearly, he liked that he could affect me, too. His hands took their time as they skimmed over my body, a torturous exploration that left me panting and squirming beneath him. I wanted more — more skin, more *him*. More than anything, I wanted to touch him like he was touching me. To trace every inch of his body with my fingertips, carve the feel of him into my mind so I'd never forget a second of this, even when I was long gone from here and he was nothing but a memory.

But that was crazy.

I kept my hands to myself, using my lips to explore him instead. I tasted the side of his neck, the delicious hollow of his throat, the hinge of his jaw. He pulled back — not far, just enough to stare down at me. His hands left my body and moved up to cup my face.

"Shit, Goldie." His forehead hit mine. He was breathing hard, like he'd run a marathon. "This isn't what I came here for."

"Oh?" My lips tipped up at the corners. "Then why did you come here?"

"To yell at you."

He probably meant to piss me off, but I snorted instead. "How's that plan working out for you?"

His whole body shook as he laughed. "Not very well."

"Funny… I think it's working out *very* well for me." The teasing note faded from my voice as I stared up at him. I knew I shouldn't say it, but the words came out anyway. "I like it when you touch me, Cade."

Long fingers threaded into the thick curls at the side of my head. I leaned into his touch like a cat, practically purring as his hand sifted through my hair.

"The feeling is mutual," he said. And then, he was kissing me again. Kissing me like he was trying to memorize me, too. Kissing me like if he didn't, he'd regret it for the rest of his life.

Without ever breaking his lips from mine, he rolled us on the bed, taking me with him so I was top. His hands slid back under my sweatshirt, skimming up my spine. And then, *whoosh*, like magic, the sweatshirt was gone and I was very nearly naked astride him, only a pair of thin cotton panties preventing me from being in my birthday suit. Meanwhile, he was still fully clothed.

I wasn't self-conscious by nature, but the way Cade was looking at me in that moment, even if I had been, I would've felt like a freaking supermodel. He liked what he saw. His eyes were half-lidded as they scanned slowly up my frame. His cock was hard as a rock beneath his jeans, pressing against his zipper.

He didn't move to free it. His hands were splayed out on my hips, holding me against him.

"Christ, you're beautiful," he rasped. "Could stay like this all night, just staring at you, and that would be enough."

My stomach somersaulted as those words slid through me, warm and unexpected. My hair fell down around both our faces in a thick curtain as I bent down to bring our mouths together again. There was a new urgency building inside me, and I poured all of it into the kiss. Cade returned it with an urgency of his own. His hands slid from my hips up my sides, tightening to pull me as close as he could get me.

I was so lost in his touch, it took a minute for the pain to register in my pleasure-dazed brain. He had no way of knowing about the bruises — not until he felt me flinch against him. Not until I gasped — this time not with pleasure.

He stilled instantly. "Imogen?"

"I'm fine," I muttered against his mouth. "Don't stop."

But it was too late. He gently moved me off him, settling me onto the bed at his side. With a quick curl of his abs, he sat up. His stare was locked on my body but his hands were unbearably gentle as he turned my torso so he could examine my back. I hadn't seen it, but I knew the impact of the bookshelf had left its mark. The florid signs of Donny's violence were blooming in black and blue across my pale skin, undeniable. I pressed my eyes closed as embarrassment cut through me.

This was *so* not how I wanted things to go the first time Cade saw me naked.

A finger traced, featherlight, over my spine. But there was nothing light about Cade's low vow. "I'm going to tear that motherfucker to pieces."

My eyes popped open. "Cade—"

"I'll fucking *kill him*."

I took a breath, then turned in his arms so we were face to face again. "Cade, honey, you're a detective. You can't go around killing people."

"Don't joke about this," he clipped. His eyes flashed up to

mine. The look on his face was dark with fury, but he seemed to be holding it — mostly — in check for my sake. "First thing tomorrow, you come down to the station with me and press charges against him."

I shook my head. "I'm not pressing charges."

Cade went deadly still. "Pardon?"

"I'm not pressing charges."

"I said no jokes."

"I'm being serious." I pulled out of his grip, putting a few inches of distance between us on the bed. "I'm not pressing charges. I'm not getting involved in this."

"Little late for that."

I grabbed my sweatshirt and jerked it over my head. My words came out muffled by the fabric. "You obviously don't understand, but—"

"No, *you* don't understand. I know you're new to town, so you don't know any better, but The O'Banion boys have been on Salem PD's radar since they were born. Four brothers, each worse than the last, with rap sheets so long and so varied, the fuckers must be competing for the criminal heavyweight title." His jaw locked tight as he struggled to keep his voice calm. "From what I can see, you and Georgia are fast friends. I like Georgia, I like her boys, but I'd be lying if I said I liked you hitching your wagon to hers."

My eyes narrowed. "And why is that?"

"Because, like it or not, Georgia's wagon is still hitched to Donny's. And I don't want you anywhere near him or his batshit crazy brothers." His face gentled a bit, some of the anger sliding out of his expression as he stared at me. "I want you safe."

Okay, so, that was a pretty good explanation.

Some of my annoyance ebbed away, but the apprehension remained. I continued to chew my bottom lip. "I still don't understand why I have to press charges. He's already in jail."

"We can only keep him in holding for forty-eight hours. Once his brothers bail him out, he'll be back on the streets."

"That's it? Forty-eight hours and a slap on the wrist?"

"With a restraining order of this nature, the scope is limited." He blew out a breath. "Trust me, no one hates the system more than law enforcement. But our hands are effectively tied here unless Donny escalates, or a judge decides he's a threat to the public at large."

"*Escalates*," I repeated slowly. "You mean if he hurts Gigi. Hurts the boys."

Cade nodded. "An assault charge from a third party would go a long way to getting him out of their lives permanently. Adds ammunition when Gigi takes her case to court, goes for full custody."

My mouth opened, then clicked shut again. I didn't have a good retort to that. He was right. But before I could admit as much, his phone began to buzz. He sighed as he yanked it out of his back pocket, eyes scanning the illuminated screen intently.

"Shit." His eyes shifted to mine. A heartbeat later, he swooped in and brushed his lips against mine in a hard, no-nonsense sort of kiss. "Gotta run, Goldie. It's the night before Halloween. Idiots are out in force tonight, and will be all weekend until the city empties out again." He shook his head. "Can't fucking wait for this holiday to be over."

I didn't even have a chance to return his kiss before he slid off the bed and started moving toward the bathroom. I heard the sound of the medicine cabinet open, then close. I heard the zipper of my small toiletry bag. I heard the sink tap running. Normally, it probably would've freaked me out that he was going through my stuff, but… this was Cade. There was nothing *normal* about him. Or about the way he acted. Or about the way he made me feel.

When he returned to me, he had two white pills cupped in the palm of one hand, a glass full of water in the other.

"Advil," he announced. "Should help with the bruising."

I lifted my hand, palm up, and he dropped the pills into it. He set the water on the nightstand, then crossed his arms over his chest to peer down at me. I tried to school my expression into something less stunned, but it was a struggle. I couldn't remember the last time someone cared enough to look after me.

To worry about me.

My hands curled into a fist around the pills.

"Uh," I said dumbly, like it was no big deal. "Thanks."

"Get some sleep, beautiful."

With one last, lingering lip-brush, he turned for the door. Before he stepped through it into the hall, he hesitated long enough to look back at me.

"We'll finish our talk about pressing charges tomorrow," he said firmly. But his voice warmed a shade as he added, "And we'll finish the rest of what we started tomorrow night at my place."

His grin was a flash in the dark, there and gone.

A second later, he was gone, too.

CHAPTER THIRTEEN

Me? A domestic housewife? Never.
A feral housewife, on the other hand...
- Imogen Warner, contemplating marital dynamics

The phone behind the espresso bar was ringing off the hook. *Again.* Gwen, who was elbow deep in a double mocha frappuccino order, turned to me with desperate eyes.

"Imogen, be a gem and answer that, would you? That's the fourth time it's rung in the last ten minutes. Clearly, someone is desperately seeking execution."

I abandoned my post behind the cash register and raced to the phone. It, like the rest of the shop, was old-fashioned, with a rotary dial and a long, curlicue cord that allowed about ten feet of free rein while chatting. I plucked the receiver from its cradle and lifted it to my ear, surprised by the heft of it in my hand.

"You've reached The Gallows, Imogen speaking. How can we hang you today?" I chirped down the line — just as Gwen had instructed me that morning. The boss was a big proponent of puns, often sending patrons on their way with a *"Swing by again sometime!"* or a *"See you on the other side!"* (How she pulled this off in a way that was cute, not cringey, I didn't quite understand.)

"Hello?" I prompted when I received no reply. "Is someone there?"

Again, I was met with silence.

Or... not quite silence. When I strained to listen, I could hear someone breathing — a creepy, ragged sort of panting that seemed to shudder straight into my ear and settle in my brain. Instantly, my skin broke out in gooseflesh.

"Hello? Is someone there?"

Still, nothing.

Nothing but the creepy breathing, anyway.

My heart was pounding, but I told myself I was overreacting. It was probably just some local kids messing around. Halloween was all about youthful trickery, wasn't it?

"Let me guess: my refrigerator is running, so I better go catch it?" I drawled, rolling my eyes. "Thanks a lot."

I set the phone back in its cradle, chucking to myself. That chuckle died when the phone immediately started ringing again.

What the heck?

I jerked it back to my ear. "You've got The Gallows."

Silence.

"Hello?"

A shuddering breath hit my ear. It sounded like the grim reaper himself was on the other line.

"Oh, great. You again." My eyes sought the gold patina ceiling in annoyance. "Please, go find someone else to prank. I've got about three hundred lattes to make and no time to entertain you. Okay?"

More ragged breathing.

Perfect.

"Happy Halloween, mouth-breather," I muttered, slamming the phone back down.

The prankster must've chosen a new victim after that, because the phone didn't ring again for the rest of the day. Which was good, seeing as we were slammed. I'd been well warned that Halloween was the busiest day of the year here in Salem. Despite the warnings, the reality of it still shocked me. The streets outside the shop were already shoulder-to-shoulder when I hopped off my bike at 8:45AM — and growing more so by the hour as revelers arrived from all over the country. Apparently, this year's Haunted Happenings were set to draw nearly a million visitors to the city this weekend alone, from families with youngsters to college-aged friend groups.

Practically everyone was in full costume as they wandered from shop to shop. I felt markedly out of place in faded jeans, a peasant-style blouse, and a pair of ultra-thin calfskin gloves as I walked the three blocks to The Gallows. A boring spot of neutral in a kaleidoscope of face paint, plastic vampire fangs, creepy masks... Pirates, witches, zombies, serial killers...

I'd never seen such variety or creativity on display. Though, it must be said, I would've preferred not to see the guy dressed like the creepy clown from Stephen King's *It*. He was scary enough to give me nightmares for weeks, standing there on the corner holding a single red balloon, staring at me with unblinking eyes as I rushed past.

However hair-raising the ensembles, everyone had one thing in common when they stepped through the door to The Gallows: they had money to burn and caffeine cravings to soothe. Even with Sally and her friend Agatha — a pear-shaped lady with the tartness of a Granny Smith — manning the mystical curiosities section in tandem, Gwen and I could barely keep up with the constant demand up front.

If I wasn't washing out mugs or clearing tables, I was scribbling on to-go cups and helping fill espresso orders. On top of that, I had four walk-in requests for tarot readings before lunch, and two appointments on the books for the afternoon. Not that I was complaining. At this rate, I'd soon be able to buy one of Puck's souped-up, special-edition Batmobiles.

Okay, maybe not.

I wasn't exactly rolling in it. But if things kept up this way, I'd be back on the road in my repaired rust-bucket before the week was out. (For some reason, that thought didn't thrill me quite the way it would've two days ago.)

"Hey, sweet costumes!" The guy at the front of the coffee line was grinning wide, looking back and forth from Gwen to me. "The Sanderson sisters, right? Man, I love *Hocus Pocus!* Must've watched it a hundred times growing up. Did you know they filmed it here in town?"

"Uh, no, I didn't," I admitted. "I like your costume too."

His grin got bigger. He looked like a high school kid, all gangly limbs and acne-ridden cheeks. But his costume was undeniably cool. (Han Solo had always been cool, would always *be* cool, if you wanted my honest opinion on the subject.)

As for my own outfit, I hadn't had much choice in the matter. Gwen had shoved it into my arms the minute I walked in the door that morning and told me to head into the stockroom at the back to change. When she'd found the time to whip together coordinated costumes, I did not know — and, frankly, was too startled by her appearance to ask.

She was dressed as Winifred Sanderson, in a flowing green dress with ultra-deep bell sleeves. Her red hair was teased out to maximum volume in a pile of curls atop her head. There were twin spots of rouge on her high cheekbones, à la Bette Midler in the movie.

"I'm not doing my hair like that," was all I could manage to say.

She'd scoffed. "Sarah Sanderson wears her hair down. Keep it just like you have it, all those loose waves around your shoulders... It's perfect. Now go get changed! We open in ten."

Waggling her fingers at me, she'd pitched her voice into a hag's cackle. *"Fly, my sistah, fly!"*

It had been simpler to comply than resist.

My own dress was maroon, full-skirted, and flowed to my feet. It had a cool corseted bodice that made the best of my B-cups, and a coordinating purple cape that draped over my shoulders. It even matched my gloves. As I stashed my jeans and blouse in the back room and shimmied into the witchy attire, I had to admit, it was nice to be included.

I took teenage Han Solo's order, then moved immediately to the next customer, hardly able to take a breath between them. In a way, it was good the store kept me so busy. With my thoughts occupied by costumes and customers and clients, I had no time to fixate on my plans for the evening.

Dinner with Cade.

At his house.

A house which, I could only assume, included a bedroom... And in that bedroom, a bed. One where we could finish what we'd started last night, just as Cade promised...

Fine, I admit, maybe I had *a little time* to fixate on my plans for the evening. I managed to pull myself back before I got swept up in a full Cade-daze that would result in singeing my skin on the steamer-wand or messing up tarot meanings. (Most of the time, anyway.)

Around 3PM, Gigi swept through the doors with Rory in tow. He was in high spirits — no doubt aided by copious sugar intake at school — and dressed in his kickass alien space invader suit. Sure, there were a few lopsided seams (I blamed the limoncello) and one of the adhesive plastic flight-activator panels was coming unglued from his forearm... but all things considered, I thought Party City couldn't have done any better.

"Imogen! Imogen!" He raced to the counter, ignoring the long line of waiting customers. "Guess what?"

"What, bub?" I asked, leaning over the counter to him.

"I won best costume in the contest! Out of all the other second graders!" Rory yelled, throwing his hands up over his head in celebration. "I got a whole bag of mini-Snickers as a prize!"

That explained the energy.

"That's awesome, Rory." I gestured down at myself. "Do you like my costume?"

His light brown eyes swept over my witchy attire with a skepticism that only a seven-year-old could pull off. "It's fine, I guess. But next year, you should totally be a space invader with me."

Next year?

My heart lurched.

Gigi was still swimming upstream through the dense cluster of waiting patrons. "Sorry, sorry, not cutting, just catching up with my son…" She bumped her hip against Rory's as she slid up to the counter beside him. "Make some room for your mother, will you bub?"

Rory slid over and began to eye the sugar packets at the creamer station.

Just what he needed.

Gigi had cat ears on her head, but otherwise looked the same as she had that morning at breakfast, in jeans and a light pink blazer. Her eyes swept me top to toe, then flickered over to Gwen and did the same.

"Sanderson sisters, huh?" Her brows arched. "Can I be Mary?"

"Sorry, Flo will be here in an hour and she already has dibs," Gwen called from the milk fridge, laughing. "Next year, we'll find a theme that works for a foursome."

There it was again.

Next year.

My heart gave another lurch.

"I'm thinking Spice Girls," Gigi murmured.

"Weren't there five of them?" Gwen kicked the fridge door shut with her foot and joined us at the counter. Her bell sleeves were so long, they dragged across the floor when she tipped her torso sideways to lock eyes with the couple in line behind Gigi and Rory. They were beginning to look impatient.

"This is kind of an emergency," she informed them solemnly, as though we were discussing nuclear codes instead of costume options. "We'll be with you as soon as we can."

"Seriously?" the man groused.

"Are you aware we have an excellent selection of crystals with calming properties?" Gwen did her patented gameshow host hand-flourish. "I particularly recommend the blue lace agate for you, sir. It's a natural mood balancer. Inspires tolerance and patience..."

I clamped my lips together to keep from laughing.

The man looked absolutely baffled when Gwen turned away from him and resumed our conversation without missing a beat.

"How about Teletubbies?" she asked Georgia. "There were four. Laa-Laa, Po, Dipsy, and the scary one."

"Tinky-Winky?"

"Like I said, the scary one."

"Can you imagine trying to sit down in those things? Or use the bathroom?" Gigi looked aghast. "Pass."

"Okay, then you suggest something."

Gigi's brows were furrowed in thought. "What about *Teenage Mutant Ninja Turtles*?"

"Possible..." Gwen's lips twitched. "Though I'm not sure Graham will approve a costume that involves nunchucks."

"That's probably a good call on his part," Gigi murmured.

"How about the Flintstones?" Gwen gestured toward her hair. "I could be Wilma."

"And who are we supposed to be?" Gigi jerked her thumb at me. "Barney and Fred?"

I snorted out a laugh.

"Relax, Bam-Bam," Gwen said breezily. "We have a year to brainstorm. We'll come up with something better."

"*Mooooom.*" Rory, who had until this point been waiting

patiently, began tugging on his mother's arm. "Let's goooo, already! We'll be late for trick-or-treating!"

"It's not even close to dark, bub. We have tons of time."

"But Declan and the older kids are all going to leave without me if I'm late!"

"They won't. I promise. But if they do, who cares?" She bumped her hip playfully against his. "You and me will walk house to house just the two of us, like we did last year and the year before and… Yep, every other year since you were born."

Rory looked positively horrified at the idea of trick-or-treating with his mother while his big brother had fun without him. "*Mooooom*! I want to go on my bike with Declan! You promised I could, you can't take it back now!"

Gigi looked up at the ceiling for patience.

I glanced at Rory and whispered conspiratorially, "You want a hot chocolate before you go?"

He licked his upper lip, which still bore traces of his Snickers binge. "Duh!"

"Are you trying to kill me?" Gigi lamented. "*More* sugar?"

I winked at Rory. "Whipped cream?"

"Double duh."

"Coming right up, bub."

By the time we closed for the night, I should've been dead tired. Instead, I was buzzing with nervo[illegible] and it didn't take a genius to figure out why. For most of the day, I'd managed to put all thoughts of Cade out of my mind. But once the store emptied out, there were no more distractions. Nervous butterflies began to swarm in my gut as doubts raced through my head.

What was I getting myself into, here?

Why had I agreed to this in the first place?

I blamed the lip-brush.

(The man gave really good lip-brush.)

If I were smart, I wouldn't dig myself any deeper. I would put down the shovel, pocket my earnings from the past two days, and head straight over to Puck's garage. I would—

Shit!

Was that the time?

I let out a small scream as my eyes snagged on the clock. Cade would be here in a half hour to pick me up and I still had a metric ton of cleaning to do before I could clock out for the night. The chairs were askew, the couch cushions were covered in napkins, the books were all out of whack.

I could hear the faint refrain of Flo's off-key humming as she moved around the back of the shop, sorting crystals and candles, righting overturned essential oil bottles and rearranging incense sticks. Gwen had disappeared into the storeroom ten minutes ago to tackle an emergency inventory order. We were almost out of espresso beans, to-go cups, and gift bags — not to mention half our stock.

I set the last of the clean coffee mugs on the rack to dry, then rushed over to the local author table, which appeared to have been rocked by an earthquake, given the state of the books piled on top of it. My hands froze on a copy of *The House of Seven Gables* by Nathaniel Hawthorne when the front door opened with a tinkle of bells.

"Read the sign!" I called without looking, reaching for another book. "We're closed!"

"I'm not here for coffee."

Oh boy.

The Scarlet Letter slipped through my fingers. I braced, but still felt my heart catapult up into my throat when I turned to face him. He looked good enough to eat — and not just because I'd skipped lunch. A navy sports coat was layered over his light blue button-down shirt, making the best of his eyes. His long legs were in a pair of dark-wash jeans that made him look even taller than his six-foot-three inches. His thick hair was falling perfectly over his forehead in a sexy way that seemed styled but I knew was a byproduct of winning the genetic lottery.

"You're early," I accused, but it came out breathy.

"I'll wait," he countered, coming toward me. I was physically incapable of moving as he leaned down and planted a long, deep, brain-scrambling kiss on my lips. By the time he was done, I was clutching the lapels of his blazer and couldn't remember my own name.

He rested his forehead against mine for a second. "Been thinking about doing that all damn day."

I swallowed hard.

That made two of us.

He pulled back a few inches. His eyes scanned down my body, freezing for a moment at the corset. His fingers lightly traced the laces that bound my midsection and I sucked in a sharp breath.

"I like this costume," he said, his voice lower.

"It was Gwen's idea," I blurted.

"Yeah?" His blue eyes glittered with heat. "Remind me to thank her."

Oh.

Oh boy.

"Okay," I whispered, even more breathy than before.

"Fuck, you're cute." He tapped my nose with his finger. "You need help with anything before we go?"

"Um. No. I just have to straighten up these books, then get changed in the back."

"Don't change on my account." His lips twitched. "I like the witchy getup. Makes me wonder what you've got on under all those layers." He paused, leaned in, and whispered against my lips. "I plan to find out. *Soon*."

My mouth went dry.

"Though you might get some looks from the boys at the station if you wear that to press charges against Donny." He glanced at his watch, brow furrowing. "We're short on time tonight if we want to pass out candy. Probably better we go tomorrow morning, anyway."

"I haven't agreed to pressing charges," I reminded him.

"Not yet." He leaned in an inch, eyes locked on mine. "I plan to be... persuasive."

I fought the urge to slam my mouth against his. "Isn't that witness tampering, detective?"

He just smirked, turned on a heel, and stalked over to the espresso bar, where he settled his tall form onto one of Gwen's girly, gold-legged stools. Most men would've looked ridiculous sitting there, but he pulled it off like that stool had been crafted specifically for his ass — long legs stretched out before him, elbows planted on the edge of the counter. Totally at ease.

I swiped at my face to check I wasn't salivating like a St. Bernard and forced myself to turn back to the books. Honestly, it wasn't fair. He had no right to be so hot all the time. It was messing with my head! And—

"You plan to sort those books or stand there frozen for the rest of the night?" Cade called from behind me. "Not that I mind the view. The way your ass moves in that swishy skirt..." His words tapered off into a growly sound of appreciation.

God, I was so screwed.

A feminine squeal came from the mystical curiosities section. "Detective Hightower! You're here!"

Flo raced up the two mahogany steps that led into the front. She was dressed as the third Sanderson sister in a getup much like mine, only her hair was sprayed within an inch of its life into a gravity-defying updo that resembled a lopsided witch's hat. Her gorgeous features were lit up in a grin as her eyes landed on me.

"Gwen and I will finish up here, Imogen. You should go." Her brows waggled suggestively. "You have *plans*."

Cade chuckled.

"So do you," I contended, crossing my arms over my chest.

"Yes, but our plans aren't until later." She looked at Cade, her grin widening. "The Bay Colony Coven invited Gwen and I to spend Samhain the old way."

"The old way?" Cade asked.

"Yep. Dancing naked under the moonlight. It's going to be *awesome*." Her eyes shifted to me. "Too bad you're going to miss it, Imogen."

Normally, I would not classify dancing naked with a dozen octogenarians as *awesome* but, hell, this was Salem. Normal had gone out the window the second my car began to smoke on the bridge into town. And I had to admit, after working with them, Sally and Agatha were a hoot. I'd be lying if I said I didn't want to meet the rest of their coven.

"Hey, maybe you can still come!" Flo exclaimed. "Were aren't meeting in the sacred grove until midnight. Gwen and I could pick you up on the way—"

"Imogen will be naked at midnight, but not in a sacred grove."

We both whipped our heads around to look at Cade when he spoke. He was still sitting on the stool, legs planted out in front of him, but his arms were now crossed over his chest and his expression was serious as a heart attack. My cheeks began to burn with a fierce blush as his words processed belatedly.

"Please tell me you did not just say that in front of Florence!" I hissed, mortified.

"Goldie…" He shrugged, totally unapologetic. "It's the truth."

"You still can't just say things like that!"

His lips were twitching. "Too late."

"Cade!"

"Now I'm thinking my naked-midnight plans are significantly less awesome than yours." Flo's face scrunched up as her thoughts wandered. "Maybe I'll get Desmond to meet me in the sacred grove after the coven departs… Do a little dance of our own…"

I began to chew my lip. My cheeks were still flaming in a deep blush as I met Cade's eyes. He, for the record, looked not at all embarrassed that he'd just announced our impending sexual exploits for the world — well, only for Flo, but *still* — to hear.

"Don't you look at me like that, Cade Hightower."

His eyes went crinkly. "How am I looking at you, Goldie?"

"Like the cat that got the cream!" I threw my hands up. "It's annoyingly self-satisfied, seeing as you haven't even *sampled* the cream yet!"

When I said that, his smirk disappeared and he full-on grinned. It was such a good grin, even Flo stopped murmuring about her tawdry midnight rendezvous to watch him do it.

"Something you should know, beautiful," he said, rising off the stool. "You standing there with your arms crossed over your chest in that tight corset you're wearing isn't as much of a deterrent as you seem to think it is. In fact, it's just giving me a very nice preview of what's to come."

"Oh wow," Flo whispered.

She could say that again.

My knees wobbled and my stomach flipped. "Cade—"

He wasn't done. He took another step toward me, eyes never shifting. "So you can either go get changed into something that doesn't make me want to rip it off you with my teeth in front of your friend—"

"Oh *wow*," Flo repeated.

"—or you can get your own early preview, up close and personal, of what my expression looks like when I'm satisfied," Cade finished. "Your choice."

My whole body spasmed.

He saw it, and his grin widened.

"I'll, uh..." I whispered. "Just... go get changed."

He chuckled as I turned and ran — yes, *ran* — into the storeroom.

Cade lived in a brown shingled fixer-upper with a postage stamp of a front yard and an attached single-car garage off the side. It was smack in the middle of an area called Juniper Point on the north side of town. Like his house, the neighborhood itself was small — just a handful of narrow streets jammed onto a spit of land surrounded mostly by water. This meant many of the houses — Cade's included — boasted ocean views from their bedroom windows and beach access from their backyards.

Unlike the rest of the houses we passed, however, Cade's was in need of some serious TLC. The lawn was mowed, but he had no other landscaping. Not a flower or shrub anywhere to be seen — not in the barren garden beds that stretched along the front path, not in the empty boxes that lined the porch rails, not in the hanging baskets that swung lightly in the crisp October breeze.

Leaves crunched under our feet as he led me from the driveway to the porch. His neighbor had a huge maple tree, which was currently a riot of red and orange, vibrant even in the dark. In another week or so, its graceful branches would be totally bare.

Not that I'd be here to see it.

The drive itself had taken only ten minutes, but this part of the city felt markedly different from downtown. I could tell with only a quick glance around that it was a family neighborhood. People took care of their homes, took pride in their properties. That was clear as day from the fresh paint, the meticulously trimmed hedges, the hand-painted mailboxes.

Cade's street wasn't quite as crowded as the ones outside The Gallows which was a bit like saying the Bahamas weren't as hot as the inner circles of Hell — but trick-or-treaters abounded. Parents walked their young ones down the sidewalks, holding plastic candy buckets as they moved from house to house. Cade's was the only dark spot on the street. The rest were brightly illuminated, their front doors left ajar in welcome. Many were sporting festive inflatable decorations on their front lawns, or had gauzy spiderwebs stretched across their facades.

"You don't have decorations," I noted as he steered me up onto the front porch. His stairs were slightly warped with age.

"Nope. No time. I'm not here all that much," he said, fiddling with his key in the lock. Before he opened the door, he paused to look at me. "Brace."

"For what?"

He didn't answer, just swung the door inward. As I had (foolishly) not taken the opportunity to brace, I was wholly unprepared when a ginormous black puppy barreled through the door and directly into my legs.

Two paws hit me in the stomach.

My ass hit the porch.

I went down with a low *oof* of surprise, but quickly recovered. My gloved hands automatically lifted to scruff the puppy's thick coat as he trampled me with full-body enthusiasm. I couldn't contain my squeals of laughter as a wet pink tongue licked furiously at my face, covering me instantly in saliva.

"Socks!" Cade boomed with quiet authority. "*Sit.*"

The puppy sat. Though, he couldn't quite contain his excitement — his tail was wagging so forcefully across the porch, it rocked his entire fluffy body back and forth. He was panting with the effort to follow orders, his tongue lolling out one side of his mouth. His glossy brown eyes were fixed on me as I sat up, wiping at my face with the sleeve of my blouse. He was looking at me like he thought I was the greatest thing he'd ever seen in his short time on this earth. Better than milk bones and kibble and all the toys in the pet store.

At least, he was — until Cade dropped into a crouch beside me and murmured, "Come here, boy."

I was instantly forgotten.

In the throes of doggie adoration, Socks barreled forward on massive paws he hadn't quite grown into yet. (He was going to be big, that was certain.) He made impact with the full force of his body, but Cade didn't go back on his ass. He merely grinned as he began to scruff the thick black fur behind Socks' ears. The puppy let out a series of happy sounds — half yelp, half whine. It was clear Cade was his favorite human of all time.

"Who's my good boy?" Cade asked in a soft voice meant only for his dog. "Who's the best boy?"

A warm, fuzzy feeling — one I was becoming alarmingly accustomed to — began to radiate through me as I watched the two of them. There was a gentle look on Cade's face I'd never seen before.

I'd give just about anything to have him turn that look my way.

I banished the insane thought as I climbed to my feet. "You didn't tell me you owned the cutest puppy ever to exist."

Cade craned his head back to look at me, his hands still deep in Socks' fur. "You didn't ask."

No, I supposed I hadn't.

Cade ushered us into the house and shut the door. Socks' nails clacked against the hardwood as he scampered around in circles by our feet, trying to capture our attention. The foyer came into full view when Cade flipped on the lights. It was sparsely furnished, with only a small entry table and a utilitarian mat to wipe your shoes. There were at least four pairs of big boots piled in the corner. No artwork anywhere to be seen on the walls. No personal touches.

"Okay, tour starts now and won't take long, seeing as this place could fit in a crackerjack box," Cade said, steering me into the adjacent room with one hand at the small of my back. "This is the living room."

I glanced around, taking in the sectional, the television, the coffee table, the doggie crate in the corner… and not much else. Only a few chew toys littered across the floor. Like the foyer, I saw no art, no knickknacks. It was a nice space, with big windows and a vaulted ceiling that gave the illusion of more square footage, but it was decidedly empty. The walls looked like they'd been freshly skimmed, but needed priming and painting.

I pushed down the urge to ask him how long he'd been living here. Weeks? Months? Since he moved to Salem a year ago? Given the state of things, I'd guess not long.

"Moving on," Cade murmured, spurring me forward through a wide archway into a surprisingly large kitchen. The ceilings were high here as well, and even in the dark, I could tell the windows looked out over the backyard, to the Atlantic Ocean. I'd bet it was a beautiful spot to stand and sip coffee in the morning. That said, it was crying out for new countertops and I'd bet the appliances were old enough to apply for a driver's license.

"Bedrooms and bathroom are down that hall." He dipped his chin toward the back corridor that fed off the kitchen. "The master is decent size. The smaller one will probably end up an office, though I fucking hate the thought of bringing work home with me."

I digested that in silence.

Cade Hightower was not the kind of man who sat behind a desk. He was made for the field. A born extrovert, who thrived on human connections. I'd noticed that about him from the very first time we met.

"And that concludes our tour."

I met his eyes. "It's nice, Cade. Really nice."

"It's not," he corrected, sounding amused. "But it will be. Eventually. Right now, it's a work in progress. I've been here four months. In those four months, my big plans for renovation got somewhat sidetracked by the adoption of the sock-monster."

I smiled as I looked down at said monster. He was licking the floor. "Sounds to me like you have your priorities straight."

"Glad you think so."

Before I could chicken out, I slipped my small leather backpack off my shoulder and unzipped it to retrieve the package I'd stashed in there this morning. "Speaking of Socks… I, uh… got him something."

Cade stilled in the middle of the kitchen. "What?"

Socks gave up on licking the floor, plunked down on his master's boots, and immediately started chewing his laces.

"Goldie?" Cade prompted.

Damn and blast.

Maybe this was a bad idea. But it was too late to reverse course. I had no choice but to soldier on. "It's nothing big. Just something I saw in the window of a pet store on my way to The Gallows this morning. It's probably stupid and I don't even know if he'll like it. I mean, I've never had a puppy, I have no idea what they like, but…"

Avoiding Cade's eyes, I tore open the gift bag and pulled out the plush dog toy. It was shaped like a ghost and squeaked when you squeezed it — I knew because I'd done precisely that when I wandered into Wag, the pet shop just down the block from Gwen's store, and made my purchase.

Suddenly, Cade was standing in front of me. His hand slid under my chin and he applied faint pressure, forcing me to stop avoiding his eyes. "You got my dog a gift?"

"Um… yes? Is that okay?"

He kissed me. It was a hot kiss. A toe-curling, breath-stealing, butterfly-inducing kiss. It was so good, I lifted up onto my tiptoes to deepen it. Cade pulled me closer, and the plush toy let out a loud squeak as it was compressed between our bodies.

We broke apart, both laughing.

Socks barked up at us. His dark glossy eyes were locked on the ghost toy in my hands. I looked to Cade for confirmation before I knelt down and gave it to him. The second his razor-sharp puppy teeth sank into the fabric, it was torn from my grip. Moving so quickly he was no more than a black blur of fur, Socks scampered into the living room to be alone with his new toy.

"I think it's safe to say he likes it," Cade murmured.

I didn't even try to fight my smile as I turned to him. His eyes moved to my mouth and went gentle. I remembered his words the other day, after we ate lunch in the park.

That smile — on the rare occasion you've actually let me see it — is like a gift. Fucking breathtaking.

My stomach clenched as more butterflies exploded to life inside it.

Cade tore his eyes from my lips and turned away. He stepped nimbly over Socks' stainless steel water bowl to get to the fridge. "You want something to drink?"

Liquid courage couldn't hurt. In fact, it might drown the butterflies that were beginning to swarm as the full implications of being here — in Cade's house, watching him move around his kitchen like we'd done it a million times before — sank in.

"Sure."

"Beer, wine, water?" He peered around the open fridge to look at me. "I can also shake a mean margarita, but I'm out of limes."

I blinked at him. "I'll have anything. I'm not picky."

"Not what I asked."

"I mean it. I'll just have whatever you're having. "

His brow furrowed. "But what do you want?"

"Whatever's easiest."

He sighed, closed the fridge, and came back to me. He was, I could not fail to notice, wearing his *serious-discussion* face.

Oh no.

He didn't stop moving until he was standing directly in front of me by the kitchen island. "Imogen."

"Um. Y-yes?"

His hands cupped my cheeks, then slid into the curls at my temples. "I know you're not used to this, so I'm giving you a pass until you have some time to adjust. But when I ask you what you want, I'm not asking for my health. I actually want to know. And I want to know so I can give it to you."

"I was just trying to—"

"I know exactly what you were doing. But your tendencies to go with whatever's easiest or most convenient, 'cause you're terrified to be an imposition? They're not going to fly around here."

My eyes narrowed. "Maybe I'm just being polite."

"Well, stop it." His lips hit mine — hard, firm, no-nonsense. "I don't want polite. I want real. You get me?"

I managed a nod, though my throat felt oddly tight.

"Now," he muttered. "What do you want to drink?"

I wasn't going to win this one. So, I sighed, then said, "A beer sounds good."

"Then beer it is, beautiful."

With another brief lip-brush — which, if you wanted my thoughts on the matter, lasted not nearly long enough — he released me from his hold, turned, and strode back to the fridge. He yanked out two bottles of hazy IPA from a local brewery called Notch. I'd walked past it twice on my first day in town, taking notice of the sun-drenched patio full of happy people drinking beer.

Cade popped the caps off the top of our IPAs, then clinked his bottle against mine and took a long sip. I watched him swallow, the cords of his throat at work an oddly mesmerizing sight. When he caught me staring, I quickly averted my eyes and took a long sip of my own.

"I'm going to take Socks out to pee, then I'll get started on dinner," he said. "You're on candy duty."

"Candy duty?"

He jerked his chin toward the bowl sitting on the kitchen island. It was full of dozens of snack-sized Hershey Bars, Reese's Cups, Almond Joys, Milky Ways… It seemed he'd purchased every conceivable variety of chocolate on the market. There was enough candy there to supply an army of children.

"Imogen?"

"I'm not sure…" I took another fortifying sip. "I mean, I…"

"Spit it out, Goldie. Socks has no doubt already eaten half the stuffing in that ghost toy, and he'll continue to do so even if it means having an accident on my floors."

"Right." I sucked in a breath. "I've never done this before, that's all. I don't know the protocol."

He stared at me. "You've never passed out Halloween candy?"

I shook my head.

"It's pretty self-explanatory," he said, staring at me like I had a few screws loose. "Just think of the times you went trick-or-treating as a kid, only this time you're the one opening the door, not knocking on it."

"But I never—" I clamped my lips shut, changing my mind. I didn't want to talk about this after all. I shouldn't have even brought it up.

His voice went quiet. "Never what?"

"Um..."

"Never what, Imogen?"

Damn and blast.

"I never went trick-or-treating," I admitted in a rush. "Or, if I did, I don't remember."

Cade was silent. Emotions flared across his face, but he locked them down into a smooth mask so fast I thought I'd imagined it. He just stood there, expressionless. Waiting for me to explain.

I didn't plan to tell him. It wasn't like me to willingly expose myself. But I couldn't seem to keep the words from spilling out of me, now that I'd started.

"My parents died when I was pretty young and I... It was..." God, why was this so hard to talk about after all these years? "I don't really know how to explain it... I mean... It's not..."

"Take your time."

I sucked in a breath. "I don't remember them. Not well. I have some memories, but they've sort of gone to watercolor with time. Faded out, you know? Until I can't be sure what's real and what I imagined."

Cade was holding himself very still. I got the sense this was intentional — as though he knew, if he came to me now, I'd clam up again. His voice was oddly controlled as he asked, "Don't you have any pictures?"

"I had some, but I can't access them."

"You can't *access* them? What does that mean?"

"It's complicated," I hedged. "I had a whole book of photographs, but it was left behind when…"

I shook my head, not wanting to think about all I'd left behind when I fled Florida at fifteen. And definitely not wanting to open that can of worms with Cade.

Not now, not *ever*.

"There weren't all that many of them, anyway. I was only five when it happened."

"Fuck," he cursed quietly. "I'm sorry."

I shrugged and sipped my beer. "Anyway, I went to live with my uncle after that and he wasn't the kind of man who… He didn't think things like costumes and candy were…" I chewed my lip. "Trick-or-treating wasn't a thing I got to do, I'll just leave it at that."

Cade's eyes were very sharp as they scanned my face. He was in full detective mode. (A.K.A. human-lie-detector mode.) After a few more seconds under his scrutiny, I feared he'd see everything about me. Every secret I'd ever had, every shame I'd ever buried.

Thankfully, the ringing of the doorbell shattered the intensity of the moment. A chorus of kids yelling *"Trick or treeeeat!"* followed.

"Showtime." Cade swapped his beer for the candy bowl, then grabbed my hand. "Don't worry, I'll show you the ropes. You'll be a candy-passing pro in no time, Goldie."

CHAPTER FOURTEEN

I'm 30 days sober!
(Not in a row, just this year.)
- Imogen Warner, cutting back on tequila

"That's the last of it," I called, flipping out the porch light to discourage any stragglers. I toted the empty bowl back to the kitchen where Cade was loading our dirty dinner plates into the dishwasher. "We're officially out of candy and closed for business."

He looked over his shoulder to smile at me. "Can't believe they went through it all. I'll have to buy a pallet next year."

"Don't think I didn't see you sneaking those Milky Ways," I teased him. "Now some poor kid is going home with an empty bucket."

"I'm sure they'll survive." His eyes moved past me to the living room. "Socks still out?"

"Like a light," I murmured. When I'd passed by, the puppy was fast asleep in his doggy bed, a puddle of drool forming beneath his slackened jowls. "I guess tearing apart that entire plush toy really tuckered him out."

"Mmm," Cade hummed, moving toward me.

I watched him approach, feeling my pulse slowly pick up speed. The evening, until this point, had been remarkably mellow. Aside from the brief, emotionally fraught blip about my childhood earlier, we'd kept the conversation light for the past few hours.

Cade, I learned, was no slouch in the kitchen. He'd whipped together a caesar salad with homemade dressing and fresh ciabatta croutons sautéed in garlic and oil. It was freakishly good, especially when paired with baked potatoes and topped with hand-breaded chicken cutlets.

Though I offered to help, I spent most of the dinner prep-time darting back and forth from the front door. The doorbell seemed to ring every ten seconds as a parade of kids from infancy to their mid-teens in a wide variety of colorful costumes marched up Cade's porch steps seeking candy. Sometimes Cade came out to say hello to his neighbors, but mostly it was just me manning the door, the puppy racing circles around my feet. (Socks took quickly to his role as support staff in the candy-distribution system, greeting everyone with tail wags and tongue swipes.)

I kept a lookout for Rory and Declan in the bedlam, but I knew from their chatter at breakfast that they planned to stick closer to their own neighborhood tonight. Gigi may've allowed them modicum of freedom, but that freedom was limited to the two-block radius surrounding The Sea Witch. If their bikes weren't back in the rack by eight on the dot, they'd be grounded for life. No doubt I'd hear all about their escapades tomorrow.

I was looking forward to that.

Not only was Cade a good cook, he was also funny. Throughout the night, he made jokes — sometimes at my expense, more often at his own — and told stories about his crazy family. Born and raised in Maryland, though none of his siblings lived there anymore. He was the youngest of three much older sisters and a self-proclaimed "accident" — one his parents were thrilled about, even though they'd not planned on starting over with a newborn in their late forties. Now, they were in their late seventies and had uprooted to a retirement community on the sunny shores of North Carolina, where their days were full of pickleball and potlucks.

His sisters were all married, all had boatloads of kids, and all scattered across the continental United States, which meant Cade didn't see them often but, when he did, he saved up his vacation time to stay for longer than a few days. After seeing him with his dog, I could only imagine how he was with his nieces and nephews.

I'd bet he was a great uncle.

The more I learned about him, the more I got to know him, the harder it was to hold him at arm's length. He was slowly but surely working his way beneath my defenses — despite my best efforts.

The first time I'd clapped eyes on him, I'd scoffed at the idea anyone could be so genuinely altruistic. So inherently decent. It was alarming to realize just how wrong I'd been to doubt he was a good person.

Even *more* alarming?

He seemed to think I was a good person, too.

I didn't know what I'd done to pull the wool over his eyes. I didn't know why he looked at me like he thought I was someone worthy, someone pure, someone who fit seamlessly at his side. Someone who could meet his neighbors and sit in his kitchen enjoying a home-cooked meal. If he knew who I was, if he knew how I'd lived these past ten years, that look would be gone in a heartbeat.

So, I didn't tell him.

I just enjoyed myself. I soaked him in like a sponge, sucking up as much Cade Hightower as humanly possible so I could enjoy it later, when life went back to normal and the Imogen Warner International Tour of Misery commenced once more.

"You want dessert?" he murmured now, stopping before my stool. The overhead lights were dimmed low, softening the angular cut of his cheekbones, the chiseled line of his jaw. His thick hair was falling over his forehead in that particular way that always made me ache to push it back for him

God, he was gorgeous.

Unfairly so.

I shook my head. "Still full from dinner."

His hands landed on my thighs. Even through my jeans, his touch was warm and solid. I tried — failed — to keep my breaths even as he slowly parted my legs and stepped between them. My hands found his waist, holding on as my head tipped back to keep his face in sight.

"Do *you* want dessert?" I asked breathily.

In lieu of an answer, his lips hit my neck, nibbling a path up to the pulse point that was thudding madly on the underside of my jaw. His tongue tasted the skin there. I shivered at the sensation as pleasure spiraled through me, a slow furl from my head to my toes. My hands slid around his back as I arched against him, pressing my breasts to his chest, desperate to get as close as I could manage.

"Don't need dessert, but I can think of something sweet I'd like on my tongue," he murmured a second before his mouth hit mine. Then, in a blink, I was being lifted up off the stool. My legs wrapped automatically around his waist as he carried me out of the kitchen, down the hall, into the master bedroom, kissing me the entire time.

Earlier, I'd been curious what his room might look like.

In this moment, I couldn't care less.

I landed on the bed.

Cade landed on me.

Yes.

Finally.

We were equally ravenous, equally eager to reignite the passion we'd sparked the night before. I worked the buttons of his shirt with shaky hands, struggling to undo them with my gloved fingers. He took over, moving so fast Clark Kent would be impressed. I spared a second to examine his bare chest up close for the first time. Pure, primal appreciation flared in my stomach as I saw the washboard abs, the distinct divots of his six-pack, the faint smattering of hair that covered his pectorals. I couldn't help myself — I leaned in to plant a kiss over his heart, then drifted a few inches down to flick his nipple with the tip of my tongue.

He loosed a low growl of desire as he tipped my face back up to his. His mouth slammed down on mine in an all-consuming kiss, one that only broke apart long enough for him to whisk my blouse up over my head and toss it away. Then his mouth came right back down and claimed mine, hard and hot and so freaking *deep* I could feel it move all the way through me. In my bones, in my bloodstream, in between my thighs.

I made a mewling, desperate sound, unable to articulate all that I was feeling, just knowing I needed more of it. More of him.

Now.

His hands found the clasp of my bra and then, *whoosh*, it too was gone. My jeans and underwear followed suit quickly, as did his. Eventually, the only thing left were my delicate calfskin gloves — the ones with the little buttons at the wrists. He tweaked one of the buttons with the pad of his thumb, his eyes locked on my face to gauge my reaction. My breath caught and I went still, wondering how I was going to explain this to him without sounding like an utter freak. Knowing, even if I found the words, telling him the truth might scare him off.

Or *turn* him off.

I'd been dreading this moment, however inevitable. In a way, I was surprised we hadn't gotten here sooner. Most everyone else asked at some point or another. Hell, Sally had asked me just this morning.

What's with the glove collection, sugar? You a cat burglar by night?

Flo and Gwen had broached the subject yesterday afternoon. Even Gigi had wondered openly about my odd fashion choice, blurting out her curiosity after several lip-loosening glasses of limoncello.

I gave them all the same canned answer I always used.

The skin on my hands is super sensitive.

A half-truth.

A big omission.

My heart pounded faster and faster. Cade stared at me, studying my face carefully in the darkness. I readied myself as much as I could, knowing he was about to ask even as I prayed he wouldn't. Maybe it was selfish, but I didn't want to lie. Not to anyone — but especially not him.

Just when I was ready to throw in the towel and confess... Cade, being Cade, proceeded to stun me senseless. To shatter all my preconceived notions about how people operated.

He didn't ask.

He just leaned forward, pressed his lips to the inside of my wrist, and set my gloved hand back on the bed. There was understanding in his eyes — an awareness that shocked me.

Did he know, somehow?

How could he know?

Then, he was kissing me again, and all thoughts of gloves and secrets went straight out of my head. There was only this moment. The two of us, naked on the bed, limbs tangled. Desperate to taste, to touch. We explored one another — hands and mouths skimming everywhere we could reach.

He was so strong, so muscular. His body was like my own personal playground. A jungle gym, built for climbing. The feeling of all that taut, tanned skin moving against mine was so good, I was panting after only a few short minutes. And my first glimpse at his cock — long and hard and visibly throbbing with desire — made me so wanton with need, I wrestled him onto his back, determined to get my mouth around him.

I'd barely traced the tip with my tongue when Cade put a stop to my fun. With laughable ease, he flipped me onto my back, then pinned me to the bed as his weight settled between my hips. For a breathless second, as I felt the glide of his shaft through the slickness of my core, my mind went blank with need. I was sure he was going to drive himself deep inside me — and I was ready for it.

Beyond ready.

I was borderline *begging* for it.

Instead he moved away, shifting down my body for some fun of his own. I would've been disappointed if it didn't feel so damn good. His lips skimmed over my collarbone, then took a long detour at my breasts, sucking and licking my nipples until they were peaked with lust. I gasped his name as he moved down to circle my navel with his tongue, and again as he shifted to the apex of my thighs. I felt his warm breath there and nearly chewed through my bottom lip in sheer anticipation. Then, I felt his unmistakable smile curve against the most sensitive part of me.

"Dessert," he whispered.

His tongue speared inside and I bucked up off the bed. My limbs electrified with pure sensation; my thoughts turned to static. His hands locked onto my hips to hold me still as he fucked me expertly with his mouth, lapping and sucking my clit until I was cursing god and seeing stars.

There was no slow build, no warning sign — the orgasm slammed into me like one of my visions, all at once, stealing all conscious thought. He continued to eat me as I rode it out, wave after wave of aftershocks shaking me from head to toe, residual tingles pulsing at my core.

Christ.

I'd never come like that.

Never.

It was off the charts.

Amazing.

Life-altering.

Cade kissed his way back up my body, until our faces were aligned. When our lips met, I could taste myself on his tongue. The intimacy of that instantly reignited my dimming sparks of need. It throbbed through me anew, a hollow burn, and I wrapped my arms tight around his back.

"You taste even better than I imagined." He nipped my bottom lip as his hand slid between my legs. "Can't wait to feel you around my cock, beautiful."

"Please," I moaned as his fingers found my clit, circling in the wetness there. My hips jerked; I felt hypersensitive after my orgasm, but the pleasure was already building again.

"You ready for me?"

I nodded as I kissed him, unable to form words. He circled faster, gradually increasing his speed until I was panting into his mouth.

"Yeah, you're ready for me," he grunted, his voice throaty.

With his mouth pressed against mine, I felt the words form before I heard them. My hands slid down the strong planes of his back to cup his ass. I used all my strength to urge him closer, needing him inside me, *now*; needing him to erase all the space keeping us apart.

"Not yet, greedy girl." He pushed up slightly with one hand planted in the mattress beside my head. "Imogen, listen to me."

I cracked open my eyes to look at him. His expression was intent; his eyes were flaring like blue fire.

"I saw birth control in your makeup bag last night when I got you Advil," he told me, flat out. "Is it yours?"

I managed a nod.

"You take it regularly?"

I nodded again.

"Good." He paused a beat and his forehead came down to rest on mine. His breaths were labored as he tried to keep his control in check. "You want me to use more protection than that, say the word and I'll suit up. But I've got to say, beautiful, the urge to drive myself inside you bare is damn near killing me."

Fuck.

That was so hot I nearly orgasmed again.

"I want you inside me," I whispered. To confirm this, my hands put even more pressure on his ass. "Please. Nothing between us. Just you and me."

He groaned at my words, kissing me at the same time. Then, he shifted his hips slightly and I felt him there, poised at my entrance. My breath hitched as he pushed in — not all the way, just an inch, letting me acclimate to his size. There was a lot to acclimate to, but I didn't care if he hurt me. I wanted it all, every rigid inch of him, everything he had to give me.

"Please," I begged.

My clit throbbed relentlessly as I waited for him to push deeper. He didn't. He just stayed there, teasing me with a taste of him as his lips ghosted over mine. I started to lift my hips, but he made a growly sound that stilled me.

"Waiting for it," he whispered, eyes locked with mine.

Waiting?

Waiting for *what*?

God, was he trying to torture me?

I couldn't wait anymore! I was going to explode into a million pieces if he didn't move soon.

"Cade—"

"There it is."

The second his name left my lips, he drove fully inside, sheathing himself to the hilt. He was so deep, I damn near felt him in my throat. It was borderline painful to take all of him, but I didn't care. Especially as he began to move, pounding into me over and over.

"Say it again," he demanded, hand fisting in the sheet beside my head.

I'd say anything he wanted, in this moment.

"Cade."

He stroked deeper, harder, faster.

"Again," he ordered, his voice ragged.

"Cade," I breathed.

Thrust after thrust, each harder than the last, drawing gasps and moans from the innermost part of me.

"Fuck, you feel good," he rasped between kisses. "So fucking tight."

I locked my legs around his hips as my hands dug into his back. His pace increased to a ferocious rhythm — one that threatened to send me over the edge into another orgasm. When he felt me nearing the point of no return, he slowed his pace to prevent it. The orgasm receded slightly, and I made an unhappy noise in response.

He chuckled, but the sound was ragged against my lips. "Not yet, greedy girl. Wait for me. We're coming together."

"Please—"

"Together."

Fuck.

I kissed him harder, lost in a sea of sensation. My tongue stroked his as his unflagging thrusts drove me nearer and nearer to utter delirium.

I was close.

I'd been close since we started, to be honest, but I was even closer now. Cade was close too. I could see it in his face; feel it in his body. The tightness there, the intensity. Like a bowstring set to snap.

Eventually, we were both panting too heavily to kiss, but we kept our mouths together and our gazes locked. Breathing each other in as we moved.

I didn't know how much longer I could hold the orgasm at bay.

Not very long. My limbs were flexing, my whole body beginning to convulse as the constant thrum of pleasure centered at my clit pitched up to a higher decibel than I'd ever felt before. Higher even than the orgasm he'd given with his mouth between my legs. I could tell this second one was going to be huge.

Mammoth.

Unstoppable.

My fingers scored into his back as it began to crescendo. "Cade—"

"Let go, beautiful," he growled. "I'm right there with you."

He rasped my name as his cock planted deep one last time. Then, with a rough pump of his hips he spilled into me, head thrown back as it consumed him fully. I orgasmed in a brilliant burst of rapture, coming so hard I forgot my own name, forgot his name, forgot everything except the bliss of being there.

In his arms.

In his bed.

Lying there with him inside me, everything in my fucked up world felt unbelievably right for the first time in as long as I could remember. Because when Cade Hightower was holding me, I didn't want to run.

I wanted to stay right where I was.

A pair of lips moved slowly along the exposed planes of my back. I was facedown on the bed, totally spent. Cade had effectively fucked me senseless. Not once, not twice, but three times.

Three glorious times.

Resulting in four glorious orgasms.

Now, it was late and we were lying in the dark, our legs tangled up together on top of the sheets. He traced absent shapes into my skin while I caught my breath.

"How's the bruise today?" His warm breath fanned down my

spine, where I knew I still bore traces of Donny's wrath. "Still sore?"

"Not really. Though I can't feel much of anything at the moment. I lost feeling to my extremities sometime around orgasm three."

He chucked, the sound low and brimming with masculine satisfaction.

"I mean it." I pushed up on my elbow to catch his eyes. "I don't think my legs are functional anymore. You may have to carry me around for the rest of eternity on a litter. Like Cleopatra."

His lips twitched. "Pretty sure you need at least two men to carry one of those."

"Once Socks gets a bit bigger, we'll rig up a harness to his back. He can take one side, you can take the other."

His grin was a flash of white in the dim room. "Sounds like you've got it all figured out."

"It's that or a saddle. Socks is only a few months old and he's got to be nearly fifty pounds already. By the time he's full grown, I'll be able ride to him around the yard like a stallion."

He chuckled. "That, I'd pay good money to see."

My reply was swallowed up by a yawn.

Cade shifted into a sitting position with his back against the headboard, and rolled me gently so I was plastered along the length of his side. I snuggled into his heat, my arm sliding around his waist as he pulled the sheet up over us.

"You tired?"

"Mmm," I hummed.

"Then sleep."

My eyes flew open. "Here?"

"No, in Socks' crate." He scoffed. "Yeah, here."

"Aren't you going to bring me back to The Sea Witch?"

"No."

I attempted to pull away so I could get a look at his face, but his arm tightened around me, preventing so much as an inch of space between us. I blinked at the wall of his chest, confusion rippling through me.

"What do you mean, *no*?"

"You're sleeping here tonight."

I was?

"I am?"

"Mhm."

"But… it's our first date."

He said nothing for a moment. When he did speak, there was subdued laughter in his voice. "Thanks for pointing that out, Goldie. Astute as ever."

My teeth chomped playfully on his pectoral in retaliation. "I'm just saying, sleepovers aren't really a first date thing."

"You have a lot of first dates?"

The question was thrown out in a deceptively casual way. But the sudden tension emanating throughout the hard body beneath mine told a different story. "Um…"

"*Um* isn't an answer."

"Well, excuse me, detective. I didn't realize post-coital cuddles were going to include an interrogation."

The tension in his body magnified. "Interrogation?"

"Yes!"

"That's funny, seeing as I haven't asked you a damn thing since you breezed into town," he said, and he did *not* sound happy. "Haven't demanded any answers, even though I could have. We both know I could have, Imogen."

A lump lodged in my throat.

He was right, but I wasn't about to admit it.

"Christ," he cursed. "I thought I was making some progress here. You, earlier, opening up about your past... Not much, just a crack, but more than you've ever given before. And, hell, I'll take a crack. I'll take whatever you give me." His head thumped back against the headboard and I knew he was looking up at the ceiling, even though I couldn't see him. "Here we are again, though. I can't ask a single question without you freezing up and freaking out."

"I am not freezing up," I hissed. "*Or* freaking out!"

"You are."

I tried to pull away again and, once more, found my efforts halted before they even began. "Would you let me go?"

"No."

"I need some space!"

That was when *he* moved — hooking me under my armpits, he hauled me up his chest so I was splayed on top of him like a human blanket. My hands had no choice but to brace against his shoulders; there was nowhere else to put them. Our eyes were locked, our faces aligned perfectly. We were both breathing hard. And, I might add, still naked as jaybirds.

"You don't need space," he informed me, a furrow forming between his dark brows. "You've had so much space for so damn long, you don't know how to begin to let anyone in anymore."

My mouth dropped open to refute him, but he was on a roll.

"How many towns have you blown through in the past ten years, Imogen? How many decent people have you scraped off because you were too chickenshit to drop those guards you've got up?"

"You don't know what you're talking about," I snapped.

"Pretty sure I do," he countered. "You think it's easier for you to uproot your whole life and start over than it is to actually put down roots somewhere. You think holding everyone at arm's length means they won't be able to hurt you. But you've got it all twisted in that beautiful head of yours. Keeping everyone at bay isn't keeping you safe. It's keeping you isolated. You aren't just alone; you're lonely." His tone gentled slightly. "That doesn't take a detective to deduce. Anyone who looks at you for longer than a moment can see it."

I flinched in his hold, hating his words. Hating him for saying them. Hating even more that they were true.

"I knew the first time I saw you that you were running from something in your past," Cade said, reaching up to trace a finger down my cheek. "I get that you aren't ready to talk about that. Not yet. Not to me. But one of these days, Imogen, you've got to decide someone is worth the risk."

I sucked in a sharp breath.

"If you want that someone to be me, I'll be there in a heartbeat to listen." His whole hand shifted to cup my face — it took all my strength to keep from leaning into it. "If that's someone else, like Georgia or Florence or Gwen, they'll be there for you, too. Like it or not, in the short time you've been here, you've surrounded yourself with some pretty great people. The kind who won't let you shake them off or toss them away."

My heart was thudding far too fast to be healthy. For a long moment, all I could do was breathe — *in, out, in, out* — trying desperately to keep from spinning into an emotional tempest.

Cade waited.

Not pushing.

Not interrogating.

That was the moment I realized he'd been right, before. He hadn't pushed me for any information. He'd *never* pushed me for any information, though I was sure he had about a million questions. If he'd looked into me on his own time, using his law enforcement resources or Gravewatch connections...

The Crawford case alone was enough to inspire a thousand inquiries. (Not to mention my rather colorful childhood on the daytime television circuit.) Regardless, he'd been remarkably patient with me. Not taking a thing, at the same time giving everything. He'd carved out a safe place for me to share on my terms, not on his.

And how did I thank him for it?

I bit his head off the first time he braved asking me anything directly.

Damn and blast.

"Not a lot," I blurted.

Confusion flashed across his features at my random outburst. "Sorry?"

"First dates." I swallowed hard against the emotion clogging my throat. "I don't go on a lot, to answer your question. The last one I went on was with a guy in Atlantic City, about a year ago. He turned out to be a scumbag of the highest order — something it took me two months to learn and then six months after that to escape."

Cade's brows pulled in. "What do you—"

I cut him off. "Before him, I had what amounts to a two-year dry spell. Lots of long, romantic nights with my vibrator and a series of cowboy-themed romance novels."

"*Cowboy* themed?"

"Don't judge!"

"I'm not. Just wondering if I should go out tomorrow and buy a Stetson."

Intriguing as I found the idea of Cade in a white cowboy hat and assless chaps, I hurried on with my story. "Pre-dry spell, I dated a handful of guys throughout my early twenties, none of whom lasted more than a few months, none of whom were anything more than semi-regular sex and even-less-regular date night companions at dinner or a movie." I sucked in a breath. "Which brings us all the way back to my high school years. Seeing as I was homeschooled and spent most of my time surrounded by adults, options were pretty limited. Do you need to hear about the pimple-faced boy who popped my cherry or is that enough?"

Cade stared at me for a long beat, then leaned in and kissed me — a gentle, whisper-soft kiss the likes of which he'd never given me before. His voice was equally gentle. "It's enough, Imogen."

I nodded, too worked up to even kiss him back properly. I didn't know what I was feeling. Angry, annoyed, and — oddly enough — relieved. Sure, telling him about myself was terrifying. But it was also liberating in a way I hadn't anticipated.

I was *so* out of my depth with this guy.

"What about you?" I narrowed my eyes at him. "What's your dating history? Now that we're laying it all out there..."

He didn't hesitate to share. "I got married right after graduation to my high school sweetheart. Corinne. Things were good for a while. Good became a memory as soon as I left the academy and got my first beat in a rough part of Baltimore. My ex... She isn't a bad person, but she..." He searched for the right words, brow furrowed. "Corinne is a kindergarten teacher. Her parents were hippies. She's all about sunshine and rainbows and silver linings. A perpetual optimist."

Married.

He'd been married.

To a kindergarten teacher named Corinne.

I waited for him to go on, listening so intently I wasn't even breathing.

"That's a great quality in a woman, I'm not suggesting otherwise," Cade went on. "But she couldn't hear about my day, the shit I saw on the streets. The darkness of it. She couldn't stand having a gun in the house. She would burst into tears if she thought too long about me having to actually shoot it at a criminal." He shook his head. "I couldn't talk about a big chunk of my life. Couldn't ever bring it home to her, unload it when I needed to share."

I kept still as a stone, studying his face in the dark.

"We tried for a while. Longer than we should have, probably. But who wants to get divorced at twenty-two? I stared taking classes on the side to get my criminal justice degree, while working full time. Never home — and when I was, it wasn't great." He sighed. "Corrine knew from the start that I was headed down the track to become a detective as soon as I'd put in enough time on the force. But when I actually started taking steps toward that goal... it was more than she could handle. Way more. Eventually, the bad days started to outweigh the good."

He said this like it was simple though I was sure, at the time, it was anything but.

My stomach twisted into a knot of sympathy. Poor Cade. Finding the career he loved — but losing the woman he loved because of it. A sad turn of fate.

"One night, we finally talked it through." His lips twitched. "It took about twenty minutes to realize we were headed down two vastly different roads, and running on an empty tank full of nothing but memories from the good old days. The truth was, I couldn't go back to being the guy she fell for at sixteen — and even if I could, I didn't want to. It was better to let her go, so she could find someone that could make her happy. Better to make the cut before we did each other lasting damage or brought kids into the mix."

"I'm sorry," I whispered, not knowing what else to say.

His eyes had gone distant as he spoke, but they slid back to focus on me. "Don't be. It was for the best. She's happily married now. Has been for almost six years. Hell, I went to the wedding. She sends me pictures of their twins in the mail at Christmas."

I blinked. "Oh."

His grin twitched wider. "Yeah."

"And you?"

"Me?"

"Are you happier now?"

The grin slid away, replaced by a serious expression. There was a look in his eyes I couldn't quite decipher as they moved back and forth across my features. The silence stretched on for so long, I didn't think he was going to answer me. When he finally spoke, it was in a halting whisper.

"I've got just about everything I've ever wanted within reach." His arms tightened around me. "So yeah. I guess you could say I'm pretty fucking happy these days."

The lump was back in my throat, bigger than ever.

Cade, as if sensing I was incapable of speech, decided to

change the subject. "While we're sharing… Can I ask you about something?"

I nodded.

"Earlier, when you were talking about your parents…"

I fought the urge to tense.

"You said you couldn't access the photographs you have of them," he murmured. "What did you mean by that?"

My eyes slid away to study his headboard. My words were barely audible. "It's complicated."

He waited a beat, then guessed, "Your uncle?"

Damn.

He was too astute for his own good. (And certainly too astute for *my* good.)

"He wasn't a nice man." I forced out the words in a torrent, eager to get this over with. "He was very controlling, in all aspects of my life, until I left at fifteen. He wanted me under his thumb financially, physically, emotionally. And he'd use any tools at his disposal to make that happen. Including holding my memories of my dead parents hostage."

Cade's jaw tightened. "Physically?"

Of course he'd fixate on that part. "Cade—"

"He beat you? That fucking bastard *beat* you? The man who was supposed to be your guardian?"

Sometimes.

When I wasn't cooperative.

When I embarrassed him.

When I pushed back.

I didn't tell that to Cade. His expression was like thunder already. I wasn't about to make it worse.

"He mostly just restricted where I went," I said instead. "What I did. Who I saw."

"That's no better."

"Cade—"

"What else did that fucker do to you?"

"That's really all there is to it," I lied, blowing out a breath. "All right? It's not something I want to talk about. Not ever, but especially not tonight, which has been as close to perfect as I can ever remember. Is it too much to ask that we don't ruin it by talking about the man who singlehandedly destroyed my childhood?"

I'd gone tense as I spoke — my jaw locking tight, my hands curling into fists, my head turning away to create as much space as I could manage without physically tearing myself from his arms. Cade's hands were unbearably tender as he turned my face back to his, so I could no longer escape him.

"I doubt very much that's all there is to it, beautiful," he said softly. His gaze was brimming with understanding and sympathy instead of the rage that I'd seen there only moments before. "But since you're here in my arms, and you just admitted you think this night has been perfect, I won't push."

"I said *close* to perfect," I corrected, just to be obstinate.

"Yeah." He was smiling as he kissed me. "I'm choosing to see that as a challenge."

His hands began to move down my body as he deepened the kiss. I was already astride him, but I pressed closer. As close as I could get. My nipples hardened as my bare breasts dragged against his chest. I could feel his cock swelling between us, its length heavy and thick against my stomach. Despite the four orgasms I'd already had tonight, I was suddenly eager for another.

Until his phone started buzzing on the bedside table.

"*Christ*," Cade groaned. "Not now…"

His hands splayed across my naked hips and he moved me sideways, off his body. I made a breathy sound of protest as I hit the mattress. He chuckled, tweaking my hardened nipple playfully.

"Sorry, beautiful. That's my work phone. I'm off duty tonight. It wouldn't be ringing if it weren't an emergency."

I sat up abruptly. "What sort of emergency?"

"Could be anything. Home invasion, carjacking, mugging, DUI..." His brows were pulled into a furrow as his eyes raced across the illuminated phone screen. The look on his face morphed from annoyed to alert.

"Everything okay?"

His eyes cut to mine as he knifed off the bed, taking his phone with him. "I'm going to make a quick call and find out. Don't go anywhere."

With that, he stalked into the bathroom. I shamelessly studied his naked form until it disappeared behind closed doors. If Flo only knew how right she'd been about the quarter-bouncing properties of that firm ass...

I fell back onto the pillows with a content sigh, a dreamy smile drifting across my face.

Not two minutes later, Cade was back. He didn't cross to the bed. He walked straight to his closet and started pulling on clothes. I watched him do it, clutching a sheet to my chest as my heart began to pound and the hair on the back of my neck bean to prickle. He didn't hesitate as he reached for the heavy-duty black lockbox that housed his service weapon.

"I'm guessing everything is not all right."

His sigh was audible as he slid the gun into its holster at his belt. "I have to go to the station. There's a situation. I don't know many of the details yet. Only know it's all hands on deck."

I nodded.

Somehow, he'd utilized his superhuman speed again. He was fully dressed, except for his boots. He crossed to me as his fingers worked at the final button of his shirt.

"Stay here with Socks," he said, swooping down to bring his face to mine. "It'll be a fuck of a lot easier to get through this night knowing you're here in my bed, waiting for me." His lips hit mine — hard, almost bruising. Just the way I liked it. When he pulled back, he added, "*Naked.*"

I laughed, a throaty sound.

"I'll call you if I'm going to be long. Keep the doors locked while I'm gone. I should be back in time to take Socks out in the morning but if for some reason I'm not and he's whining, just bring him into the backyard. There's a spare house key hanging on his leash in the kitchen."

"Okay," I agreed.

He started to pull away, but my hands flew out of their own accord and landed on his shoulders. He stilled in surprise as I launched up at him for a last, lingering lip-brush.

"Stay safe out there, honey," I whispered when I was done.

His eyes flared with heat and something else. Something I didn't fully understand, I just knew it was serious. So serious, I felt it down to my bones.

Down to my freaking soul.

Cade pulled away, turned to the door, and stalked through it. He didn't look back at me. He didn't pause to say goodbye to Socks in the living room. He'd already shifted into detective mode, his shoulders broadening, his strides even, his focus absolute.

I took a deep breath, feeling a strange amount of sympathy for his ex-wife. If this gut-churning worry I was currently experiencing happened every time he walked out that door in the middle of the night, whoever he ended up with for a lifetime was going to have to be one strong woman.

For a minute, delusional as it was…

I wished that woman could be me.

CHAPTER FIFTEEN

I don't have resting bitch face.
My bitch face does not rest. It is ever vigilant.
- Imogen Warner, trying to look approachable

Cade hadn't been gone for more than twenty minutes when I wandered into the kitchen wearing the button-down shirt I'd stripped off his body earlier that night. I was too worked up to sleep. I poured myself a glass of water, drained it dry, then fished my phone out of the depths of my backpack to see if he'd called with an update. He hadn't. But, to my shock, the screen showed more than a dozen other missed calls.

Adrian, I might've expected.

Gigi, however…

That was a surprise.

My pulse kicked into high gear as I hopped up on a stool and dialed her number. It was 10:17PM, according to the clock on the microwave. In my experience, calls that came in after dark were *never* good news. I listened to the phone ring, trying to convince myself I was wrong, that the feeling of foreboding gripping my body was misguided.

Maybe she was three glasses deep in the limoncello. Maybe she wanted the inside scoop about my night with Cade. Maybe she was worried I hadn't come home to The Sea Witch and—

"Imogen!" Her voice cracked over the line, a live current of raw emotion, and I knew instantly that her reasons for calling were anything but casual. "Please, tell me you've seen Rory."

Rory?

"Not since The Gallows this afternoon," I told her. "Why? What's going on?"

"He didn't come home tonight!"

I sucked in a breath. "*What*?"

"He was with Declan and some friends, trick-or-treating. They got separated somehow... By the time Declan realized..." A note of hysteria crept into her voice. "God, Imogen, I'm in a state of panic. I've been looking for him all over, first on foot, now in the car. I've been driving the streets for the past two hours, calling everyone I can think of..."

"What about the adults who were watching the group? I thought you said some of Declan's friends' mothers were going to be with them?"

"They were supposed to be! But they were walking. They couldn't keep up, so they let the boys go ahead by themselves on their bikes." Her laugh was so bitter, I flinched. "I *never* would've let Rory and Declan go with that group if I'd known! God, I should've been there myself! If I hadn't been working..."

"Gigi, you can't beat yourself up."

"Of course I can! Who else am I supposed to blame? *Rory is lost!* There's no sign of him anywhere and I— I— I—"

"Gigi, take a breath. It's going to be okay. We're going to find him." As I said this, I was racing out of the kitchen into Cade's bedroom. I located my jeans in a tangle on the floor and hauled them up my legs with shaky hands. "Have you called the police?"

"Yes, two hours ago! They say they're out looking, but..." The devastation in her words was hard to stomach. She sounded close to defeated. "They want me to come into the station with Declan. But I have to keep looking! I can't stop. Not when he's out there somewhere scared and alone and—"

"Gigi, the police are going to find him." I yanked my blouse over my head. "Cade is going to find him. But they can't help you unless you cooperate with them."

She was silent, except the muffled sound of her sobs. I could hear her directional blinking in the background as she made a turn.

"Georgia."

"What if Donny has him?" The words came out in a fractured whisper. As though she was afraid to say them out loud. "He said it over and over last night — he wanted the boys for Halloween. I didn't let him have them and now— Now, he's taken my boy."

Shit.

Shit, shit, *shit*.

"We don't know that, Georgia," I said, though my own voice sounded not the least bit assuring. "It's possible he's just gotten lost. It's dark out. He might be close by but not sure how to get home."

Gigi wasn't listening to me. She had a one-track mind and that track led straight to her soon-to-be-ex-husband.

"This is Donny's revenge," she said darkly. "He's getting back at me. Punishing me."

"We don't know that," I repeated. "And last I heard, Donny was in lockup."

"His idiot brothers probably bailed him out already!" Her voice broke with hysteria. "I should go to his house. Or The Banshee—"

"No! Don't do that," I said quickly. The more I learned of the O'Banion-owned watering hole, the less I wanted to step foot in the place. If Gigi went off half-cocked, stormed in there demanding answers and tossing accusations...

Let's just say, I doubted Donny — or any of his brothers — would be very receptive.

"But if Rory is there—"

"Please, Gigi. Listen to me." I strove for an even tone. "If Donny really does have Rory, you going in there alone would be giving him exactly what he wants."

She was quiet, contemplating this.

"Where is Declan now?" I asked.

"He's home at The Sea Witch. Rhonda, the night manager, is with him."

"Okay. That's good." I hopped on one foot as I tugged on my socks. "And where are you?"

"I — I don't know. I'm just going in circles. The streets downtown are still so crowded and—" A sob caught in her throat. "If I don't find him—"

"Stop. Don't say that. Don't even think it." Fully dressed, I walked back out to the kitchen. "I'm going to text you Cade's address right now. You're going to come pick me up, and then we're going to decide what to do next. Together."

"But—"

"Honey, you shouldn't be alone right now. You definitely shouldn't be driving around when you're this upset." I sucked in a breath that did nothing to steady me. "I'm going to hang up and text you the address. If you aren't here in ten, I'm calling you back. If you don't answer, I'm hunting you down."

She was quiet for a beat. Her voice was almost childlike when it came again. Shattered. Broken. But she agreed.

"Okay, Imogen. I'll come."

"See you soon, Gigi."

The second the call clicked off, I texted her Cade's address. Then, I grabbed the spare key off the dog leash and shoved it into my backpack. Flipping off the kitchen lights, I crossed through the dark living room — Socks was still sound asleep in his crate, a small miracle — and pulled on my boots in the entryway. I locked the door behind me and sat on Cade's front steps to wait, jittering with nervous energy.

The streets had emptied out a bit, but they were by no means abandoned. While most of the youngsters had been home in bed for hours, there were still plenty of teenagers out causing trouble. Toilet paper streamed from the branches of the neighbor's maple tree. I saw several smashed jack-o-lanterns on the sidewalk across the street, their orange guts splattered all over the pavement. Two lanky boys about Declan's age pedaled by on mountain bikes, their costumes covered in a thick layer of what looked like shaving cream. The sharp wail of a firecracker split the sky like a scream.

Finally, a pair of headlights turned down the street. By the time they came to a stop in front of Cade's house, I was already halfway down the walk. I flew to the driver's side door and practically yanked Georgia out from behind the wheel. Before she could say a word, I pulled her into a hug.

She dissolved instantly in my embrace, sobbing against my shoulder like her world had come to an end.

I supposed it had.

"I c-c-can't," she hiccupped. "—believe this is h-h-happening."

"We're going to find him," I told her fiercely, stroking her hair. "I'm sure he's just wandered off. He'll be back home before you know it."

But the truth was, I wasn't sure.

I wasn't sure at all.

I drove Georgia's sporty hatchback station wagon, as she was in no fit state to be behind the wheel. First to The Sea Witch, where we collected a shellshocked Declan from the care of Rhonda, the dour-faced night manager. Then, to the Salem Police Department.

I'd never been to this particular station before, but I'd been in plenty of others in the past. It was a pretty brick building near the center of town, no more than a few minutes' walk from The Gallows. Twin spotlights lit up the flagpole out front, along with the large round SPD seal — the city's trademark flying witch — emblazoned proudly on the brick.

Despite the late hour, the station was a hub of activity. Uniformed officers were pouring through the tall glass doors into the dark parking lot, moving quickly to reach their cruisers, heads tilted to listen to radio chatter. I wondered if they were headed out to look for Rory.

I hoped to god they were.

I parked in a spot directly in front of the flag pole. Gigi was out of the car the second I shifted into park. She practically sprinted into the station, too distraught to remember she wasn't alone. I wasn't surprised — she was in another world, at the moment. She'd barely said two words to me on the drive. She'd kept her face pressed to the passenger window, staring out at the people on the sidewalks as we passed.

Now that the trick-or-treating was over, the city was shifting into the darker side of Halloween. One designed for adults, not kids. At its core, Salem was a college town. Plenty of twenty-somethings in scanty fishnets and clingy corsets were stalking the streets, looking for a spooky good time. The entry lines to every local bar were wrapped down the block, already at capacity. And the night was young.

The thought of Rory somehow lost in their midst…

A shiver moved through me.

I grabbed Declan's hand, squeezing tight as I led him inside. He squeezed back, but said nothing. He was normally such a chatterbox. Seeing him like this — so solemn, so shaken — made my stomach twist.

The room was surprisingly full. Several seats along the side wall were occupied by people in costumes, waiting to speak to the receptionist about issues unknown. All of them looked decidedly peeved their fun Halloween plans were ending in a fluorescent lit precinct.

Georgia didn't take a seat to wait her turn. She marched straight across the drab concrete floor, planted herself in front of the reception desk, and stared at the woman sitting behind the plexiglass partition until she stopped clacking away on her keyboard.

"There's a line," the secretary informed her, looking beleaguered. "Please wait your turn, ma'am."

Georgia didn't move an inch. Her hands gripped the edge of the desk so hard, her knuckles were white. "I'm Georgia O'Banion. I called earlier. My son— My Rory— He's missing. I was out searching, but they told me to come in."

The receptionist went pale and reached immediately for her phone. "Of course. Just a moment, Mrs. O'Banion."

"I don't *have* a moment." Gigi's voice cracked. "My boy is out there. I need to speak to someone *now*—"

"You can talk to me."

The man's voice cut cleanly through the chaotic air. We all turned toward him at once — me, Gigi, Declan, the receptionist, even some of the seated strangers — moving like marionettes on a single string.

Cade.

It had been less than an hour since I saw him last, but my stomach performed a series of enthusiastic back handsprings as soon as he came into view. His tall frame filled the mouth of the hallway that led deeper into the station. His eyes hit me and flashed in dangerous way that told me his own stomach was not in the throes of a gymnastics routine.

Oh, boy.

He was pissed.

His jaw tightened, a muscle jumping in his cheek, but he locked it down almost instantly. By the time his focus shifted to Gigi, he was the picture of calm, cool, composure.

"Georgia," he said, tone grave.

"Detective Hightower," Georgia whispered. "I— I—"

"Come on into the back with me, will you?" His voice was a carefully controlled contrast to Gigi's fragmented disquiet. He glanced at Declan as he approached. "You'll come too, Declan. We'll talk things through."

"I should be out there." Gigi swallowed visibly. There were tears shimmering in her eyes. "I need to—"

"You're right where you're meant to be, Georgia," Cade assured her. "It's good you came in. The more information you can give me, the better our chances at bringing Rory home safe and sound, as soon as possible."

She gave an uncertain nod. Without further protest, she allowed him to steer her toward the back hallway. Cade hadn't technically invited me to tag along, but Declan grabbed my hand for support and I wasn't about to tear it away. Together, we walked out of the waiting room.

Up ahead, Cade was speaking to Gigi in low, soothing tones. She was nodding at whatever he said, but didn't appear to be responding. We passed several doors, including two glass-walled holding cells where several people — again, in costume — were being detained under lock and key.

In the women's cell, a girl dressed as Dorothy from *The Wizard of Oz* was snoring lightly on one of the stainless-steel benches, drool dribbling from the corner of her mouth, while a pissed-off Raggedy Ann glared daggers at her from her position against the cinderblock wall. Teenagers, most likely, waiting to be bailed out by their parents for underage drinking or general debauchery.

They had an older barfly for company, with limp blonde hair, a cheetah-print bra that showed through her shirt, smudged lipstick, and raccoon eyes from her runny mascara. Unlike the teens, she was not in costume. (Not unless she was going as Charlize Theron in *Monster*.)

I was too busy shielding Declan's eyes from things best unseen (*i.e.* animal print undergarments) to pay any real attention to the cast of characters contained on the men's side.

Beyond the holding cells, there was a dingy kitchenette followed by a space filled with lockers and workout equipment that smelled vaguely like old socks. A handful of doors led into cluttered, closet-sized offices — most of which looked dark and empty. We passed them by without pause. At the very end of the hall, there was an interrogation-style room complete with a two-way mirror wall and chairs bolted straight into the concrete floor. I'd been in rooms just like that and had no desire to recreate the experience, thank you very much.

Cade turned down another corridor, through a locked door he used his badge to access, then to a stairwell. We climbed in silence to the second floor. This level was all one open space, with six L-shaped desks scattered across the carpeted floor, stacked high with manila folders and large computer monitors. Filing cabinets lined the walls, along with several giant windows that overlooked the parking lot below.

A classic bullpen.

That's what they called it on *Law & Order: SVU*, anyway. I half expected to see Benson and Stabler sitting at the desks, simultaneously solving crime and exchanging sexually charged looks. Alas, the only people we saw were two middle-aged cops, one a white male with a slight paunch, the other a Latina female with her dark hair pulled back in a severe bun. They were both on their phones, but disconnected when they saw Cade lead us through the doors.

"This is Chief Ted Coulter and Detective Lucia Aguilar." Cade pointed from the man to the woman as they approached, then turned back to Gigi. "And this is Georgia O'Banion, her son, Declan, and—" His unhappy blue eyes cut to me "—a friend of the family."

Both offered Georgia their hands in greeting, then nodded at me. Declan still had my hand in a death-grip. Any tighter and my bones were going to be pulverized to dust inside my glove.

"Hey there, Declan," Chief Coulter said, stooping down to snag the boy's gaze. (He didn't have to stoop far; he was extremely short-statured.) His eyes were kind, but Declan's hand still spasmed nervously around mine. "You want something to drink? A soda? A glass of water?"

Declan shook his head.

"How about you, Georgia?" Coulter asked. "Water? Coffee? Soda?"

"Coffee would be good," Gigi said. Her voice was so weak, it was barely audible. Her face was pale as a ghost. I knew, even though she was here in the room, her mind was out there on the dark streets of Salem.

"Okay. Coffee, coming right up." Coulter looked at Cade. "Conference room?"

Cade nodded, then steered Georgia toward the female detective with a hand at the small of her back. "Detective Aguilar is going to bring you and Declan into the conference room to start going over everything that happened tonight. I'll be in shortly to help explain what our next steps are."

Gigi went with Aguilar without a word, docile as a lamb. She had no fight left in her, but I knew she'd find it again soon. She was strong. She'd get through this.

For Rory.

My eyes dropped down to Declan's. He was looking worriedly after his mother. I squeezed his hand. "It's going to be okay, Dec."

His eyes flickered up to mine. The emotion in them was so stark, so hopeless, I nearly burst into tears.

"No," he whispered, breath hitching with a suppressed sob. "It's not."

Then, he dropped my hand and followed his mom to the conference room. I stared after them, feeling like I'd been socked in the stomach. I'd had no time to recover when Cade materialized in front of me. His expression was darker than a storm cloud.

"We need to talk," he clipped. "*Now*."

I swallowed hard.

This did not bode well for me.

His hand landed on my hip and he corralled me in the opposite direction. I didn't resist, though all my internal alarm bells were warning me to run for the hills. The last time I'd stepped foot in a police station…

This isn't like last time, I told myself. *This isn't Baltimore.*

My heart was a cavalry charge in my chest. The blood was roaring between my ears. I took shallow breaths, trying to stay calm as he led me through a set of doors, into a dark room. When he flipped on the overhead fluorescents, I saw it was full of filing cabinets, a copy machine, recycling bins, an industrial shredder, and other random office supplies.

The door closed with an ominous click.

I turned to see Cade leaned back against it, effectively blocking me from any misguided attempts at escape. His expression was somehow even stormier than before. So much so, it took all my effort not to shy away.

"You want to explain what the fuck you're doing here?"

The breath halted in my lungs. "Excuse me?"

"You heard me, Imogen. What are you doing here?" His eyes flashed with fury. "You're supposed to be home in bed, where I left you. Safe. Not putting yourself smack in the center of harm's way again, hitching your wagon to one that's headed over a cliff."

My mouth dropped open.

"Christ!" He cursed, running a hand through his hair. "How did you even know about this shit?"

"Gigi called me," I said, trying very hard to remain calm. Irritation was sparking to life inside me, quickly overtaking anxiety and apprehension as my primary emotion. "She was out looking for Rory, driving around. I texted her your address, she picked me up, and I convinced her to come in."

His eyes were working with thoughts — none of which he volunteered.

"What is this about, Cade? I figured you'd be happy I got her to come here, seeing as her alternate plan was storming into The Banshee."

"Her being here is not what I have a problem with."

"But you don't want *me* here." I shook my head, equal parts pissed and confused. "Why?"

He didn't answer. His head tipped down to study his boots and he took a deep breath that made his whole chest broaden.

"Cade—"

He cut me off. "You've known this woman four days."

"What does that have to do with anything?"

"She is not your friend."

It took all my resolve not to flinch. "What?"

"There is no reason for you to be here, getting involved."

"No reason?" I snapped, my handle on my anger slipping. "How can you say that?"

He didn't waver. "You are not involved in this, Imogen."

"I am," I countered.

"Then uninvolve yourself."

"It's too late for that!" I yelled.

"God fucking *damnit*!" he yelled right back at me. "I don't want you anywhere near this. Don't you understand that?"

My mouth shut with a surprised click.

"The way cases like this typically turn out—" His jaw tightened, locking down the rest of his words.

And I suddenly realized where all his anger was coming from.

Cade was afraid.

Afraid this case was going to end badly.

Afraid Rory wasn't coming home.

And he didn't want me anywhere near the fallout of that if it happened.

"Cade..."

"I can't protect you if this goes sideways," he said without looking at me. His voice was tight. "And I can't do my job effectively if I'm not thinking clearly."

"But—"

He finally looked back at me. His eyes were burning. "A seven-year-old kid is out there, lost, scared, likely in the hands of someone he shouldn't have ever crossed paths with. These first forty-eight hours are critical if he's even got a chance in hell at coming home."

"I understand that," I told him. "But—"

"I need my head clear."

I stared at him. "Okay."

"When you're near me, my head isn't clear, Imogen." He swallowed, the apple of his throat bobbing harshly. "When I'm thinking about you, I'm not thinking about all the shit I need to be thinking about tonight."

"I'm not trying to distract you!"

"You don't have to try."

I wasn't sure whether that was an insult or a compliment. We faced off for a few long moments, until the air of the copy room was brimming with so much tension, I could hardly breathe around it.

Eventually, Cade's expression softened. As did his tone when he murmured, "Come here, Imogen."

Since he seemed — marginally — calmer, I did as he said. As soon as I was within arm's reach, his hand shot out, tagged me around the back of the neck, and he hauled me against his chest. I did my best to keep stiff as his arms closed around me. He was breathing harder than usual. His mouth hit my temple, and he pressed a kiss to it.

"I'm sorry for yelling," he whispered.

I just shrugged. Or, half-shrugged. It was difficult to pull off a full shrug with my body plastered so tight against Cade's.

"None of this is your fault," he continued. "Not right for me to take it out on you."

His lips were in my hair, which felt deliciously good. It took all my strength to keep my posture rigid.

"Still, I can't help wishing, that first night, I'd brought you somewhere besides The Sea Witch. Then you wouldn't have met Georgia. You wouldn't be tangled up in this nightmare."

His logic was flawed, but I understood his intentions were pure. That made the last of my resolve melt away. I allowed my body to go pliant in his arms, then craned my neck to look up at him.

"Cade."

His brows went up.

"You're going to find him," I told him, lifting up onto my tiptoes to meet his gaze head-on. He was so tall, we still weren't quite face to face as I slid my arms around his neck. "I have faith in you, honey."

A warm, beautiful light hit his eyes, but his voice was still solemn. "We've got every available officer out looking for him, canvasing the streets. If we can get some more specifics out of Declan, we can retrace their exact route."

"Georgia is convinced Donny took him."

Cade shook his head. "Donny is in lockup in the next county. He'll be there a while. Turns out, he had an open warrant for failure to appear on a destruction of property charge."

That was a relief. "Oh. That's good news."

Cade didn't seem to agree. There was a dark furrow between his brows and that warm light vanished from his eyes.

"What?" I asked. "What is it?"

He hesitated a beat before he shared. "Most times, when kids go missing, it's just what Georgia assumed. Custody issue. One parent goes off half-cocked, decides to take the kid without permission, chaos ensues. When it's not the parent…" The furrow deepened. "Opens up a whole other realm of possibilities. We're already sending uniforms to knock on the doors of known offenders, ensure a sexual predator didn't snatch and grab."

I swallowed hard.

"Tonight isn't just any night," Cade continued. "Halloween. Fuck, the freaks are out in force in every town across America. That's especially true here in Salem. We've got just shy of a million visitors in the city this weekend. And they've come from all over the country. Some of them international. That means we aren't just looking at a local pool of suspects. If someone from out of state shoved Rory into a car trunk, he could be anywhere by daybreak. Anywhere."

Fear sluiced through me. "Oh my god."

"Imogen, I'm telling you this. *You*. Not Georgia. You understand me?"

I nodded. "Yes."

"Won't do her any good to hear this shit." He exhaled sharply. "She needs to focus on the things in her control. Let us do the rest."

"How can I help her?"

His eyes scanned my face. "You're not going to sit on the sidelines for this, are you? Even if I ask?"

"Not even if you beg, detective."

He sighed. His hands slid down my back to rest just above the curve of my ass. "Aguilar is going over everything with Georgia now, gathering all the information we need. Mainly, what he was wearing tonight along with any distinguishing scars, birthmarks... People or places he might've gone to if he was lost and couldn't get home. We already have a BOLO with his basic physical description out to every officer on the streets."

"BOLO?"

"Be On The Lookout," he clarified. "We'll be sending out an AMBER Alert statewide in a few minutes so the general public can look for him as well. We'll get a designated line set up, so people can call in with tips."

"That's good."

"Standard protocol," he said. "One stroke of luck is, we already have a shit ton of support staff from neighboring counties on deck this weekend. We knew we'd need them, with so many out-of-towners here. We'll call in more if he's not home by morning, plus local volunteers. Search parties take a hell of a lot of manpower. I've also got a call in to the Feds for additional support. We'll need them if this crosses state lines."

"Feds? As in… FBI?"

He nodded. "The Boston field office is sending an agent. It's going to be all hands on deck around here. I've reached out to Gravewatch, as well. They're the best in the business when it comes to monitoring surveillance and chasing clues. Plus, they can move in spaces I can't while wearing a badge. Knock down doors I'd need a warrant to even glance at. Question suspects with methods they don't teach in the academy."

I felt my face pale. "That's what Graham does for a living?"

"Graham does all sorts of things," he said, not quite answering my question. "Each of his boys has a different area of expertise, so to speak. Keir is a fucking ghost, can blend in any scenario and track a lead colder than Siberia. Makes him a lethal asset when it comes to chasing bond-skips. Welles is skilled in intel extraction. Sawyer is an ace at surveillance — wiring it, monitoring it, you name it."

"And the twins?"

"Far as I can tell, Holden and Hunter are good at just about everything."

I could feel my eyes bugging out of my head at this bevy of information. I managed — with brute force — to shove my rampant curiosity back down. There were far more pressing matters at hand than the men of Gravewatch and their myriad talents.

Cade's eyes slid back to my face. "Not sure when I'll see you next. Not sure when I'll be able to get home to Socks, either."

"I can go back to your place once Gigi is done here to check in on him. And, um, to feed him. And make sure he gets a morning walk." My cheeks flamed more and more as the words tumbled out. "Unless you have someone else you want to call. I know you have help..."

In fact, I'd met his neighborhood dog-walker, Jamie, only hours before when she came to the door with her kids to trick-or-treat. She watched Socks whenever he pulled a double shift.

Shit.

What was I thinking?

He didn't need me.

I swallowed hard. "Forget it, I wasn't thinking—"

"Imogen."

"Y-yes?"

"Keep thinking like you're thinking, beautiful." His forehead hit mine. His voice went low. "I like that you want to check in on my puppy. He'll like it too — way more than Jamie. I promise."

My cheeks were probably beet red, by this point. "Are you sure?"

"Yeah, I'm sure. We Hightower men — big fans of Imogen Warner."

Fuck, that was nice.

"Oh. Okay," I said like it was no big deal, even though my stomach was doing double back handsprings. "No problem. I can check on him. Whatever."

Cade grinned, totally seeing through my attempt at nonchalance. "Glad to hear it, Goldie."

"I hope you don't mind I... um... borrowed the key on his leash when I left."

"Why would I mind? I'm the one who told you to take the key."

"Right, if I took the dog out to pee," I said. "Not for—"

His brows went up. "Not for what?"

"I just didn't want you to think I was confiscating it or something."

A glimmer of humor moved through his face. "Fuck, you're cute."

Cute?

Cute?!

"I am not!"

"You are."

I narrowed my eyes at him. "Don't you need to be out canvassing the streets and flashing your badge at nefarious individuals?"

"Yeah." His lips were twitching as he leaned down and laid a kiss on mine. It didn't last very long, but I felt it in every corner of my body. When he was done, he pulled back a hairsbreadth — only far enough to whisper, "I'll call you when I can."

"Okay," I whispered back. "Bring Rory home, honey."

He didn't say anything else.

But I could see from the flare of determination in his eyes that he was going to do everything in his power to do precisely that.

CHAPTER SIXTEEN

Instead of saying "God bless you!" when someone sneezes, try a nondenominational phrase. (Such as "Ew!" or "Gross!" or "Stop that!")
- Imogen Warner, equally disgusted by everyone's germs

Flo's leg was jittering so hard, it was shaking the coffee table between us. Given that I'd consumed enough coffee in the past twenty-four hours to legally change my name to Arabica, I was feeling rather jittery myself. I was running on zero sleep — and even less hope.

It had been almost a full day since Rory went missing.

He was *still* missing.

After we left the police station last night, Gigi and I had dropped Declan back at The Sea Witch to get some sleep under the watchful gaze of Rhonda, then headed straight back out. While Detective Aguilar had strongly suggested she leave the investigation up to the professionals, Georgia was incapable of sitting on her hands while her little boy was lost. She was determined to keep looking — and I wasn't about to let her do it alone.

We'd spent the night searching what felt like every street in Salem. Sometimes in the hatchback, sometimes on foot. We checked all the spots we could think of — the playground behind his elementary school, his favorite bench on the Common, the skate park up at Gallows Hill. We even drove out to Salem Willows, the seasonal amusement park where Gigi took the kids for arcade games and ice cream in the summer months, and searched every empty gazebo along the beach.

No sign of him anywhere.

When the sun began to creep over the horizon, I'd finally convinced her to take a break. If not for her own sake then for poor Socks, who was likely wondering where his human had gone and why his morning kibble was so unfairly delayed. He'd attacked me with slobbery kisses the second we stepped through Cade's front door. When he did the same to Georgia, I actually saw the specter of a smile on her face for the first time in hours.

She'd camped out at the kitchen island to call Detective Aguilar for an update while I saw to Socks' needs — filling his breakfast bowl, then bringing him out into the backyard for a pee so long, I was positive it broke at least one Guinness World Record.

When I'd walked back into the room, Gigi was on the phone with Gwen. I wasn't sure what that conversation entailed, but ten minutes later we were back in the hatchback, headed for The Gallows.

For the record, by "*we*" I was referring to myself, Gigi, and Socks. It hadn't felt right to leave him all alone in his crate for the day. There was no telling when Cade would be free to check in on him and, besides, I didn't have a car to come back if Gigi and I separated. I'd left a note on the counter that would (hopefully) absolve me of any dognapping charges, loaded him into the back seat, and cracked a window so he could drool into the wind.

When we'd arrived at The Gallows, the brick pedestrian mall was eerily quiet compared to the hullabaloo of the past few days.

Probably due to the ungodly early hour. Most of the shops weren't yet open. The only people out and about were street sweepers and delivery truck drivers, who parked in the shop alleys to unload their inventory, their hazard lights blinking in the dim dawn light.

Gwen had yanked open the door before we had a chance to reach for the knob. She'd pulled us both inside, then pulled Gigi into a fierce hug. Florence was there too, providing caffeinated beverages and pithy commentary as we all settled in around the coffee table by the front window. Our "war room" so to speak. From there, we'd set about organizing our search efforts.

It wasn't that we didn't trust Salem PD, Gravewatch, or the FBI. But we, like Gigi, felt far too useless simply sitting around doing nothing but wait for word. Besides, Rory's disappearance was personal for Florence, as well. She was not only Georgia's friend, she was Rory's second grade teacher. She'd taught Declan, too, four years prior. She loved both boys like her own and was quick to declare her commitment to helping in any way she could.

For Gwen, the stakes may not have been quite so personal, but she still wanted to help. Because Gwendolyn Goode cared about people. She would've helped even if Rory was a stranger on the street. The more I got to know her, the more I saw how right Graham had been that first day, when he accused her of making everyone she met into her best friend. She had a habit of drawing people close, then keeping them there. It was a great quality — one I was not ashamed to admit I envied.

In another life, I would've liked to be a lot more like Gwendolyn Goode.

Upon our arrival, Gwen immediately tacked up a sign on the front door — "CLOSED TODAY FOR A FAMILY EMERGENCY" — which I thought was likely to start a riot amongst the latte-deprived hipsters. Even if they threatened to beat down the doors of The Gallows, we had far more important matters to contend with today. They'd just have to survive on Starbucks temporarily.

Oh, the horror!

At the detectives' instruction, Gigi had made an exhaustive list of every person she'd ever met since moving to Massachusetts a decade and a half ago. (This amounted to approximately half the population of planet earth, by my estimate.) After divvying up the names, we set about calling all of them. One by one, we worked our way through the list, alerting acquaintances old and new to be on the lookout for Rory, providing the details for the search party we were organizing, and sharing the designated tip-line the police had set up for anyone with information. Even with four of us chattering into our cellphones simultaneously in different corners of The Gallows, it took all morning to reach the last name on the list.

From my spot by the window display, I watched the streets slowly fill with people. By noon, the crowds were nearly as thick as yesterday. They didn't seem to care that the 31st had come and gone, that Halloween was technically over. The costumed revelry continued regardless, a constant stream of people smiling and laughing and snapping photos.

It was an oddly festive backdrop to our frantic search efforts.

Around one, Flo slipped out to buy sandwiches from the cafe next door, which we fell on like ravenous hyenas on the hunt. I ate so fast, I barely tasted my turkey and cheese. Meanwhile, Gigi picked at hers, unable to take more than a few bites. Florence, Gwen, and I traded worried glances, but said nothing.

What could we say?

If my child was missing, I wouldn't have an appetite, either.

We were all worried about her. There were bags under her eyes and despair in their light brown depths. The fact that she wasn't curled in the fetal position crying her eyes out was, in my humble opinion, a mark of unbelievable fortitude. But she never allowed herself to fall apart. Not even when she left us mid-afternoon to head back to the station for another 'debrief' with Detective Aguilar.

If they were calling her in for more questions…

They still hadn't found him.

Not the news we were all hoping for, obviously.

With the war room down to three — four, including Socks, who spent most of his day alternately chewing the elk antler Gwen found for him in one of her display cases and snoozing on one of her elegant wingback armchairs — we carried on. Gwen took it upon herself to design a missing flyer on her laptop. Flo set about posting it online, blanketing social media with Rory's picture and information, while I braved the crowds to visit the copy shop down the block. I had the clerk print two hundred copies. When I'd tried to pay, he waved me off.

"Least I can do for the kid," he said gruffly, shooing me out the door. "We locals have to stick together."

Sometimes, humans were surprisingly decent.

We divided the posters into thirds and each took off in different directions, plastering them on every streetlamp, electrical pole, and community board we came across, until the whole downtown area was covered.

Socks came with me. For a puppy, he was remarkably well trained. He didn't pull at the leash — a blessing, given how strong he was — or knock down any of the small children who ran up to him screaming "*DOGGIE!*" at the top of their little kid lungs. He didn't bark at the woman dressed like Cruella de Vil. (And, given her proclivities for fur, if *anyone* deserved to be barked at, it was her.) He did, however, take the largest doo-doo known to man in the middle of the Common, which earned me several dirty looks from the LARPers who were preparing do to battle on that same stretch of lawn.

You win some, you lose some.

By the time me, Florence, and Gwen reconvened back at The Gallows, it was nearly dinner time and we were all so exhausted, we could barely move. Except for Flo's foot, which kept up its jittering until Gwen kicked it clear off the coffee table.

"Hey!" Flo cried. "What was that for?"

"You're scuffing up my furniture."

"I thought you like that lived-in look, Gwennie."

"*So* not the point, Florence."

Flo rolled her eyes.

"I hope the flyers work," I interjected, before their squabble escalated. "At least they'll get Rory's face out there, maybe spark a memory in someone who saw him last night..."

Flo nodded. "Local news is covering it, too. Did you see all those satellite trucks? There must've been a hundred of them near the police station."

"Probably hoping for a glimpse at Gigi, the vultures," I said scathingly. It must be said, I was not a fan of the media circus that surrounded cases like this. Reporters always seemed to care more about their ratings than the families who were being ripped apart.

"Do you think we'll hear something soon?" Gwen was wringing her hands. "I'm going crazy not knowing anything. I tried calling Graham, pestering him for information, but the man is like a fortress." Her eyes lit up as they shifted to me. "Oh! You could call Cade! See if you can get the inside scoop."

"Yeah, you've got pull," Florence chimed in. "Call him!"

"I'm not calling Cade. He needs to focus on the case." I chewed my lip. "Besides, I'm not sure I have any real—" My fingers lifted to do air-quotes. "*Pull.*"

Flo and Gwen looked at one another.

"Isn't that his dog sleeping on your feet?" Flo asked.

"Uh..." I glanced down at Socks. He was, indeed, snoring on my boots.

"And isn't that the same outfit you were wearing yesterday when you left here for your date night at the detective's place?"

"Uh..." I squirmed in my day-old clothes. "Yeah."

Both of them snorted.

"Okay. Fine. I might have *some* pull. But I'm not planning to use it," I said decidedly, leaning back against the green velvet sofa.

"When there's news, someone will call. We just have to be patient."

"I'm not so good at patient," Gwen admitted.

"No kidding," Flo muttered. "All hail the queen of instant gratification."

Gwen shot her an annoyed look, then glanced back to me. "Back to brighter subjects! By which I mean your walk-of-shame clothes. I'm guessing they are indicative of a successful first date?"

A blush immediately hit my cheeks. "Um..."

"We're waiting," Gwen prompted.

"We were promised details." Flo reminded me. "It's time you deliver. *Pronto*."

I blinked at them, somewhat startled by their interest. I didn't have any girlfriends. This was uncharted territory. Swallowing nervously, I asked, "What do you want to know?

"Everything," they chorused in unison.

Shit.

"Well... I passed out candy and played with Socks. Cade made dinner. It was fine."

"Fine?" Flo exclaimed. "Just *fine*?"

I contemplated lying for a moment, then decided I was too mentally exhausted to formulate a fib convincing enough to deceive them.

"Actually, it wasn't fine. It was pretty fucking fantastic, if you want to know the truth," I spilled before I lost my nerve. "He's a good cook. He's funny. He's kind. He doesn't just pretend to listen while I'm talking — he *actually* listens, then asks follow up questions. He shares his own stuff freely, too, about his family and his interests. Did you know he rides a motorcycle?"

"Really?" Gwen's voice went a little breathy.

"Yep. In his garage. It's shiny and black." My own voice went a little breathy. "He promised to take me for a ride."

"I'll bet he did," Flo murmured with a wink.

Ignoring her, I carried on. "He knows his neighbors by name, even though he only moved in a few months ago. He thinks spending time with his puppy is worth prioritizing over home improvement projects. He wants to fix up his house himself, with his own hands." I shrugged my shoulders. "He's like some kind of fictional man I'd read about in a romance novel. Except he's *real*. And he is officially *freaking me out*."

They both beamed at me.

I finally took a breath. I hadn't meant to say even half of that aloud, but it poured out in a torrent. Part of me wanted to snatch back the words and run from the room screaming; the other part was being overtaken by that ever-increasing warm, fuzzy feeling that spread through my chest cavity, then out to all my extremities.

Gwen giggled lightly. "You are so *not* leaving town, girlfriend."

I blinked at her. "Excuse me?"

"You're not leaving."

"Actually, I am," I countered.

"Uh huh." Her grin was huge. "Sure you are."

"I wasn't even supposed to be here in the first place!"

"So? Screw *supposed to*. You're here," Florence cut in. "You might as well stay. Especially now that you have a hot, protective as hell, motorcycle-riding, gun-toting, silver fox detective who looks at you like you're a tropical oasis and he's been wandering the desert for six straight days without water."

I narrowed my eyes at her. "You can't survive six days without water."

"Not really the point I was hoping you'd take away from that speech."

Gwen giggled again.

"You don't understand," I told them, crossing my arms over my chest. "The second I rolled into this weird little town, Cade Hightower took it upon himself to mess up all my plans! Without even asking!"

"Seeing as your plans involve fleeing Salem, ne'er to return, that's fine by me." Florence shrugged. "I say mess away, Detective Hightower. *Mess away.*"

"I second that," Gwen said. "For the record."

"Listen—" I started, but was cut off by Flo.

"You know, as happy as I am to hear you think Hightower is so dreamy, can we get to the good stuff already?" She pressed her palms together, then slowly started pulling them apart. "Yell when I reach an accurate size representation."

My eyes sought the ceiling for divine intervention.

None arrived.

Damn and blast.

"Ignore her, Imogen," Gwen suggested, amusement thick in her voice.

"Fine! Keep the mystery all to yourself!" Florence dropped her hands back to her lap with a scowl. "At least confirm that his ass is as magnificent out of those jeans as it looks in them."

My lips tipped up in a small smile. "Well, I didn't have a stack of quarters on hand to test your theory but..."

Flo sucked in a breath, waiting.

"I can confirm, the detective's ass did not disappoint," I finished. "And he's a good cook, but... his skills in the kitchen pale in comparison to those in the bedroom. That's all I'm saying on the subject. Unless you plan to waterboard me, drop it."

Gwen grinned.

Flo sighed. "Fair enough."

"Anyway," I said pointedly changing the topic. "How was your naked moonlight dancing adventure with Agatha and Sally?"

"Surprisingly awesome," Gwen cut in. "You'd never know it to look at them, but the Bay Colony ladies can *party*. Canes and all."

"I'm joining the coven," Florence confided.

"You can't join the coven, Flo." Gwen rolled her eyes. "You aren't a Wiccan."

"Honorary member, then. I need to get me one of those spiffy velvet robes. You know, you should really start stocking those here at the store, Gwennie. They were cool as hell."

"Agreed."

"How does one join a coven, exactly?" I asked.

"Not sure. I'll keep you posted if I succeed." Flo stood up suddenly, crossing toward the espresso bar. "Anyone else need a coffee? My jitters are wearing off, which means it's officially time for another macchiato."

Gwen shook her head. "None for me."

"My bloodstream is already 95% caffeine," I said.

"So… that's a yes on the latte, then?"

I laughed. "What the hell, let's make it 98%. I'll need it if I'm going to last the next few hours while we wait for news."

The metallic clang of a portafilter against the counter was Flo's only reply.

"I just hate this," Gwen muttered. Her delicate red brows were pulled into a glower. "Sitting around uselessly…"

"Me too."

"There must be something else we could be doing."

"We've done everything we could think of — putting up flyers, calling all Georgia's friends and family, getting the word out on social media." I shrugged. "I'm not sure what else we can do."

Liar, a voice whispered in the back of my head. *There's one other thing you could do. You just don't want to do it…*

I tried to push the voice away, along with the surge of guilt it inspired. I didn't quite succeed. Probably because… well, the voice wasn't wrong. I *could* try to trigger a vision. But even if I made the attempt, there was no guarantee I'd be successful. There was even less of a guarantee I'd learn anything useful.

Even if there's an infinitesimal chance, it's worth a try, the voice derided me. *This is Rory we're talking about…*

I sank my teeth into my bottom lip, wishing the voice would shut the hell up. I wanted to bring Rory home. Of course I did.

Just like I'd wanted to bring little Joey Crawford home, when I walked into that Baltimore precinct with the best of intentions.

In the end, he'd come home in a body bag.

Six years had done nothing to numb the pain of that experience. I was excruciatingly aware of how wrong things could go when working with the police. The plain fact was, I didn't know whether I'd be helping or harming the investigation by getting involved. I didn't trust my own instincts when it came to my powers. They were unpredictable at best, unnerving at worst. Pretending they were the answer to all our prayers for Rory's safe return wouldn't do anyone any good.

Least of all me.

It would only lead to disappointment, blame, and, ultimately, the same ostracizing attitude that drove me out of the state of Maryland as fast as the bus could carry me.

Better to let the authorities handle it this time.

I'd learned my lesson.

Coward, the voice whispered.

"Imogen?" A voice cut into my conflicted thoughts. "Are you okay?"

My head snapped up. Gwen and Florence were both staring at me with identical looks of concern. Flo was holding two steaming coffee cups. I hadn't even heard her return.

"Sure, I'm fine." I smiled weakly. "Just tired. I could use a nap."

"And a shower," Flo added, eyeing my mussed hair. "No offense."

Gwen snorted.

"Give me a break if I'm not daisy-fresh," I grumbled, irritated. I knew I looked a fright even without her pointing it out. "Not all of us got eight hours of beauty sleep last night, Flo."

"Too busy with all the sex?"

"Too busy searching the streets for Rory," I corrected. Then, with a sigh, admitted, "And all the sex."

Flo smirked and passed me my latte.

Gwen's eyes had gone distant with thought. "Maybe I should design a website for Rory. A central page with his picture, information for volunteers, all the important phone numbers to contact…"

"That's not a bad idea," I told her, sipping my latte. (And scalding my tongue in the process.)

"Since when are you so tech-savvy?" Flo asked, skeptical.

"Since I successfully launched The Gallows' online store!" Gwen sounded rather proud of herself. "Gather round, girlfriends. I'll show you."

She bent forward, swiped her laptop off the coffee table, and cracked it open. Flo came around to our side, and we all squeezed in on the couch as Gwen pulled up her new website. It wasn't a technological marvel by any means, but it certainly served its purpose. The landing page was all black, featuring a spooky font that declared ***THE GALLOWS*** in large lettering. Like the sign out front, the 'o' was in the shape of a noose. Beneath it, a subheading read:

OCCULT TEXTS, ANCIENT RELICS, MYSTICAL CURIOSITIES, AND PSYCHIC READINGS

Beneath that, in even smaller font:

Now serving coffee!

There were several photographs of the shop, both interior and exterior. Her hours were listed in the top right corner, along with the shop's phone number. There was a (currently nonfunctional) tab for online ordering.

"I haven't had a chance to upload our inventory yet," Gwen muttered, dragging her cursor around the page with the trackpad. "But eventually people will be able to add items to their cart, purchase with a few simple clicks, and *voilà*! We'll ship them out the next business day. I think it'll give us a huge spike in sales!"

"Do you really need a sales spike?" I asked wryly. "Based on the past two days working here, you can barely keep up with the current demand. I'm surprised you're eager to add more."

Gwen waved away my concerns. "This is high season. Halloween is the busiest weekend of the year. In two days, when all the tourists go back home, you'll see what the city is actually like most of the time. Granted, we still do a fair amount of business... but nothing like your first few shifts. It can actually get a bit boring sometimes."

Boring would be a welcome change of pace.

"I think it's fab, Gwennie." Florence sipped her latte. "First stop, online orders. Next stop, world domination."

"Wait! I forgot to show you the best part." Gwen grinned excitedly as she navigated to the header bar and clicked the ***ABOUT US*** tab. A new page popped up, the top half of which was dominated by a large headshot of Gwen. She was smiling directly at the camera, head tilted slightly to one side, eyes twinkling with laughter.

It was a great photo.

"Hey! I took that!" Florence elbowed Gwen in the side. "Do I get a commission?"

"How about... You get dibs on the first velvet witch robe when I get them in stock. Deal?"

"Deal."

Gwen scrolled down slightly. The words ***GWENDOLYN GOODE, PROPRIETOR*** were displayed in bold letters under her picture. A short bio accompanied it. I only managed to read a few snippets about her upbringing before she flicked her fingers on the track pad again, scrolling down to another photograph.

My mouth dropped open.

"*Ta-da!*" Gwen looked over the moon with excitement. "Isn't it great?"

It wasn't.

Not even a little bit.

I stared in horror at the screen. More specifically, at the

photograph on the bottom half of the screen. A photograph of *me*. Judging by my outfit, it had been taken on my first day of work, but I had no idea when Gwen snapped it. It was a candid shot. I was standing in front of the green curtains of the reading room. My tarot cards were in my hand. My face was averted in profile as something out of frame made me smile. (Sally, most likely.)

"That's a great picture of you," Flo said, bringing her face closer to the screen. "You look like Rapunzel. Look at your hair! There's so *much* of it! Does it curl like that naturally, or do you spend seven hours in front of the bathroom mirror every morning?"

I was still incapable of speech. My brain seemed to have short-circuited. I read the description beneath the photo, barely able to process the words.

IMOGEN WARNER, IN-HOUSE PSYCHIC

"I didn't know what to put for your bio, since I don't know all that much about you." Gwen's voice was apologetic. "But we can always add more later—"

"Take it down," I whispered, finally finding my powers of speech.

"What?" Gwen's face whipped around to look at me. "What do you mean, take it down?"

I swallowed hard.

Tell me this isn't happening.

"I know you say you're leaving soon," Gwen carried on, oblivious to my freak-out. "But while you're here, there's no reason not to advertise your services—"

"Take. It. *Down,*" I repeated, still whispering. "Right now."

She still didn't seem to understand. She shook her head, smiling softly. "Don't be modest, there are so many people who would love to—"

"TAKE IT DOWN!" I shrieked, sounding like a horribly distorted version of myself. I jumped to my feet so fast I nearly

knocked Florence off the arm of the sofa. Socks was startled out of his puppy-slumber. "I mean it, Gwen!"

She stilled, her smile fading instantly. "Imogen, what—"

"I am not being modest and I am not joking around with you," I said, heart pounding faster and faster as I stepped around the coffee table and started to pace. I was incapable of staying still for another second. "I cannot have that online. I cannot have my picture out there. My *name* out there."

Gwen and Flo watched me pace, wide-eyed and silent. So did Socks, though he wasn't silent. He let out a low whine, as if he could sense my sheer panic from across the room.

I tried to get a handle on it, but I couldn't.

I was officially spiraling.

Run.

Now.

Get in your car and go.

He's coming for you.

"Imogen, please," Florence said gently. "Can you explain?"

My head shook back and forth rapidly as my boots clapped across the hardwood floor. I was breathing hard, nearly hyperventilating.

"Don't you understand? *He'll find me.* If that's out there..." I drew abruptly to a halt. Tears filled my eyes as my words faded to an inaudible whisper. *"He'll find me and he'll drag me back into hell."*

Gwen flinched. "Who? Who'll find you?"

A single tear slipped down my cheek. I took a deep breath. "My uncle."

And there it was.

There *he* was.

The source of all my horrors. The nightmare on my heels. The grim reaper in the back corner of my mind. The man who made my life a misery from the moment I found myself living under his roof until I finally fled at age fifteen, when I could take no more.

Not of him.

Not of the spotlight he'd pushed me into.

Not of the big plans he had for my future in Hollywood.

If I hadn't left, there was no telling where I'd be now. Dead, possibly. Miserable, most definitely. Every facet of my existence controlled, every morsel I consumed measured, every communication I made monitored. No friends. No relationships. No interactions he didn't approve of personally.

Days at the studio, recording. Nights either doing press interviews or prepping for them.

A shell of a life.

And for what?

My name in the papers, my face on the television. My fame feeding his greed, a vicious cycle without end. I trembled as memories washed through me. The ten years I spent in his house, after my parents died and left me in his care, were not something I liked to look back on. Most days, I tried my hardest to forget it ever happened. If I just kept moving forward, if I just kept running, I might go days or even weeks without thinking about it.

Until, without warning, it caught up.

And clobbered me.

For a moment, no one said anything.

There was no snarky comment from Florence, no reassuring remark from Gwen. They stared at me in utter silence, watching as the tears dripped down my cheeks, their expressions both contorted in horror and sympathy and — even worse — pity.

Expressions like that were exactly why I didn't talk about my past.

Gwen's hands gripped her laptop so hard, I feared it might snap in two. But she eventually composed herself, wiped her expression clear, and assured me, in a very calm voice, "It'll be down in two seconds."

It was more like two minutes, in actuality. Two long, excruciating, awkward minutes, during which I stood in the middle of the floor watching Gwen's fingers fly over the keyboard. Only when she closed the lid of her laptop and met my eyes again did I finally take a shaky breath and start to feel some of my panic ebb.

"It's done," she said softly. "It's down."

"Thank you," I breathed, my relief palpable. "I— I'm sorry. I didn't mean to yell at you."

"No, I'm the one who's sorry." Gwen rose to her feet and came slowly toward me, approaching like I was a skittish animal. Her eyes were soft, her expression open. "I didn't think. I was just so excited about the website, I got carried away."

"You didn't know. It's not your fault."

She shook her head. "I should've asked first. You mentioned your childhood. You said you ran away at fifteen. I didn't realize..." Her eyes glossed over with tears. "You're still running aren't you, love?"

My throat felt too tight to speak, so I just nodded.

Then, I was in Gwen's arms. She hugged me with surprising strength, compressing my ribcage until I could barely breathe. A moment later, a second set of arms closed around me as Florence joined the huddle.

"You're suffocating me," I lied.

They just squeezed tighter.

When I finally managed to extract myself, I sat down on the floor and pulled Socks into my lap. He squirmed for a few seconds, then happily settled with his body sprawled over me. I sank my fingers deep into his thick fur and began to scruff his neck, his ears, his jowls. I didn't look at Florence or Gwen as they sat down on the couch. I kept my eyes on the puppy, knowing it would be easier to speak about this if I pretended no one else was in the room with me.

"When I was a kid, I was sort of..." I sucked in a breath. "Famous."

The air went still.

"Not Taylor Swift level or anything," I hurried on. "It wasn't on a national scale. This far north, people probably wouldn't know me. But in the southern states — mainly in Florida, where the show was based — I had a pretty substantial following."

"The show?" Gwen asked quietly.

"It was just a daytime television program. Local syndication, at first. Then, later, it got picked up by some of the cable providers. Eventually, it became one of the most popular time slots in the afternoons." I swallowed hard. My fingers rubbed Socks' ears and he sighed in blatant appreciation. "*The Child Clairvoyant*. Dumb name, I know. But it got people to tune in."

"Oh my god!" Flo screeched.

My head snapped up to her.

She was looking at me with stunned disbelief — and clear, undeniable recognition.

Damn and blast.

"I knew you looked familiar!" Her eyes were riveted to my face. "For days now I've been racking my brain, trying to figure out where the hell I know you from! That's *it!* I used to watch that show all the time when I was a kid. My grandma was *obsessed*. She never missed an episode!"

"Go figure," I muttered glumly.

"You look the same! I mean, older now, obviously. But you still have that JonBenét Ramsey child-star look about you. Those super light blue eyes! That gorgeous blonde hair! Jeeze, now that I see it, I can't believe I didn't before." Flo looked at Gwen. "Did you ever watch the show?"

"No." Gwen's lips twitched. "We didn't have cable TV in the trailer park. Even if we did, my Mom wasn't big on the witchy-woo-woo, if you recall. That's why she and my Aunt Colette had such a falling out." She paused. "Well, that and the fact that my mom was a raging bitch with a penchant for meth."

My eyes widened.

"Right," Flo muttered, then looked back at me. "Anyway, this is so freaking cool, Imogen."

"It's really not, I assure you."

"It is!" she insisted. "You're totally famous!"

"I *was*," I corrected. "I'm not anymore."

"So that's what you ran away from?" Gwen guessed. "When you left home at fifteen... It was to escape that showbiz life?"

I nodded, then heaved a heavy sigh. "My uncle was also my manager. It made our relationship less avuncular, more..." I searched for the correct word. "Authoritarian."

Gwen grimaced.

Some of Flo's enthusiasm visibly dimmed.

"Whatever he said, I did. I didn't get to pick what I wore, what I ate, who I talked to. He told my stylists how to dress me, the makeup people how to do my eyeliner, the hair techs how to braid my hair—"

"Oh my god! The *braids*! I remember the braids!" Flo touched her own dark, glossy hair. "God, growing up, I wanted nothing more than to have hair like yours."

I snorted. Florence looked like Lana Condor mixed with hints of Nina Dobrev. She could be on a freaking Vogue cover. "Are you kidding?"

"No! Those braids were so cute!"

"They didn't feel so cute when a woman in the hair and makeup trailer was yanking them into my head at six in the morning so I could step onto the studio stage and perform for twelve hours straight in front of the cameras."

Flo frowned. "Right."

"What exactly happened on this show?" Gwen asked. "I assume, from the name, something of the supernatural variety..."

"Guests would sign up, audition for a chance to come on an episode. They'd sit across from me on the soundstage — all in front of a live studio audience, of course — and I'd take them by the hand and try to trigger a vision. Usually, the people they brought on the show had experienced some sort of loss and were seeking closure. A message from the other side." I shrugged, feeling sheepish. "It was cheesy and exploitative and once I was old enough to realize that my uncle and the studio executives were taking advantage of desperate people for money and ratings…"

"You left," Gwen finished for me.

I nodded. "I wanted to leave for a long time before I finally got up the guts to run away. But I was young. I had nowhere to go. I was scared. And the first two times I tried, my uncle dragged me back, kicking and screaming."

"Jesus," Flo muttered.

"The production people tried to throw more money at me. They thought a better trailer, fancier stage, bigger budget would make me want to keep being *The Child Clairvoyant*." I snorted. "They didn't know the money didn't matter to me. I never saw a dime of anything I made in my contracts or in my residuals. My uncle — acting as my manager — controlled all the finances, and paid himself from my earnings. I never saw a dime. I still haven't, to this day."

"That fucking asshole!" Flo yelled.

"Guess that explains why you're working in my coffee shop instead of sitting on your pile of millions," Gwen murmured.

"Better here than there, trust me on that." I smiled at her. "And I like working here."

She smiled back. "I'm glad."

"Hello? How are you two *smiling* right now?" Flo sounded outraged. "Imogen just said that her dickhead uncle stole all her money! Am I the only one who finds that out-fucking-rageous? Not to mention ill-fucking-legal?"

"I appreciate your wrath on my behalf, but there's nothing I can do about it."

"That cannot be true," Flo said instantly.

"Every time I've tried to fight my uncle, I've lost. I don't just mean physically. I mean *financially*. He controls the purse strings. When I ran away at fifteen, I left him with the keys to the kingdom. And I'd do it again." I blew out a breath. "A life on the run is better than the one I had with him."

Flo and Gwen looked at one another, seeming to conduct an entire conversation without words in the space of a heartbeat. Whatever conclusion they came to, we never had a chance to discuss.

The front door of the shop swung open, bells tinkling.

Several tall male forms strode through it.

CHAPTER SEVENTEEN

I once dated a dude who genuinely believed "going viral" had something to do with chlamydia.

- Imogen Warner, watching a cat video with 12 millions views

Graham, Welles, and a blond man who could've been Chris Hemsworth's body double in Thor stepped through the door of The Gallows. (Given the amount of muscles on display, he'd have no difficulty picking up the mythological hammer.) They'd barely cleared the threshold when Socks tore out of my arms and barreled toward them. His furry body slammed full-tilt into the blond behemoth's legs. Besides a teensy twitch of his lips, the man showed no reaction to the fluffy assault.

"Hey, babe." Graham nodded at Gwen, then swiveled his head in my direction. "Imogen. Florence."

Flo waved. "Hello, boys."

"Hi, Graham. Hi, Welles." I clambered to my feet and turned to the man I hadn't met. "Hi... Um, sorry, I actually don't know you yet."

"Sawyer," the blond said succinctly. His eyes were a dreamy shade of blue. Not quite as blue as Cade's, but…

A close second.

Stop thinking about Cade's eyes, you obsessed loser.

Gwen flew across the shop to her boyfriend's side. "Any news?"

Graham shook his head. His mouth was set in a frown. "Nothing yet."

Gwen's eyes filled with tears. "Nothing? How can there be nothing? He's been missing almost twenty-four hours!"

"Baby. I'll find him." Graham leaned down and brushed his lips against hers. He gave good lip-brush. It looked almost as good as Cade's.

Another close second.

Must. Stop. Thinking. About. Him.

God, I was so screwed.

"What are you doing here?" Gwen asked when Graham pulled away from her.

"We were nearby. Figured you'd be here. Guessing those posters plastered around town are your handiwork?"

Gwen nodded, then gestured to me and Flo. "The three of us did it. We thought getting Rory's face out there in the public eye might help someone remember something."

"You thought right, baby." He exhaled sharply, nostrils flaring. "We'll take all the help we can get, at this point. It's like the kid's gone up in smoke. No sign of him anywhere. And, trust me… we've looked."

Gwen appeared very close to losing the battle against her tears. "There must be some sign of him. Someone must've seen something. Or caught something on camera."

"We've spent the day pouring over surveillance from all over the city, trying to pin down the kid's last known location." Graham's eyes shifted to Sawyer briefly. "We'll keep going through it but as of now, we have nothing. Either the kid wasn't where his brother claims he was and we're looking in the wrong location, or..."

"Or what?" Flo cut in.

Graham's brow furrowed. "Someone grabbed him. Stuffed him in a car trunk and drove off, yanked him inside a house and hid him... No way of knowing."

We all fell silent, brooding over that grim possibility.

"The longer he's missing, the less of a chance he's just lost somewhere," Graham continued reluctantly. "The greater the chance..."

"Someone took him," Gwen whispered.

Graham nodded.

"It is odd we haven't found his bicycle," Welles put in, in a bid for a silver lining. "Usually, if someone grabs a kid, they're in a hurry. They wouldn't take the bike with them. No point. Just more evidence you have to get rid of later along with the body."

I pressed my eyes shut.

The body.

"Welles," Graham clipped. "Think who you're talking to right now."

"Shit," Welles muttered, chastised. He tucked a lock of hair that had escaped his man-bun behind his ear. "Sorry."

"It's fine," I told him, even though it really wasn't. Nothing about the past twenty-four hours was anything resembling fine.

"I talked to Hightower a few minutes ago," Graham said.

My heart leapt at the mention of Cade. (*Had I mentioned how screwed I was?*)

"Did he give an update?" Gwen pestered. "Are the police having any better luck?"

"No update. No ransom note. No viable tips. No nothing. So far, they have jack. Same goes for the FBI," Graham said bluntly. "Tomorrow morning, Georgia is going to make a statement for the press. Plead for the safe return of her son. Rarely works, but it's worth a shot. At this point, anything is worth a shot."

Graham's sharp green stare cut to me. There was something working in the depths of his eyes. A question he didn't ask, though I got the feeling he wanted to. I felt the intensity of his gaze like a physical weight against my skin and wondered how Gwen hadn't developed a case of scoliosis in their short time dating.

His eyes finally moved away.

I took a shaky breath.

"Told Hightower I'd get Imogen home safe and sound," Graham explained. "Welles will bring her."

I looked at Welles. "You will?"

He nodded. "Yep."

"You don't mind?"

"Nope."

Forcing myself to look away from his bright, hazel-gold eyes, I turned to Gwen. "Are you opening the store tomorrow?"

She shrugged. "I guess it depends what happens with the search. It feels weird to go back to business as usual when Rory is missing..."

I worried my bottom lip with my teeth. On Sundays, The Gallows had abbreviated hours, opening late (noon) and shuttering early (four). Mondays, we didn't open at all.

"Just call me, whatever you decide," I told her. "If you want me here, I'll be here."

"Will do," she said, giving me a quick hug goodbye.

Florence wandered over and did the same. "See you later, superstar."

I rolled my eyes.

"Superstar?" Sawyer asked. Besides his name, it was the only word he'd uttered since his arrival.

"Imogen here is famous," Flo informed him happily. "She was a child star."

Sawyer's lips twitched. "Was she, now?"

He didn't say it like a question. He said it like an inside joke — one Flo wasn't in on.

He already knew.

"You already knew!" Flo accused, coming to the same conclusion.

Gwen looked up at Graham. "Did *you* know Imogen was famous?"

Graham nodded.

"What? *You knew?*" A thick vein of accusation ran through her words. "How could you know?"

"For the hundredth time, baby… I'm a private investigator," Graham said pointedly.

"Just because you're a PI doesn't mean you're all-knowing, all-powerful. Hello? That's Santa. And last I checked, you do not have a belly like a bowl full of jelly."

"This morning, then?" His smirk was amused. "Think that's the last time you conducted a thorough examination of my body…"

"Don't you flirt with me, Graham Graves!" Gwen snapped, but there was no heat to her words.

I looked at Welles. "Take me home, please."

"You got a leash for the dog?"

I jolted slightly at his question. I'd nearly forgotten Socks! I seriously needed to get some sleep.

"Um… yeah. Right over there, on the coffee table."

Before I could move to get it, Welles crossed to the coffee table, scooped up Socks' leash, and snapped it onto the puppy's collar without a word. He then proceeded to march, Socks in tow, to the door and jerk it open for me to walk through.

"Let's go," he said, hazel-gold eyes on mine. "I have shit to do tonight that doesn't include chauffeur duties."

Oh, boy.

He was *bossy*.

I waved goodbye to everyone and bustled toward the door.

Before I stepped through it, I mustered the courage to turn back. My gaze sought Graham's sharp-edged green one. It seemed to cut into me like a blade. Fighting the urge to shy away, I forced myself to ask the question I knew, if I didn't, would haunt me all night.

"Cade," I whispered softly. "Does he know, too? About me? About… my past?"

Graham's eyes flared with emotion. He gave a shallow nod of confirmation.

Shit.

Cade knew.

Of course he did. It wasn't exactly a secret. Still, I felt my stomach clench and my thoughts begin to spin in a dangerous direction. One that told me to run, run *now*, run before things began to deteriorate.

"Imogen," Graham said.

My unfocused eyes flew back to his face. It was set in a very serious expression. "Y-yes?"

"Who you are is not who you were," he said in a flat, matter-of-fact tone that was oddly comforting. "Hightower knows that. We all know it. Why don't you?"

Why didn't I?

I had no answer for him. So, I gave a lame little goodbye wave, turned on my heel, and walked out the door.

Welles was not chatty by nature. I learned this on the ride home, during which he said approximately five words. (Two of which were "buckle up" and three which were profanities he muttered at other cars as he weaved in and out of the thick Saturday evening traffic in the black-on-black SUV.)

I stared out the window as we drove, feeling like I'd been tossed down a flight of stairs. Then, kicked for good measure when my body hit the bottom. I was exhausted — physically, mentally, emotionally. My limbs were leaden. Even my hair was tired. I couldn't decide what I needed more desperately, a shower or a meal — I just knew I wanted both to be of the *hot* variety.

Caught up in the numerous aches and pains of my body, I failed to notice Welles was not driving in the direction of The Sea Witch until we turned onto Cade's street.

"Um..." I glanced over at him. "I thought you were bringing me home?"

Welles didn't even look at me. "Give me about twenty seconds, babe. You'll be there."

"Not *Cade's* home. Home, home. My home. The Sea Witch."

"Motels aren't homes."

"It's more of a bed and breakfast, actually. They do a sweet continental spread—"

"Babe," he cut me off.

"What?"

"We're here." His chin jerked toward the windshield.

My sleep-deprived brain tracked the movement. Sure enough, he'd pulled into Cade's driveway while I was yammering on about breakfast.

"But..." I shook my head. "I didn't ask to come here. I didn't even want to come here."

"Hightower wants you here," he said, like that explained everything. Like that was sufficient reasoning for dropping me off at the house of a man I'd had precisely *one date* with. (And, okay, one orgasmic night of post-date activities the likes of which womankind had never before experienced.)

"I don't live here," I informed him stiffly, resolving not to cave to any macho-man antics. "I'd really prefer it if you'd bring me back to The Sea Witch."

He shook his head as he shifted into park.

"But all my clothes are there. My phone charger is there. And, most importantly, Georgia is there. I need to check on her, because I'm sure—"

"Don't care."

I blinked. "You don't *care?*"

"Nope."

I stared at him, too stunned to speak.

Welles spoke instead. "I've got shit to do and no time to do it so I'm not going to sugarcoat this for you," he said bluntly. "Hightower has had a long fucking day, a miserable fucking day, searching for a kid that's likely going to come out of this damaged, if he comes home at all. And when you get home from a day like that, one of the few things that can make it better is having your woman waiting for you in your bed, to obliterate some of that misery with her hands and her mouth and her body." His eyes flickered over my face, then moved to linger on the loose curls that framed it. His grip tightened on the gear shifter. "You want to know how I know that?"

I sucked in a breath.

I was so *not* sure I wanted to know.

Welles told me anyway. "I know because I've also had a long, miserable fucking day. And I wouldn't mind having you improve it for me."

My stomach did a somersault.

"Hightower made it clear he wants you in his bed," he went on. "You have problems with that, take it up with him. I'm just the delivery service." Then, his voice dropped a shade lower and his eyes ignited, going from heated hazel to molten gold. "You decide you don't want to be in his bed, babe... You give me a call, yeah? I'll bring you to mine instead."

With that insane comment still hanging in the air, he swung open his door and alighted from the SUV without another word.

Damn.

And.

Blast.

I heard the lift gate open as Welles retrieved Socks from the back. He didn't wait for me. He just started up the walk to the house, allowing the puppy enough free rein to sniff the front lawn as he went. With no other choice, I hopped out and followed after them.

I stopped on the top step, prepared to make one last plea. "Maybe I can call Cade to clarify—"

"Key," Welles cut me off.

"Excuse me?"

His hand extended my way.

I stared at it like it was about to self-destruct.

"House key," he clarified. "I was told you have it."

His chestnut brown brows were arched. Those incredible gold eyes were full of frustration — and exhaustion. He'd had a long day. Longer than mine, given that he'd spent it scouring the streets for signs of Rory. After he dropped me off, he was probably headed right back out to keep searching.

Some of my resolve slipped away.

"Babe." His fingers waggled with impatience. "You planning to produce the key or am I going to have to strip-search you for it?"

I jolted at the prospect of Welles conducting a top-to-toe examination of my person. My cheeks flamed a bit as I muttered, "You don't have to strip-search me."

I reached for my backpack, fished the key from the depths, and handed it over. Welles opened the door, pushed me lightly at the middle to herd me inside, then passed over the leash. He did all of this without stepping so much as a toe over the threshold, his badass combat boots planted firmly on the porch.

"Lock it when I leave," he ordered. "Lot of assholes out stirring up trouble tonight. One last hurrah before Halloween finally fucking ends."

I nodded, gripping Socks' leash tighter. "Um. Okay. Will do."

He turned and started jogging down the steps. His broad frame cast a long shadow across the lawn as he moved beyond the beam of the porch light.

"Thanks for the ride, Welles!" I yelled after him when he

reached the driver's side door. Then, for reasons unknown, my mouth formed the words, "If it's any consolation, there are about three zillion women within a ten-block radius who'd be more than willing to turn your day around!"

He paused to look back at me. Even in the dark, I could see the flash of his grin. I thought I heard him mutter something, but I was too far away to make out what. He got into the car and drove off, flashing his headlights at me as he backed smoothly out of the driveway.

I closed the door and glanced down at Socks. He looked as tired as I felt. His eyes were drifting shut, tongue lolling out one side of his mouth. His gangly limbs were splayed out on the hardwood, like he couldn't quite hold himself upright. Impossible as it seemed, his endless reserves of puppy energy had finally been depleted.

"Same here, buddy," I informed him, crouching to his level. "I'm so past ready for a snooze, it's not even funny."

His head tilted, listening to my voice.

"Unless you want dinner first..."

His head tilted the other way.

"Kibble?"

He sat up suddenly and loosed a low woof. He knew that word.

"Okay." I scratched him behind his ears, then unhooked his leash. "Dinner first. Then, a thousand years of sleep. Do you think Cade will care if he comes home and finds you cuddled up in bed with me instead of in your crate?"

He barked again.

"I agree," I told him, smiling. "He won't be mad at all."

A pair of lips skimmed along the slope of my shoulder blade. I was on my side, curled into a ball around a pillow. I could feel the warm weight of a canine form sprawled in the crook of my legs.

An even warmer weight pressed itself to my spine as a distinctly human form settled behind me, spooning my body with his larger one.

My eyes cracked open. "Cade?"

"Shh. Sleep, beautiful," he said, his voice husky. "I didn't mean to wake you."

"What time is it?"

"Late. Almost midnight."

"Is there any—"

"No," he answered my question before I could even ask it. "No news."

Damn.

His arm slid around my midsection and pulled me closer. His callused palm slipped up under the hem of the t-shirt I'd borrowed from his drawer after my shower. My breath caught in my throat as his light touch traced my bare skin. I was highly aware that I wasn't wearing my gloves. If I touched him right now…

I curled them into tight fists.

"Cade…"

"I like this," he murmured against my hair. "Coming home to you here, in my bed."

Welles had been *so* right.

His lips touched the nape of my neck — not a passionate kiss, a soft one. Featherlight. Almost like he didn't intend for me to feel it. Except I did, and it felt so good, it set off sparks of desire deep inside me. I shifted my hips backward, seeking closer contact. My mouth went dry when I felt the hard length of his cock against my ass.

The sparks of desire flared into full flames.

My fingers curled into the sheets. He may not have meant to wake me but I was *definitely* awake, now. Though I could feel the clear indicators of his desire, he didn't act on it. Didn't take things any further. His hand stayed at my midsection, not moving either higher or lower to explore more of my body.

He thought I was tired.

Sleeping.

He was content to just hold me, denying his own needs to ensure mine were met.

God, that was sexy.

Welles words from earlier echoed in my head. *When you get home from a day like that, one of the few things that can make it better is having your woman waiting for you in your bed…*

"You had a bad day," I whispered into the dark. Not a question, a fact.

"Yeah," he agreed gruffly. His forehead pressed harder against my hair and his arm squeezed reflexively tighter.

"So did I," I admitted.

He said nothing, just nodded. His breath was warm against my nape.

I swallowed hard, summoning my nerve. Then, I whispered, "You want to make it better with me?"

His body went still as the words processed. Then he moved, *fast*, hand flashing up to cradle my face. Turning it so his mouth could capture mine, he kissed me — a long, hard, deep kiss. His tongue in my mouth. Tasting me. Savoring me.

Kissing him back, I tried to turn in his arms, but he didn't let me move from our spooning position. His hand left my face to move down my body, pausing briefly to cup my breast, then continuing down, down, *down*. The anticipation of his touch was like a drug in my veins. I was panting into his mouth even before his fingers slid between my legs.

I hadn't had any clean underwear to put on after my shower, so I wasn't wearing any. Cade growled low in his throat when he made this discovery. A sound of surprise, but also satisfaction. His fingers slid into the slickness there — I was already wet for him, *aching* for him — and found my clit without any fumbling.

I gasped into his mouth as he began to work me, circling until the passion built to a breaking point. It didn't take long at all until I felt the first throbs of an orgasm pulsing through me.

"Cade," I begged against his lips. "I'm close."

"Good," he muttered.

I was on the cusp of coming when I felt him reposition behind me. His hips shifted slightly and then, with one smooth thrust, he drove into me from behind.

Oh.

My.

God.

I came instantly, crying out Cade's name like a benediction. From this angle, he filled me completely. Each stroke sent a brilliant shiver through my every nerve ending. He'd been deep last night, but this was unreal. So deep, I almost couldn't take all of him. So deep, it almost hurt. And I loved it, every rock-hard inch of him, pumping in and out of me with perfect rhythm.

His fingers kept circling at my clit as his hips pinioned. Harder, faster, fuller. Elongating the orgasm until another one built directly in its wake. The sensation was mind-numbing, nerve-fraying. All I could do was clutch the sheets, holding on for dear life as the pleasure pitched up to new heights.

"Bend your knee for me, beautiful." Cade's voice was ragged. "And tilt your hips."

I did as he said. My spine arched to give him more access; my knee cocked up on the bed. I hadn't thought it was possible, but he slid even deeper, the thick tip of his cock hitting a place inside me I'd never felt before.

God.

It was almost too much. *Too* good. Sex had never been like this for me. Not once. Not ever. And once I left him, I feared it never would be again. He'd ruined me for all other men.

In that moment, I was too lost to care.

My head craned back as his lips continued to devour mine. His tongue was in my mouth, kissing me so hard I couldn't breathe around it. The second orgasm slammed into me, a blinding thunderbolt that electrified every square inch of my body. Cade came no more than a second later, grunting a low oath against my mouth, his whole frame going tight as he spilled into me in long, endless thrusts.

It took a long time for me to come down from the high he'd brought me to. From his ragged breathing, I figured I'd done the same for him. I laid facedown on the pillow, incapable of movement or speech, in the best possible way. When he finally pulled out, a tender pang shot through my core. I'd be sore for a while. I'd bet tomorrow I'd still feel the mark of him deep inside me.

I liked that.

I liked that *a lot*.

"Going to clean up," he murmured, pressing a lingering kiss to my shoulder blade. His voice was thick with emotion. "Thanks for being the only bright part of my day, beautiful."

I smiled against the sheets.

Then, still smiling, I fell asleep.

I moved around Cade's kitchen as quietly as possible. Socks, bless him, was being cooperative in this regard. He shadowed me silently as I opened cupboards and rooted around in the depths of the fridge, his large paws padding gently against the hardwood.

Cade was still asleep. He was dead tired. He hadn't even stirred when Socks began to whine to go out around six-thirty. Nor had he woken when I slid out of bed, scooped up the puppy — *god, he was heavy!* — and left the room, shutting the door behind me with a soft click.

Bleary-eyed, I'd taken Socks out to do his business. Then I fed him, filling his bowl with kibble and exchanging his stale water for fresh, yawning the entire time. I was not a morning person.

Never had been. But I was even less of a *cleaning-up-puppy-pee-after-an-accident-on-the-living-room-floor* person, so I figured I didn't have much of a choice in the matter.

After seeing to Socks' needs, I saw to my own. I was no longer merely hungry; I was starving. Last night, I'd been too tired to do much more than shower and face-plant in Cade's bed. Now, acid was threatening to burn through my stomach lining if I didn't eat something.

I was happy to discover Cade's fridge was stocked with eggs, bacon, and sliced sourdough bread. I put the bacon in the oven to crisp, then cracked six eggs into a bowl and started to whisk. I wasn't sure how Cade liked his eggs, but I figured he'd be hungry when he woke up, too.

I was standing at the stove, mid-scramble, when an arm slid around my middle and a pair of lips hit my nape. A happy shiver rippled through me.

"Good morning," I breathed, leaning back into his heat.

"You didn't wake me," Cade grumbled. His voice was still gruff with sleep.

"You looked tired."

"I am," he said. "Still would've preferred to start my day with you, naked, in my arms."

"Socks needed to go out."

His hands slipped into my t-shirt. "Mmm."

Oh boy.

My hand tightened on the spatula. "And you need a solid breakfast before you go to work."

"Mmm," he hummed again. His hands diverged, one going southward to slip inside the boxer shorts I'd borrowed from his drawer — they were huge on me, I'd had to roll them four times at the waist — the other moving up to cup my breast.

My breath hitched as his thumb brushed across my nipple. "Cade, I'll burn the eggs."

He said nothing. Just reached around me and turned the burner knob, shutting off the gas.

"There's bacon in the oven."

He shut that off, too.

Good thing I hadn't yet pushed down the lever on the toaster. The sourdough would be scorched by now.

"Cade, your breakfast—"

"Eggs are great, beautiful. But right now, there's something else I'd rather eat."

Holy shit.

All thoughts of breakfast flew right out of my head. He pulled the spatula from my limp hand and set it on the counter. Turning me around to face him, he lifted me into his arms with his hands beneath my thighs, then carried me three steps to the kitchen island. I quickly found myself deposited on top of it. Even more quickly, I found the boxers ripped down my body and tossed across the room.

The only thought in my head as he spread my legs and knelt between them was that, suddenly, I saw the merits of becoming a morning person. Then, his tongue hit my clit and I didn't think anything at all.

Looking back, I was glad the day started on such a high note; the rest of it was one long, downward spiral into despair and depression. Rory had been missing for more than a day. The situation was no longer just dire.

It was desperate.

After Cade left for work — and left me stranded at his house — I'd called Gwen to find out if The Gallows was opening for business at noon, as scheduled. I wasn't at all surprised when she informed me the hipsters could wait another day for their turmeric-ginger lattes. The search party took precedence.

She graciously offered me a ride there — one I happily accepted. More so when I saw her car. She drove a badass, vintage, turquoise blue Ford Thunderbird from the late 1960s, which she'd inherited from her eclectic Aunt Colette. (Along with nearly everything else she owned.) It was the exact model Thelma and Louise drove off the cliff at the end of the movie, and kept in absolutely pristine condition.

Classic Gwendolyn Goode.

An hour before volunteers were set to gather at the elementary school, Gwen drove me to The Sea Witch. She waited around while I took a shower and changed into my last clean pair of jeans and a ribbed, pale pink sweater that perfectly matched my suede gloves. I was getting down to the bottom of my duffle; I'd have to find a laundromat soon, otherwise swing by that thrift shop I'd seen around the corner from The Gallows to replenish my closet. When I'd left Atlantic City, I'd unfortunately also left the majority of my clothing behind. (Adrian had no doubt tossed them down the trash chute of his high rise the second he realized I wasn't coming back.)

We were hoping to see Gigi at The Sea Witch but instead, Rhonda the night manager was manning the desk, looking dour-faced as ever in the daylight hours. She informed us that Georgia was at the police station with her mom and sister, who'd flown in from Oregon on a redeye in a show of support. At noon, Gigi was scheduled to give a statement to the public during the SPD press conference.

I was glad she'd have family there, standing by her side. God knew her O'Banion relatives wouldn't be doing the same. I sent her a text to let her know I was thinking about her as Gwen drove us to the elementary school. There were already dozens of people there when we arrived. I searched the crowd for Cade's tall form, but only saw Chief Coulter in the crowd, standing on the perimeter with several agents in FBI windbreakers.

The search party was both well organized and well attended.

Volunteers came out in droves to help law enforcement comb neighborhoods, abandoned lots, graveyards, and tracts of woods that abutted the city. We were divided into groups and assigned to different sectors. Tracking dogs, trained to follow the scent of Rory's pajamas, moved with each unit. The sight of the little silver spaceships on the fabric made my eyes fill with tears. I looked away so they wouldn't fall.

There were other dogs, too. No one told me, but I knew what they were. Cadaver dogs. I didn't like to think about what they were trained to sniff or why we needed them today. When I did, my throat felt too tight to draw breath. They moved with agility, as did their handlers, alert eyes scanning their surroundings along with the crowd.

Before he'd rushed out the door for the day, Cade confided over a hurried breakfast of scrambled eggs and toast that the search party was a two-pronged effort. The police were looking for leads, of course, but they were also looking closely at the volunteers.

Sometimes, the perpetrator inserts themselves into the investigation, he'd told me, looking grim. *Adds to the thrill of the crime.*

I tried not to stare at the dozens of locals who showed up to help, but it was easier said than done. The possibility that whoever had taken Rory was wearing the same orange VOLUNTEER vest as me... searching the same grid of land.... pretending to help solve the very atrocity they had committed...

My teeth ground together with rage as I walked, eyes to the ground, just as the FBI search coordinator had instructed.

Gwen and I were assigned to the same sector of the dog park, along with Florence and her boyfriend Desmond, who I finally had a chance to meet properly. A professor of folklore at the local university, he was handsome in a quiet, bookish sort of way. He had dark blond hair, nerdy glasses, and ink splatters on his fingertips. He also seemed to worship the ground Florence walked on.

I liked him instantly.

Overhead, the whir of helicopter blades was a constant soundtrack to our search efforts. They flew in low loops over the harbor, where divers were scouring the depths beneath the docks. Their panoramic cameras zoomed in on the men in neon green uniforms scattered across town, searching dumpsters behind local businesses and warehouses.

More fodder for the 24/7 news cycle.

Later that night, when the search party broke apart, Gwen dragged us all back to her house. We sat on her sofa, watching that same helicopter footage play on repeat, and a bitter taste gathered on my tongue. The bobble-headed newscaster was just doing her job, but I still glared at her through the screen as she read off her teleprompter.

"Waste Management employees searched dozens of dumpsters this afternoon across the Salem area. Though authorities did not officially confirm this activity was related to Rory O'Banion, the boy who went missing on Halloween night, a source close to the investigation confirmed that all possibilities, from rescue to recovery, are on the table," she parroted. "Police, FBI, and private investigators continue to work in tandem to solve this mystery that has gripped one of New England's oldest communities..."

The screen went dark as Florence jammed a finger violently against the power button.

"I can't watch anymore," she declared. "The way they're talking about Gigi... Seriously, the constant coverage just seems cruel, at this point."

Gwen had recorded the press conference. We'd huddled around her television to watch it, and all found it difficult to stomach. Detective Aguilar had spoken at length about the measures they were taking to bring Rory home. Then, Georgia had a chance to make an appeal of her own — standing in front of the station at a podium in an elegant pantsuit, her voice shaking slightly as she pleaded for the public's help. Her mother and older sister flanked her sides for support. They both had Gigi's light brown hair and foxlike features.

That was difficult enough to watch, all on its own. But the way the news anchors and so-called "experts" discussed her afterward... Making not-so-subtle digs at her decision to allow her boys out after dark on Halloween... Questioning her judgment in trusting other chaperones to watch them while she worked...

It was enough to make me want to smash the television into pieces.

"Delivery is on its way," Gwen announced, sashaying back into the living room. She nearly tripped over a paint can as she rushed toward the sofa, cursing under her breath when she stubbed her toe. Her house was a bit of a hazard.

Gwen lived in a huge, drafty old Victorian (also courtesy of Aunt Colette) that overlooked Salem Common. It was currently in the throes of major renovations. On the first floor, only the kitchen and dining room appeared to be complete. The rest of the rooms were covered in the detritus of home improvement — paint cans and drop cloths, electric sanders and putty knives. Her television was currently balanced precariously on milk crates, and surrounded by ladders.

She plopped between us on the sofa. "Hope you like Indian, 'cause that's what we're eating."

"Sounds good to me," I said. Anything sounded good, at this point. We'd skipped lunch.

"Can you drink tequila with Indian food?" Flo asked, eyes on her task. She'd lined up three shot glasses on the coffee table and was pouring Patrón up to the brims.

Gwen nodded. "You can drink tequila with anything."

"Great." Florence slid shots toward Gwen and me, then curled her fingers around her own. "Bottom's up!"

They were so full, we had to bend over the table and slurp straight off the top before we could lift them into the air for a cheers. The tequila burned down my throat — but it was a pleasant burn in comparison to Gigi's limoncello lighter-fluid.

Originally, we'd planned to cancel girls' night. It didn't seem appropriate. Then again, after the last forty-eight hours, none of us had ever needed a drink quite so badly.

"Do you think we should call Gigi?" I asked. "Check in on her? I know her family is in town, but..."

"Those fucking newscasters," Florence muttered darkly, refilling our shot glasses.

"Forget the newscasters," Gwen said, wincing. "Whatever you do, don't read the comments on social media. People are awful. Just awful. The lack of humanity on display..."

I chewed my bottom lip until Flo shoved my shot glass into my hand. "Drink."

We drank.

We ate Indian food when the delivery guy arrived.

We chatted about inconsequential things, trying to keep our thoughts off Georgia. Off Rory. Off the ongoing investigation.

I wanted to call Cade. Not for an update. Just to hear his voice. I resisted the urge, knowing he was busy with far more important matters. Still, my heart flew up into my throat when my phone began to buzz on the coffee table.

I set down my margarita — Gwen had whipped up a batch sometime between the naan and chicken tikka masala — and yanked it toward my face. It took my eyes a second to focus.

Those margaritas were *strong*.

I'd expected to see Cade's name flashing across the screen. I saw Georgia's, instead.

"Gigi?" I said as the call connected. "How are you holding up, honey?"

"Imogen."

Her voice sounded strange. Not frazzled, not heartbroken.

Determined.

A fissure of disquiet shot through me. "Georgia, what's going on?"

"I just got back from the station."

"Okay, honey. That's good."

"It isn't."

My eyes flew back and forth from Flo to Gwen. They were both staring me with identical looks of concern. "Why not? Did something happen?"

"They don't believe me."

My heart started pounding faster. "Believe you about what?"

"Donny."

"Donny?" I echoed, trying to remain calm. "What about Donny?"

"I know it was him, even if the police don't believe it." She was still speaking in that eerily detached voice that sounded nothing like her own. "He's got Rory. He's got my boy. And I'm going to get him back."

"Georgia, honey, listen to me," I pleaded, rising to my feet and beginning to pace. "Donny was locked up when Rory went missing. There's no way he could've taken him. Remember?"

"Then it was his brothers. Mickey or Shane or Nick. Any of them. All of them. They're messing with me, because I'm messing with Donny. They want to hurt me."

"The police already talked to them. You know that. You're just tired and overwhelmed and not thinking clearly right now—"

"I'm thinking clearly," she snapped, a tiny bit of emotion cracking through her numb demeanor.

"Okay, Gigi. Okay." I swallowed hard, trying to clear the lump from my throat. "When did you last sleep? When did you last eat?"

"That's not important! What's important right now is that I'm going to get Rory back. I just wanted to tell you so you knew — so *someone* knew — before I go in there."

This was sounding worse and worse. "Go in *where*? Where are you?"

There was no answer.

"Are you with your mom? Your sister?"

Again, no answer.

My eyes moved to Gwen. She was on her feet, standing close. Her face had gone pale. "Why don't you come over here to Gwen's house? Flo and I are here, we can talk through this—"

"No." The word was so soft, I had to strain to hear it. "I'm going in. I'm getting him back."

"Georgia!" I was frantic, now. "Where the hell are you going?"

"The Banshee," she whispered.

That's when the line went dead.

CHAPTER EIGHTEEN

I'm going for broke, here!
Wait. Scratch that. I'm already broke.
- Imogen Warner, checking her bank statement

We were too drunk to drive, so Gwen made a call to arrange a ride for us. I figured she'd hail a taxi or maybe ask one of Graham's minions to ferry us to The Banshee before Georgia did something immensely stupid involving Donny's batshit crazy brothers. I was so busy pulling on my boots and frantically redialing Gigi's number, I didn't pay all that much attention to who Gwen was dialing.

Our getaway vehicle pulled up to the curb. Not a cab, nor a black-on-black badass-mobile, but an ancient-looking minivan that had seen better days.

Sally was behind the wheel.

Agatha was riding shotgun.

Oh boy.

The passenger window cranked down. "Get in, already! You girls are slow as molasses!"

"*This* is who you called?" Flo hissed as we rushed down the front steps toward the street. "The Golden Girls?"

"I didn't exactly have many other options!" Gwen hissed back. "All the Gravewatch boys are out in the field!"

"You could call Graham."

"No way!" Gwen protested. "You know how he feels about the O'Banions. Specifically, about me being near them."

"They did try to kidnap you," Florence pointed out.

I gasped. "*What?*"

"Mickey and I had a teensy issue involving my previous psychic, Madame Zelda." Gwen shrugged, like this was a minor detail instead of a monumental one. "Gravewatch resolved it."

I blinked at her, not sure how to respond to that.

Gwen turned back to Florence. "Look, the bottom line is, if I call Graham, he'll tell us to stand down. Do you guys *want* to stand down?"

I sucked in a breath. "No."

"No," Flo concurred. "I just wish our backup had not been born before the Industrial Revolution."

"I heard that!" Agatha yelled form the passenger seat.

Gwen giggled.

So did I.

(What could I say? We were still drunk on tequila.)

We all studied the peeling side-panel of the minivan for a long beat in silence. Eventually, Florence sighed, then reached for the handle.

"Oh well," she muttered. "Beggars can't be choosers."

We rolled open the door and clambered into the back. Sally and Agatha were turned around in their seats, peering at us in the dark. There were still curlers in Sally's hair. Agatha appeared to be wearing a nightgown.

"Um..." I blinked at them. "Did we wake you?"

"It's 10PM on a Sunday night," Agatha groused. "Of course you woke us, you dingbat."

"Sorry." Gwen grimaced. "It's kind of an emergency."

"Don't call Imogen a dingbat," Sally chastised. Her eyes moved to mine. "Ignore Agatha. She's always cranky, but she's *especially* cranky after eight."

"I am not! But if I'm missing my beauty sleep, there better be a good reason." Agatha pinned Gwen with a severe look. "You said there was trouble, Gwendolyn?"

"Yes. It's our friend Georgia O'Banion."

"The mother of that missing little boy?" Sally's thin white brows shot up toward her hairline. "Have they found him?"

"No, he's still missing."

Sally and Agatha looked at one another.

"Horrible. Just horrible. Reminds me of that other case — the Thurman girl. Remember, Ag? She just vanished without a trace one night…"

"Of course I remember, Sal. Whole town was in an uproar looking for her." Agatha's brows pinched inward. "That must've been… what? Fifteen, twenty years ago?"

"At least," Sally said, shaking her head. "Strange case. Very strange. And very sad."

"Okay," Florence interjected, patience dwindling. "Normally, I might care more about some long-past case involving another missing kid, but tonight we don't have time for your tangents. *Comprende?*"

Agatha shot her a look. "This is why you never win when we play canasta. No patience."

"No ability to see the big picture," Sally added.

"What?" Flo gaped. "You said I was getting pretty good!"

"We lied," they chorused.

Flo looked truly aghast at this news.

"Sally, Agatha…" Gwen waded into the squabble. "The thing is, we're pretty certain Georgia is about to walk into a dangerous situation involving the O'Banions."

Sally gasped. "Oh! That's not good."

"Our thoughts exactly. She needs a bit of backup — that's where we come in." Gwen leaned forward in her seat, swaying slightly from the Patrón still coursing through her veins. "I'll explain more on the way. Just drive, Sally. *Fast*."

Sally needed no more encouragement. The minivan took off like a shot, peeling away from the curb with a screech of tires that left the scent of burning rubber in the night air.

Taking a deep breath that did nothing to calm me, I reached for my seatbelt.

I'd seen The Banshee my first night in town, when my car had broken down. It had looked foreboding then; now, it seemed even more ominous. The facade was dingy, with missing shingles and a boarded-up window. The illuminated sign was peppered with rust.

Gwen, Florence, and I stood on the sidewalk outside, shoulder to shoulder, studying the line of motorcycles parked at the curb and listening to the clatter of pool balls that spilled out the open windows. (It had taken some arm-twisting, but we'd managed to convince Sally and Agatha to wait in the minivan across the street.)

"Whatever you do," Flo said. "Don't touch anything."

"Or let anyone touch you," Gwen added.

I chewed my bottom lip. "Maybe I should call Cade."

"The O'Banion boys will go apeshit if the SPD storms into their bar." Gwen shook her head. "Besides, they're busy searching for Rory. If we call them, we take them away from that."

She was right. Still, a flutter of nerves occupied my stomach. They vanished in a puff of smoke as a female scream — Gigi's scream — split the night.

"I know you know where he is, Shane! Tell me where my boy is!"

We all looked at one another for a heartbeat. Then, we rushed for the door. We practically fell through it, the three of us one big tangle of limbs. It was only by the grace of god that we didn't sprawl onto the sticky bar floor. (Seriously, it looked like it hadn't been cleaned since Salem was founded in 1626.)

The rest of the place wasn't much better. I'd seen a glimpse of it in my vision the other night, when I'd touched Donny, so I knew not to expect five-star service and designer decor. But the events I'd witnessed took place about a decade ago. Things had deteriorated significantly in the years since. *Shabby* was too nice a word to describe it.

Seedy came closer.

The bar stools had visible foam peeking out of the cracked leather. Several were sporting duct tape. The pool table in the corner had chipped legs and fraying green felt. Three of the neon beer-brand signs had burned out and never been replaced. The bar-top was cloaked in a layer of grime I could see clear across the room. The whole place smelled of cigarettes, mildew, stale beer, and body odor.

The clientele was, if you could believe it, even less appealing. A handful of burly men were clustered around the pool table with sticks in their hands. Several more were planted on stools, nursing beers. But it was the two giants standing behind the bar who caught my attention. Firstly, because they looked like Donny — bushy red beards, brooding demeanors, built like a walking advertisement for anabolic steroid use. Secondly, because they had Georgia cornered behind the bar, her back to the wall of liquor bottles. Thirdly, because one of them had his ham-sized fist wrapped around her throat.

I didn't think, I just reacted. So did Florence and Gwen. We all launched into motion at once, running full tilt at the bar, screaming our heads off.

"Let her go, you bastards!" (Gwen.)

"I'll shove your balls so far down your throat, you'll choke on them!" (Flo.)

"You hurt her, you're dead! You hear me? *DEAD*!" (Me.)

Gwen and I headed for the end of the bar, where the counter lifted up on hinges to allow entry. Florence took a different approach. She vaulted over the bar like an Olympic hurdler, then executed what I can only describe as a full stage dive. I don't know how she managed it so gracefully. She only knocked over one beer with her foot, which sent the barflies scurrying for cover.

Gwen and I could only watch, along with the rest of the patrons in the establishment, as she sailed through the air, arms extended out in front of her. She hit one of the O'Banions — the bigger of the two — square in the back. He grunted in shock as she took him down to the floor.

One down, one to go.

The other brother still had Georgia by the throat. The moment we were in range, Gwen and I fell on him like wild animals, using everything in our arsenal to inflict damage — nails scratching, fists punching, palms slapping. I would've used my teeth, too, if I'd had the chance.

"What the fuck?" he yelled as my fist connected with his eye socket. "Stop hittin' me! Crazy fuckin' bitches!"

We did not.

If anything, we got slightly more violent.

"LET!" *Punch.*

"HER!" *Slap.*

"GO!" *Smack.*

He finally released Gigi. Unfortunately, it was only so he could backhand me across the face. Seeing the blow coming, I ducked in time.

Gwen didn't.

His knuckles cracked across her beautiful cheekbone and she flew backward into the bar. Several bottles crashed to the ground, shattering on impact around her feet.

"No!" I screamed. "Oh, god! Gwen!"

She looked dazed by the blow, but she was still standing. I

rushed toward her — as did Gigi, who gasped an outraged, "Are you okay?"

Gwen nodded.

Gigi squeezed her upper arm, then hurried past her to the opposite end of the bar, muttering something about ice.

My pale pink gloves curled into furious fists as I turned back to the O'Banions. Rage was simmering in my veins, so strong I could barely keep a handle on it.

"You just hit my friend!" I snapped, glaring daggers at the man before me. He had a creepy tattoo crawling up the side of his neck and the coldest eyes I'd ever seen.

At my angry words, he shrugged.

Shrugged!

My rage quadrupled.

Florence finally stopped wrestling with the giant on the floor and found her feet. Her mouth dropped open as she saw Gwen holding a bag of ice to her face, courtesy of Gigi, who was hovering by her elbow looking just as angry as I felt. Despite the ice, Gwen's cheek was already beginning to swell.

She'd have a killer bruise tomorrow.

Florence's dark eyes were brimming with fury as they shifted to the man who'd delivered the blow. "You are so fucked," she informed him, her voice seething. "You do realize that, don't you?"

"The bitch was attackin' me in my own fuckin' bar!"

"The *bitch* is Graham Graves' girlfriend," Flo continued. "And he's going to burn your bar to the ground when he finds out you just hit his woman."

The man paled slightly, making the tattoo on his neck stand out even more starkly against his skin. His eyes cut to Gwen, widened, then moved to his ginormous brother. "Fuck. Is it her, Nick?"

"Knew she looked fuckin' familiar," the bigger brother

growled. "Last thing we need is Graves on our ass again. We only just got done with that clusterfuck Mickey started…"

Neck-tattoo looked at Georgia, lip curling in distaste. "You miserable cunt, you've been nothing but a pain in our fuckin' asses since the day Donny dragged you home."

"Don't call Gigi a cunt!" I snapped, pointing a finger at him. "Don't talk to her at all, in fact! If you have something to say, you can say it to me. Or, preferably, don't say it at all. No one gives a single shit what you or the genetic anomalies you call brothers have to say."

"Don't recall talkin' to you." He leaned close, dark eyes flashing. His lips were twisted in a cruel smile as he added, "*Cunt.*"

Florence gasped. Her lips parted, but the sound never reached my ears. This was because, at that exact moment, the door behind us swung open.

Agatha and Sally flounced through it.

Shit.

In the dingy bar, they were admittedly an incongruous sight. Between the hair rollers, the nightgown, and the fuzzy bunny slippers…

My teeth sank into my lip, holding in a laugh. Or a scream. I couldn't quite decide.

"What the fuck?" Nick hissed, reeling back. "Who invited the geezers?"

"Old folks' home is down the road," Shane added, brows furrowing. "Though from the looks of you two, would save time to head right to the funeral parlor next door."

All hell promptly broke loose again. We all started shouting at once.

"Don't you talk to Agatha and Sally like that!" (Gwen.)

"Don't you talk to them *at all*, you cretins!" (Me.)

"I'll take you down again, asshole! Just try me!" (Flo.)

"Your mother would be ashamed of you!" (Gigi.)

Then, Sally and Agatha joined the fray, chatting amicably as they approached.

"You call this a bar? I've seen toilet bowls cleaner than this place!" (Agatha.)

"We may not have much longer to live, but I sure hope we're here long enough to see it condemned by the city!" (Sally.)

The O'Banion brothers looked at one another in confusion.

I fought the insane urge to giggle.

"Oh! Maybe they'll turn it into a Trader Joe's." (Agatha.)

"I *love* Trader Joe's. They sell a great frozen cheesecake. Not as good as mine, but then… Whose is?" (Sally.)

"ENOUGH!"

This was a new voice. One we hadn't heard before. It came from the doorway and, automatically, we all turned toward that direction. I was stunned to see the Graves twins, Holden and Hunter, standing two steps inside the frame. They were both dressed in all black, from their boots to their leather jackets. And they did *not* look happy. In fact, if their inky blue eyes were anything to go by, they were aggressively *un*happy.

This may or may not have had something to do with the ice on Gwen's rapidly reddening cheek.

"Thought we taught you this lesson already," Holden — actually, it might've been Hunter, I couldn't yet tell them apart — growled, lethal gaze locked on Shane and Nick. "You put your hands on a woman, there are consequences."

"Time for a refresher course," Hunter (Holden?) added.

"No one invited her here," Shane spat, crossing his beefy arms over his chest. "She walked in and picked a fight."

"We did not!" Gwen cried. "He had Gigi by the throat!"

"He was hurting her!" Flo added.

"If I'd hurt her, she wouldn't be standin' there shootin' her mouth off at me," Nick muttered. "After the shit she pulled, throwin' accusations about kidnappin' our own fuckin' nephew, siccing the fuckin' Feds on us... Bitch deserves whatever hurt I dish out."

The twins did not move, but both of their gazes snapped to Georgia, then shifted down the line to me, then Flo, then Gwen in perfect sync.

"*Out,*" Holden/Hunter barked. "Car's waiting at the curb."

It wasn't immediately clear who, specifically, he was speaking to. Thus, no one moved. It wasn't until he took two strides closer, crossed his arms over his chest, and growled "*Move your asses. Now.*" that I realized he meant all four of us.

Well, six, including Agatha and Sally. Though, they were already wandering toward the door, staring at the twins with the same lovelorn expression I imagined I wore when I was deep in the third act of a cowboy romance novel.

"What does *now* mean? Get in the fucking car!"

We jolted into motion at Hunter/Holden's barked command. I grabbed Georgia by the hand and dragged her with me as I rounded the bar. Flo did the same with Gwen. We had to squeeze past the O'Banions in the process, and I resisted the urge to scratch out their eyeballs with my fingernails.

Barely.

"You come back here, Georgia, we got problems," Shane called after us when we were halfway to the door.

Gigi's hand convulsed around mine.

Before I could snap back, one of the twins did it for me.

"You got plenty of problems, O'Banion," he said flatly. "But none include any of the women in this room. We clear on that?"

"Stay out of this, Graves," Nick warned. "This is family shit. Doesn't concern you."

"You're right," Holden-maybe-Hunter agreed. "It is family shit. *My* family shit. That's my brother's woman holding ice to her cheek. She's family. I promise you, he will have something to say about you putting your hands on her."

"So will I," Hunter-maybe-Holden murmured, a slow, scary grin spreading across his face. "Soon."

Oh, boy.

All six women filed out the door, the twins on our heels. Sally's minivan was now double-parked directly behind the row of motorcycles, blocking them in. One of the black Gravewatch SUVs had pulled up directly behind it — still running, hazard lights flashing. As we watched, another vehicle pulled to a stop in the lineup.

A brand new Ford Bronco.

Given the way Gwen sucked in a breath at the sight of it, I had a pretty solid suspicion who was behind the wheel. This suspicion was confirmed when the door swung open and Graham Graves stepped down onto the street. He looked scarier than ever, his expression set in stone. His eyes had gone dark with fury and they darkened more still as they swept over Gwen, taking in the sight of the ice on her cheek.

"I think I'm in trouble," Gwen whispered from beside me.

I didn't respond. I was too busy watching yet another vehicle pull to the side of the road. A black, unmarked police cruiser. One I recognized even before Cade alighted from it.

His expression was just as unhappy as Graham's. When he spotted me standing in the crowd, his brows pulled into a deep furrow and the muscle in his cheek began to tick with barely-contained rage.

"I think I am, too," I whispered back.

The ride back to Cade's house was tense to begin with. It grew even tenser when I hopped out of his car along with Georgia at The Sea Witch.

Make that *attempted* to hop.

His hand flew out and caught me around the wrist before I got so much as a finger on the door handle. Georgia had already disappeared inside. I was on my own.

Damn and blast.

"Where the fuck are you going?"

"Um..." I hedged, not really wanting to piss him off further. "Inside?"

He shook his head.

My eyes narrowed.

"You're sleeping at my place," he said in a tone that told me arguing would be futile. "We have shit to discuss. Privately. If that discussion gets loud, I don't want to do it in a motel with paper-thin walls."

He anticipated *yelling*?

That was not exactly an enticement to go with him. I had no intentions of stepping even a pinky toe inside his place, seeing as I had no clothes there and no desire to spend the night with someone whose general disposition brought to mind a ticking time bomb. However, I had a feeling any protests to that effect would fall on deaf ears.

Cade was not in a listening mood. Determination was etched across his features. I saw it in the set of his jaw, the clench of his teeth, the deep fissure between his flinty blue eyes. In a bid to avoid poking the bear and further provoking his fury, I made my voice as mellow as possible.

"I can't sleep at your place, Cade. I don't have any clothes there."

He contemplated this for zero point three seconds, then released my wrist. His eyes remained locked on mine as he shifted across the center console, into my space. It took all my courage not to cower back against the leather seat as he came closer. And closer. And still closer, until he was *right freaking there*, a scant inch away.

"Then pack," he ordered tersely.

"Pack?"

He gave a shallow nod. "Pack your shit. You're staying with me."

"I am not staying with you!" I declared, immediately deciding I would, in fact, poke the bear because the bear was being kind of a bossy dickhead, at the moment.

"Goldie, you already are. Or have you forgotten you spent the past two nights in my bed?"

Shit.

He had a point there. But I wasn't about to admit it. "That's different."

"How?"

"Why would I check out early?" I countered. "I have two more nights here. I prepaid for a full week."

"Yeah, and you aren't paying for another one."

"What does that mean?"

"It means I'm currently working eighteen-hour days, and I'd like to spend the handful of free hours I get to myself not chasing you down at notorious biker bars or two-star motels with flimsy door locks. I'd like to know when I'm coming home at night that the best part of my day is already waiting for me in my bed, wearing one of my t-shirts, cuddled up with my dog." He was still glaring at me, hard and uncompromising. "You get me?"

My mouth had fallen open. I closed it with an audible click of my teeth. Long before I'd recovered my composure, he starting talking again.

"You can either pack or I'll go upstairs and pack for you."

My eyes bugged out of my head. "You will not!"

"You have ten seconds to decide," he informed me. His voice dropped to a mutter. "Wouldn't be the first time Georgia let me borrow a key to your room."

He was right about that. Still, I maintained my glare. "Crashing at your place is one thing. That's just sex. If I check out..." I shook my head. "That's insane. That's basically like *moving in!*"

He stared at me.

A semi-hysterical, panicked laugh shot from my lips. It was not a good sound. "I'm not moving in with you. For the record."

He continued to stare at me.

"Cade—"

"Ten seconds are up," he announced. He reached for his door handle.

"Wait!" I cried.

He stilled and looked back at me.

"I'll go pack," I grumbled unhappily. I shoved open my door and, just before I slammed it, yelled, "But I'm *not* checking out!"

I stomped up the front porch steps, jerked open the creaky screen, then shoved my way through the door to the reception area. Rhonda was sitting at the front desk, looking bored out of her skull. She barely made eye contact with me as I thundered inside — not that I blamed her. I doubted my expression was one of warmth and openness, at the moment.

It didn't take me long to shove my belongings into my duffle bag. I didn't have all that much stuff and, after years of travel, I'd gotten quick-packing down to a science. Unfortunately, this meant I didn't have enough time to cool down. I was still steaming mad as I stomped back down the stairs to the reception room, blasted my way out the door to the porch, and tramped to the idling SUV. When I threw my duffle on the floor and hopped up into the passenger seat, Cade looked like he was fighting a grin.

"You break that door slamming it off its hinges, the chief is going to bust my balls."

I rolled my eyes. I hadn't slammed it *that* hard.

He chuckled. Apparently, he was over his anger.

That made one of us. I, for one, didn't see anything amusing about this scenario.

At all.

We drove to his place in total silence. The silence continued as we parked — this time, he pulled all the way up the driveway and, after hitting a button on the visor to trigger his garage door, steered the SUV into the bay beside a sleek black motorcycle.

A tiny crack formed in my icy resolve as I stared at the bike through my window.

Cade would look seriously hot straddling that bike.

He grabbed my duffle bag — annoyingly considerate, even when we were in a fight — and carried it from the car to an inner door which led into his kitchen. Socks greeted us the second we stepped over the welcome mat. Another crack in my icy resolve formed as Cade dropped down into a crouch and performed a full doggie rub-down, ears to rump.

"Good boy," he murmured, his deep voice back to its normal calm tones. "You chew anything you weren't supposed to, today? Huh?"

Socks' answer was a wet tongue-swipe across Cade's cheek.

Cade chuckled.

He dropped my duffle by the hallway entrance, grabbed Socks' leash, and snapped it on.

"I'm taking him for a walk," he informed me, striding across the kitchen to the French doors that led out into the backyard. "He's been cooped up all day."

I watched them go, feeling suddenly unsure. Out of place. The past two nights I'd stayed here, I hadn't thought about what it meant. I was so caught up in all the fantastic sex, I didn't really contemplate that I was, for all intents and purposes, shacking up with a guy. Not just any guy, either. An amazing guy (when he wasn't being majorly bossy) who had, in the span of a week, effectively flipped my entire world on its head.

After Adrian, I'd sworn never to get involved with anyone else. My heart was going into retirement. Sex was one thing. But actually caring about someone? Letting them know me? Getting to know them?

That scared the breath out of me.

Far more than bar fights with the O'Banion brothers.

My buzz from the margaritas had officially worn off. I wandered to the fridge and pulled out a beer, taking a long sip to settle my nerves as I waited for Cade to return. This took quite a while. So long, my beer was halfway gone by the time he stepped back into the kitchen.

Socks bounded my way the second he was free of his leash, running circles around my feet. I wanted to hop down from my stool and greet him, but Cade's eyes were on me, holding me in place as effectively as shackles. He set the leash down on the counter and came at me, not stopping until he was standing less than a foot away. His hip hit the counter. He reached out and closed his long fingers around the beer bottle, brought it up to his lips, and took a long, deep pull.

I felt my mouth go dry as I watched him swallow.

"Cade—"

"No."

My brows shot up.

"I get to talk. Then you get to talk." He didn't sound angry anymore, but he didn't exactly sound happy, either. "Then, if I don't like what you have to say, I'll do more talking. It's called a conversation. Realize it might be new to you, seeing as you're allergic to sharing and your whole M.O. is about keeping everything self-contained."

"I am not—" I snatched my beer back. "—*allergic* to sharing."

"You are."

"Why would I need to share? You seem to know everything about me already." My eyes narrowed into a glare. "Graham told me you know about my upbringing. The TV show. All of it. I'm guessing that means you knew about my dead parents, too, even before I told you?"

He flinched.

I'd scored a point. Somehow, it didn't make me feel any better.

"And that means you know about me. That I'm..." I couldn't make myself say the words out loud.

His eyes flickered down to my gloves and lingered there for a beat before returning to my face. "Yeah, Imogen. I know you're a clairvoyant."

My heart clenched. *Hard.* "Do you even know what that means?"

"I know it goes beyond parlor tricks and tarot cards." His stare bored into mine. "I know you don't wear those gloves 24/7 to make a fashion statement."

My breath caught.

"What else did Graham tell you?" he asked, eyes scanning my face.

Who you are is not who you were.

That's what Graham had said. He was wrong, though. I wasn't on television anymore, but I would always be that girl.

The girl people couldn't see.

I wasn't incorporeal. I didn't have powers of invisibility, or a special cloak, or a genetic quirk that allowed me to mimic the natural camouflage of a chameleon. But, growing up, even when the show was at the pinnacle of its success, when I was signing autographs in the street and smiling for selfies with fans…

People couldn't see me.

Not the real me, anyway.

The girl they saw on silver screens, on tabloid magazine cover spreads, in viral click-bait articles that circulated whenever a case I'd advised on became national news fodder?

She was a fiction. A fabrication, carefully curated by my uncle. (Along with a team of professional stylists.) And the sad fact was, no one really noticed, or even cared. No one expressed all that much interest in discovering who I was once the cameras stopped rolling and the stage lights dimmed.

To be fair, even if they had, I rarely gave them the opportunity. Back then, the real Imogen was only ever allowed up for air in the brief intervals between filming, when I stepped away from the perfectly orchestrated sets and closed the door on scripted public appearances.

That version of me — *Real Imogen,* the one who didn't smile like a pageant-winner or dutifully follow orders to perform or wear her hair in those ridiculous American-Girl-Doll-inspired platinum pigtail braids that they hoped would keep me young and fresh in the eyes of viewers for years after I'd outgrown them — had spent so long in the dark, it was hard to let her up into the light.

Real Imogen remained a mystery to me, even now.

Fake Imogen was gone, but not forgotten.

Never forgotten.

Nor was my deep-seated fear that no one, ever, would care enough to look beyond the surface. To find the heart of me beneath.

The true me.

For whatever reason, in that moment, a memory of Cade popped into my head. We'd been standing in his kitchen only a few nights before. He'd asked me what I wanted to drink and insisted I tell him my preferences.

When I ask you what you want, I'm not asking for my health. I actually want to know. And I want to know so I can give it to you.

Shit.

He'd really said that.

Your tendencies to go with whatever's easiest or most convenient, 'cause you're terrified to be an imposition? They're not going to fly around here.

Double shit.

He'd said that, too.

I don't want polite. I want real.

Triple shit.

I was so totally screwed.

"Imogen." Cade called me back to reality.

My eyes flew to his. "W-what? Sorry, did you say something?"

"Where did you just go?"

"I'm right here."

"You're sitting two inches away from me but your thoughts are in another universe."

Christ, he was perceptive.

I took a sip of my beer and averted my gaze. "Why does it matter?"

"Not sure what it's going to take for you to realize that everything you do matters to me." His hand found my chin and he turned my head so I was no longer able to avoid his stare. "That includes putting yourself in harm's way, storming into a bar owned by men you know are dangerous."

"But Gigi—"

"I know. Your friend was in trouble. You were only trying to help. Instead, you could've gotten yourself seriously hurt. I warned you once before, the O'Banion boys have rap sheets longer than your arm and are all too happy to add a few more lines. More than a few of those charges are for violence against the women in their lives. Not just assault. Rape of every variety — attempted, date, statutory. The list goes on."

My eyes went wide.

His jaw clenched. "I wasn't a big fan when you put yourself on Donny's radar. Can't say I'm any more of a fan that you're now on his brothers' radar, as well."

"I wasn't trying to get myself on their radar," I protested softly. "I just thought about Georgia walking in there alone, no backup—"

"The police could've been her backup. Not you, Gwendolyn, Florence, and two eighty-year-olds with arthritis and expired licenses."

"Sally's license is expired?"

"For about six years now, yeah."

"Huh. I guess that explains the state of her minivan."

His lips twitched, but the humor quickly vanished as he got back to the matter at hand. "I don't need to be worrying about you and your friends going off the rails, getting calls that you're engaged in an altercation at The Banshee. Not when I have a lot of other shit I should be worrying about."

"I never asked you to worry about me."

"You don't need to ask. You're in my life. I care about you. That means I'm going to worry about you. I'm going to show up when you need me. I'm going to do it even when I'm pissed off. I'm going to do it even when *you're* pissed off. That's how a relationship works."

I blinked, struggling to process that concept.

A relationship.

With Cade.

"Any of this sinking in yet? No? Not at all?" He paused to stare at me for a while. A long while. "You're lucky I find that hard-headed mindset of yours endearing, instead of annoying."

I narrowed my eyes at him.

"And that I know that sharp-tongued mouth of yours has other talents besides frowning at me for being right or reaming me out for telling the truth."

My eyes narrowed further.

"And that I recently learned your—"

"I'd quit naming body parts if you ever want to enjoy access to any of them again," I suggested icily.

Cade grinned, entirely unapologetic.

I promptly changed the subject. "How did you guys even know we were there? We didn't call anyone. The twins just showed up unannounced and ordered us out..."

"Gravewatch has the whole place wired."

"What? *Wired*?"

He nodded. "Not exactly a legal wiretap, you understand?"

"Uh... not really, no."

"Graham has his way of doing business, I have mine. His way doesn't always follow the letter of the law, which puts us at odds sometimes but, more often, is mutually beneficial. In this case, I didn't ask why he had one of his men put eyes inside The

Banshee, and he didn't tell. Better that way for all parties involved." He exhaled sharply. "I'm just relieved his surveillance guy was paying attention tonight when Georgia sauntered in. Even more relieved he rang the alarm when he clocked you, Gwen, and Florence roll up ten minutes later."

I had to admit, I was pretty relieved about that as well. If the twins hadn't arrived when they did, there was no telling how the night would've turned out.

Cade took the beer out of my hand, set it aside, and proceeded to cage me in, arms bracketing the counter, the heated wall of his chest trapping me on the stool. My heart began to pound faster as he bent forward to bring our faces together.

"I'll say one more thing, then we can drop this. You do not run full-tilt into danger again without calling me or one of the Gravewatch boys first. You do not put yourself at risk. You do not put your friends at risk. Hard as it is for you to wrap your beautiful brain around, you aren't alone anymore. Stop living your life like you are."

My throat was lodged with emotion. There was a telltale prickling at the backs of my eyes. I was horrified to discover I was about to start crying, right there in Cade's kitchen.

My phone began to buzz on the counter with an incoming call.

Saved by the bell!

Cade pulled back slightly so I could answer. I was so relieved to have an interruption to this conversation, I didn't even glance at the screen before I accepted the call and lifted the phone to my ear. I was expecting to hear Gwen's voice.

Or Gigi's.

Or Flo's.

Even Sally's wouldn't have been a surprise.

Instead, I heard someone else.

"About time you answered, dollface," Adrian snarled, his melodious voice turned ugly. "We need to talk."

CHAPTER NINETEEN

The only muffin top I care about is the kind they sell at Dunkin' Donuts.
- Imogen Warner, feeling body positive

All the blood rushed out of my head.

Fear rushed in.

Peripherally, I was aware that Cade was still close by — his arms bracketed around me on my stool, his intent gaze locked on my face — but I barely noticed his presence. All my focus was on the phone in my hand; the man's voice coming through it.

"We don't have anything to talk about," I whispered.

"How about the fact that you royally fucked me over? Huh?" Adrian yelled so loud, I flinched. "How about the fact that you bolted in the middle of the fucking night — no note, no explanation. Leaving me alone to deal with Viggo and his boys. They have my balls in a fucking vise over this! The residency—"

"I told you I didn't want a residency."

"No one turns down a six-month gig at The Palace."

"*I do!*" My heart was thundering. "I told you, Adrian—"

Cade's whole frame stiffened and his expression changed. I was too caught up in the phone call to see it, or realize what it meant. Oblivious, I kept speaking.

"—I'm not doing another show. Not television, not live on stage, not *anything*. I must've told you that a dozen times. You didn't listen. You made the arrangements with Viggo all on your own. If your balls are in a visc because of it, well, that's on you. Don't put it on me."

"When did you turn into such a screaming bitch?"

"Probably around the same time you turned into an abusive manipulator! Or maybe it was the time you shattered my snow globe, just because you knew how much it mattered to me! Maybe it was the time you put your hands around my neck and made me spend a month wearing goddamn turtlenecks!"

Cade's frame, already stiff, went ramrod. It was a good thing I didn't notice his face, in that moment. If I had, I probably would've fallen off my stool.

I pulled in a ragged breath. "And, might I add, it was *June!* June is not a turtleneck month, asshole!"

"Doll..." Adrian's voice turned cajoling. A familiar tool in his gaslighting arsenal. "We were always hot and heavy. Explosive. You want that kind of fire, you also get the burn—"

At this point, Cade was done.

The phone vanished from my hand as he yanked it away. I (belatedly) lifted my eyes up to his face and felt my heart quail at what I saw. Not anger. Not even rage. This was pure, undiluted *wrath*. And all of it, every terrifying ounce, was directed straight down the line at the man on the other end.

"This is Detective Caden Hightower, Salem Police Department," Cade clipped into the phone, his voice totally controlled even though his eyes were burning like blue fire. "Lose this number. You don't, I will dedicate every bit of my time and every one of my resources to personally fucking you over. And I will take pleasure in doing it."

Adrian said something I couldn't make out, though I strained my ears to hear. Cade listened for approximately zero-point-three seconds, then cut him off again.

"I don't give a fuck what you think you're owed here. Imogen isn't giving you a goddamned thing. Not her time, not her explanations, certainly not an apology. Not ever again. I already knew you were a piece of shit; this conversation is just further confirmation. You call her again, you even think about calling her, I will do exactly what you do with dog shit: throw it in the fucking bin and let it rot in a landfill somewhere for the rest of time."

A tremble moved through me.

"That's not a threat or a warning," Cade growled. "It's a vow."

With that, he disconnected the call. Then, he proceeded to shut the phone off. I watched, wide-eyed, as the screen went completely dark in his hand. When he set it on the counter, my eyes finally shifted up to his face. I sucked in a breath. His wrath was still burning bright. If possible, even brighter than before. His jaw was clenched, the telltale muscle ticking in his cheek. His voice came out tight — like he didn't trust himself to speak.

"*Explain*."

"Cade—"

His jaw went even tighter. "Not asking."

(*i.e.*: he was telling.)

Oh boy.

I hurried to explain. "That was Adrian."

He waited.

"My ex." I swallowed hard, trying to remain calm. "From three months ago. I told you about him the other night."

His nod was curt.

"Okay, well..." I searched for the right way to explain. Then, I quickly realized there wasn't really a *right* way to spin the saga of my abusive, asshole, ex-boyfriend, so I just went with the truth. "Adrian and I met in Atlantic City. I was working as a waitress at one of the casinos. I started out on the main floor, but eventually got moved up to the high roller section. It was the kind of place where the casino owners brought their VIPs to impress them. Bottle service, reserved lounges, tabletop hookahs… anything they wanted, we arranged." I blew out a long breath. "One night, Adrian came in. He knew everyone and was a big deal with the casino crowd. He played poker. High stakes. He was pretty good at it, too. Won a lot of money."

Cade continued to wait, listening intently.

"What he wasn't so good at was saving that money. He spent almost everything he earned. Blew it on ridiculous things. He needed the fanciest penthouse. The most expensive luxury car. The highest quality wool suits, tailored to his specific measurements."

The next part was harder to admit aloud.

I forced myself to continue anyway. "He swept me off my feet at the beginning. Gourmet dinners, nights on the town. A trip to New York City at Christmas, with the nicest suite at the Ritz-Carlton, overlooking Central Park. I can't lie — for a while, I enjoyed not being the one serving the drinks when I stepped foot in a nightclub or restaurant."

Cade nodded.

"He could be fun. He took me dancing, taught me to throw darts. If we ate at a steakhouse with a piano, he'd sit at it and serenade the whole place with Sinatra songs. Cue the applause." I huffed out a bitter half-chuckle, remembering how he'd dazzled me back then.

Foolish, foolish girl.

"Everywhere we went, everyone else seemed so convinced he was special. When he walked into a room, it was like Zeus himself had descended down from Mount Olympus to mingle among the mortals," I said. "It was nice to think someone like that, someone special, thought *I* was special, too. It was even nicer to think…"

My tongue felt thick. I couldn't get words past it.

"Take your time, Goldie," Cade said, his voice no longer brimming with rage. "I'm not going anywhere."

I pressed my eyes closed. I couldn't look at him for this part. I didn't think I could bear to see the pity in his expression when I made my pathetic admission.

"I wanted so badly to believe someone could love me," I whispered, barely audible. "Looking back, I realize I'd been lonely a long, long time when I met him. I guess I just needed someone. Anyone. And I convinced myself that Adrian was that someone." My voice cracked. "How stupid is that?"

Two hands landed on my neck, sliding gently across my skin in a soothing gesture.

"Not stupid at all, Imogen," Cade said, and there was no pity in his voice. Not even a shred of it. "It's human."

Trembling, I opened my eyes. I'd been so afraid to see him looking at me like I was the ultimate loser. But his expression was gentle, his eyes were soft. It was a look I'd seen before — the one he made when he greeted Socks. I didn't know what it was, but it was pure and it was beautiful and just seeing it aimed in my direction made my heart clench like he'd wrapped his whole fist around it.

I wanted him to keep looking at me like that forever, but I knew I had to finish the rest of the story. To expel it from my system so we could move past it.

"He wasn't violent at first," I confessed in a whisper.

Cade flinched, his hands jolting on my neck, but his expression never wavered.

"I didn't realize he was spending more than he made. I didn't realize the lifestyle he was indulging in was totally unsustainable. I didn't realize he was in deep with the casinos, and getting deeper with every game he lost." My lips twisted in a grim smile. "When he found out about my past — *The Child Clairvoyant* — he was over the moon. I'd never seen him so happy. He thought it was the answer to all his financial woes."

Cade scoffed darkly.

"One of the guys he owes money to is named Viggo. A big fish in the Atlantic City cesspool, with connections in all the entertainment circles. He arranged for a six-month residency at The Palace. A live show on stage. And me as the main attraction." I paused. "Adrian didn't even ask me first. He just agreed."

"Asshole," Cade muttered.

"No question about that. Unfortunately, Viggo and his boys are even bigger assholes. They started putting pressure on Adrian when he couldn't get me to say yes. Then, Adrian started putting that pressure on me. It was a domino effect."

"Don't make excuses for him."

"I'm not. I'm just trying to paint the picture of why he flipped—"

"He didn't flip. He showed you his true colors." Cade's voice was tight. "Men who put their hands on women don't just start one day, out of the blue. Whether it was the residency or something else, he would've eventually turned violent. That's his nature. Don't give him more credit than he deserves. And don't look for reasons to justify why he did what he did to you." He leaned in. "The reason is that he's a goddamn scumbag. And if I ever cross paths with him, beautiful... He better pray I don't have my gun on me."

"Cade..." I whispered, shocked but also strangely touched. I didn't know what else to say. I planted my face in his chest and slid my arms around his waist, holding on as tight as I possibly could.

"Done talking about this asshole," he declared, his mouth pressed against my hair. "He's taken up enough of your life. He doesn't get another fucking minute."

I nodded against his chest.

"You're getting a new number, soon as we can get to the phone store."

I nodded again.

"You're not going to fight me on that?" He chuckled in disbelief. "That's a first."

"Why would I fight you? I was already planning on changing it, I just haven't had a chance. Things have been a bit..." I looked up at him and shrugged. "*Chaotic* around here."

"That's putting it mildly."

"I can't believe it's been forty-eight hours and we still don't know anything."

The words hit him like a bucket of ice water. There was a heavy pause before he spoke. "Not for lack of trying."

"I'm sorry, I didn't mean to imply—"

"I know you didn't."

With a light neck-squeeze, he released me. Reaching for my beer bottle, he brought it to his lips and chugged down the rest in one long gulp. Then, he walked to the fridge, pulled out another one, snapped off the top, and took a long pull.

I watched him do this in silence, nearly chewing through my lip. I didn't know what to say; how to make this better for him. I knew how hard he was working. I also knew how much pressure he was under. I'd seen firsthand the toll a case like this could take on those assigned to solve it. There were shadows under his beautiful eyes and I didn't doubt he'd soon have a few more steaks of silver at his temples from the stress.

Lucky for Cade, the look worked for him.

A few minutes passed and he didn't speak another word. His hands splayed out on the countertop. He stared down at them for a while in deep reflection. Intermittently, he took long sips of his beer.

What he did *not* do was share his thoughts.

He probably thought he couldn't, I realized belatedly. His ex-wife had never wanted to hear about his day. Her fragile disposition couldn't handle the darkness he was keeping pent up inside.

But I wasn't fragile.

I could do this for him.

Be this for him.

"It might help if you unloaded some of that weight off your shoulders, honey," I murmured softly.

His head came up. "Not much to say that won't depress you."

"I'll be depressed whether you share or not. If you need to talk, I'm here to listen."

His eyes warmed a bit, some of the bleakness disappearing as he looked at me. "I'm just tired."

"You haven't been sleeping much."

"I can survive without sleep. What I'm really tired of is looking into Georgia O'Banion's eyes every time she comes down to the station for an update, and telling her we have jack shit." He shook his head. "I don't blame her for storming The Banshee tonight. If it was my kid out there missing..."

He'd never stop looking. Never stop trying. Because when Cade Hightower loved someone...

He never let them go.

The thought made my heart flutter.

"It doesn't make sense. We've searched the whole damn town. Covered the neighborhood those kids were in with a fine-toothed comb. There's no trace of Rory." He took another pull of beer. "Search party today was a bust. Scuba divers didn't find a damn thing under the docks. Cadaver dogs didn't catch a scent. Trackers couldn't sniff out a trail."

"That's got to be frustrating."

"Frustrating doesn't cover it." His lips twisted in a humorless smile. "I've spent the past two days knocking on sex offenders' doors, scouring surveillance footage, and squeezing information from every source I've got on the streets. All amounting to precisely fuck-all in the way of a credible lead. In between, I'm swallowing down condescending remarks from FBI agents who don't know their asses from their elbows when it comes to small town mentality, as far as I can tell. The way they're stomping around, marking territory like this is some bureaucratic beauty contest… Fuck, it's no wonder the locals won't talk to them."

I'd seen the agents in their suits and dark shades, standing apart at the search party. Watching, not interacting. I'd also seen how differently the SPD officers and detectives moved through the crowd, greeting people by name, offering hands to shake and words of thanks to the volunteers.

This was their city. They cared about the citizens — and would continue to care long after the Feds piled into their government-issue vehicles and rolled out of town again.

The agents were likely remaining objective on purpose. It was protocol — evaluating the situation with detached eyes so they could catch any blind spots the police might miss. I had no doubt they were highly intelligent and well trained. But the way they were going about it wasn't going to get anyone around here to approach them with information. It came off as aloof. Arrogant, even.

In my experience, New Englanders had very little patience for arrogance. They were, on the whole, salt of the earth people. No bullshit, no bravado.

Cade's thoughts were in line with mine. "What the Feds don't seem to get is, folks choose to live in a quirky place like Salem *because* it's a little offbeat, not in spite of that fact," he said, shaking his head. "Maybe the city got famous for pinning scarlet letters, but things are different now. Everyone is welcome here. Gay, straight, black, white. Christian, Muslim, Wiccan, Atheist. Young, old, every age in between. That's not to say there's no racism or sexism or crime. But generally, people around here are accepting of each other. They look out for one another. The SPD understands that."

"And the FBI doesn't?"

"They breezed in and took over day one. All ego, zero action. They treat Chief Coulter like he's a country bumpkin fresh off the farm, and Aguilar like she's working her first case. She used to be a homicide detective in Miami, for Christ's sake."

"I didn't know that."

"You wouldn't. Zero ego, all action — that's Aguilar. She doesn't brag, she just gets the job done. Can't help wondering if we'd have better results without all the federal red tape." He pinched the bridge of his nose, as though he might quell a headache. "It would be one thing if they were getting results. But they're not. We're moving on day three and haven't found a single clue. And Rory..."

"Is running out to time," I finished when he trailed off into silence.

His hand dropped to press against the counter. His frame was rigid with tension. He was struggling to keep his emotions in check. Watching him, it was difficult to keep my seat. I wanted to fly across the kitchen to him. To wrap him in my arms and assure him everything was going to turn out okay. But I couldn't do that. There were no assurances here. Nothing I said could take this weight off his shoulders.

"I wish there was something I could say to make this better for you," I said, feeling utterly useless. "I wish there was something I could do—"

Cade's whole frame jolted, an involuntary response he quickly hid behind a blank mask.

My brows went up. "Cade?"

"Can't."

"What?" I asked, confused.

"Can't do it." He shook his head, fighting some inward battle I didn't really understand. "Can't ask you."

My confusion mounted. "You can't ask me what?"

His eyes hit mine — and I knew. I *knew.* I saw in their conflicted blue deaths what he was struggling to say.

Or *not* say.

"I just stood here in this kitchen, not ten minutes ago, watching your face crumble as you talked to a man who tried to use you for what you can do," he murmured, eyes never shifting from mine. "I don't want to be that kind of man. Don't want any common ground with that scumbag. And, Christ, here I am, about to do it anyway. Even though I know it'll cut you. Even though I know I have no right to ask you. Even though I know getting involved in this is the last thing you'd ever want to do, after the last time."

Last time.

Baltimore.

Joey.

My voice was choked with emotion. "You... You know?"

He nodded shortly.

"You know about Baltimore," I whispered, the words barely audible.

He nodded again. His jaw was clenched so tight, I thought his teeth might crack.

Tears glossed my eyes. I started breathing too hard, too fast. Hyperventilating. I couldn't contain my panic. My shame. My guilt. It was too much. I wanted to disappear. To blink out of existence, never to be heard from again.

Cade saw me starting to spiral. He pushed off the counter and came toward me. "Imogen—"

"No." My hand flew up to ward him off — one pink glove, extended out like a shield. It was shaking visibly. "Don't come near me. Not right now."

He stopped moving immediately.

I sucked in a gulp of air, trying desperately to tamp down my rampaging emotions. "I don't do that anymore. What you're asking—" I took another ragged gulp. "I can't get involved in a case like this. Not again."

"I know the Crawford situation didn't go well. But before that, you helped solve a dozen different cases up and down the eastern seaboard."

My lips parted in surprise. "How do you know that?"

"Goldie, your name pops up in so many cold case files, you could have your own true crime podcast. I mapped your whole path up the coast, those first few years, starting when you left home at fifteen. Everywhere you stopped — Orlando to Annapolis — if you could help, you helped."

"Guess you were pretty thorough when you looked into me," I said, a note of bitterness sluicing through my voice.

"Yeah. I was. That's why I know you aren't some con artist bilking desperate families for money. You aren't looking for payback or credit. You're definitely not looking for fame." He didn't move closer, though I could tell he wanted to. His hands were fisted at his sides with the effort to keep from coming to me. "I don't know how your abilities work. I don't care. What matters is, you're the real deal, Imogen Warner. You have a gift. And until you hit Baltimore, you were pretty generous when it came to sharing that gift with others."

"There's a reason I stopped."

He nodded. "What happened with the Crawford case was a miscarriage of justice in every regard, Imogen. The fact that it blew back on you is bullshit. And I know you think it's your fault—"

"No! You don't know. You may *think* you know," I said staring at him through my tear-glazed eyes. "You may think you understand. But you weren't there. You didn't see how it went down. You didn't hear what they said about me. You didn't see the look on that mother's face when they told her the news. You didn't—"

"I did."

I flinched. "You did what?"

"I did see how it went down." He took two steps closer, ignoring the hand I still had up to hold him off. "Because I was there."

He was there.

No.

No, that wasn't possible.

My hand fell limply to my side. My body pushed backwards, automatically seeking distance from him when he continued to come toward me. I didn't stop moving until my spine hit the counter's edge. A dull throb moved through me — I was still sore, thanks to Donny — but I barely felt the pain. My brain was stuck on what Cade had just said, and incapable of moving past it to another thought.

"You were there."

He nodded. He was watching me carefully, like he wasn't sure how I was going to react to this information. Like he thought I was about to bolt. There was a wariness to his expression I'd never seen before. I didn't like seeing it there, but I couldn't blame him for it, either.

I wanted to bolt.

I'd never wanted to bolt so much.

He stopped five feet from me, and didn't move a muscle. His boots were rooted to the floor, his arms were crossed over his chest. He was utterly silent.

"How is that possible?" I forced myself to ask after a series of deep breaths that did precisely nothing to calm me. "You weren't there."

"I was."

"I'd remember you if you were there!"

"You don't believe me?"

I shook my head. I didn't. I *couldn't*. If he was there... If he knew me... That changed everything. Everything I thought I knew about us. How we'd met. How we'd started.

Everything.

"Go on, then." Cade's hand lifted toward me, palm out. "Touch me. See for yourself what I remember."

"*What?*"

He waggled his fingers.

My spine was like an iron rod. My voice was raw. "Don't mock me."

"I'm not. I'm being perfectly serious," he said — and I could tell from the gravity in his eyes that he meant it. "I've got nothing to hide. Told you your first night in town, I'm an open book. If you want to go riffling around inside my head looking for answers, have at it. There's nothing in there I wouldn't tell you myself, if you asked."

I stared at his hand in horror — not at his suggestion, but at the realization that *I wanted to*. I wanted to touch him, more than I'd ever wanted anything in my life. More than I wanted my parents back, alive and breathing. More than I wanted my uncle to evaporate in a puff of smoke. More than I wanted Adrian to leave me the hell alone.

I wanted to slide my hands across his skin, to feel that thick silver-threaded hair against my fingertips. I wanted to see if, beneath the perfectly packaged exterior, he was just as kind and strong and warm as he seemed to be.

But...

What if he wasn't?

What if I touched him and saw nothing but darkness? What if, like Adrian, his thoughts were full of deceptions and trap-doors, lies and disappointments?

He'd be knocked right off that pedestal I'd put him on, his Hero-Hair nothing but a foolish hope. And, selfishly, I wanted to keep him there. Crystalized in my memory forever, a rare unblemished chapter of my sad, twisted tale.

"No," I said flatly, pressing harder against the countertop. "Just... Just tell me."

Cade's eyes flashed with strong emotion as his hand slowly dropped back to his side. He locked it away before I could decipher what it was, settling his mask of composure firmly in place.

"I was just a beat cop back then, not a detective," he said

without delay. "I wasn't in the bull pen. I was out canvassing the streets like everyone else. Looking for the Crawford kid."

"Joey," I whispered.

"Joey," Cade repeated. His voice was a soft blow, straight to the heart. He sucked in a breath, then continued. "That night, when you first came in, I was on duty. My shift had just started, and it was chaos at the station. Phones ringing off the hook with leads, press hounding us for answers. The parents out front, crying as they gave their statement. Everyone was rushing around, utter bedlam. Everyone… except you."

I was no longer breathing.

"I walked through the waiting room and there you were. Just sitting there, totally still. Totally calm. Like the eye of a hurricane." His jaw clenched tight. "Stopped me in my fucking tracks."

God.

He was telling the truth.

I remembered that night. I remembered sitting there in that waiting room like it was yesterday. I'd been nervous. This wasn't like any of the other cases I'd consulted on. I wasn't giving a tip to solve a home invasion or bringing a cold case back into the warm light of day. This was a missing kid. He was still out there.

And he was in danger.

Unsure as I was about getting involved in something so serious, I knew I wouldn't be able to live with myself if I didn't follow through on the vision I'd had earlier that evening. I'd been nineteen at the time. Working at a diner, trying to scrape together enough in tips to afford my share of the rent in a shitty apartment I split with two roommates in a sketchy part of town. Barely able to afford food and bus fare.

The man had come in late, ordered dinner to-go. He'd barely made eye contact, let alone conversation. But he bumped into me when he hurried for the door, knocking the tray I was bussing right out of my hands. My *bare* hands. I didn't like to get my gloves dirty when I was clearing tables and wiping food scraps.

Funny how one vain, inconsequential choice can damn you for all time, isn't it?

When we collided, I'd nearly gone sailing. Instinctually, I'd grabbed hold of the man's arm, to stop my descent. And—

Bam.

Purple sparks had exploded at my temples.

The door to the basement is locked. The man makes sure before he leaves the house. Not once, not twice.

Five times.

Five locks.

Three deadbolts, two chains.

His new pet can't get out, the man assures himself as he gets in his car and drives away. Even if he were tall enough to try and climb out the window, it's barred from the outside.

A perfect cage.

The man is not soothed by this knowledge. He feels jittery. On edge. He was careful. Careful and quick. But what if someone saw him carry the boy inside? What if those nosy neighbors of his come poking around, asking questions they have no right to ask?

Then they'll get what's coming to them, that's what.

The man is no fool. He's been planning this a long time. No one is going to mess up his plans. Not the busybody down the block, and not the goddamned police.

He learned a few things in the war, watching his friends blown to bits by landmines. How to rig a booby trap, for one. How to get the pressure plates just right, so when a man steps down on one…

Lights out.

If his traps don't take them out on their way in, he has enough fire power to blast apart a whole SWAT team long before they reach the basement.

Armor-piercing bullets are great.

Hand grenades are even better.

He isn't going down without a fight. And if anyone tries to take away his new pet... He'll take them all down in a hail of gunfire the likes of which this city has never seen.

I'd slammed back into my head, nauseous and reeling. It was a miracle I managed to swallow down my vomit before it spewed all over the man's shoes. He'd made a low grunt of displeasure, ripped his arm out of my grip, and raced for the door.

Eager to get home.

To Joey.

His pet.

The thought had nearly sent me to my knees. I'd wanted to run screaming in the opposite direction, horrified by the images in my head, even more horrified by what they meant for that little boy. Instead, I moved to the door.

The man had hustled out so quickly, I was worried he'd already vanished. But when I reached the exit, I saw his truck, an older model red pickup, pulling out of a spot in front of the diner. Whipping out my order pad, I'd jotted down his license plate number just before he peeled out into traffic.

I waited until he was out of sight, then stepped out the door. My manager had called something after me — probably wondering where the hell I was going in the middle of my shift — but I didn't stop. Not to explain. Not even to take off my apron. I walked into the dark night, hand gripping my order pad, pulse roaring between my ears. And I didn't stop walking until I'd reached the police precinct five blocks away. The one I passed every day on my bus ride to work.

I'd informed the receptionist I had information — urgent, vital, important information — about the Joey Crawford case, and begged to speak to the detective in charge as soon as possible.

Take a seat, she'd told me. I'd have to wait.

So, I'd waited.

And waited.

And *waited.*

Fifteen minutes passed.

Twenty.

Thirty.

Forty-five.

Each second that ticked by was agony. Didn't they realize they were wasting time? Didn't they know they were pissing away Joey's chances at a future?

The only way I could keep from screaming at the top of my lungs was to stay totally still. Completely self-contained. The second I acted the least bit crazy, any information I had would immediately be dismissed as the hysterical rantings of a madwoman.

So I sat.

And sat.

And *sat.*

Even though it damn near killed me.

As for Joey…

It *did* kill him.

"They should've listened to you," Cade said now, calling me back to the present with a jolt. "That night, when you first walked in… they should've taken what you had to say more seriously."

I didn't have a response to that — mostly because I fully agreed.

"I was there, on the other side of the glass, when they finally pulled you into the interrogation room. Even before that night, I knew Jennings was an incompetent idiot. Third generation BPD, promoted up the chain with the helping hand of nepotism, regardless of the fact he had about three functioning brain cells."

My lip curled at the mention of the lead detective on the Crawford case. He was a prick of the highest order. I had no doubt he was also the 'anonymous source close to the investigation' who'd sold me out to the press.

"I couldn't believe he thought you were lying. Anyone with eyeballs could see you weren't fucking around for a laugh."

"It's not exactly normal," I murmured, shrugging. "Most people find what I can do… difficult to accept."

"Skepticism is healthy. But Jennings was a straight-up asshole to you from minute one. Didn't listen when you said the perp was a jumpy motherfucker. Didn't listen when you said the whole place was rigged to blow." Cade's face contorted into a look of disgust. "If we'd gone in soft, like you said, we could've taken him into custody. That SWAT team would still be alive. And so would Joey Crawford."

My chin jerked to the side. My eyes bored holes into the cabinets.

He was wrong.

"Imogen."

I didn't look at him.

He closed the gap between us in two big strides, not stopping until he was in my space — his body pressed against mine, his heat sinking into me. I had no choice but to tilt my head up.

"It wasn't your fault," he told me, voice intent.

I swallowed.

"It wasn't, beautiful. You did what you could. You tried. That's all anyone can ever do." His forehead hit mine, pressing gently. "I won't ask you to get involved again if you don't want to. It has to be your decision. But I need you to know, if you do take that chance again… it won't be like last time. This isn't Joey. This is Rory. And I'm not that asshole Jennings. I'm not going to hang you out to dry. Neither is Coulter or Aguilar."

"You can't promise me that, Cade."

"I just did."

"It's not that simple—"

"It is. It is that simple." His face was so close, I felt his exhale against my mouth. "You can trust me, Imogen. I'd never hurt you. You have to know that by now."

"I do know that," I whispered.

"Saw you six years ago. Lost you then, but I never forgot you," he confessed. "A week ago you walked back into my life and I knew I'd do anything I could to keep you from walking out of it again."

God.

My heart squeezed. My eyes were abruptly full of tears. "Cade—"

"I think you've had about as much as you can take for one night," he cut me off. "And I can't stand seeing that haunted look in your eyes for another goddamned second. So now, I'm going to carry you into my bed and I'm going to fuck you until it's gone. Until you're looking at me that way you do — soft, dazed, desperate — when I'm deep inside you and you're about to come for me."

I had to admit, that sounded good.

His mouth hit mine at the same moment he scooped me up into his arms — one going beneath my knees, the other supporting my back. He didn't stop kissing me as he carried me into his bedroom, where he did exactly as he'd promised.

Twice.

CHAPTER TWENTY

Why did we stop putting men on the moon? Let's put them all up there. Starting with my exes.
- Imogen Warner, conversing about space

Later that night, I made a decision.

I was on top, straddling Cade on the bed. He was deep inside me, filling me so completely my breaths hitched with each downward stroke. I rode him slowly, taking my time. Earlier, we'd been frantic for each other. Desperate. Now, I was savoring it.

Our hands were locked together, the long, tan lengths of his fingers intertwined with my pale pink gloves. He was looking up at me, eyes half-lidded with lust, lips parted slightly as he watched me move. We were both close to release. I could feel the tension gathering in me, like a storm about to break, and increased my tempo. His hips lifted off the bed to meet my downward strokes, impaling me from below, hitting my g-spot perfectly.

God, that felt good.

"I'm almost there." A moan vibrated from my throat. "Are you coming with me?'

"No."

My breath caught. "No?"

"Want to feel your hands on me," he rasped.

My stomach somersaulted. "What?"

"Need your touch, beautiful." His fingers flexed around on mine. "No gloves. No walls between us."

"But—"

His hips drove upward again, deepening our connection. I cried out in pleasure, protests long forgotten. I was about to come, and he was asking me — god, I could barely even keep track of what he was asking me. All logic, all reason, was being tuned out by the white noise of desire.

Cade was determined. His hips drove up with another powerful thrust. "Touch me, Imogen."

"I can't," I gasped. "I— I'm—"

Coming.

Through the thick fog of my orgasm, I heard him say something else. Something I barely processed at the time, too overcome to think straight.

"You will," he growled, grinding into me. "Someday, you will."

Then, he came too — with a ragged groan and a full-body shudder that matched my own. When the aftershocks faded, I collapsed onto his chest, incapable of holding myself upright. My forehead found the crook of his neck, where his pulse was pounding like a battle drum. His hand moved through my hair, rhythmic strokes that made me snuggle closer.

I was sated in a way I hadn't been maybe… ever. I felt safe and warm and supported. But I also felt unquestionably strange. I couldn't put my finger on why; couldn't decipher what, exactly, I was feeling.

Until it finally hit me.

Home.

That's what I felt.

Lying there in Cade's arms, I felt like I was finally home. And for a girl who'd never had that... not since she was five years old...

There were no words.

None in the English language, at least. (I didn't speak any other languages, but I doubted they had words to describe that feeling, either.)

"Imogen?" Cade rumbled.

"Mmm?"

"Earlier, when you were on the phone—"

I tensed slightly.

"—you mentioned something," he went on cautiously. "A snow globe. You said that douchebag smashed it."

Christ, he never missed a single detail. No wonder he was a detective.

I sighed. "Is there a question in there?"

He squeezed my hip at the sassy comment. "You know the question, smartass."

"It was from my parents," I admitted after a long beat of silence. "One of the last things I had to remember them. They bought it for me when I was four, during our first trip to Disney World. It had Cinderella's castle inside and when you shook it, these purple sparkles floated all around. It was beautiful."

His hand tightened on my hip again — this time, a soothing gesture instead of a scolding one.

"One night last spring, Adrian had a bad run of luck at the poker table. He smashed half the stuff in his penthouse." I swallowed hard, trying not to remember that night too clearly. It hadn't ended well for me. "Including my snow globe. He chucked it at a wall and it shattered to pieces."

"I'm sorry, Goldie."

"You didn't do it."

"No. But I'm going to fix it."

"Fix it?"

He nodded. I couldn't see it, plastered so tight against his side, but I felt him do it.

"What does that mean?" I asked. "How are you going to fix it?"

"Firstly, by making sure that fuckwad never comes near you again," he said flatly. "He contacts you, I want to know about it."

"Okay."

"Let's hope he's smarter than that."

Adrian was many things; *smart* was not one of them.

"Cade, you really don't have to get involved in my drama. You have enough on your plate right now."

He rolled me off his chest onto the bed, then came up on one elbow so he could look into my face. "Anything that hurts you, anything that even tries, I'm getting involved. Whether it's that asshole ex or your asshole uncle."

My stomach turned to stone. "My uncle?"

"Already put in a call to one of my contacts in Orlando," he confirmed calmly. "He'll get back to me with whatever he finds out."

"Cade!" I practically screamed, not calm at all. The very opposite of calm, in fact.

I shoved away from him with all my strength, instinctively trying to flee. He didn't let me get far. His arm was like steel as he hauled me back against his body and rolled on top, effectively pinning me to the bed with his weight. I thrashed for a few seconds, a useless endeavor.

"Settle down, Goldie."

I glared up at him. "I will not *settle down*! I cannot believe you're poking into my uncle without my permission!"

"Really? You can't believe it?" He scoffed. "You can't believe I'd find out someone fucked you over, forced you into a life of show business against your will, performing like a trained monkey at a circus for his benefit, and *not* have a reaction to that? You can't believe I'd learn that same someone stole all your money, left you penniless at fifteen years old when you'd finally had enough and took off, and *not* try to punish the bastard?"

Gwen and Flo had big freaking mouths. One of them must've spilled the beans about my financial woes. (I was guessing Gwen. She folded faster than a beach chair whenever confronted with her boyfriend's naked body — a fact she readily admitted after several shots of tequila.)

I continued to glare up at him. "I'm not your problem to fix, Cade."

"You're right. You are not a problem, Imogen. You are a purpose."

Damn.

That was a nice thing to say. Hearing it took some of the wind out of my sails. I persevered anyway. "Please understand... That part of my life is over. I want to keep it that way."

"You're still running from it. That means it's not over."

My lips pressed together.

"Only way you'll be able to stop running is if this shit is finally dealt with," Cade declared. "And I don't want you running anymore, beautiful. I like you right where you are." He gave me more of his weight, as if to underline his point.

Double damn.

Not only did the move feel deliciously good, that was an even nicer thing to say. Still, I was determined to make him understand.

"My uncle... He is not someone you want to mess with, Cade. He has some powerful friends and deep connections. Before I left Florida, I tried to sue for emancipation. He threatened to have a psychiatrist declare me mentally incompetent. Told me he'd get one of his judge buddies to put me in a conservatorship, so I'd *never* be free of him, even after I turned eighteen."

"Fucking bastard."

"Finally, something we agree on."

"You aren't a kid anymore, Imogen. He can't touch you — not legally, not physically. Not even emotionally, so long as you don't let him." He bowed his head, aligning our faces in the dark. "He's kept you in a cage of fear for so long, you don't know what freedom feels like. I'm going to make sure that changes. I'm going to make sure you're free and clear if it's the last thing I do."

Free.

Free and clear.

Triple damn.

Tears filled my eyes in a sudden rush. "That's too much. I can't ask—"

"You didn't ask. I offered. And, frankly, even if you tell me to stop, I'm not going to. I might not be able to undo the hurt in your past. But I can sure as fuck make sure there's no more in your future."

"That's—" My voice cracked. The tears spilled over.

He kissed them away, his lips soft against my cheeks. "Sleep now, beautiful. It's late and I have to be out of here early."

That's when I decided.

To trust.

To try.

To take a chance.

"Wake me before you go," I said shakily.

"Why? You should sleep in a bit. The Gallows is closed on Mondays."

"I know." I took a breath. "But I want to come with you. I want to help with the case. To try, at least. I might not be any help, but if there's even a small chance I can bring Rory home…"

Cade's body went solid beneath mine. There was a long moment of silence before he took a breath and murmured, "You sure?"

"I'm sure."

He didn't say anything else. But his arms tightened around me until I could hardly breathe. His lips hit my hair to press a kiss there. And I knew, without any words, he was telling me that he was proud of me.

Sun streamed through the window of Georgia's sunny yellow kitchen. I stared at the chip on the corner of the wood tabletop, wondering where to begin. Declan sat across from me, looking like a shell of the little boy I'd known before. His expression was closed off, his eyes cast down at the bowl of cereal in front of him. It looked completely untouched.

On our way to The Sea Witch, Cade shared his suspicions that Declan knew more than he was telling the police.

The kid's clammed up. Won't say more than a handful of words. It's bigger than guilt. It's fear. Something's got him spooked. And we need to know what.

Sitting there, studying Declan, I could see Cade was right. He was afraid. He was practically trembling.

"Declan," I called softly.

He didn't look up.

"Dec. Honey, look at me."

Finally, he lifted his gaze. It was brimming with emotions — the strongest of which was sheer, unadulterated terror.

"You know none of this is your fault, don't you?"

He shifted slightly in his chair, uncomfortable with my question.

I kept at him. "You know no one blames you for Rory disappearing, right? Not me, not your Mom. Not the police."

He shifted again. On the table, his hands knit together into a ball of worried white knuckles.

"It's going to be okay."

His eyes pressed briefly closed as pain flashed across his features. I recalled he'd had a similar reaction on Halloween, at the police station, when I'd assured him everything would be fine.

"Declan?"

He finally spoke, forcing out the words in an empty tone. "It's not going to be okay. It's *not*."

His eyes opened again, and there was a horrible bleakness in their depths. Thank god Cade was keeping Georgia occupied in the other room under the guise of official police business. She would've gone straight into panic mode, seeing that look in her son's eyes.

"It's my fault," he confessed. Tears started streaking down his face. *"It's all my fault."*

He began to sob, too worked up to say anything else. I tried twice more to gently prod an answer from him, but he couldn't give me one. He sat there, trembling like a leaf, too broken to say another word.

Under the table, I pulled my gloves off and laid them on my thigh. I felt a bit like trembling, too, if I was being honest. But my hand appeared remarkably steady as I slid it across the tabletop.

Slowly, so as not to scare him, I took Declan's bare hand in mine. A sob caught in his throat as I squeezed reassuringly.

Just once.

That was all I had the time for.

With a flash of purple in my peripherals, I was swept away.

The boys ride through the shadowy streets, pedaling fast. Their veins are pure sugar; their grins are wide. Plastic candy buckets shaped like jack-o-lanterns are looped over their handlebars, clacking each time they round a bend.

This neighborhood is the best. The big houses on the hill near the golf course always have the king-sized candy bars. The boys aren't supposed to come here. It's too far. But as long as they're back home by eight, they won't get in trouble. Plenty of time to stock up on more sugar, then head to the woods for some spooky fun.

Fun with the witch.

The Witch of Salem Wood.

They've all heard the ghost stories about her. Tonight, they're going to see for themselves. They have it all planned. They've even invited a few other kids in their sixth-grade class — but they'll probably all be too scared to show up.

Lame.

He's not scared. He's with his friends. All six of them are the same age. Eleven. Way too old for chaperones tagging along, ruining their time.

The one exception is the boy at the very back of the bike brigade. The little one, struggling to keep up as they ascend higher and higher up the hill, clicking their gears and standing up on their pedals to keep momentum.

Only a bit farther, now.

"Declan!" The youngest boy calls, his voice breathy with exertion. "Wait for me!"

The older boys laugh and keep pedaling.

Onward, upward.

"Dec!" The youngster tries again as they hit the midway point. The reflective panels of his costume catch the streetlights with each pedal-turn. "Please!"

"Go home, you baby!" His brother's voice carries back from a long distance. "You're not supposed to be here anyway!"

"But I want to come with you!"

"Tough!"

"I want to see the witch!"

The older boy finally stops riding to look back. His face is annoyed. His friends are leaving without him. "You can't come, Rory. You'll be too scared."

"I will not!"

"Will too," the older boy counters. "You'll start crying and screaming. Then, she'll steal your soul away, just like the legend says!"

"Nuh-uh!" the little boy cries, but his voice is less certain. "I can be quiet."

The older boy shakes his head. "You're too much of a scaredy cat."

"I'm telling Mom you called me names! And that you went to the woods, even though you're not supposed to!"

"Fine! Whatever. Tattle like you always do, you big blabbermouth. You still aren't coming."

"But, Dec—"

The older brother glares at the younger harshly enough to cut off his protests. "Don't you get it, dummy? No one wants you here. Go back down the hill to the chaperones. And do me a favor: find your own friends."

With that, the older brother turns his back, grips his handlebars tightly, and starts pedaling again. Up the hill, into the dark. He doesn't look back. He doesn't see the determined set to the younger boy's shoulders as he fixes his eyes on the top of the hill. And he doesn't hear the words that drift into the night.

"I'm not a scaredy cat. He'll see. They'll all see. I'll prove it to them."

The vision changed, morphed into something new. It was the same night, but darker. Later. And the boys were no longer on the streets, but deep in the woods.

The boy holds the flashlight under his chin, casting the planes of his face in ghostly yellow light. He affects a deep warble as he tells his tale, trying his hardest to instill fear in the hearts of the small group who've gathered in the deepest stretch of the woods.

He's determined to impress his crush. He didn't think she would show up, but there she is, sandwiched between two of her friends on the hollow log, looking cuter than ever in a neon pink wig. He doesn't know what her costume is, and he's too nervous to ask.

He wants her to think he's cool.

He needs her to think he's cool.

"Beware the Witch of Salem Wood. The old hag made from stick and vine," he croaks, trying not to laugh. "She'll steal your soul, drink your blood. But of her sins they'll find no sign…"

The three girls titter nervously. Two of the boys in the group inch closer to each other. The woods are very dark. The boughs creak in the wind, an eerie sound all around them.

"If you hear her creeping near — moaning, groaning, in the trees," the boy recites from memory. "Keep still and quiet through your fear, or her next victim you will be."

A girl on the other side of their circle drops her flashlight. They all let out sharp screams as it clatters into the leafy undergrowth. Their alarm is quickly covered with embarrassed coughs and chuckles.

The tale is reaching its end. The boy infuses his voice with as much rasp as he's able for the grand finale. "For if you make a single sound, your very voice is hers to keep… Until you're buried in the ground, another word you'll never speak…"

The boy trails off. The clearing falls totally silent. Until a sharp crack echoes from the tree line — like a boot, snapping a twig in two. They all go still, collectively terrified.

Is someone out there?

Has the witch come to steal their souls?

No, look — it's just a rabbit, hopping through the brush.

The moment passes and soon, they're all laughing again.

It's fun to be scared.

That's what this night is all about. That, and the candy of course. The boy searches for the best, biggest king-sized bar in the bottom of his bucket. When he finds it, he plucks up his courage and carries it across the clearing to the girl in the pink wig.

She smiles when she sees him coming.

It's the best Halloween he's ever had.

I jolted out of Declan's head and back into my own with the same whirlwind velocity as always. He was still seated across from me, but his expression had shifted from one of devastation to one of confusion. No doubt because my hand had gone limp in his and I'd essentially slumped over onto the table like a rag doll.

"Are you okay, Imogen?"

"Of course," I lied.

With a deep breath, I straightened, pulled back my hand, and attempted a smile. It was shaky and, from the concern on Declan's face, did little to assuage his worry. The fog of the vision was still thick in my head, clouding every thought, but I pushed my way through it.

I had to focus.

"Can I ask you something?"

He hesitated, then gave a shallow nod.

"On Halloween..."

His whole frame tensed.

"Declan, honey, you won't get into any trouble. I just want to know where you went that night. With your friends, in the woods."

His eyes widened to huge orbs. "How do you know about that?"

"It doesn't matter, bub. I just do."

"But— but—" He spluttered, looking close to tears again. "Rory wasn't with us. I left him behind, that's why he's lost. I left him. I didn't want him tagging along. I said a bunch of mean things..." Horror flashed through his features. "You aren't going to tell Mom, are you? She'll never forgive me if she knows it's my fault. She'll hate me. Like she hates Dad."

There it was: the source of his fear. The reason he'd kept silent, these past few days. He was terrified he'd lose his mother's love. Terrified he'd never be forgiven. The realization made my throat lump. I spoke through it, trying to keep my emotions in check.

"Like I told you before, Declan, this isn't your fault."

He lost the battle against his tears. They streaked down his cheeks in a torrent, relentless. I got out of my chair, moved around the table to his side, and yanked him into a tight hug.

"Shhh." I breathed against the messy brown curls at the top of his head. "It's all going to be okay, honey. But I need you to be brave. I need you to tell me the truth about what happened that night. I know you're scared of getting in trouble. But wherever Rory is right now, he's scared too. He wants to come home. And you can help him do that."

"O-okay." He hiccupped violently. His whole body jerked with the force of it. "Okay, Imogen. I'll tell you."

Three hours later, Gigi and I sat side-by-side on stools at Gwen's kitchen island, watching intently as Sally demonstrated the crucial twelfth step in her raspberry cheesecake recipe. (Steps one through eleven had also been crucial, for the record.)

At Gwen's insistence, we'd driven over an hour ago in Georgia's sporty hatchback for lunch with "the girls." I was expecting Florence. I was not expecting Sally and Agatha. Yet, there they were — Sally at the stove, Agatha embroiled in a marathon round of canasta with Flo in the living room.

I was on edge. I'd been on edge since my vision and only grown edgier afterward, when I talked to Cade about what I'd seen. His mouth was no more than a flat line by the time I finished speaking.

"If Rory followed the older kids to the woods that night," he said, shaking his head slowly. "We've been looking in the wrong fucking place."

He'd left soon after, pressing a quick kiss to my lips before he strode through the door. I'd kept Gigi company for a while in the reception area. Technically, she wasn't on the clock, but she said sitting at her desk was the only thing in her life that felt remotely normal, anymore. Her mother and sister were there too, staying in rooms on the third floor. Like Gigi, they were kind and welcoming, with foxlike features and shiny brown hair. (Unlike Gigi, they did not have a goofy sense of humor or a proclivity for homemade limoncello.) When Gwen called, they'd happily taken over the front desk duties, rushing Gigi out the door with promises to look after Declan and any guests who wandered in.

I'd said goodbye to Declan before I left, barely getting a response. He'd descended again into a pit of grief and guilt. I feared he'd be stuck there forever if we didn't bring his brother home soon.

Even after we got in the car and drove away, my thoughts had returned again and again to the vision. Something about the scene in the woods was nagging at me, like a loose thread that begged to be tugged and tugged until the whole sweater unraveled. I had the strangest sense that I was missing something, here.

Something huge.

Something important.

I just couldn't put my finger on what.

"Imogen, sugar, you're not listening to me," Sally chastised, calling me back to the present. "You'll end up with lumpy preserve if you don't whisk it right."

"Sorry." I exhaled sharply, then shifted my focus to her. "I'm just distracted."

"What's on your mind?"

I hesitated. I wasn't sure this was the right topic of conversation. Georgia was sitting right beside me. Then again, Sally was a practicing Wiccan. And she'd lived in Salem for decades. If anyone would know about the legend...

"Spit it out," Sally said, pointing her wooden spoon at me. The tip was stained red with raspberries. "No point teaching you my secret recipe if you aren't able to learn it. The sooner you unload, the sooner we're back to the truly important matters. Cheesecake, for instance."

"Of course," Gigi said, snorting softly. "Life's one true purpose."

I shot her a quick smile, then went for it. "It's kind of an odd question."

"My favorite kind." Sally's eyes twinkled. "Go on."

"I was wondering if you'd ever heard of a local legend about a witch..."

"Lots of witches in Salem's history," she said wryly. "You'll have to be a wee bit more specific, dear."

"Right." Color hit my cheeks. "Um... well, the one I'm referring to is called The Witch of Salem Wood. Have you heard of her?"

Sally scoffed and set down her spoon. "I certainly have. But she's not a real witch. She's just a local legend the kids made up decades ago."

"It's an old ghost story. Everyone who grew up around here knows it," Gwen chimed in, eyes narrowed in thought. The swelling on her cheek had gone down, but she was still sporting a bruise. "Every year, kids go into the woods and try to freak each other out, telling it under the moonlight. It's sort of a local tradition, like Bloody Mary in the Mirror. Florence and I used to recite the rhyme to each other at midnight during sleepovers. We'd scare ourselves silly and wouldn't sleep a wink all night."

"What is the legend, exactly?" I asked.

"Pretty standard stuff." Gwen shrugged. "An old hag wanders the deepest stretches of the woods. If you come across her, you have to stay quiet. No screaming. Otherwise, she steals your voice."

"And your soul!" Flo called, looking up from her canasta cards.

"Poppycock," Agatha declared.

"The legend or my meld?" Flo asked.

Agatha sighed. "Both, dear."

"Stories like that are what give real witches a bad reputation." Sally shook her head. "People shouldn't spread them around."

"Tell that to the kids in my second-grade class." Florence abandoned her cards, admitting defeat against Agatha, and wandered over to join the conversation. "They've all got the rhyme memorized. Recess is like one long spoken-word performance. Come to think of it, Georgia, your Rory is always the ringleader—" Flo froze, realizing what she'd said. "Oh, god. I'm sorry. I didn't think..."

We all held our breath.

Gigi managed a tremulous smile. "It's okay. Really. I like talking about him. It's better than people avoiding the subject, acting like he never existed." She took a shaky breath. "Declan taught him the story a few months ago. For weeks, the two of them would sit up in bed way past their curfew, holding flashlights under their chins, telling it over and over again. Giggling up a storm. I used to burst into their room, yelling at them to shut the lights and get to sleep." Her posture crumpled inward. "If I could go back... I'd give anything to be lying in my bed, listening to them laugh through the wall."

My heart gave a sympathetic pang.

Florence came unstuck from her spot in the middle of the kitchen. Moving to Georgia's side, she slung an arm around her slim shoulders and hugged her tight.

"Rory will be back in his bed, safe and sound and driving you crazy, before you know it," she said. "You just have to hold on a little longer."

Gigi nodded. But, looking at the defeated slump of her shoulders, I wondered how much more she could take before she broke completely.

My thoughts wandered back to the vision I'd had this morning. Back to Declan and his friends in the woods, fighting their fear as they heard the wind howling through the trees and phantom footsteps on the fallen limbs.

"Where did the story come from?" I glanced around the kitchen. "When did it start?

Gwen shrugged. "No idea."

"I could ask Desmond," Florence offered. "He's a big local history buff — it sort of comes with the job description as a professor of New England folklore. If there are real origins to the legend, he'll probably know."

"I'm also a big local history buff," Agatha interjected, shouldering her way up to the counter beside Florence. "It's called being eighty-one years old and having ears."

I snorted out a laugh.

Agatha turned her sharp gaze on me. "That urban legend's been floating around nearly half a century, now. You talk to the locals, they'll tell you there have been sightings of this so-called *witch* for years, deep in the woods. Mostly at night. Campsites disturbed, food and supplies gone missing…"

"Ag's right," Sally added. "There have been whispers for ages. But it wasn't until maybe fifteen years ago they gave her that name. *The Witch of Salem Wood.* Right around the time…" She glanced at Agatha. Her brows went up in silent question.

Agatha nodded in confirmation, then murmured, "Yes. The Thurman girl."

"I thought so." Sally shook her head. "Such a shame, what happened. Horrible. Just horrible."

The Thurman girl. They'd mentioned her once before, during our hair-raising drive to The Banshee. We'd had other priorities at the time — namely, rescuing Georgia from the O'Banion brothers — but now, my interest was piqued.

"What happened to her?" I asked. "Who was she?"

Sally's eyes shifted to Georgia for a moment. "Maybe it's better not to talk about this. It might be upsetting."

We all looked at Gigi.

She sat up straighter on her stool. Her face was set in a stubborn expression. "Tell us. I want to hear."

"Are you sure?" Sally heaved a sigh when Georgia nodded. "All right, dear. Annie Thurman was the last child who went missing in Salem."

Every particle of air in the room turned solid with tension.

"Fifteen, maybe twenty years ago," Sally went on. "She was playing in her backyard on a summer afternoon, then — *poof*!

Gone. Her folks thought she'd wandered off to play with her friend down the street. Until night fell. She never came home."

"A five-year-old girl, gone without a trace. The whole town was in an uproar, as you can imagine," Agatha added, getting in on the story. "Search parties organized, flyers posted on street lamps. Police going door to door, neighbors searching their yard sheds and swimming pools."

Sally shook her head. "No sign of her anywhere."

"Just like Rory," Gigi whispered.

"How have we never heard about this?" Florence asked, her voice stunned. "A case like this would've been national news!"

"At the time, it certainly was. But you were no more than a little one yourself when this happened. You wouldn't remember." Sally took a long breath. "And, of course, the story died down when she came home."

The air, already tense, turned even tenser.

"She came home?" Georgia asked, and there was a thread of something in her voice that broke my heart clean in half.

Hope.

"She did," Agatha confirmed. "Wandered out of the woods nearly a week after she'd first disappeared. A passing car spotted her on the side of the road. Not a scratch on her."

"She was dirty, of course. A few scrapes and scratches from being outdoors… A bit of sunburn. Slightly dehydrated. But physically, she was completely unharmed." Sally hesitated. "Except, of course…"

We waited.

Sally and Agatha traded another glance — one that made all the hair on the back of my neck lift straight up. Whatever they were going to say next…

It wasn't good.

"Just tell us," Gigi pleaded softly. "Tell us the end."

"She never spoke another word," Agatha said, a fissure of sorrow in her voice. "Not the day she returned, not in the weeks or months that followed. Not ever. Whatever she saw in those woods, whatever she experienced in her time out there… It rendered her totally mute."

"Horrible," Sally said. "Just horrible. We were all shocked. I can't imagine how her parents felt, getting her back only to…" She trailed off at Georgia's sharp intake of breath. "I'm sorry, dear. I told you this story wasn't one you'd want to hear."

"I'm fine," Gigi lied. "I want to know. Tell us the rest."

Florence hugged her tighter. I shifted my stool closer so I could press my thigh against hers beneath the counter.

Agatha cleared her throat. "The Thurman family was wealthy. The father was a doctor, the mother a lawyer. They paid for the best medical experts in the state. ENTs. Surgeons. Specialists. Speech pathologists. All of them said the same thing. Her vocal cords were fine. It was selective mutism. Psychologists figured she must've had some kind of trauma while she was missing. But they never learned what. Never found a suspect in her disappearance, either."

"How can that be?" Gwen shook her head. "A child was gone for a week, and the police had no suspect?"

"Technically, they had no evidence of a crime being committed. By all accounts, she might've just wandered off. There was no way to confirm she'd been taken by someone. She wasn't abused, wasn't injured."

"She never spoke another word!" Flo exclaimed. "I'd say that's evidence enough that something happened out there in the woods!"

"Even so, there was no proof. No explanation. And no answers," Sally murmured. "Generally, a situation like that makes people uncomfortable. They need someone to blame, some answer as to why a thing like that happened."

"Which brings us back to the legend," Agatha said. "The Witch of Salem Wood."

"They created a villain because there wasn't one." My mind was racing nearly as fast as my pulse. "And the legend was born."

Gwen nodded slowly. "The witch who steals your voice. Makes sense."

We all fell silent. It was a lot to process. I wanted to ask what had happened to the Thurman girl after her diagnosis, but I was highly conscious of Georgia sitting beside me, barely holding it together. I'd have to ask Sally or Agatha another time.

"Desmond is going to flip over this story," Florence said finally, shattering the heavy silence. "The birth of a local legend... that's like crack cocaine to the man. Oh *god*, I bet he'll want to do a deep dive. Do you know what that means? I'll tell you what it means! Another academic journal submission. Another paper it'll take eons for him to write, locked away in his study. Another peer review process." She said the words *peer review* like they tasted foul. "I might as well prepare for six months of playing second fiddle to this fictitious witch. She's about to be the main lady in his life."

Gwen stifled a laugh. "At least he's no longer in his Sleepy Hollow phase. Remember when he started insisting that *Ichabod* is a solid name if you ever have kids?"

"Don't remind me," Florence grumbled. "There's a reason the jury's still out on whether or not I'll reproduce."

"Can we get back to my cheesecake, now?" Sally interjected, sounding impatient. "I'd like to get the batter into the springform before I expire."

The emotionally charged air dispersed as we dropped the subject of Salem's homegrown ghost story. We quickly shifted the conversation into calmer waters, keeping to light topics as the cheesecake baked and eventually came out of the oven. It smelled heavenly and looked divine. There wasn't a single crack in its lightly browned top.

"Water bath," Sally said with satisfaction. "Makes all the difference."

She insisted it couldn't be eaten for hours, needing to cool completely before it could be sliced and served. Frankly, I thought it was cruel and unusual punishment to sit there salivating while we waited for it to reach room temperature.

The sharp ring of the doorbell distracted me from all thoughts of dessert. Gwen left the kitchen to answer it and returned with Cade in tow. We all took deep breaths as his handsome frame filled the doorway. He nodded hello to everyone, but his eyes found mine. There was a serious look in their depths that made my heart skip a beat.

Something had happened.

"Imogen," Cade said softly. "Can I talk to you for a minute? Privately?"

I very nearly vaulted off my stool. In a second, I was across the room, standing in front of him. He grabbed my hand and led me through Gwen's foyer, then into the adjacent living room, steering me around paint cans and drop cloths with ease. We stopped in the corner, eyes locked. For a minute, he didn't say anything.

I was in no mood to wait.

"You found something?" I guessed, hardly daring to hope.

His nod made my heart skip another beat.

"We found something."

CHAPTER TWENTY-ONE

I'm not procrastinating.
I'm on a side quest.
- Imogen Warner, putting off responsibilities

I stared down at the red bicycle. The chain had fallen off its track, but otherwise it looked undamaged. There were several unopened chocolate bars scattered around it, as though a plastic candy bucket had been upturned, but no signs of the bucket itself.

Or its owner.

We were in a dense stretch of woods that abutted the golf course, not far from the local high school. You could actually see the edges of the overgrown soccer field if you squinted through the foliage. Not twenty feet away, a dirt walking path wound its way to a parking lot.

Yet, they'd missed it.

All the search parties, all the volunteers... And they'd still missed it. Probably because the investigation was focused primarily on the other side of town, in the area where Rory and Declan were supposed to be that night.

Christ.

"It's a fifteen-minute bike ride from here to The Sea Witch," Cade said from beside me. "Nearly an hour on foot. We had no reason to think they'd come all the way out here. Could've been days — even weeks — before someone found this, Imogen."

I glanced over and found he was looking at me.

"First clue we've had since this all started," he murmured, keeping his voice soft so as not to draw the attention of the uniformed officers who were roping off the entire area with crime scene tape. "And we only have it thanks to you."

I looked swiftly away. The expression on his face was too much to process, right now. It was more than gratitude or pride. Infinitely more. Infinitely *better*. I tucked it away for later examination.

"Am I going to get in trouble for disturbing a crime scene?" I asked, brows lifting as I stared at Rory's bike.

"We've already dusted it for prints and swabbed for DNA. Pictures were taken of the scene. There's nothing for you to disturb." Cade stepped closer. His voice was still hushed. "Coulter is in the loop about your involvement. So is Aguilar. They weren't over the moon about bringing you on as a consultant at first, but I talked them around. Finding the bike erased whatever lingering hesitations they might have had."

I eyed the two officers still loitering nearby. "But—"

"Buckley! Grieves!" Cade called over my shoulder. "Do me a favor. Take five, will you?"

The officers nodded and, without a word, walked out of sight.

Problem solved.

Having no more credible reasons to delay, I dropped down into a crouch. As I pulled off my gloves, I couldn't help pointing out the obvious.

"There's no guarantee this will work, Cade. It's not like touching a human being. Most of the time, when I touch an object, nothing happens. There needs to be a very strong emotional trace in order to trigger a vision."

"Only asking you to try, Goldie."

"I just don't want to disappoint you if—"

"Not possible," he cut me off.

Damn and blast.

There he went, being nice again.

I set my gloves down on the ground, took a deep breath, and reached out to touch the rubber grip of the handlebar, where a small boy's fingers would wrap as he rode.

Dazzling violet starbursts erupted in my eyes.

I blinked once.

And disappeared into Rory's head.

The boy is scared, but he doesn't let it show. The woods are darker than he thought they would be. There are no streetlights here to illuminate the shadows.

He doesn't want his brother to yell at him again, so he's keeping back from the group. Off the path, in the trees. Out of sight. He can hear the older boys up ahead, laughing as they head deeper into Salem Woods. Their flashlight beams bounce over tree trunks in the distance.

He pedals faster, not wanting to lose them in the dark. His tire hits an unseen divot and his bike pitches forward. He tries to brake, but it's too late. He sprawls, headfirst, over his handlebars. He hits the ground hard, the impact snatching the wind from his lungs.

His palms shred on the rough earth. His candy bucket topples, spilling his precious loot in all directions. Sticks tear at his space suit. Tears gloss his eyes at the sudden shock of pain.

But he is determined.

He won't be left behind.

Not tonight.

He'll show Declan he's no baby. And he'll get the last laugh, in the end. When he sneaks up on them during the ghost story...

They'll all scream.

They'll all be the scaredy-cats, then.

Not him.

The thought makes him forget all about the pain. He gathers his scattered candy bars, shoving them back into his bucket before he loops it over one arm. He has no choice but to leave his bike behind. The chain is off its track and he doesn't know how to fix it.

Mom always does it for him.

He clicks on his flashlight and continues on foot, grinning to himself as he moves through the dark trees, following the sounds of laughter up ahead.

The vision faded out.

When I came back to myself, I was slumped in Cade's arms, the earthen ground hard beneath us, a tree trunk at our backs. He must've grabbed me the second I was swept away.

I dropped my head into my hands, biting my lip to contain a frustrated scream. I'd gotten practically nothing from the vision. Nothing useful. Just a few seconds of Rory, and absolutely no clues about what had happened to him.

"Imogen?" Cade's voice was soft.

I shook my head, not wanting to tell him.

"Goldie..."

"It's not much."

"*Not much* is better than the *nothing* we currently have."

He had a point.

I dragged in a harsh breath. "It was dark. He was riding after Declan and his friends, keeping off the path so they wouldn't see him. His bike hit a hole here, and he flipped over. His candy bucket spilled. He scraped his palms to hell when he landed. If you find traces of blood, they're probably his." I stared at the oily black bike chain, hanging limply off its track. "The chain fell off. He didn't know how to get it back on, so he left the bike behind."

Cade waited. He was still holding me, his arms warm and strong, his firm chest supporting my limp frame. This many visions in one day was taking a heavy toll on both my body and my mind. I could barely hold my head up. It would take a while before I was ready to attempt something as vigorous as standing.

"He continued into the woods on foot," I said, still seeing Rory's image in my head. "After the older kids. He wanted to sneak up on them. Scare them, while they were telling ghost stories. To prove he wasn't a baby."

I looked into the tree line. The woods were thick at the perimeter, and only got thicker as you moved deeper toward the clearing where Declan and his friends had gathered that night. Cade had told me on the drive here that the tracking dogs were already being deployed throughout the area, but it could take days to cover it all.

It was more than just a matter of searching the hundreds of acres of trees, ferns, and foliage. One side of those woods backed up to a sheer rock face which dropped several hundred feet down into a century-old stone quarry; the other side eroded into a thick wetland of tidal marshes. In between, there were streams and ponds, creeks and rivers — the biggest of which flowed straight out into the Atlantic.

A large area of difficult terrain. Not ideal to begin with; even less ideal when factoring in that it was already twilight.

They'd be searching in the dark.

My thoughts moved to little Annie Thurman. Lost out there for nearly a week. She'd come back alive, but forever changed. I didn't want that fate for Rory. For Declan. For Georgia. I didn't want to live in a world without Rory O'Banion's happy giggle, his mile-a-minute chatter, his quick-fired questions. I wanted him back at The Sea Witch with me, complaining about the broken waffle machine and debating whether or not Pluto should be reinstated as a planet.

Cade's mouth brushed my temple. "We're going to find him, Imogen."

"Alive?" I couldn't help asking, my voice shattered by exhaustion and grief. "Unharmed?"

Cade didn't answer.

And that, in its terrible way, was answer enough.

Cade brought me back to his house, kissed me hard beneath the porch light, then turned right back around to join the search in the woods. Socks and I stood in the doorway, watching him leave. The set of his shoulders was determined as he strode to his SUV, climbed inside, and roared away.

He did not look back. He didn't even flash his headlights. He was in detective mode, laser-focused now that they had an actual lead to follow and a proper lock on the location.

He hadn't had a full night of rest in days, but he wasn't about to take a break. Time was of the essence. And, given the chance, Cade Hightower would put others' needs before his own every time.

"Your Dad is pretty awesome," I told Socks. "Did you know that?"

His tongue lolled happily out one side of his mouth. I took this as confirmation.

"Yeah, I guess you do." I rubbed his floppy ears. "Come on, we have laundry to do and dinner to eat. I'm going to order a pizza. I'm guessing you're going with kibble again?"

He whined softly.

I took that as a *yes*.

"How about a walk around the block before dinner?"

He barked and jumped up, recognizing the word *walk*. I grinned at him as I retrieved his leash.

"Inquiring minds want to know: what are your thoughts on

cuddling? You've been sleeping on my feet the past few nights, which is nice, but I think we're ready to take it to the next level..."

He barked again as I clipped on his leash and led him to the back door.

"Cuddles it is, then. Glad we're on the same page, Socks."

My arm was nearly yanked out of its socket as he bounded down the back steps, into the yard.

I woke to the soft tones of Cade shooing Socks out of his spot on the bed. His weight hit the mattress and his bare chest curled into my back.

"Goldie, I love that you and my dog are bonding. That said, I don't love coming home to him drooling on my pillow and spooning my woman."

"Mmm?" I hummed, still barely conscious. "What time is it?"

"Past midnight."

"The search?"

"Called off until the morning. Fog rolled in around ten. We couldn't see shit. Too dark to make much progress that deep in the woods." His arms slid around my waist and he tugged me closer. "We'll start fresh when the sun comes up."

I wiggled back into him, fitting my hips to his. He was, I realized with a bolt of desire, completely naked. My gloved hands curled into fists against the sheets.

"Cade?"

"Yeah?"

"Are you tired?"

"Fucking wiped," he muttered against my hair. There was a beat of silence. "You want me to fuck you."

My mouth dropped open. "I do not!"

"Don't lie, Goldie." He chuckled, amused. "You suck at it."

"I do not suck at lying!" I declared, then proceeded to lie

immediately. "And I do not want you to fuck me, Cade Hightower!"

"You sure about that?"

His hand moved up beneath my t-shirt to cup my breast, the pad of his thumb whispering over my nipple. I arched into him, biting my lip to contain a moan.

Nope, I wasn't sure at all.

"Fair warning, beautiful," he rumbled. "I'm beat. This is going to be fast and rough."

Another bolt of desire shot through me — this one centered straight between my legs.

"Fast and rough sounds perfect," I breathed.

He grinned against my neck a second before his finger hit my clit. It felt good. More than good, it felt *brilliant*. I let him work me for a while, building my pleasure in slow circles until I was wet and writhing against him. At the same time, my hand moved up and down his shaft, pumping until he was throbbing with need, his breaths reduced to thready pants at my nape.

We were both nearly there when he repositioned us — jerking me up onto my knees with his hands at my hips, he pulled my ass into the air and thrust inside.

Yes.

God, yes.

I gripped the base of the headboard as he pounded into me from behind. Fast and rough, just like he'd promised. I never wanted it to stop, but I couldn't hold off for long. The orgasm crashed through me and I came so hard, I blacked out for a minute. I was so lost in the throes, I didn't even hear Cade follow me over the edge a few seconds later, grunting my name as he poured into me.

When I came back to my senses, I was half sprawled on Cade's chest. He'd knit our fingers together and was stroking his thumb across the back of my gloved hand.

"You don't have to wear these in this bed," he said gently. "You don't have to wear them at all. Not if you don't want to."

I sucked in a sharp breath. "Doesn't it freak you out? That I might touch you and see something you don't want me to?"

"No."

"But—"

"Open book, Goldie," he reminded me. His eyes found mine in the dark. "Might actually save me some time, you knowing my thoughts before I have to tell you."

"Hilarious."

"Wasn't kidding." His eyes crinkled up at the corners. "You want to know what I'm thinking now?"

"Not particularly."

"I'm thinking I'm glad your car is such a steaming piece of crap that it broke down in my town. I'm thinking I'm glad you've been too busy making friends and walking my dog and fucking my brains out to ask me a single question about the repair status of said car."

My mouth fell open.

Cade wasn't done. "I'm thinking you *not* asking about your car means you're finally realizing you have no desire to get your fine ass back in that driver's seat and leave this place in your rearview, because what you've found here — intentionally or not — is the best thing you've had in years. Maybe in your whole damn life. And I'm thinking that's going to play nicely into my plans, seeing as I have no intentions of letting you ride off into the sunset without me."

My mouth was officially hanging open.

"You having a stroke or just processing?"

"Processing," I muttered, like total idiot. Because, well…

I was!

Cade grinned.

"I don't see what there is to grin about, Cade Hightower."

"Then you're fucking blind."

I glared at him. "What exactly is happening with my car?"

"I talked to Puck this afternoon. The part he ordered should be in by tomorrow night. He'll have your shitbox up and running by mid-week."

"Excellent."

"Not the word I would've used," he muttered, voice losing all humor. "You talking about leaving doesn't exactly thrill me to bits, beautiful."

I held his stare for a long moment, ignoring my thudding heart. "You knew when you met me, I'm not one for standing still."

"Because of your uncle." A statement, not a question.

"You're not getting the scope of my situation. If I stop moving… if he finds me again…" I shook my head. "I'm not getting dragged back into that life."

"You're the one not getting the scope, here. If he comes at you again, if he even tries, I'll stop him. He'll have to go through me to get to you."

"Cade—"

"That means he's going through the full force of the Salem Police Department."

"Cade, I just—"

"He'll also have to go through Georgia. And Florence. And Desmond, which isn't saying much, seeing as he's a nonviolent professor who uses his hands to grade papers, not to fight. But it's still something."

"But—"

"He'll also have to go through Gwendolyn Goode. With Gwen comes Graham. And with Graham comes a fuck of a lot of badassery all on his own but, if that isn't enough, also comes with the additional force of Gravewatch at his back. That's a whole legion of highly trained men who'd enjoy nothing more than pounding a dick like your uncle into the dirt."

"I get what you're trying to say but—"

"And then there's Sally, Agatha, and their entire Bay Colony Coven. Can't say I'm hip on the witchy woo-woo, so to speak, but I do know I wouldn't want a dozen Wiccans on my ass, cursing me to Hell."

I could no longer formulate any excuses or interjections.

"I see I'm finally making my point," Cade murmured, scanning my face. "You have a network of protection here. A strong one."

"I don't want anyone protecting me because they feel sorry for me."

"Tell me you're kidding."

"I'm not kidding. I don't need their pity."

"It isn't *pity*, Imogen. People around here like you. They like being around you. You're a good friend and a good person. Why is that so difficult for you to understand?"

I blinked at him. I didn't really have an answer to that.

"Yeah," he muttered, scoffing. "That's what I thought. Now, can we go to sleep? I have to be up in four hours."

"Okay," I whispered, totally overwhelmed. I couldn't stop my mind from replaying the words he'd just said. Mostly, though, I couldn't stop my heart from clenching as a now-familiar feeling stole through my body.

Home.

In these strong arms.

In this warm bed.

In this strange town.

I was finally home.

And, crazy as it was....

I didn't ever want to leave.

When I woke up the next morning, Cade was already gone. The puppy was asleep beside me in his spot, snoring lightly, his jowls slackened on the pillow. I sat up against the headboard and spotted a note on the nightstand. Socks lifted his head when I reached across his furry form to nab it.

There was a short message scrawled in Cade's blocky handwriting.

Goldie—

Gone to search for Rory. If I get a break, I'll swing by The Gallows. If not, I'll see you tonight. Could be late — don't wait up.

And don't wear anything to bed.

(Yes, that includes the gloves.)

– C

I pressed the note to my chest as a flurry of idiotic, lovestruck butterflies burst to life in my stomach. I tried to hold onto my annoyance at his bossiness — *Who did he think he was, ordering me to sleep in the nude?* — but it was an impossible task. Joy was coursing through my bloodstream, invigorating my whole body.

Until I saw the alarm clock.

"Shit! Is that the time?" I shrieked, scrambling off the bed. "Socks, I'm going to be late! Come on, boy, let's move! Gwen will be here any minute!"

By the time I'd fed Socks and brought him into the backyard to do his business, I had about thirty seconds remaining for myself. I took the fastest shower in human history, pulled a pair of jeans and a fitted v-neck sweater out of the dryer (I hadn't had the energy to fluff and fold last night, truth be told), and ran a comb through my damp curls. I was dabbing on a bit of mascara when I heard a beep from outside.

"Bye, Socks!" I called, racing through the living room. "Don't chew anything! And try not to pee on Jamie's shoes!"

Jamie, Cade's dog-walker, lived three houses down, had lime-green hair, and had made a rather successful business out of caring for all the pets in the neighborhood, from cats to iguanas to puppies to pythons. I'd met her in passing on Halloween, when she brought her kids to the door for candy. At the time, I thought the badass iridescent mohawk was part of her costume.

It was not.

She sported it full time.

I locked the door and raced down the front walk, where a turquoise muscle car was idling. The Thunderbird. Gwen was in the front seat, looking chic in a pair of tortoise cat-eye shades, a semi-sheer silk blouse, and high-waisted trousers that made her legs seem longer than should be anatomically possible. Her bruise was better today, turning yellow at the edges as it healed.

"Thanks for picking me up," I said as I settled into the passenger seat. "Cade says I should have my own wheels back by tomorrow or the next day."

"No problem." Gwen shot me a smile as she steered away from the curb. "It feels a little strange, opening the shop while the search is still ongoing..."

I nodded. Neither of us felt great about the prospect of making smalltalk with customers, stocking books, and serving coffee — not while Rory was still out there. But The Gallows couldn't stay shuttered forever. And not just because the hipsters would stage a revolt. Gwen had a business to run. I had bills to pay. Life went on.

Even when you didn't want it to.

Even when it felt impossible.

We parked downtown in a spot on the street not far from the brick pedestrian zone. I was stunned silent by what I saw when we approached The Gallows. The whole strip was abandoned. Gone were the costumed tourists, the ghost tours moving in groups, the teens snapping selfies in the stocks. Gone were the musicians busking for tips, the food vendors pushing combo-meals, the pop-up shops hawking homemade wares. It was totally, completely…

Empty.

"Where *is* everyone?" I asked, wondering if I'd stepped into an alternate reality.

Gwen chuckled as she slid her key into the front door lock. "I told you — once Halloween is over, the whole city empties out. This is normal for a Tuesday morning. Welcome to Salem, eleven months out of the year. I think you're going to like it."

She was right.

I *did* like it.

And I liked it even more as the day waned on. I liked the slower pace. I liked being able to catch my breath between coffee orders. I liked that the tables were full of college students typing quietly on their laptops, instead of tourists shouldering each other out of the way for souvenirs. I liked that Gwen and I could chat as we worked, that the milk fridge never ran dry, that we could eat our lunch at a speed that didn't cause indigestion.

I did two tarot readings in the afternoon and took my sweet time with each of them. Both tipped generously, and made arrangements to come back again in a few weeks. I sent them on their way with the small appointment cards I'd found in one of Madame Zelda's desk drawers, unable to suppress my smile.

I had repeat customers.

Regulars!

It was a good feeling.

Towards the end of the day, I manned the shop alone for a few hours while Gwen was in the back interviewing potential baristas and busboys. We were in a late-afternoon lull. Most of our customers had wandered out when their caffeine buzz wore off after lunch. I took the opportunity to spritz down all the tables and wash the growing stack of dirty mugs.

When the door swung open, my head whipped toward it. I was hoping it would be Cade — I'd been hoping all day — but Sally swept through the door instead. She was wearing a bright yellow dress that made her already generously endowed chest appear truly gargantuan. In her hands, she had two plastic Tupperwares stacked on top of each other. Agatha, wearing a shapeless house dress, trailed on her heels.

"Hi, Sally. Hi, Agatha."

"Hello, dear." Sally glanced around, eyes sweeping the shop, taking in the handful of students still camped out at the espresso bar; the lone man perusing the bookshelves. "Glad to see things are finally back to normal around here. The whole town can breathe again now that the tourists are gone."

"Good riddance," Agatha declared, plunking down into one of Gwen's plush armchairs.

I fought a grin. "It's, uh... definitely a nice change of pace. Are you here for coffee?"

"No, just popping by to drop this off." Sally set one of the Tupperware on the counter beside the cash register. "There are two slices in there, one for you and one for Gwendolyn. Cheesecake."

My mouth watered. "You didn't have to do that."

"Trust me, she did," Agatha called. "She has to spread the calories around, otherwise she eats the whole thing in one sitting and drags me out to shop for new dresses a size up."

"You're one to talk!" Sally fired back. "How many biscotti did you eat after dinner last night? Seventeen?"

"They're a digestif!"

"Keep telling yourself that." Sally looked back at me. "Next she'll be saying tiramisu is a well-balanced breakfast food."

I grinned, but it slipped somewhat as I held her gaze. "While you're here, can I ask you something?"

"Sure, sugar."

"Yesterday, when we were talking about Annie Thurman, I

wanted to ask but... It didn't feel right. Not with Georgia sitting there."

"Poor woman," Agatha muttered.

"She's being very strong. Still, I can't imagine how she gets herself out of bed in the morning." Sally's fingers tapped the top of the Tupperware in her hands. "She's my next stop. Figured she and her boy could use a little pick-me-up."

"That's nice of you."

Sally's lips curved up. "It's the very least I can do."

"That said, we'd like to get there before the sun sets," Agatha cut in. "So, if you've got something to ask..."

"Right." I blinked. "Um... I guess I just wanted to know what happened to Annie after she came back home."

Sally's expression darkened. "Oh..."

So did Agatha's. "*Oh.*"

My stomach flipped. "What? What is it?"

"Her parents... well, like we told you yesterday, the Thurmans were a prominent family in town. Big reputations even before the case threw them into the spotlight," Sally explained. "I guess it got to be too much for them. The whispers about Annie's condition. The suspicion that blew back on them. They didn't handle it well when all their money failed to fix their daughter. They picked up and moved not long after."

"They didn't just *move*." Agatha laughed bitterly. "Those folks started a new life somewhere else, where no one knew about what happened. Popped out another child. A fresh start, that's what they called it. But we all knew they just couldn't stand their perfect family no longer looking like a page ripped out of *Coastal Living* magazine."

My stomach flipped again. "And Annie? What about her?"

Agatha's voice got even more bitter. "They threw her in the looney bin."

Surely that couldn't be true. "*What?*"

Sally exhaled sharply. "Ag, they don't call it the looney bin anymore."

"A mental asylum, then," Agatha amended.

"They don't call it that either, Ag. *Psychiatric ward.* That's the term."

"I don't care what they call it, Sal! The fact remains, they tossed that girl away like garbage."

"Is that true?" I asked Sally, eyes wide. An unpleasant feeling snaked its way through me, coiling in my gut. "It can't be true."

Sally's eyes were a bit misty. "I wish it weren't. But yes, last I heard, her family put her in a long-term care facility for treatment. She's spent most of her life there at Oak Grove, over in Danvers."

My words came out as a hiss of outrage. "How could they just leave her?"

"Can't rightly say. Though, I suspect that whole experience changed them just as much as it changed their daughter. I don't pretend to know what living through something like that does to a person. I pray I never know." Sally's lips flattened into a frown. "In the meantime, I hold my grandbabies as close as I can every time I get the chance. There are no guarantees in this life."

I gripped the edge of the counter for support. I'd already been walloped this week by everything that had happened with the search, the visions, the emotional roller coaster that was my relationship with Cade... Hearing about Annie Thurman's sad fate was yet another crushing blow. I couldn't help worrying Rory's story would end the same way. Even if we found him, there was a strong possibility he'd never be the same.

"Imogen, dear? Are you all right?"

My eyes flashed up to Sally and Agatha. They were both standing, now, and staring at me with matching looks of concern. I didn't know what to say, so I just shook my head.

I wasn't all right.

None of us were.

"Don't lose hope, sugar." Sally reached across the counter to cup my cheek. "The search party hasn't given up on Rory. Neither should we."

I managed a nod.

"It's too bad Annie Thurman can't talk," Agatha murmured, shaking her head. "If anyone knows the secrets of those woods, it's her."

They left shortly after, sweeping back out the door with the same dramatic flair I'd come to expect from them when making an entrance or exit. It wasn't until later that night, when the shop was closed for business and Gwen and I were intermittently downing bites of cheesecake while cleaning up the messy mystical curiosities section, that Agatha's words fully processed. And, when they did, I stopped in my tracks, a chunk of rose quartz in my hand.

It's too bad Annie Thurman can't talk. If anyone knows the secrets of those woods, it's her…

She couldn't talk.

Not with words.

Not out loud.

But...

"Imogen?"

My wide eyes swung to Gwen when she said my name. My voice came out stiff. "Annie Thurman."

Gwen blinked in surprise. "What about her?"

"I need to see her."

She stared at me like I had a few screws loose. "Pardon?"

"I don't have time to explain," I said, shaking my head. "Can you give me a ride to Oak Grove in Danvers?"

"Sure, of course. I'll drive you anywhere you want. But… isn't Oak Grove…"

I nodded. "A psychiatric hospital."

"And we're going there… *why?*"

"Because that's where Annie Thurman lives. And I'm going to talk to her."

Now, Gwen was not only looking at me like I had a few screws loose; she was looking at me like I'd come unscrewed completely. But she merely straightened her shoulders, planted her hands on her hips, and nodded.

"Let's hit the road, then. We can be there in twenty minutes. Thirty, tops." She paused. "But we need to swing by Flo's duplex on the way. If we leave her out of this she'll drive us so crazy, we'll be the ones institutionalized."

CHAPTER TWENTY-TWO

Immaculate conception is one thing. But THREE wise men in the same room? That seems improbable.
- Imogen Warner, having a religious experience

I wasn't certain what to expect of the Oak Grove Psychiatric Center. Something out of a horror film, perhaps, with graying cinderblock walls and a gloomy atmosphere akin to a penitentiary. Instead, we were met with a well-kept brick building situated on a surprisingly lovely campus, with lush green lawns, towering willow trees, and a gently flowing creek.

Graceful wrought-iron fencing wrapped the entire property. We rolled through the automated gate without issue and parked in a lot directly in front of a wooden sign that said **RECEPTION** in gold lettering, illuminated by two spotlights.

There weren't many cars in the lot. That didn't surprise me much. It was dinnertime. Most visitors had probably come and gone for the day. When we first walked in, I was worried we'd be turned away at the front desk, but the receptionist hardly blinked when we said we were there to visit Annie Thurman. After asking us to sign our names in the check-in book, she rattled off a room number and buzzed us through a heavy wood door into the ward.

The patients here clearly weren't violent offenders. There was no security anywhere, so far as I could see. No bars on the windows. No restraining straps on the beds. Each room we passed was personal in design. Different paint palettes, different furnishings, different decor on the walls. No bland state-funded watercolors, here, that was for sure. And definitely no hospital food. The dinner trays being ferried into each room by uniformed care aids both looked and smelled gourmet.

Agatha and Sally had made it clear the Thurmans were wealthy. After seeing this place, I thought their fortune must be closer to billions than millions. The going rate for a suite in a private care facility of this caliber had to be astronomical. And if Annie had been here for two decades...

My brain couldn't begin to fathom the cost of care on that scale.

Her room was located at the end of the hall, off a windowed alcove furnished with lots of armchairs and bookshelves. It was dark outside, but I imagined it was a pleasant enough spot to sit and read during daylight hours. Florence and Gwen chose to wait there. We didn't want to overwhelm Annie by storming in all at once.

I was going in alone.

Her door was ajar. I rapped my knuckles against it to announce my arrival before I pushed it open wider. She was sitting in a chair by the window, staring out the crisscrossed pane into the dark. She looked around my age, maybe a few years older. Her dark hair was pulled back into a low ponytail at her nape. I could see her features only in profile, but what I did see was quite pretty.

"Annie?"

She didn't turn at the sound of my voice. She didn't even flinch.

I took a few steps farther into the room.

"Annie, my name is Imogen Warner."

Still, she gave no indication she'd heard me.

"Would you mind if I spoke to you for a moment?" I cleared my throat. "I'm sorry to disturb you so late, but... It's important."

She continued to stare out the window.

I took a few more steps, then slowly lowered myself onto the matching armchair at the window with my body angled toward hers. She either didn't notice my presence or didn't care to acknowledge it.

Maybe this was a bad idea.

Still, we were already here. Asking a few questions couldn't hurt. I steeled my shoulders and took pains to keep my voice steady.

"Annie, I don't want to upset you. But a young boy has gone missing in the woods—"

It was almost imperceptible, but her body jolted.

She was listening.

I continued. "The police are out looking for him. They've been looking for days. But it's like he's vanished into thin air... just like you did all those years ago."

A tremble moved through her.

Shit.

I had to tread carefully, here. The last thing I wanted to do was cause her any more pain. She'd been through enough already.

More than enough.

"If there's anything you can tell me about the woods... What you saw there... Any details at all..." I took a deep breath. "It would really help, Annie."

This time, when I said her name, her head turned. She looked me dead in the eyes. I fought the urge to shy away from the devastating emptiness I saw there. Her gaze was totally vacant. Vacuous. Whether it was from the trauma she'd endured or the medications she was taking, I couldn't begin to guess.

I found myself blinking back tears as I struggled for the right way to continue. As usual, I opted for the plain truth. "I know you can't communicate verbally. I'm hoping you'll be open to speaking to me another way."

The faintest glimmer of curiosity crept into her eyes. That was a good sign, I thought. And I'd come this far already. Might as well keep going.

"It's going to sound crazy — trust me, I know — but... When I touch certain things... When I touch certain people..." As I spoke, I looked down at my hands and began to peel off my gloves, one fingertip at a time. I laid them on the seat cushion beside me, cleared my throat, and summoned the courage to finish. "I'm able to see things normal people can't see. Memories. Thoughts. Fragments of their lives."

Annie was still staring at me. Not calmly. No longer detached. Her wide eyes flickered over my face, back and forth, a rapid movement that I found vaguely unsettling.

I forced myself to sit still.

"You may not believe me," I whispered. "Hell, you may immediately call for a nurse to toss me out of your room just for coming here tonight. But if there's even a chance you might be able to help me understand—"

I never finished the rest of my sentence. Before I could say another word, Annie Thurman reached out and grabbed my hand so hard, my bones were nearly crushed.

With an explosion of purple sparks, she pulled me under.

Hopscotch on pavement.
Pink sidewalk chalk.
Mother yells, Father sighs.
White linen tablecloth.

Annie Thurman's mind wasn't like any other mind I'd ever

been inside. Most visions came as a singular memory; one crystallized moment in time. They played out like a motion picture before my eyes.

Annie's thoughts were not a movie; they were a medley. An ever-changing, ever-shifting montage of thoughts and emotions, memories and fragments. They rushed at me in a blur, morphing so fast I could barely make out what I was seeing before another wave of purple sparks dissolved them into something else.

Woods in the dark.
Wind in the trees.
A cry in the night.
Little girl lost.

It was like the film reel had been cut apart and spliced back together all out of order. Not one cohesive vision, but a jumbled stream of them.

A marsh bird calls.
Floors creak underfoot.
Two eyes in the corner.
Stay quiet, don't speak.

One after another, they rocked through me, tearing at my mind until it threatened to shred under the pressure.

Morning breaks bright.
Toads croak in the mud.
A slippery climb.

Rusted railroad tracks.

Finally, I emerged from her head with a ragged gasp that burst from my throat. I didn't know how much time had passed. The hollow ache in my bones suggested years, but I knew it had only been seconds. Annie was looking at me with that same intent look as before — her empty eyes shifting back and forth.

Back and forth.

Back and forth.

I tried to smile at her as I straightened from my slumped position against the back of the chair. My lips felt numb. My whole body did. Exhaustion battered at my temples, spurring a monster of a migraine to life.

I'd never felt so tired. Not in all my life. Not even when I was on television, having daily visions at my uncle's command.

No wonder Annie never spoke. I'd spent twenty seconds in her head and barely made it out alive. She'd been locked in there twenty years.

She continued to stare at me.

"Thanks for talking to me, Annie," I croaked. My voice was utterly drained. "If it's okay... I'd like to come back again to visit sometime. But only if you want me to."

Maybe, with enough practice, I could decipher some of her dizzying mind-scape; make a connection through the chaos.

She didn't smile. Her expression didn't change in the slightest. But her eyes looked a little less vacant as she gave a barely-there nod.

"Okay," I whispered. "Then I promise I'll be back. Soon."

With a tired smile, I stood, grabbed my gloves, and left her behind. At the door, I glanced back one last time. She was staring out the window again. Into the darkness.

I wondered what she saw there. I wondered if it was as scary as the fragments I'd seen inside her head.

Swallowing down the lump in my throat, I stepped into the hall.

Gwen and Florence were (understandably) bummed that our trip to Oak Grove was a bust. If I was being honest, I was rather bummed, as well. I'd known going in that it was a long shot. I'd known better than to get my hopes up that I'd miraculously discover a clue that would lead us straight to Rory.

And yet…

Disappointment curdled in my stomach the whole ride back to Cade's house. It lingered long after I waved goodbye to Gwen at the curb; after I let myself in the front door with the spare key; after I walked Socks around the block to do his nightly business. It lingered after I fed Socks dinner, and wolfed down my own. (Cold leftover pizza — not exactly a delicacy, but it did the job.) And it continued to linger even after I stripped off all my clothes and climbed naked into bed, as instructed.

The clock on the bedside table read 8:56PM. It could be hours still before Cade came back, but I was too tired to wait up for him. My body felt like it had been run through the garbage disposal.

I wished I knew where he was. If he was still out searching, or back at the station. Since he'd never made it into The Gallows, I was guessing that meant he hadn't had a break all day. He'd be just as exhausted as I was when he finally dragged himself home. Probably more so.

Lying in the dark under his dove gray duvet, I used his landline to dial his cellphone. I listened to it ring several times before it kicked over into voicemail. His deep rasp hit my ear, setting off a full-body tingle.

"You've reached Detective Caden Hightower, Salem Police Department. Please leave a message…"

I didn't bother.

Not a second after I'd hung up, the phone rang in my hand.

"Hello?"

"You naked?" Cade asked, his voice a low rumble.

"Maybe." My lips tipped up in a grin. "You coming home anytime soon?"

There was a long pause.

"Cade?" I prompted.

"I like that," he murmured. "You calling my place *home*."

A happy flutter moved through my stomach. "You know what I meant. It's just an expression. Don't get ahead of yourself."

"Too late, beautiful."

I rolled my eyes. "So, are you?"

"Am I what?"

"Coming back here soon?"

He blew out a sharp breath. "Not sure. We've been out all day, searching. Still have a lot more ground to cover. It's slow going. The quarry is deep. The woods are thick. The marshes are worse."

"I'm guessing that means you haven't found anything."

He was silent.

I took that as confirmation. "Damn it."

"Much as I'd rather stay on the phone with you all night, knowing you're naked under my sheets on the other side of the receiver…" His voice took on an edge of frustration. "I've got a lot of shit to do. May not be there for hours."

"I don't want to keep you. I just… I have something I wanted to tell you."

"You've got thirty seconds."

Shit, he was bossy sometimes.

At warp-speed, I described my visit to Oak Grove, and the fruitless vision I'd had there. When I was finished, Cade was quiet. Processing.

"Cade?"

"I'm here."

"You're not saying anything."

He sighed deeply. "Imogen, I know you're eager to help in any way you can. It's tempting to look for connections where there aren't any."

"But—"

"I get that there are similarities between Annie Thurman's disappearance and Rory's. I do. And I'm not saying you're off base. I'm just not convinced a case from eighteen years ago is in any way related to what's going on now."

His words were a blow to my self-confidence.

"You don't believe me."

"It's not that I don't believe you." His voice went gentle. "But, even if you're right, you said it yourself: Annie Thurman isn't talking. Not to me with words, not to you with your visions. Why would I waste my time on a dead end?"

A dead end.

He thought I was grasping at straws. And hell, maybe I was. But it still hurt, hearing he thought my hunch was essentially a fool's errand.

"Imogen." Cade sighed, sounding worn out. "I really need to go."

"Wait! One more thing." I forced myself to set aside my wounded pride and ask. For Rory's sake. "If the evidence box from the Thurman case is still in storage at SPD, maybe there's something in there that could spark a vision. Maybe—"

"Imogen, enough," Cade clipped.

My mouth clicked shut.

He'd never used that tone with me before.

"*Fuck*. Look, I don't want to hurt you, but I don't have time for this right now. I'm knee-deep in pond water. I've spent twelve hours wading through creeks and riverbeds, looking for the body of a seven-year-old." His frustration was so raw, it hurt to hear. "Forgive me if some old case files aren't my number one priority tonight."

I couldn't help flinching.

"This shit will have to wait," he went on.

This shit.

This.

Shit.

He'd been all too happy to use my abilities when he needed a break in his case. But when I had an idea of my own, suddenly those same abilities were inconsequential. As were my opinions.

So much for my role as a consultant.

"Of course," I said stiffly. My voice had gone totally cold. Arctic level chill. "I'm sorry for suggesting it. In the future, I won't bother you with *shit* like my thoughts or feelings or instincts."

"Imogen—"

"I'll let you go."

"God damnit, will you just lis—"

I jammed my finger against the receiver button, disconnecting the call. Then, I shoved off the covers, stalked across the room to Cade's dresser, and pulled out one of his t-shirts. Followed shortly by a pair of my underwear, fished from the duffle on the floor, and a pair of gloves, swiped from the top of the nightstand.

No way in hell was I sleeping naked.

Not anymore.

I didn't want to sleep there, *period,* but I had no way to get back to The Sea Witch and it was too late to bother anyone for a ride. So, I crawled back into bed, piled a metric ton of pillows in the middle of the mattress, and jerked the covers right up to my chin. Socks watched me do this from his post by my feet, his head canted to one side in curiosity.

"Your Dad can be a real jerk sometimes," I informed him, still in the subzero grips of my anger.

The puppy let out a low whine in response, settling his head on his front paws.

Despite my bone-deep exhaustion, it took me a long, long time to find sleep.

Sometime in the middle of the night, I blinked awake as the mound of pillows rustled against the sheets. A second later, they disappeared completely, sailing off the bed and onto the floor. A broad chest hit my back, warm even through the fabric of my t-shirt.

"You still pissed?" Cade whispered, mouth at my ear.

I glared into the dark in total silence, my frame stiff with hurt and anger.

"I'll take that as a yes."

I continued to glare into the dark.

His hands skimmed up my hips, then settled on my stomach. His touch was soft, not seductive. Still, it felt so good, I had to steel myself from melting against him.

His voice dropped until it was barely audible. "I'm sorry, beautiful. You were only trying to help and I shut you down instead of listening."

My chin jerked.

"I know it's no excuse for taking it out on you, but you caught me at a shit moment, after a long string of other shit moments, which started the second I left this bed this morning. You want to be pissed at me for that, be pissed." His sigh gusted over my neck. "I'm still going to hold you close. Even if you're mad as a hornet, being here with you is still the brightest spot of a pretty fucking dark day. The only bright spot, frankly. So, I'm soaking it in, as much as I can get. And I'm taking it with me tomorrow when I go back out into that darkness."

Damn it to hell.

How could I be mad at him when he said things like that?

I couldn't.

It was physically impossible.

He pressed a kiss to my nape. Then, he pulled me even closer, until his whole body was wrapped around mine like a cocoon of strong limbs.

I didn't say anything. But, after a few seconds, I allowed my body to soften against his as the anger bled out of my system.

The last thing I felt before I fell back asleep was Cade's smile against my skin.

When I woke up in the morning, Cade was gone.

Again.

For the second day in a row.

I didn't like how we'd left things last night. Were we still in a fight? I didn't think we were. Most of my anger had melted away while he held me as we slept. And whatever small shred remained disappeared when I walked into his kitchen and spotted the evidence box sitting on the island.

THURMAN was written on the side in blocky black marker.

My eyes prickled, a telltale sign of impending tears. He must've gone to the station last night after he was done with the search. Even though he'd had a horrible day. Even though he was dead tired. He'd still made a special trip. Gone out of his way. Dug through god only knew how many files to find this.

For me.

I totally should've slept naked.

Before I could even fully process the monumental gesture that was the evidence box, I heard a loud, rhythmic beeping sound coming from outside. I wandered to the front of the house, Socks shadowing my every step, and pulled open the front door. To my surprise, a bright yellow tow truck was in the process of lowering my shitbox car into Cade's driveway. I rushed barefoot out into the cold morning, rubbing the goosebumps from my forearms and wishing I'd pulled on something other than my denim cut-offs when I got up.

"Hey!" I waved down the driver as he detached his rig from the undercarriage. "That's my car!"

The man in coveralls glanced with undisguised disgust at my vehicle. "Congrats," he said drolly.

"Is it fixed?"

"Fixed is a relative term. It runs, if that's what you mean."

"That's what I mean."

"Then you're in luck."

He lobbed the keys at me. Springing into motion, I managed to catch them before they careened to the ground.

"What do I owe?" I asked, somewhat dreading his answer. "Do I pay you directly or will Puck send me a bill?"

"It's covered."

My brows sailed upward. "What?"

"The repairs," he said with a shrug. "They're covered. Paid for. You're square."

"But— But— " I spluttered. "I haven't paid anything!"

He nodded and glanced at the clipboard in his hand. "Bill was paid by one Detective Cade Hightower."

"*What*?!" I shrieked. "Why would he pay? It's not even his car! That's crazy!"

The man pinned me with an amused look. "Guessing the fact that you're standing there on Cade Hightower's front walk wearing Cade Hightower's shirt with Cade Hightower's dog sitting on your feet is a pretty good indication of why that bill is paid. You have further issues with the matter... I suggest you take it up with one Detective Cade Hightower."

My mouth was hanging open — which left me woefully unequipped to formulate a reply as the man turned around, got in his truck, and drove off.

Blast.

Snapping my fingers at Socks, I marched back up the walk into the house. I proceeded to march straight into the kitchen, where I tossed my keys onto the island with a loud clatter.

"Bossy, overbearing, madman," I muttered, running my hands though my messy hair. "That's your Dad I'm talking about, for the record."

Socks answered by swiping his tongue at the crook of my knee. I took that to mean he wanted breakfast.

"Okay, boy. I won't hold this against you. It's not *your* fault you were born to a wannabe superhero with great hair who insists on solving all my problems, being unbearably good in bed, and making it impossible for me to hate him."

He licked my leg again.

I dumped a large helping of kibble into Socks' bowl, then poured cereal for myself. My options in the cupboard were... Raisin Bran, Raisin Bran, and, you guessed it, more Raisin Bran.

Yuck.

Cade needed some new breakfast options. Now that I had wheels again, I was going to hit the grocery store ASAP and load up on some non-disgusting cereal alternatives.

I shoveled spoonfuls down my throat at the kitchen island, eyes locked on the evidence box. I had yet to open it, but I couldn't stop wondering what was inside. I rinsed my bowl in the sink, then moved back toward the counter, drawn in like a moth to the flame.

Removing the lid, I reached into the box. My fingers landed on a clear evidence bag. Inside, there were clothing items belonging to a young girl. A paisley blue cotton shirt with ruffled sleeves. A pair of tiny jean shorts. Two small sneakers, once white-soled, now dirt-streaked.

I held my breath as I unsealed the bag and touched the items one by one.

Nothing happened.

No shower of purple.

No visions.

Blowing out a frustrated breath, I set that bag aside and reached back into the box. There wasn't much else. A few police reports printed on official SPD stationary — again, triggering nothing — and some handwritten notes from the lead detective on the case, yellowed with age. I skimmed them briefly but they didn't reveal anything new in the way of information.

At the very bottom of the box, there was one more evidence bag. It was minuscule, no bigger than the size of my hand. It held a girl's gold locket. I wondered why the Thurmans had never collected it. Maybe, in the aftermath, they didn't want anything associated with that awful chapter of their lives. Maybe they'd simply forgotten.

My fingers shook a bit as I traced the heart-shaped pendant through the plastic. The gold was tarnished. Its tiny hinges were hanging loose.

Annie had worn this piece often.

Before I could talk myself out of it, I dumped the locket into my palm — and fell straight to the kitchen floor in a dead faint as the vision consumed me.

The little girl hates lamb chops. She hates the formal dining room, and the linen tablecloths, and the way Mother and Father glare at each other when they think she's not paying attention.

She likes to eat dinner at her friend Emma's house, instead. Emma has four siblings, all of them louder than the last. Emma's parents smile at one another. They don't serve lamb or game hen or escargot. They order Chinese food and eat it right out of the cartons, everyone yelling about egg rolls and tossing fortune cookies around.

The little girl looks at the big house up the sloping lawn. Any minute now, the maid will come out and call for her. Any minute now, she'll have to sit at the big table, hands folded on her lap, and force down bites of icky fancy food.

She'd rather be at Emma's.

She wants to live at Emma's.

She doesn't look back as she rushes toward the trees. She's not supposed to cut across the golf course, but it's faster than going the long way around. If she goes fast, she can be there in time for crab rangoons. She's never had a crab rangoon before — she doesn't even know what a crab rangoon is — but she wants to, desperately. Last time, Emma's big brothers devoured them all before she got a taste.

The girl hurries across the fairway. It is the middle of summer, still warm though it's twilight. A secret thrill moves through her as she races around sand pits and flagsticks. Her parents will be furious. But they are always furious, these days. Her thrill shifts to panic as she spots a golf cart coming straight for her.

If she's spotted, they might take her back home!

She darts into the trees.

She can find her way from there.

It's not far.

The vision shifted with meteoric sparks of purple.

The girl is lost.

Terribly lost.

Hopelessly lost.

The trees seem to multiply all around her as the sun slips lower and lower on the horizon. It is dark and growing cold. She should have been there by now. But there is no sign of Emma's house. No sign of any house at all. Just more trees, more leaves, more ferns. Mosquitos sting her bare arms and legs. She slaps at them.

Go away, stupid bugs!

Maybe she should turn back. But which way is back? Which way is home? Every direction looks the same in the lengthening shadows. Reeds and roots under her feet; bushes and boughs swaying overhead.

The girl is growing frantic. Her parents will be worried. And the girl loves her parents, even though she sometimes questions if they love her in return.

She rounds a bend and spots a path ahead, aglow in the moonlight.

A path!

A path will bring her home. A path will lead her out.

But the path is not the salvation she thinks it is. As she gets closer, a figure steps onto it, out of the shadows. The girl sees the gleam of two eyes in the dark as it comes at her.

A monster!

Dirt-streaked. Silent, even as it moves closer. Reaching out with ragged nails…

She tries to run, but she slips on a mossy stone.

Water seeps into her white sneakers.

Two hands close over her arms.

More sparks.
More purple.
The vision shifted yet again.

The girl wants to run, but she is too tired. She hasn't slept in days. The monster in the cabin keeps her wide awake. Creeping around in the dark. Her limping gate echoes oddly against the crooked floorboards. Her hair is a wild tangle down her back.

The monster never speaks.

She gives her food.

She gives her water.

She gives her a blanket.

But she never, ever speaks.

Just stares and stares, until the girl thinks she will be pressed flat under the weight of that unflinching gaze.

What does the monster want from her?

She does not ask. She does not dare say a word, does not dare make a sound. She thinks maybe if she's quiet enough, the monster will forget she's there. Maybe, if she's good, the monster will let her leave.

On the fifth morning, the girl wakes alone in the cabin. The monster is gone. Out, somewhere, in the woods. She dashes for the door and out into the daylight. It is blinding after so many days spent in darkness.

She walks and walks.

Away from the cabin, down a short dirt road. Past a broken down car, red with rust. Through a swampy marsh, her sneakers making slurping sounds. Up a slippery slope, grabbing tree roots to keep from sliding back down.

At the top of the hill, she finally sees something new. Something besides bark or leaves or moss or grass.

Railway tracks.

Shiny in the sun.

The girl knows tracks mean trains, and trains mean people.

She scrambles up the bank.

She starts to walk.

Following them home.

Every step, wondering if the monster will follow here there.

If the monster will follow her forever.

I ripped violently out of the vision. I was lying on the kitchen floor, cold tile seeping into my skin. Socks was standing over me, his glossy eyes on my face. As soon as I blinked awake, his pink tongue swiped my cheek, leaving a trail of drool up the entire left side.

"*Gah!*" I raised my arms to shield my head. "Socks! Quit it!"

He scampered over my prone form without apology, paws pounding into my stomach. I rolled out of his path before he could flatten me completely.

When I'd recovered slightly (from both puppy paws and the visions) I pushed myself up into a sitting position. My fatigued mind was spinning. But beneath the exhaustion, there was an undeniable current of excitement. Annie's memories had finally yielded some answers about the mysteries of the woods.

Train tracks.

A slope.

A marsh.

A dirt road.

And an abandoned cabin, deep in the swamp.

If I could retrace Annie's steps from that train track… Follow her trail back to the start…

I worried my bottom lip with my teeth.

It was a long shot.

I knew that.

Even if I found the cabin, there was zero guarantee Rory would be there. There was no assurance the "monster" in Annie's memory from almost two decades ago had anything to do with this new disappearance. There was a high probability I was once again setting myself up for disappointment.

I reminded myself that Cade hadn't seemed exceedingly enthusiastic about this particular lead. That it was foolish to get my hopes up for nothing.

And yet…

A voice deep inside me was screaming to trust my instincts, for once. To embrace this gift I'd been given instead of shutting it out, locking it down. To finally take off the proverbial gloves and embrace who the hell I was meant to be.

I figured it was time I listened to that voice.

Past time.

A half hour later, the doorbell rang.

"Coming!" I hollered, tugging on my sneakers. "Just a sec!"

It was probably Jamie, coming over to check on the puppy. Or Gwen, thinking I needed a ride to work. Or Sally, dropping off cheesecake. Or a Mormon missionary, attempting to convert me.

The doorbell went again.

I waved goodbye to Socks, who was happily making a mess of a rawhide bone in the middle of the living room, and yanked open the door. "Sorry, sorry. I was—"

My words dried up.

Gwen wasn't standing on the porch.

Neither was Florence.

Or Georgia.

Or Sally.

Or Agatha.

Or even Jamie-the-dog-walker.

It was a man. A man with thick, dark hair and sultry bedroom eyes. A man in an expensive wool suit. (Which, I might add, was way too tight for him, exposing his ankles and hugging his chest muscles in a ridiculous way that I'm sure he thought was the pinnacle of fashion.) A man who, when our gazes snagged, looked at me like he wanted to rip my throat out with his bare hands.

"Adrian," I breathed.

His fist cocked back and, before I could even attempt to duck, he punched me square in the face.

I was out cold before I hit the floor.

I came to as I was being dragged down Cade's front steps, toward a bright red Ferrari that was idling by the curb. *Of course* Adrian drove the most ostentatious car on the market. It practically screamed "I'm rich!" in a desperate sort of way that wasn't fooling anybody. I'd told him as much, back when we were dating. He'd not taken the slight in stride. (*i.e.* He shattered an heirloom Tiffany lamp on the floor in a fit of rage.)

I had no desire to be kidnapped. Not ever. But I definitely did not care to be kidnapped in a freaking Ferrari the color of a Cheeto.

Not.

Freaking.

Happening.

"Let go of me!" I screeched, starting to struggle as we reached the walkway. "I mean it, Adrian! Let me go!"

"Shut the fuck up!"

"I will *not!*" I elbowed blindly at his gut. *"Shut!"* I clawed the length of his arm. *"The fuck!"* My heel connected hard with his shin. *"Up!"*

"Had about enough of your shit, dollface." He grunted in pain as I landed another kick to his leg. "Making me drive all the way up here…"

"I didn't make you do anything!" I snapped, furious. "How did you even find me?"

"Gotta admit, those automated search alerts are handy as fuck. You popped into my inbox a few days back. Two clicks and I had you," he said, voice somewhat labored as he struggled to haul me down the walk. "Imogen Warner, brand new psychic at some shop in Salem. Your picture and everything, right there on the page."

Damn.

I kept struggling, but his hold was like iron.

"Couldn't be that easy, I thought. No fucking way." He scoffed again, still dragging me toward the curb. We were close, now. "Then, I called. And, surprise surprise, who answers the fucking phone?"

Me.

I had.

The creepy breathing, the prank call on Halloween — that was Adrian on the other line.

Damn, damn, *damn.*

"Now, you're coming back to A.C. with me. You're gonna make this right with Viggo."

"I'm not going *anywhere* with you!"

We were almost at the curb.

"You've made my life a real fucking mess." His arms went tighter around me — crushingly so. One at my neck in a chokehold, the other at my midsection. I could hardly breathe. "And now, you're going to clean it up."

"*Fuck!*" I gasped, fighting for air. "*You!*"

"Oh, you'll fuck me, baby." His voice gained a lascivious edge. "We'll fuck until you remember how good we were together."

I thrashed violently against his grip. I tried to scream, but he was now cutting off my oxygen completely.

He started to say something else, but his words were overshadowed by a deep, warning growl. It was coming from the front porch, and it was ominous enough to stop Adrian in his tracks.

"What the—"

My eyes shifted in time to see Socks vault off the top step. His oversized paws hit the path and then, in two bounds, he'd reached us. His razor-sharp puppy teeth sank into Adrian's exposed ankle.

"*Fuck!*" he bellowed. "What the fuck!"

Surprised by the attack, his arms loosened enough for me to slip out of his grip. I dropped to the sidewalk like a stone, then scrambled toward the path on my hands and knees. Meanwhile, Socks continued to snap at Adrian's ankles, until the man was backed up against his car door.

"Get the fuck away from me!" He kicked out at Socks, who easily dodged.

Good boy.

"Get away! Fucking psycho mutt!"

I rose to my feet, heart pounding, eye throbbing.

"Imogen!" a voice called from down the block. "Everything okay over there?"

I turned and spotted Jamie on her front lawn, holding a hose. She was watering her mums. Her face was contorted in concern as her eyes moved from me to Adrian and back.

"I'm fine, Jamie," I called. Then, my gaze swung around to pin Adrian with a glare so intense, I wished looks were in fact capable of killing. "He was just leaving."

Adrian glared back at me. His bedroom eyes flickered over to Jamie, then shot down to Socks — who had momentarily paused his sharp-toothed assault — before returning to my face.

"This isn't over," he hissed, rounding his Ferrari to the driver's side. "We have unfinished business, doll. If I were you, I wouldn't get too comfortable in this new little life you're building for yourself."

"And if I were you," I returned. "I wouldn't show my face here again. My new boyfriend is a detective. You spoke to him on the phone, remember?"

He paled slightly.

"I'm guessing you do, seeing as you must've looked up his address to track me here." I smirked. "Good. That means you'll know exactly who is beating your ass to a pulp if you show up again. My advice? Leave Salem. Don't come back."

Adrian sneered at me, yanked open his car door, and slid inside. He roared away from the curb in his gaudy sports car, leaving a streak of skid marks across the pavement. When he was gone, I glanced down and found Socks sitting, per usual, on my feet, tongue lolling out the side of his mouth.

"Exciting morning, huh?"

He woofed.

CHAPTER TWENTY-THREE

The only person who wants a gold ring more desperately than a girl in a five-year relationship goes by the name of Gollum.
- Imogen Warner, reading Tolkien

I raced down the side road, holding the steering wheel steady with my knees. I used one hand to press the bag of frozen peas to my face as the other dialed Gwen's number. As soon as it started to ring, I toggled the speakerphone function and tossed the cellphone into the center console tray.

"Hello?" Gwen's voice sounded tinny through the speaker.

I was too busy squinting at the rusty street sign up ahead to respond. I was sixty-three percent sure that was where I was supposed to turn, but the letters were so faded I couldn't be certain. I probably should've spent more than twenty seconds studying the directions before I backed out of Cade's driveway and took off.

Was it a right or a left after the railroad crossing?

Shit.

I didn't have the luxury of getting lost. My car was running on fumes. In the passenger seat, Socks was hanging his head so far out the window, I worried he was going to fall out.

"*Hello*?" Gwen repeated. "Anyone there?"

"Hi! Sorry!" I steered onto yet another side road. This one led past a sketchy-looking encampment of tents and tarps. I *so* did not want to run out of gas in this neck of the woods. "It's Imogen."

"So says the caller ID," she said wryly. "What's up? You need a lift to the store?"

"No, I have my car back."

"That's great news! You can park on Essex, there were a bunch of open spots—"

"I'm not coming in today."

"Oh. That's not-so-great news." She paused. "Please tell me you're not currently driving out of town, ne'er to return?"

"Driving, yes. Out of town, no..."

As I drove to my destination, I filled Gwen in on my plans. I figured *someone* should know where I was going, seeing as I was headed into the marshlands all alone, where I would quite possibly come face to face with an honest-to-god bog witch who stole the souls of innocent children. I didn't even know what a bog witch *was*, let alone how to confront one. I'd already had my ass kicked once today, and the sun was barely up.

Adrian's handiwork was ugly as ever. There was a serious shiner blooming over my left eye socket. (Hence the frozen peas.) Cade was going to go apoplectic when he saw it. Unless, of course, I was murdered by the Witch of Salem Wood before he had a chance.

"So, anyway," a note of hysteria crept into my voice, but I plowed on. "If I never return from this little walk in the woods, feel free to call Cade and tell him that Socks is with me."

On the other end of the line, Gwen was uncharacteristically quiet.

"You should probably also tell him to send some sort of rescue squad," I tacked on.

She was still quiet.

"Also, while you're at it, tell him to buy some better cereal options, for the love of god. I mean... Raisin Bran? *Raisin Bran?* What am I, a triathlete?"

Still, nothing in my ear but quiet.

"Gwen? Did I lose you?"

"Nope," she said, sounding weirdly out of breath.

"Are you running?"

"Yep."

"Why are you running?"

"Well, it's sure as shit not for my health. I do not run in three-hundred-dollar heels if I can help it." She panted into the speaker. "Where exactly are you headed?"

"Why?"

"Why do you think?" Her eye roll was almost audible. "You're not doing this alone."

I sat in my car in the dirt lot at the edge of the train tracks, fiddling with my keys. There was no one around, so far as I knew, but I was jittery with paranoia and nervous energy.

I wasn't sure about this.

Not remotely.

Through my windshield, I eyed the rusted-out school bus that had been left to rot here since the late 80s, if I had to wager a guess. Its sides were covered with at least a generation's worth of graffiti. Trash littered the ground around it, along with dozens of discarded tires, their treads worn smooth. Several discolored mattresses had been dumped unceremoniously into the ditch that ran along the railway.

The longer I waited, the more anxious I became. I'd been here twenty minutes already. I wasn't waiting another twenty. If Gwen didn't show up soon...

Socks gave a low whine from the passenger seat.

I glanced over and saw the turquoise Thunderbird rolling into the lot, tires kicking up a cloud of dust. Tossing my peas onto the floor — they were mostly thawed mush by this point, anyway — I hopped out. Socks followed, testing the limits of his leash as we rounded the hood.

Gwen slid out of the driver's seat, dressed in jeans, sneakers, and a t-shirt that said *SLAY*. It was the most casual outfit I'd ever seen her wear. Her long red hair was swept up in a pony tail. The bruise on her cheekbone looked much better, barely visible under her concealer.

"*Slay* in the Gen-Z sense of the word, or the Buffy sense of the word?" I asked.

"Buffy. Obviously." She grinned. "I have matching sleep-shorts that say *Chosen One* on the ass."

The passenger door flew open unexpectedly. I felt my eyes widen as Georgia glided out of it. They went even wider when Florence half-fell out of the back seat, nearly tumbling to the dirt in her haste.

"Where the eff are we?" Her gaze swung around, halting abruptly on my face. "And what the eff happened to your eye, Imogen?"

Gwen and Gigi both swooped in for a closer look.

Embarrassed, I reached up to cover the shiner. "My asshole ex is in town. Paid me a surprise visit this morning."

"Oh my god!" Gwen gasped.

"Are you okay?" Gigi asked.

"I'm fine. I don't even think it's going to bruise very badly."

No one looked convinced.

"Fucking hell. As if we don't have enough problems to deal with." Florence scowled. "Remind me again why we aren't calling the police for backup with this little search party at the far edges of civilization?"

"Because, I'm not dragging anyone else all the way out into the sticks until I'm absolutely sure it's not a wild goose chase. Which is why I planned on going—" I shot Gwen a pointed look. "*—alone*."

She merely shrugged. "Forgive me if I didn't want you *dying* alone on this wild goose chase of yours."

"Is it still a wild goose chase if there are four of us going?" Flo's brows lifted. "Or does that make it a wild geese chase?"

I looked heavenward. "Lord, help us."

"I don't care if it's a dead end," Gigi interjected. "What if it's not? The police still have so much ground to cover in the heart of the woods, it could be days before they get all the way out here to the fringes."

This was true.

Cade had told me they were centering their search around the clearing where Declan had met his friends, moving methodically outward in a grid to cover every inch of territory. It was a painstaking, thorough, time-consuming procedure. One that was measured in days, not hours.

"If there's even a tiny chance we could find Rory out here, I want to check it out," Georgia insisted. Her voice went softer as she added, "Whatever you saw, whatever you felt... I trust your instincts, Imogen."

My breath caught. I hadn't realized, until that moment, that Georgia knew about my visions. I hadn't told her — hadn't wanted to get her hopes up unfairly — but someone else must have spilled the beans.

Was there anyone left in this town who didn't know all my secrets?

Not likely.

A few days ago, that knowledge would've made me feel exposed. Uncomfortable. I would've had to fight the urge to disappear. But now, as I stared around the circle from Gwen to Florence to Georgia, I didn't feel judged. I didn't feel like a lab rat or a bug under a microscope. I didn't even feel like Fake Imogen. They were looking at me — the *real* me — and there was no judgment in their expressions. No suspicion or calculation.

Only openness.

Only trust.

I swallowed hard.

"All right," I whispered, tilting my chin toward the old railroad tracks. "We'd better get going."

We walked for nearly an hour, following the tracks deeper and deeper into the woods. The trees were so tall, they blocked most of the sun even when it reached its apex in the midday sky.

"I've lived in this town all my life, but I had no idea there was so much wilderness back here," Florence called, bringing up the rear.

"Where are we, anyway?" Gwen asked. "Somewhere behind the quarry?"

"Not anymore," I murmured, scanning the terrain ahead. Looking for something — anything — I recognized from Annie's memories. "We're closer to the marshes."

"Does the city own all this land?" Georgia looked around at the thick woods to either side. "The state?"

"No idea. The state probably owns the tracks. The rest..." I trailed off with a shrug.

"I just hope axe-wielding hillbillies don't come out of the trees and chop us to bits for stepping on their turf," Flo said cheerfully. "Have you seen those *Wrong Turn* movies? Sheesh!"

We continued walking.

Continued searching.

Mostly in silence, just trudging along, listening to the birds chirping in the trees overhead. The wind stirred fallen leaves around our feet into tiny vortexes of orange and red. Occasionally, a squirrel or bunny would dart across our path, and Socks would nearly yank my arm off trying to chase them down.

I gnawed on my lip as the minutes ticked on and on without a single sign we were going the right direction. I was starting to doubt my own memory. Were these even the right tracks? I thought they were, but… Maybe I hadn't seen what I thought I did. Maybe I was so desperate for a clue that would break this case wide open, my mind had conjured up—

"There!"

Georgia screamed and started running in a dead sprint toward a clump of low-lying bushes about twenty feet off the tracks. We all burst into motion, close on her heels. Socks barked happily, thinking it was a game, but the rest of us didn't make a single sound. I felt like I was running in slow motion, my limbs water-logged by anxiety and dread. My heart, on the other hand, was in fast forward, thudding triple-time.

I watched my friend drop down into the dirt. She made an awful noise — a whimper of raw emotion that pierced me through the gut. Her hands shook violently as she pointed into the wild juniper bush.

There, snagged on one of the branches, was a piece of stiff reflective material. It gleamed faintly in the sunshine. I gasped, recognizing it instantly as one of the flight-activator panels we'd glued onto Rory's space invader costume.

"Oh, *shit,*" Flo whispered.

"Is that—"

"Rory's." Gigi cut off Gwen's question in a trembling voice. "It's Rory's."

I couldn't say a word. I was stunned silent.

We'd found something.

We'd actually found something.

Georgia reached out as if to touch it, but pulled back at the last moment. She knit her hands together in front of her chest and started rocking slowly back and forth. Over her head, Gwen, Flo, and I all traded panicked glances. I was sure my own expression mirrored the shocked looks they were both wearing.

"What the fuck do we do now?" Flo hissed quietly, eyes darting down to the top of Gigi's head.

"Why are you asking me?" I hissed back.

"You're the one who dragged us out here!"

"That doesn't mean I have a plan!"

"Shut up!" Gwen snapped, reaching into her back pocket for her cell. "We're going to call for help. That's what happens now."

Right.

Of course.

We'd call Cade, he'd appear with a full cavalry—

"Hellfire," Gwen cursed.

"What?" I asked, seriously not liking the look on her face. Not one bit.

She held up her cell. "No service. We must be out of range."

"Seriously?" Florence pulled out her own cellphone, glanced at the screen for a few seconds, and then screamed at the top of her lungs. "*Fuck!*"

Birds erupted from the trees overhead.

"Okay," I said slowly, mind racing. "Here's what we'll do. I'll wait here. You guys will bring Gigi back to the car. You can call for help once you're back near civilization. There was service in the lot where we parked."

Gwen shook her head. "I don't think—"

"We absolutely aren't leaving you *alone* out here!" Flo exploded, cutting her off. She leveled me with a glare. "Have you never seen a horror movie? The gang splits up and ten seconds later… cue the chainsaws."

I looked pointedly down at Gigi. She was still rocking slightly back and forth, eyes fixed on the reflective panel. "She can't stay out here."

At my words, Georgia stopped rocking. She pulled in a breath, the sound ragged in her throat. Slowly, she got to her feet. When her eyes met mine, they were burning with determination. There was a set to her shoulders I'd never seen before.

"I'm not going anywhere."

"Gigi—"

She turned to Gwen and Flo. "You two are going back to the car, getting help out here as soon as you can. Imogen and I are going on ahead."

"That's not—"

Gigi cut Flo off before she even began. "So help me god, Florence Lambert, if you make one more snappy little comment about scary movies or fictional villains, I will *scream*. You want to talk horror? I've spent the past four days *living it*. Every hour without my boy, every minute, every damn second without him..." Tears misted her eyes as her finger jabbed down toward the juniper bush. "That, right there, it the first tangible piece of my son I've seen since he went missing. So, you get your ass moving down those tracks. You do it now. Or I swear—" She leaned toward Flo, expression menacing. "I will *make* you move."

Florence didn't turn tail and go. Not immediately, anyway. First, she stepped forward, wrapped Georgia in her arms, and squeezed. Hard. Then, she grabbed Gwen by the hand and the two of them high-tailed it down the tracks, back the way we'd come.

"Don't do anything stupid!" Flo screamed back at us over her shoulder. "We'll be right back!"

When they were out of sight, I looked over at Georgia. Her gaze was heavy on my face. There was a question in her eyes. A plea. I knew what she wanted without her needing to ask aloud.

"Imogen..."

"I'll try," I told her, passing Socks' leash into her hands, then kneeling in the dirt. "But I can't promise anything."

She nodded, clutching the leash so hard her knuckles turned

white. She knelt next to me, hauling the squirming puppy up against her side.

I looked for a long moment at the shiny material in the bush. I took a huge breath, the kind I'd take before I dove deep underwater. And then, before I lost my nerve, I reached out and ran my fingertips down the length of the flight activator panel.

A wave of purple washed me away.

The boy realizes the depth of his mistake when his flashlight flickers out. He smacks his hand against the bottom, but the batteries are dead. He sticks the useless thing into his candy bucket and keeps walking.

He has already walked for so long. So very long.

Too long.

He is tired. So very tired. His legs ache with each step. But he can't stop now. He has to make it to the clearing, where the older kids are gathered.

He's been there twice before, but never at night. And always with his brother to guide the way.

Were there railroad tracks, last time?

He thinks there were.

He cannot really remember.

The woods are different in the dark. The branches pull and tear. The wind bites with sharp teeth. He shivers in his thin costume. His shredded palms sting from the crash off his bike.

He wants to go home.

Not the hotel.

He hates the hotel.

He hates his brother, too.

It is the worst Halloween he's ever had — even before the fall. He tumbles over the unseen tree root, face-first. His arms pinwheel. His candy bucket sails into the air, then clatters to the ground somewhere out of sight. The ground rushes up to meet him, slick with wet leaves. He tries to stand, but slips again — this time down a sharp incline. He feels his costume shredding as he slides past bushes and branches; feels his flight panels tearing loose…

We retraced Rory's steps in total silence, moving through the woods like two ghosts. It didn't take us very long to find the incline where he'd slipped. We spotted the upturned candy bucket first, its orange hue dulled by dirt and leaves. Dozens of shiny wrappers were scattered on the ground around it. The mud was disturbed, deep rivets made by scrambling limbs.

This was where he'd tumbled.

We did not pause to even look too closely. We were caught in a current of urgency, driven to keep moving by some invisible gravitational force that called us forward.

Down the slope.

Into the marsh.

It took a long time to pick a safe path to the bottom. It was steep enough to see why Rory had fallen. One wrong step on a slippery patch of leaves would spell disaster.

I carried Socks in my arms as we made our careful descent, muscles straining under his weight. God, he was heavy. In another few months, he'd weigh more than I did. At the bottom, we scanned the area for more signs of Rory. There was nothing, at first. Georgia called out for him, screaming his name over and over again until her voice went hoarse.

There was no response.

If someone was around to hear us, they were not making themselves known.

She grew more and more frantic as we searched the area, her breaths coming faster as the minutes dragged on without success.

"He was here," she muttered, shoving at a thorny bush until her skin tore. "There must be something…"

It was Socks who found it, in the end. His sharp nose led him to a patch of sodden leaves, where he snuffled around until he unearthed the source. My airway closed up when I saw an unnatural shape amidst the brambles. A boy's sneaker, the treads full of mud, the laces hanging loose.

Rory.

"Georgia," I called, voice halting. I dropped to my knees in the mud. "Come here."

She was at my side in an instant. I heard the sob catch in her throat, but I did not turn to look at her. I was already reaching out to touch the sneaker. Hoping like hell it would trigger something.

I'd never been so relieved to see that telltale violet cloud over my eyes.

The fall lasts forever.

Longer than the slide at the water park the boy tried out last summer. Longer than the hill he and his brother sled down in the wintertime, when it snows.

Down, down, down.

He cannot stop it. It is too steep, too slick. He wonders how he will ever make the climb back up to the top. It will take all night.

When he finally hits the bottom, he jolts to a stop against the unyielding earth. His ankle burns with a fiery pain he's never felt before. Broken or simply sprained, it doesn't matter. He can't put weight on it when he tries to stand. He can't walk more than a few steps. It is swollen to twice its normal size.

He loosens his shoelaces, then tugs off his sneaker to ease some of the throbbing agony. It does not help much.

Tears track down his cheeks, drip off his chin.

He yells and yells.

For his mother. For his brother. For anyone.

But there is no one around to hear.

Not for a long, long time.

Not until nearly dawn.

When, finally, she *comes.*

His scream tapers off abruptly when he sees her limping closer, moving through the trees like a phantom. He does not dare make another sound. He knows what will happen, if he does. He knows the legend by heart.

The witch has come to carry him away.

We weren't alone out here.

The thought haunted me as I shook off the head-spinning aftereffects of the vision.

I did not tell Georgia what I'd seen. Not all of it. Not the very end. She didn't need to know about the woman in the woods who'd carried her boy away, into the night.

The Witch of Salem Wood.

Rory's childlike mind had leapt to the most natural conclusion, conjuring up a terrifying figure out of a familiar ghost story. But nothing I'd seen in his memories suggested anything remotely supernatural. The brief glimpse I'd gotten of her — that limping gait, that wild hair — only confirmed what I'd already suspected.

Whoever she was - whatever she was - Rory's monster was the same as Annie's.

If he had been taken, there was every chance he was still out here somewhere. Perhaps even in the same cabin where she'd kept Annie, all those years ago. And if he was… I didn't think it wise to give ample warning of our arrival by shouting at the top of our lungs.

"Imogen—"

"Give me a minute, Gigi," I pleaded softly. "I'm trying to remember the way."

I pressed my eyes closed for a moment, conjuring the vision I'd seen in Annie's fragmented memories. Playing it over and over, until it was clear in my mind.

Away from the cabin, down a short dirt road. Past a broken down car, red with rust. Through a swampy marsh, her sneakers making slurping sounds. Up a slippery slope, grabbing tree roots to keep from sliding back down…

We weren't far.

Half a mile.

Maybe less.

I opened my eyes. "Gigi."

She looked at me. There were tears in her eyes — but precious little hope. "Yeah?"

"I know which way we have to go," I told her, trying to sound confident even though, inside, I was anything but. "It isn't far. But if you can't stay quiet, you have to stay here and wait for me. Can you stay quiet?"

She hesitated a beat, then gave a small nod.

"Okay." I swallowed hard. "Then let's go."

I led the way. Georgia, true to her word, stopped screaming Rory's name. We crossed a marshy stretch of swamp, shoes squelching in the muck. Socks was up to his chest in it, his black fur caked brown by the time we hit dry ground on the other side.

The trees here were thinner than those in Salem Woods. Not towering maples or willows, but skinny silver-barked pines and twisted sycamores. Foxtail reeds and salt marsh grasses lined the banks of the estuary. I heard the croak of toads in the algae-blooming shallows and the warbling call of blue herons hunting prey.

Socks shook himself dry, sending sandy water droplets flying in all directions. He seemed no worse for wear, despite his filthy state. Both Gigi and I were shivering, but we kept going. There was no turning back.

Not now.

We were getting close. There, on the bank, was the rusted-out car, mostly hidden by overgrown bushes. There, just beyond, the dirt path through the trees.

Trading a glance, we followed it, not daring to speak, hardly daring to breathe. The narrow way curved to the left, we came around the bend, and—

There.

A clearing.

And, smack in the middle of it…

A cabin.

Almost a shack, in fact. Tiny, ramshackle, and in a state of total disrepair. Its wood was rotting away. One strong gust of wind might reduce it to timber. The entire dwelling canted to one side. There were visible holes in the roof. What remained of the front porch had crumbled, either from the constant barrage of time or the crashing waves of coastal storms.

Perhaps at one point, it had been a nice place to live. A quaint cottage by the sea, perfect for fishing in the marshes and soaking in the splendors of nature.

That time was long gone.

It looked uninhabited. A place for ghosts and spiders and — I had to admit — evil witches in a children's tale.

I gulped in a bracing breath as we stared it down.

Maybe Florence wasn't so far off when she mentioned the axe-wielding hillbillies…

Georgia and I moved toward it, side by side, Socks tromping along below. Our feet trailed wet splotches on the ground. I'd never been one for physical violence, but I found myself grappling with the strangest urge to arm myself as we closed the distance to the front porch.

I wanted a gun.

Or a taser.

That, or a really, really thick stick.

Gigi's foot hit the bottom step. It creaked ominously under her weight. In the quiet of the clearing, the noise echoed like a gunshot, rebounding off the tree line.

Shit.

We both froze.

Another noise hit my ears. A shuffling sound. Not from Gigi's shoes — this was coming from inside the cabin. Coming closer to the door. I braced for whatever was about to step through it. Sensing my tension, Socks began to growl — a low rumble that was surprisingly foreboding, given his typical disposition.

The door screeched open, dragging against the floorboards on uneven hinges. A figure stood in the threshold, leaning on the frame for balance. There was a makeshift splint on his ankle, made from wood slats and strips of cotton.

His mouth opened to speak.

And what he said was—

"Mom?"

He was covered in dirt.

His neon green costume was in tatters.

But he was alive.

He was breathing.

We'd found him.

Rory.

His eyes were wide as saucers as they swung from me, to Socks, and finally, to his mother — at which point they filled to the brim with tears. Georgia made a strangled sound — half shout, half wail — and launched herself at his tiny frame. She covered his dirt-streaked face in a flurry of kisses. His cheeks, his forehead, his jaw. Everywhere her lips could reach. Between kisses, she chanted his name over and over. Like a mantra. Like a spell.

"Rory... Rory... Rory..." She was sobbing, now, her voice a broken whisper. But I knew they were good tears. The best tears. Tears of a woman granted her dearest wish. "Oh, Rory. You're here, bub. My god, you're here. I can't believe you're actually here."

His spindly arms lifted, closing around her back as he hugged her. His voice was a croak. "*Mom…*"

Tears filled my own eyes as I watched their reunion. I had to look away to keep them from falling. Deep inside me, joy and gratitude warred for dominance. My heart felt as though it might burst within my chest, unable to contain everything I was feeling.

Socks whined and strained his leash.

I thought he was trying to get to Rory. But when I looked down, I saw he was staring toward the tree line on the other side of the clearing. My own gaze swung up, following his. My body locked with alarm, all my joy vanishing in an instant. The blood in my veins turned cold as ice.

There was something — someone — standing in the shadows, under the twisted sycamore by the edge of the estuary. I couldn't make out much detail. Only the vaguest silhouette of a human. I could almost be convinced it was just a trick of the light. That there was no one standing there at all.

Except for Socks.

He saw it, too.

Saw her too.

A woman. One with wild hair and a lopsided frame. The living fragment of a whispered legend.

The Witch of Salem Wood.

She was real.

Somehow, she was—

The unmistakable whir of helicopter blades drew my gaze suddenly skyward. On the horizon, flying low, a police chopper was headed our way.

Clearly, Florence and Gwen had found cell service.

My heart lurched as I saw the helicopter coming closer. I didn't have many dollars in the bank, but I'd bet every last one of them that Cade Hightower was sitting inside it, those piercing blue eyes scanning the marshes below for signs of life.

He'd come to bring us home.

All of us.

Relief surged through me, sharp as a knife. By the time I pulled my watery eyes away from the impending rescue and looked back at the sycamore, where the strange figure had been...

No one was standing there.

The shadows were empty.

Whoever she'd been...

Whatever she'd wanted...

She was gone.

CHAPTER TWENTY-FOUR

Pack your bags, we're going on a guilt trip.
- Imogen Warner, being read to filth

I'd always hated hospital waiting rooms. The first memory I had of sitting inside one, I was only five. They'd rushed my parents there after their accident. Mom was DOA. Dad held on for a few days, only to slip away a bit more with every passing hour.

It was awful. All of it. Every last moment. But the *waiting* — the waiting was the worst part.

Waiting for him to live.

Waiting for him to die.

Waiting for the fates to swing like the cruelest of pendulums, one way or the other.

I'd been too young to fully understand what was going on. All these years later, the memories felt distant when I looked back. Watercolored and weak. But the one thing I did know for certain, even at five, was that waiting rooms were the worst place on planet earth.

The air, so heavy in my lungs. The fluorescent lighting overhead, buzzing like a timer that's run out. The yellow wallpaper, meant to be cheerful, no doubt, but instead the jaundiced pallor of the terminally ill.

We'd all gathered as the afternoon crept on. Appearing one by one. In pairs and trios. In groups and clusters. Until everyone I'd met since coming to Salem seemed to fill the waiting room to bursting.

Sitting there, looking around at all of them — Sally, Agatha, Gwen, Graham, Florence, Desmond, Declan, Georgia's mother, Georgia's sister, Welles, Hunter, Holden, Sawyer, Detective Aguilar, Chief Coulter, Rhonda the night manager, and a sun-tanned gentleman with salt-and-pepper hair I'd since learned was Mr. Monteith, owner of the illustrious Sea Witch Inn, who'd flown in from Florida to show his support — for the first time in my life, waiting didn't seem so very bad.

Their collective presence closed around me like two arms in an embrace. I didn't feel the horror or the grief or the anxiety anymore. Only the love. The hope. The family.

Home.

The door to Rory's room opened. Everyone sat up a bit straighter in their chairs as Cade and Gigi stepped out into the hallway. Gigi's eyes were swollen from crying, but there was a relieved smile on her lips. Cade looked relieved, too. But his expression changed when his gaze found mine in the crowded room. It went totally gentle. His eyes were shining with pride and something stronger — something that made my whole heart clench. I could hardly pull breath into my lungs when he was looking at me like that.

"He's okay," Gigi announced to the room at large, her voice breathy. "His ankle isn't broken. They say he can go home tomorrow morning."

The wave of relief that washed through the room was palpable. Chief Coulter and Detective Aguilar shook hands with the FBI agents in the corner. Gwen leaned deeper into Graham, and his arm went tighter around her shoulders. Desmond smiled indulgently at Florence as she looked to the ceiling and dropped an enthusiastic f-bomb. Agatha and Sally were both grinning wide.

The Gravewatch men took the news in typical stoic stride. Still, Welles ran a hand through his long hair and shook his head. Sawyer's eyes were crinkled up at the corners. The twins, who were leaned back against the far wall, both exhaled in tandem.

I reached over and squeezed Declan's hand. He squeezed back, hard, and when I looked over, I saw his dark brown eyes were shining with emotion.

"It's over now, Dec. You can breathe."

He nodded, blinking rapidly.

"Go to your Mom, honey."

I didn't have to tell him twice. He launched out of his chair and hurried across the crowded waiting area, weaving through the cluster of burly Gravewatch men who were standing at the center of the room, looking totally out of place in their black leather jackets and combat boots. When he reached Georgia, he took a huge breath. I knew he'd lost the battle against his tears. His voice was thick with them.

"He's really okay?" he whispered up at her.

Her hand lifted to tuck an errant curl behind his ear. "He's okay, bub."

"Can I see him?"

"Of course you can. He's been asking for you."

Declan's arms flew around her middle, so hard she rocked back on her heels. I saw her arms come up to return the hug, then lost sight of them both as they were enfolded into the arms of Georgia's mother and sister.

Cade appeared before me. I hadn't even seen him move. But there he was, standing two feet away, his hand extended. I took it, allowing him to pull me up out of my seat without a word of protest. He tugged me down the hall for some privacy, steering me carefully around the legs and purses that cluttered the floor, along with Socks, who was snoozing under my chair, too tired to even notice when I passed his leash into Desmond's ink-stained hands.

It had been a big day for him.

Technically, I didn't think dogs were allowed in hospital waiting rooms. But no one was going to question it when said dog arrived in the company of the entire Salem Police Department, a fleet of FBI agents, and a squad of the most elite private investigators on the east coast.

Cade stopped at the end of the hallway, out of earshot of the rest of the group. He looked tired, but the tension that had consumed him for the past few days had finally vanished. An undeniable weight had lifted off his shoulders. He dropped my hand — but only so he could cup my face with both of his, tilt my chin up, and capture my mouth in a soft, sweet kiss.

"How are you holding up, beautiful?"

"Me?" I stared into his eyes, thinking I could drown in those blue depths and not care a bit. It would be a great way to die. "I'm fine."

"I haven't had a chance to talk to you, with everything that's happened these past few hours."

This was true.

It had been chaos at the scene once the cavalry arrived. I wasn't sure what Gwen and Florence had said when they finally found cell-service, but it was enough to mobilize a huge law enforcement response. Only minutes after I'd first spotted the inbound chopper, officers had descended like locusts on the abandoned cabin — most of them dressed in full tactical gear, armed and dangerous. (And, ultimately, disappointed that there was no enemy around to fight.)

A search of the cabin revealed Rory was the only one there.

All that urgency, all that testosterone, all that ammo... For nothing. I had a feeling it was a bit anticlimactic for the commandos.

As for me, I was too relieved to feel anything else. Rory was alive. And, despite his dirty appearance, he was seemingly unharmed. Just happy to be in his mother's arms again.

The two of them had sat on the edge of the clearing, wrapped tight in an embrace, whispering to each other under their breaths, until paramedics arrived and peeled Rory away for an exam. They came on foot, carrying a stretcher and medical supply bags. There was no other choice. The forgotten patch of marshland was completely inaccessible by car.

Technicians had arrived in droves, wading through the swamp with their kits held high over their heads. They'd immediately begun cataloguing every inch of the cabin's interior, collecting evidence, taking photographs. Meanwhile, officers and agents searched the swampy salt-marsh for any sign of the woman who'd taken Rory.

So far, there were none.

She was like a ghost. If I hadn't seen her with my own two eyes, I wouldn't believe she existed at all. The responding officers didn't seem entirely convinced of that fact, even after Rory told them what had happened to him; even after I described what I'd witnessed.

I supposed, when all was said and done, they'd wanted a better villain. Someone they could pump full of bullets in a Hollywood-style gunfight, or parade in front of the press as the feather in the cap of their search efforts. Chasing a strange, silent recluse through the misty marshes wasn't exactly the ending they'd envisioned for this mission.

Still, I knew they'd keep looking for her. Everyone from the lowest-ranking beat cop on SPD payroll to the director of the Boston FBI field office had questions about her role not only in Rory's disappearance, but also in Annie's. Aguilar was out for blood. Coulter was adamant they needed answers. Even Cade, who was generally very level-headed, was having a difficult time coming to terms with the situation.

I'd never forget the moment he'd finally stalked out of the

trees that afternoon and spotted me there, standing in front of the cabin at the center of that chaotic scene. I was trying my best to stay out of the way as agents streamed past on all sides, as officers spoke rapid-fire into their radios, as gun-toting commando types jogged into the thigh-high waters, searching for clues. The tide was coming in, making it even more difficult to traverse the water-logged terrain.

Socks, who had caught sight of the trained canine unit several moments prior, was already pulling at his leash to get to them, thinking to make a new friend. The pulling turned to full arm-wrenching when his glossy eyes locked on his master, emerging from the tree line on the heels of Detective Aguilar and Chief Coulter.

(It must be said, the butterflies in my stomach were having a similarly enthusiastic response.)

Cade.

He'd stopped short when he saw us, visibly rocking back on his heels, looking for all the world like someone had socked him in the stomach. This may have had something to do with the fact that I was covered in mud from the thighs down to my toes, with a shiner blooming on my eye. Not necessarily my best look of all time.

His eyes had dropped to my feet and worked slowly up the length of me. Throughout, his face remained oddly blank. I couldn't tell what he was thinking. What he was feeling.

Was he annoyed?

Was he mad at me?

Was he going to yell?

It took him a few seconds to recover — after which, he'd strode across the clearing, hauled me into his arms, and kissed me.

Hard.

Not a chaste peck that said, 'I'm happy to see you.' Not an appropriate lip-brush that took into consideration the number of onlookers milling about. It was a full on, no holds barred, long, deep, wet kiss. With tongue. A kiss that said, 'to hell with everyone watching, to hell with everyone in the whole damn world, I can't live another second without your mouth on mine and I don't care who knows it.'

It was unquestionably the best kiss of my life.

Pulling back, he'd traced his fingers along the bruise I knew was turning my entire eye socket blacker and bluer with each passing hour.

This, he did not do hard. This, he did soft. Like he was afraid, if he touched me, I might shatter to glass in his hands.

"I'm fine," I'd told him.

"You're standing there with a fucking black eye, beautiful. You aren't fine." His mouth had gone tight. "Did the fucker who took Rory do this to you?"

"No! No," I said quickly. I wasn't thinking about the repercussions when I blurted, "It wasn't her. It was Adrian."

He went still.

Ultra still.

And when he spoke, he did it in a rumbly, intense, scary voice that sent shivers down my spine.

"Adrian Lombardo did this to you?"

I didn't think it was good that he knew my asshole ex-boyfriend's full legal name. But I also didn't think it was a good moment to discuss that small detail.

"I'm okay, really. It looks worse than it is."

Cade's eyes were aflame. *"I'm going to fucking kill him."*

"Um..." I'd swallowed nervously as my eyes flitted past his enraged face to the bevy of law enforcement officials around us. "Cade, honey, maybe we should talk about this at another time."

Ideally, when there were no potential witnesses to his murder confessions.

"Later," he'd vowed tightly. His jaw had been set like stone. I knew he meant business.

Now, it *was* later. Four hours later, to be exact. He still looked like he meant business. His unhappy eyes scanned my battered face, lingering on the bruise.

"Wish you'd let me call over a doctor to look at that," he muttered, not for the first time. "We're in a damn hospital. There are a hundred of them around here who'd be happy to help."

"I don't need a doctor. It's just a bruise. It'll heal."

"You should put ice on it."

"I already did," I said. "By the way, I owe you a bag of frozen peas."

His lips twitched. "I'm sure you're good for it."

We stared at each other for a while. There was a lot to discuss. So much, in fact, I didn't really know where to begin. Between our fight last night, the evidence box, the car repairs, the Adrian incident, and the Rory rescue...

I decided to tackle the most pressing issue first.

"Has Rory said anything else?" I asked, brows high on my forehead. "Anything more about what happened out there?"

Cade shook his head, frustration creeping into his face. His teeth ground together. "No. Still the same story."

My stomach twisted. Glad as I was that we had Rory back safe and sound, I felt strangely unsettled about the whole thing. Mostly because Rory was adamant the woman in the woods hadn't harmed him.

She'd *helped* him.

After he fell down that slippery incline, he'd been hurt. Injured. He'd laid at the bottom of that hill for hours, calling for someone to come.

Finally, someone had.

According to Rory, she'd carried him across the marsh, to the ramshackle cabin. She'd given him a blanket and fashioned a rudimentary brace for his twisted ankle. And, for four days, she'd tended to him — bringing food and water.

She never spoke.

Never touched him, except to check on his splint.

"Do you believe him?" I asked.

Cade exhaled a sharp breath. "He has no reason to lie. He's talking. He's eating. Doesn't seem scared or even particularly shaken up, given what he's been through. Doctors checked him over, top to toe. He's healthy, besides the ankle. Psychiatrist said the same thing."

"That's good news."

He nodded. "Mhm."

"You don't seem convinced."

"I just—" Something flashed in his eyes for a moment before he locked it down.

"What is it?"

"Wouldn't mind being certain, that's all." The apple of his throat bobbed as he swallowed. "But I hesitate to suggest— To ask if—"

"Out with it, Hero-Hair."

"Goldie..."

"Out. With. It."

He sighed. "It might put my mind — and Georgia's mind, especially — at ease, if you'd... You know..." His eyes were intent. "Talk to him."

Comprehension flashed through me. "You want me to touch him and trigger a vision, to see if his story aligns with what actually happened."

Cade gave a shallow nod.

"Let's go, then." I turned and started walking toward Rory's room without delay. A hand flew out and caught me before I made it more than a few steps.

"Imogen, wait."

My brows were high on my forehead when I met his gaze again. He looked deeply conflicted.

"What is it?" I asked, confused.

"I didn't mean right now."

"This shouldn't really wait, though. Right? Isn't this whole shebang sort of time-sensitive?"

His lips flattened. "You still don't have to do this."

Was he crazy? "I totally have to do this, Cade."

"You don't," he repeated firmly. "You got Rory back for us. You've already done enough."

"We may have him back, but we still have no real answers. If I can help provide some, I want to do it."

He said nothing, jaw clenched tight.

"What's this about?"

He blew out a long breath. "You look like you're about to fall over."

"Gee, thanks."

His eyes narrowed. "How many visions have you had today?"

"Um..." I chewed my lip.

Too many.

My mind felt stretched too thin, too far, like an elastic band about to snap.

"Yeah," he muttered, reading the answer on my face. "That's what I thought."

"I can still do it. One more won't kill me."

I didn't think so, anyway.

"You've had a long fucking day, Imogen. You've been beaten. You've tracked miles through the woods and marsh. Your clothes are damp with mud. And you've been pushing yourself to the limit, mentally." He shook his head. "The rub of it is, I'm the one who asked you to do it. But I can't help feeling guilty as hell, knowing the toll it takes on you."

He was worried about me.

"Honey," I whispered, sliding my arms around his waist. My head was tipped up to hold his anxious stare. "I'll be fine."

"You say that, but you don't know what it's like — watching you go limp when a vision hits you."

"It's only for a few seconds."

"Yeah. A few seconds of not knowing whether you're going to come out of it. A few seconds of pure fucking terror, wondering how the fuck I'd carry on with my life if you didn't."

God, that was sweet.

I couldn't speak around the lump in my throat, so I pushed up onto my tiptoes and pressed my lips to his in a light kiss. It was meant to be light, anyway, but he kissed me back — deep, wet, delicious — until we were both breathing hard.

"I'll come back, Cade," I told him.

"You promise?"

I nodded. "I promise. Because, for the first time in my life, I have something worth coming back to."

His eyes flared with emotion.

Then, he took me by the hand and led me down the hallway, into Rory's room.

I fell asleep on the ride home from the hospital, slumped over in the passenger seat of Cade's SUV. I was so worn out, I didn't wake when the engine turned off. Or when the driver's side door opened. Or even when a strong set of arms scooped me out of my seat and carried me up the dark front path, to the house. It wasn't until Cade's boot hit the porch that my heavy eyes finally blinked open.

"Are we home?" I murmured, still half-asleep.

"Yeah, beautiful." Cade's voice was warm. "We're home."

Thank god for that.

The vision I'd had back at the hospital hadn't killed me, but it came pretty damn close. Rory had been fast asleep when Cade led me into his room. There were deep circles under his eyes and a hydrating IV was hooked into his arm, but otherwise, he looked fine.

He looked like Rory.

I'd lowered myself gently onto the chair at his bedside and taken his frail hand within both of mine. I wasn't sure if my exhaustion or Rory's unconscious state was to blame but, in any case, my vision was brief and, despite my highest hopes, offered precious little in the way of explanations.

The witch never speaks.

Not with words, anyway. The boy does not think she knows how. Or maybe she's forgotten, after all this time alone in the marsh. He wonders how many years she has been out here.

Too many.

She is old. Older than his mom. Not quite as old as his grandmother.

He wants to ask her to take him home, but he does not say a word. He does not risk it, remembering the legend.

She'll steal your soul, drink your blood…

Somehow, the boy does not believe that is true. He was scared at first, but as the hours pass, his fear slips away. The rhyme is wrong, he decides. The witch is not evil, like everyone says. She doesn't seem to want anything from him, least of all his voice.

She is taking care of him. Helping him. He does not know why, but he can see she is trying her best. She brings him a dusty blanket to warm up and smears something gooey all over his swollen ankle when she props him up in bed. It's thick like mud, sticky as sap. And it smells strange as it dries. After a while, though, the throbbing isn't so bad anymore.

He wonders why she stays in a place like this. There's some furniture – a bed, a dresser, a few wax candles on the table. Moth-eaten curtains on the windows. A potbelly woodstove, crackling in the corner beside a stack of logs.

But nothing else. And no one else.

Doesn't she get lonely?

Doesn't she get bored?

No television, no Nintendo games, no phone, no electricity. No running water, even. She brings him a cup from the well-pump in the backyard, passing it to him and gesturing for him to sip when he hesitates. His hands shake as he lifts it to his lips. He is thirsty enough to down the whole thing in two gulps.

After, she retreats to her side of the small cabin and watches him from the shadows. He watches her back from the corner of his eye, too curious to keep his gaze averted. Eventually, his eyelids droop closed with exhaustion. The last thing he thinks before he falls asleep is that, maybe, she does *get lonely all by herself.*

Maybe that's why she's brought him here.

Maybe she wants a friend.

Ultimately, the vision had given me nothing – not about the so-called witch's identity or her motives in taking Rory. The only thing it did confirm was that he had been telling the truth. She hadn't hurt him. She'd done what she could with the rudimentary supplies at her disposal to keep him healthy, hydrated, and healing.

For Georgia, that was enough.

For the investigators on the case, however…

It didn't even come close to assuaging their need for answers.

Cade set me down on the front porch so he could open the door. I swayed on my feet, dizzy with exhaustion, until he steered me gently inside. Socks hurried in after us, making a beeline for his water bowl. He trailed dirty paw prints through the whole house on his way there. He was a muddy mess, but doggie-bath-time was a problem for tomorrow. (Imogen-bath-time took precedence.)

Cade led me straight to his bathroom and turned on the shower. While the water got hot, he helped me strip out of my mud-caked clothes, piece by piece. Off went my disgusting sneakers, straight into the garbage bin, followed by my still-damp socks. He peeled the jeans down my legs, the denim stiff with dried marsh water, followed by my undies. They, too, sailed toward the trash bin. Same with my ruined gloves — which he removed with such painstaking care, a lump formed in my throat as I watched him do it.

My sweatshirt was the last clothing item to go. He reached for the hem and stilled for a moment, studying the front. The Baltimore Ravens logo was faded from a million wears. I'd had it forever. Years and years. I couldn't even remember where I'd gotten it, if I was being honest. But I'd never throw it out. It was cozy and warm and oversized in the best sort of way. Even if it took ten washes to get the muck out of the fabric, I was keeping it.

"Don't throw that out," I whispered as Cade whooshed it up over my head. "It's my all-time favorite article of clothing."

"Yeah?" His lips curved in a smile. The sweatshirt was still in his hands. His thumb absently traced the lettering.

"Um... yeah." I narrowed my eyes at him, not understanding the weird look on his face. "What's going on with you?"

He just shook his head, not sharing his secrets as he carefully folded the dirty sweatshirt, set it on the sink vanity, and ushered me into the shower.

The moment the cascading water hit my head, I forgot all about clothing. Nothing in the history of the world had ever felt so good as that hot shower. I didn't reach for the soap right away. I just stood there, letting the stream crash down on my head, watching rivulets of mud flow down the drain.

Cade joined me a few moments later. His naked body pressed against my back as he reached around me for the bar of soap. He lathered it in his hands, then set about washing every part of my body — moving from my feet up my legs, over the curve of my ass, across the planes of my stomach. I stood perfectly still as he gently soaped my skin. I kept waiting for his touch to shift into something seductive, but he was intent on his task.

I sucked in a breath as he reached my breasts, but he didn't linger there. He moved to my neck, then down my arms. Eventually, he turned me around so he could do my upper back. He covered every inch of me — with one blatant exception.

My hands.

He let me do those myself.

When I was clean, he moved on to my hair. His strong fingers lathered my scalp with shampoo, then conditioner. It felt so good, I leaned back against him to hold me up. His chest was slick with water, warm and strong. And though it had been made perfectly clear he had no intentions of taking this touch any farther than pure care, I could no longer help myself. I turned around so we were face to face and looked up to meet his gaze.

His thick, dark hair was dripping wet, falling over his forehead. In the steamy air, the blue of his eyes was bolder than ever. I arched my body against his, pressing my breasts flush against his chest, and almost whimpered at the contact.

He sucked in a breath. "Imogen..."

"Kiss me."

"You're barely conscious, beautiful."

"Fine," I said, pushing onto my tiptoes, winding my arms up around his neck — careful not to touch his skin with my bare fingers. "Then I'll kiss *you*."

And I did.

My lips hit his, demanding. He met that demand instantly, mouth opening over mine, tongue sweeping inside. His hands slid down my back to cup my ass and he jerked me against him. I gasped when I felt his cock ramrod stiff against my stomach. He swallowed down the sound, never tearing his lips from mine. Deepening the kiss until I couldn't breathe, couldn't think. Until I could barely stand.

I wanted to touch him, so badly it almost hurt. I knit my fingers together behind his neck instead.

"Cade." My mouth tore away, just long enough to take a breath. My plea was ragged. "Fuck me. Please."

His teeth skimmed down my throat, nibbling and tasting as he stooped toward my chest. His tongue circled my peaked nipple, then he sucked it into his mouth.

My toes curled against the porcelain tub. "Cade—"

"Here or in our bed?" he muttered, moving to the other breast, where he inflicted the same mind-blowing torture.

"Here," I breathed, arching as his teeth clamped down on my nipple and tugged.

Hard.

Fuck.

My eyes fluttered closed. "I need you inside me."

His fingertips curled into my upper thighs as he hiked me up into his arms and pinned me against the tile wall. I felt the thick ridges of his cock sliding along the wet folds of my core, teasing me with a preview of what was to come.

"You want me, beautiful?"

"Yes," I gasped when his hips shifted slightly, allowing the tip of his cock to inch inside. "God, yes."

"How do you want me?"

He slid in another inch and my mind blanked with bliss.

Until he stopped.

"Don't stop," I breathed.

I needed more. My legs tightened around his waist, desperate for it, but he held back.

"Imogen," he prompted in a growl. "Look at me."

My eyes, which had drifted shut, snapped open. His face was close, his expression fierce with need.

"Tell me how you want it, greedy girl, or you won't get it at all."

That was so hot, I nearly orgasmed just hearing it.

"Tell me," he ordered.

"Hard. Rough," I confessed in a rush. "Don't be gentle."

He grinned — a grin of such dark promise, it set off a full-body tingle from the top of my head to the tip of my toes. And, without another instant of delay, he made good on that promise.

He slammed inside me, burying himself to the hilt. We both cried out at the sheer pleasure of it. He gave it to me just as I'd asked. Hard, rough. There was nothing gentle about the way he fucked me, nothing even close to gentle about the orgasm that rocked through my frame a few short moments later. I'd barely finished coming when another began to build, spurred on by the relentless drive of Cade's hips, the brutal pace he maintained as he gripped my ass with unflagging strength.

The second time I came, he came with me.

His forehead planted in the crook of my neck, where my pulse was pounding twice its normal speed. His breaths were just as ragged as mine. But his voice was full of satisfaction when he muttered, "Christ. Just got you clean, now I have to start all over again…"

I laughed as he set me back on my feet and grabbed the soap.

CHAPTER TWENTY-FIVE

I'm on my way! There's a bunch of traffic.
- Imogen Warner, stepping out of the shower

Later, we were lying on our sides in bed, facing one another. The room was dark. For once, the heavy weight of a furry body was not sprawled across my feet. Socks had been shut out for the night, ruled too filthy for bed-access by Cade. (For the record, I — pushover that I was — had advocated to let him track muddy prints all over the duvet, but was overruled.)

"Thought you were tired," he murmured, staring at my face.

"The double-orgasm kind of woke me up."

His lips twitched, but all amusement drained from his expression as his eyes shifted to my shiner. "Tell me about this morning. Adrian."

"Maybe I am tired after all…"

"Imogen."

"Fine, fine," I muttered.

He'd already heard about most of my morning — back at the hospital, I'd told him all about the vision Annie's locket had triggered; how it had set me on the path to the marsh and, eventually, led me straight to Rory. But I'd been able to avoid telling him about Adrian's surprise visit.

Until now.

I gave him a brief synopsis, sparing no details but also attempting to gloss over some of the parts I knew would fray at his last nerves. Besides a brief lip-twitch when I described Socks' puppy-teeth taking advantage of a trendy ankle-bearing suit, he had no reaction at all.

"He said that?" he growled when I drew to a close. "That this isn't over?"

"I think we've established Adrian's instincts of self-preservation are seriously lacking."

"He'll try again. To get at you."

"Maybe." I shrugged. "If he does, he won't get me. I'm not going back to A.C. with him. I'm not going anywhere with him."

"Still, I want you out of The Sea Witch. Officially checked out."

Since my pre-paid week had been up two nights ago and all my stuff was already gone from the room, I was guessing Rhonda the night manager had taken the liberty of checking me out. But that didn't mean I wasn't planning on checking back in, as soon as the dust settled. "Cade—"

"Imogen." His face was hard. Unyielding. "This isn't open for discussion."

I narrowed my eyes at him. "You're very bossy."

"No, what I am is pissed off your idiot ex thinks he can dig out from the mountain of shit he's buried himself under using you as a goddamned shovel." His eyes glittered with menace. "Now that Rory is home, I can dedicate my full attention to making sure that never happens."

I wasn't certain I liked the sound of that. "Maybe you should let me deal with it myself, Cade."

"No."

"What if I *want* to deal with it myself?"

"Too bad. I'm dealing with it."

I sucked in a calming breath. "At this juncture, perhaps we should discuss your propensity for 'dealing' with my problems without asking me first. My car repairs, for instance."

"What about them?"

"You paid for them!"

"And?"

"And, that's crazy!"

"Why?"

"Because it isn't your car to repair!"

Cade's eyes narrowed a shade.

Uh oh.

He leaned in an inch.

Double uh oh.

"Goldie," he said, sounding pissed. "Did I or did I not tell you I was going to give you your freedom?"

"Uh..."

"Did I or did I not tell you I was going to get you free and clear?"

"Uh..." I swallowed.

"*Uh...Uh...* what?" His patience was expiring. "Pretty sure I recall telling you."

"You told me," I whispered.

"Yeah. I did." A muscle jumped in his cheek. He seemed to be struggling for control, but his voice was steady. "Step one of that is your car. It's fixed — at least, for a while. You're no longer dependent on anyone for rides. You want to, you can get in that car tomorrow, drive out of this town, and never come back."

My heart twisted painfully.

Why did that — something I'd wanted since I was first marooned in Salem — sound more like a punishment than a reward?

"Step two of making you free is cutting Adrian Lombardo out

of your life. For good, this time. Already told you I have plans for that. Plans I'll be executing tomorrow, first thing."

It was probably better for all parties involved if I didn't ask the specifics regarding that particular step of Cade's plan. (Plausible deniability, and all.)

I thought he was finished after those two steps, but he spoke again. And what he said nearly made my head spontaneously combust.

"Step three is Florida."

My breath caught. "Florida?"

"Yeah. Florida." He stared at me. "And that step's already done."

What was he saying?

"Done? How can that be done?"

"You know I called my contact down in Orlando. Asked him to do some digging into your uncle."

I gave a hesitant nod.

"Well, I finally heard back from my guy today," Cade said. His eyes went soft, as did his tone. "Your uncle is dead, Imogen. He died three years ago. Pancreatic cancer. It took him quick — three months between his initial diagnosis and hospice care."

I shook my head, rejecting this information.

No.

No, that wasn't possible.

"He can't be dead," I choked out in a strangled voice that sounded not at all like my own. I sat up suddenly on the bed, feeling the need to move but not knowing where to go. My spine pressed into the headboard. Without it, I might've fallen over.

Cade sat up too, moving close to look directly into my face. "He's dead, beautiful. He can't hurt you anymore. You're free of him."

I was free of him.

My eyes flooded with hot tears. "But— But I—"

"But what, Imogen?" he prompted gently, when I choked into silence.

"I've been running from him. All these years, I've been running..." I shook my head rapidly. "I was running from a ghost?"

Suddenly, I was in Cade's arms. They were tight around me, holding me together as I fell apart. I sobbed against his neck, unable to contain all the emotions raging inside me.

My uncle was dead.

My nightmare was over.

And the worst part was... it had been over for a while, now. Three years. I just hadn't known it. I'd been so terrified of confronting my fears head-on, I'd kept running long after I could've stopped. Kept walking that tightrope. Never settling anywhere, never putting down roots. Never truly belonging.

Maybe if I hadn't been so conditioned to constant flight... Maybe if I'd chanced looking back over my shoulder every once in a while...

"Shhh," Cade breathed against my hair. His hand moved up and down my spine in soothing strokes. "Don't waste any more tears on that man, beautiful. He doesn't deserve them."

I pulled back a bit, so I could look into his face. The expression I saw there made my throat feel tight. I wished I had a camera so I could take a snapshot, but I didn't need one. As long as I lived, I'd remember Cade Hightower's face in that moment. It was burned into my memory like a brand.

"You ready for the rest?"

My brows arched. "The rest?"

"Step four of making you free," he said slowly, eyes never shifting from mine. "Is your estate."

I blinked. "My estate?"

"Your money. All the royalties from your time on television," he explained.

"My uncle spent it."

"Not all of it. There's a fuck of a lot left. We're talking eight figures. And that's just the primary accounts my guy was able to scrounge up with a cursory search. Give him a few more days, he'll sniff out the rest."

I blinked at him again, struggling to process this.

"There's also the house. Your uncle had no kids to inherit it. Even if he had, he bought it with your money. It's yours, if you want it."

My blood ran cold. I hated that house — that prison. "I don't want it."

"You'll sell it, then. It's huge. Palatial. Should sell for at least two million."

I swallowed hard, trying to reconcile this information with reality. "Then... that means I... I'm..."

"Fucking loaded," Cade said, grinning at me. "Yeah. You've got enough cash to live comfortably for the rest of your life, anywhere you want."

"Anywhere I want," I repeated dumbly.

He nodded, grin slipping a bit. "Yeah, beautiful. You want to go home... Well, now you can do that."

"Home?"

"Florida."

"Florida isn't home."

A fissure of confusion appeared between his brows. "Isn't that where you lived with your parents?"

"Yes," I murmured. "But Florida isn't my home anymore, Cade. I'm not going back there."

"All right, not Florida. Somewhere else, then. Must've been somewhere you liked living, these past ten years. Or, somewhere you've always dreamed of living."

For once, I was silent.

He kept going. "You want a beach bungalow in Maui? It's yours. You want a ski chalet in Switzerland? You can have it. Hell, you have enough money for both, if you want them."

My heart was pounding.

My mind was racing.

I didn't understand.

Did he want me to leave?

I thought he wanted me to stay.

I thought…

"I don't ski," was all I could think to say.

"Point remains." He shrugged casually, but his eyes remained intense. "You can go wherever you want. You're free."

I was free.

That's when I understood.

He was giving this to me.

My freedom.

No strings.

No expectations.

He was letting me know, if I wanted to go, he wasn't going to hold me here. He wasn't going to cage me in. He wasn't a new captor, swapped out for Adrian or my uncle. He'd promised I'd be free and clear.

And Cade Hightower always kept his promises.

My heart squeezed again — this time not in a painful way. In a new way. In an *I think I might love you* way. In an *I don't think it, I know it* way.

I held his eyes and took a deep breath. "I can go anywhere?"

"Anywhere."

"But… What if I want to stay here?"

His whole frame tightened.

I kept going. "What if I want to stay in Salem? What if I want to stay with you?"

His answer was a kiss. A bruising, thorough, amazing kiss that resulted in me sprawled mostly across his chest, my legs straddling his hips, my breaths reduced to choppy pants.

"You're staying," Cade growled against my mouth. His eyes were burning like I'd never seen them before.

"If you'll have me."

His hips shifted and he drove inside me, filling me with his length in one smooth thrust. My breath snagged in my throat as he ground deeper.

"I'll have you," he gritted, the double meaning of his fierce declaration not lost on me.

I rode him, slowly at first, then faster and faster as the pleasure built. Our eyes were locked the entire time. I wanted to tell him I loved him, but I was too scared. It was too soon. I wanted to tell him that he'd changed my life, but it was too much. I couldn't say it. Not out loud, anyway.

Not with words.

There was only one way I could think to convey my feelings.

With touch.

My touch.

I released my death-grip on the headboard and brought my hands into the space between our bodies. I held them there a moment. Suspended. Waiting. Cade's lips parted on a soft gasp as he realized what I wanted. He gave a tiny nod.

"Touch me, beautiful," he rasped. "Been waiting six years. Can't wait anymore."

Before I lost my nerve, I lifted both hands up to cup his face.

A sea of purple sparks swallowed me whole.

The first time the man sees her, his world rocks off-kilter.

She is sitting in the precinct waiting room wearing a waitress uniform straight out of the 1950s. Frilly white apron, little cap sleeves on her pink button dress. It's ugly. But the woman wearing it is the farthest thing from ugly the man has ever seen.

She is exquisite.

It is more than her cascading pale platinum curls, partially restrained by a plastic clip at the back of her head. It is more than her eyes, clear as the water of a lake on a summer day, scanning the chaotic room around her with an unshakable serenity. It is more, even, than the way she holds her petite frame — so perfectly still, so self-contained. Like the eye at the center of a hurricane.

It is all of her.

One glimpse, and she has him by the throat.

She is young. Too young for him, in any case. Still, the man cannot tear his eyes away. Not as someone calls her name and she gets to her feet, relief briefly contorting her delicate features. Not as she follows the receptionist out of the frenzied waiting room, into the back hallway.

The man is meant to be out on the street, starting his shift. His partner is waiting for him in the cruiser outside. He can't afford to get written up. Not now, when he's trying his damndest to make detective. But the man cannot stop his feet from turning — not toward the door, not the direction he is meant to go, but into the back hall.

After the woman.

He has no explanation for the strange pull he feels in his gut. Yet he is powerless to stop it. He finds himself standing in the back of the interrogation room, where a crowd has formed to watch Jennings take her statement. Her voice is just as he imagined it would be. Like musical notes, light and melodic, even as she says the strangest things. Things that cannot possibly be true.

Can they?

He stares through the two-way mirror, knowing she cannot see him, even when she turns those bottomless eyes his way. Through the glass, her gaze cuts like a knife, straight to the heart. There is no deception there. Only truth. Only pain.

A lifetime's worth of pain.

He stays for her whole statement, listening to her speak. The other officers in the room make jokes. They laugh. They call her a quack, a fraud, a charlatan.

But the man makes not a sound.

Just stares at the woman, wondering who put that pain in her eyes. Wondering what he'd risk, just to get a shot at taking it away.

Purple sparks shifted, stealing the scene away. The vision changed.

The second time the man sees her, his world stops turning.

It is late. The middle of the night. The station is a storm of grief and pain and rage. Officers are processing the news. Some crying, some cursing, others completely silent. In the lobby, phones ring off the hook without reprieve despite the late hour. The receptionist is too devastated to answer.

More press camp out on the curb outside as the night creeps on, desperate to get this fresh horror filmed in time for the morning broadcast.

A whole SWAT team, dead.

Six good men, never coming home.

No justice for the boy who was taken.

No punishment for the man who did the taking.

It is the worst case scenario. It is nightmare-fuel.

The public will demand answers, as soon as first light breaks and they turn on their televisions to see the news. This miscalculation is a career-ender for Jennings — and Jennings knows it. No amount of nepotism can save him, not this time.

The man is headed home for the night. His shift is over. He cannot be here anymore. He would rather be at home alone to process his grief. Even the emptiness of his new apartment, the one he moved into after the divorce was finalized, is better than being here.

He changes into plainclothes in the locker room, then heads out. He is halfway down the hallway when he hears Detective Jennings shouting at someone. He isn't surprised. Jennings has to take his rage out somehow.

He rounds the corner and stops in his tracks.

The recipient of Jennings rage is none other than the woman he saw the night before. The clairvoyant. The one who gave them the lead. The one he hasn't been able to stop thinking about since.

"I'm not going down for this fuck up!" Jennings is shouting directly in her face. "I'll make sure everyone knows this is on you!"

The woman does not respond. She stands there, spine stiff, and takes the verbal lashing without cowing. Clearly, it is not her first. She has taken many such lashings before, the man would stake his badge on that.

"You should be the one to tell that mother what happened to her son!" Jennings roars, spit flying, hitting her cheeks. "You should be the one to face her! You're the one responsible for his death!"

The woman flinches. It is a slight movement – barely noticeable – but she cannot quite hide her pain.

"You're responsible for all their deaths," Jennings tells her, slamming a hand against the wall beside her head. It is a fierce blow, nearly a punch. She barely moves. It's like she's expecting the strike.

The man feels something ugly twist deep in his gut.

"Don't go anywhere," Jennings snarls. "We're not done. Not even close."

The detective leaves, but the man does not. He stands there, watching the woman. She is utterly still, holding herself in that self-contained manner. Locking in her emotions through sheer force of will.

But he can see, no matter how she tries to hide it, she is trembling. It is cold in the precinct and she's not wearing a jacket. Before he can stop himself, he's reaching up to pull the sweatshirt over his head. He grips it tightly in his hands as he moves toward her, his measured strides eating up the distance between them. The logo on the front is a purple eagle, emblazoned with the words **BALTIMORE RAVENS**.

When he gets close, he sees the tears shimmering on the surface of her incredible eyes. She looks up at him through a fog of grief and horror. She does not see him. Not really. Her gaze goes straight through him — even as he reaches out and places the sweatshirt in her shaking hands.

"Put this on," he tells her. "You're shivering."

He does not trust himself to say anything more. To do anything more. His chest feels tight as he turns and walks away. When he reaches the hall, he looks back in time to see the woman pulling his sweatshirt over her head. It is laughably large on her. But the sight of her wearing it makes some of the tension bleed out of his body.

She's going to be okay.

Maybe not tonight, but someday.

The man is sure of it.

In fact, he plans to make sure of it — personally.

Purple sparks hit me. The vision changed yet again.

The third time the man sees her, his world starts turning again after six long years of stopped motion.

He's tired. It's been a long day. This time of year is always hectic. Halloween brings out the crazies in full force. He is eager to get home, take his dog for a run, and clear his head.

He is not particularly thrilled by the sight of the broken down car steaming on the dark block in a not-so-great stretch of town. He is even less pleased to see a female form bent over beneath the hood.

He flips on his directional.

He'll help her, then head home.

She hears him coming. He's halfway to her car when she ducks out from beneath the hood and rounds toward him. He sees nothing but legs, at first. Long, shapely legs, still somewhat tanned from summer, in a pair of denim cut-offs so sweet they make his cock twitch to life inside his jeans.

Christ.

What is he, sixteen? He really needs to get laid if he can't make it through a traffic stop without getting hard.

His eyes jerk up to the woman's face and he prepares to ask her the usual questions. But the words dry up before they leave his lips. His whole body locks in shock. And deep beneath his feet, the world — stagnant for six long, endless fucking years — starts spinning again on its axis.

Her.

It's her.

He stares into a set of bottomless eyes, incapable of speech. She's looking right at him, waiting for him to start. He knows he should be saying something, but he can't seem to manage it. He watches her head tilt sideways in confusion; watches her hands curl into tiny fists at her sides, like she's frustrated with him.

"Uh… Hi," she says, clearly annoyed. "Can I help you with something, officer?"

That voice. Melodic as a song, even when she's pissed.

She's cute when she's pissed.

He can barely hide his grin.

As he drinks in the sight of her, something inside him falls into place. Like a puzzle piece he's been searching for without success, finally clicking in. Completing the whole picture.

Yeah, the man thinks to himself. She can help him with something.

A whole lifetime of somethings.

Starting now.

The vision released me with a lurch.

I came to, breathing hard. My eyes hit Cade's. He was watching me carefully. We were still connected — he was planted inside me, not moving, just holding me there, his arms locked tight around me.

"Beautiful, you back with me?"

I leaned forward and kissed him. And kissed him. And kissed him some more, pouring everything I wanted to say into my lips. My hips rocked against him, a rhythmic grind that sent spirals of pleasure through me. Wave after dizzying wave.

"You weren't the only one, you know," I confessed in a cracked voice. Tears were tracking down my cheeks, unstoppable. "You made my world start turning, too."

I saw Cade's eyes flash with a fierce, intense look — one I felt all the way down to my bones. Moving like lightning, he flipped me onto my back and flung up my legs so he could drive into me, deeper than ever. I felt my orgasm build to a fever-pitch. I was close, seconds from coming.

He could feel it.

His hips kept driving, but he stopped kissing me. I didn't know why — until he rasped something against my lips. Something that made my tears gather all over again.

"I love you, Imogen."

The tears slipped out of my eyes. "Cade—"

"Fell in love with you the first moment I saw you."

God.

"Love at first sight," he muttered. "And will be, till my last."

Those words, in combination with his deep strokes... I couldn't hold it off anymore. I came. And he came with me, driving into me over and over, wringing every ounce of pleasure from both our bodies until we were a tangle of limp limbs on the bed.

Afterward, I laid on his chest, my bare hands skimming up his chest. Allowing myself to explore his skin without any more barriers, as I'd wanted to for so very long. I slid my fingers up into his thick, perfect hair. It was just as soft and silken as I'd imagined. Leaning in, I whispered the words against his lips before I kissed him. And it wasn't half as scary as I thought it would be, saying it out loud.

In fact, it wasn't scary at all.

"I love you too, Cade."

The next morning, Cade brought me to the police station for what he called a "debrief" — which, upon arrival, I learned was basically just a meeting with Chief Coulter, Detective Aguilar, and two agents from the FBI field office in Boston.

Cade sat close by my side as I walked them through everything that had happened the day before. Occasionally, someone would cut in with a question or request a clarification but, for the most part, everyone simply listened. The only sound in the conference room was my voice, the faint patter of rain on the windows, and the light scratch of four pens unanimously jotting down notes.

When I was done, the Feds closed their notebooks, got to their feet, murmured their goodbyes, and left the room. I got the sense neither of them was particularly thrilled with my involvement, and were eager to get the hell out of Salem altogether.

Chief Coulter stood, but he didn't leave. He stared directly into my eyes and offered me his hand.

"Very grateful for your help, Miss Warner," he said solemnly, pumping my glove up and down in a vigorous handshake. "The force owes you a debt. The whole city does."

"Oh." I blinked in surprise. "I didn't do much."

"You did more than you had to. And, if you hadn't, Rory O'Banion might still be out there alone in the marshlands."

"I was happy to help, Chief Coulter."

"Good. Another case like this ever comes up, we'll need your help again." He finally released my hand. "You plan on sticking around?"

My eyes flickered briefly to Cade, who was fighting a grin. "Yes," I told Coulter. "I think I am."

Cade lost the fight against his grin.

"We'll give you a call if we have any follow up questions. We've still got units out there, searching the woods for the suspect. So far, there's no sign of her." The chief's gaze moved to the window, where cold rain was pelting the panes. The world outside was gray and dreary. "We'll keep looking," he murmured. "If she's out there, we'll find her."

I couldn't help thinking he didn't sound totally confident that they'd succeed in said search.

Detective Aguilar stood, drawing my gaze. Her expression was stern as ever, but her eyes were warm as they held mine.

"I heard about the Crawford case," she informed me bluntly. "Most people who've been burned like you were by the system wouldn't want to get involved in something like this. Not again. Had to be hard to trust that we wouldn't scapegoat you if this shit had ended differently."

I said nothing.

What could I say?

It *had* been hard.

"Frankly, I wouldn't have blamed you for telling us to go fuck ourselves," Aguilar continued.

Cade snorted.

"What I mean to say is... *thank you,*" she finished. "Thank you for working with us to bring that little boy home. Believe me, it will not be forgotten around here. Not by me, not by anyone in this station, not by anyone in this town."

With that, she filed out of the room, followed by Coulter. The second the door closed behind them, Cade nabbed me around the back of the neck and hauled me into his arms. His voice was warm, but soft.

"She's right, you know."

I said nothing. My throat felt thick.

"Proud of you, Imogen."

Tears prickled at the backs of my eyes.

I didn't say it.

But I was pretty proud of me, too.

CHAPTER TWENTY-SIX

Like my internet connection, I am occasionally unstable.
- Imogen Warner, attempting to connect to wifi

Our second "debrief" of the day was less official, in that it happened in the sleek downtown Gravewatch office instead of an actual police station, and the guest list included Florence and Gwen in addition to the bonafide investigators.

A pretty blonde receptionist named Brianne led Cade and me to the glass-walled meeting room in the back, with a prime view of Salem Harbor. Everyone was already there, waiting for us to arrive. Graham, Welles, Hunter, Holden, Sawyer… and a new man I'd never seen before.

I'd thought the Graves brothers were intense, but this guy… *Whew*. This guy made Graham, Holden, and Hunter look positively chill. He was tall, dark, and dangerous. Just standing there in the corner of the room, he exuded a magnetic energy that made it difficult to tear my eyes away. Gwen and Florence were both staring at him with blatant appreciation. I had to avert my eyes, afraid if I stared too long in his direction, I might drool.

"Coffee, anyone?" Brianne asked. Her eyes shifted restlessly between the twins and the man in the corner, as though she couldn't decide who was the most appealing of the three. "Keir? You want anything?"

Keir?

Of course the mega-hot guy had a mega-hot name.

None of the men said a word.

"Tea?" Brianne tried again. "Water?"

"We're good," Graham clipped at her from his spot at the head of the table. "Close the door on your way out, would you?"

Brianne physically cowed at the dismissal and practically bolted from the room.

I settled in at one of the empty seats, across from Florence. Cade dropped into the spot beside me.

"So?" he asked, eyes on Graham. "Where are we? Any progress?"

Graham flipped open the file folder that was laid out in front of him and tapped a finger against the top page. "Welles spent last night scouring old land records, trying to chase down who lived in that cabin. He can start us off."

I looked at the other end of the table, where Mr. Man-Bun himself was seated. He'd leaned all the way back in his chair, looking relaxed. But his hazel-gold eyes were alert. When they snagged on mine, he shot me a playful wink.

Cade scoffed.

Welles heard it. His lips twitched as he began. "Did some digging into old town zoning. The cabin where we found Rory was one of a whole string of other cabins just like it. Seasonal places, for the most part — no heat, no running water. Mostly used by local families for fishing and bird watching, from what I read in the official records. Some of them were razed to the ground back in the 1990s, but most of them were just left there to rot away."

"But why?" Florence interjected impatiently.

"In the early '80s, when the state laid those new railroad tracks through town, the road that led out there was cut off. The whole strip of salt-marsh became inaccessible. I guess they figured it was easier to relocate a few families than re-route the whole train."

I thought of the vintage car rusting on the dirt road that led to the cabin. Someone had left it there decades ago, and never come back for it.

"Is that legal?" Gwen asked, head tilted to one side. A long red tendril fell into her face. "How could the town just decide to cut off access?"

"It's called eminent domain," Graham explained, reaching over to tuck the tendril behind Gwen's ear. "Basically, the law gives the state the right to claim property — even private property — whenever they see fit, so long as they have proper justification. Happens more often than you'd think."

"So, the cabin was abandoned..." I murmured, mind racing. "What about the families who lived there? Is it possible someone stayed behind, even after the land was seized?"

"That's where our story takes an interesting turn," Welles said. His eyes flickered to Sawyer. "You want to take this part?"

All gazes snapped to the blond behemoth. His blue eyes were not piercing like Cade's. They were dazzling. Dreamy. It was like looking into a Van Gogh painting.

"Nope," he said succinctly.

Man of few words.

Got it.

Welles looked past Sawyer to the corner of the room, where Keir was leaning. "I know better than to even ask you to chime in."

Keir's only response was the slight curl of his mouth at one corner, lifting into a half-smirk.

Suddenly, my own mouth felt remarkably dry.

"*Wowza,*" I heard Florence whisper under her breath from across the table.

She could say that again.

Welles snorted, and our gazes swung back his way.

"Since no one else is feeling verbose..." He continued. "There were a few stories in the paper. Most of the families who were evicted were all too happy to take the money and run. But one or two tried to fight."

He cocked his chin toward Graham, who was in the process of pulling an old news clipping from the folder in front of him. He slid it across the table to Cade, and I leaned over to get a look at the bold black letters across the top.

HOPES DERAILED: SHRIVER FAMILY LOSES FIGHT AGAINST STATE IN EMINENT DOMAIN BATTLE

Beneath the headline, there was a photograph of what I could only assume was the Shriver family. A man, a woman, and one small child, all dressed in simple clothing, and standing in front of a familiar cottage. The little girl was no more than four or five years old. She was leaning back against her father's legs, holding her mother's hand. I stared at her tiny features, pixilated beyond recognition by the deteriorated paper. Her dark hair, long and wild even then.

My throat felt clogged.

"What is it?" Gwen asked, straining to see from across the table. "What does it say?"

Cade read the snippet of typeface printed beneath the photograph aloud, so everyone could hear.

"We've spent most of our savings on this legal battle," Mr. John Shriver told reporters, adding he was concerned his family has been rendered effectively homeless after the court's decision. "I don't know how we'll live. I don't know where we'll go. My family has been on this land since they came over on the Mayflower. We don't intend to just walk away from it."

His wife added the couple is especially concerned about their young daughter, if they have to start over somewhere new. "Our Marcie was born mute. She has a hard enough time communicating with us, with the people she knows around here," Mrs. Samara Shriver stated. "What will she do in an unfamiliar place? How will she get along in a big city? This is the only home she's ever known. This is the only place she feels comfortable. And you want us to take that away from her?"

When Cade fell silent, we all looked at one another. For a long moment, no one said a word.

"Couldn't find any records on the Shriver family after that," Welles said finally. "None of their daughter going to school. Nothing in the form of an address, a work history… Nothing. No death certificates for either of the parents, either. It's like they just vanished into the marsh."

We all contemplated that for a moment.

"Is it possible they never left?" Gwen finally asked, looking from Graham to Welles. "That's what you're saying here, isn't it? That this family stayed on their land, even after the state effectively cut off their resources?"

"Not saying that. But…" Graham sighed. "Not *not* saying it, either."

"There were signs of life in the cabin beyond just a transient shacking up for a few days," Welles said. "Camping equipment. Fishing rods. Casting nets and lobster traps. Some of it new, most of it old. All of it an eclectic mix of brands and styles." He paused. "My guess? Stolen, not purchased."

"It explains why the whispers started, that there was something in those woods," I murmured. "All those campers and hikers who claimed their packs were pilfered, their supplies picked over…"

"There was food in the cupboards," Cade added. "Good chunk of it was labeled SALEM PANTRY. Whoever lives there – or *lived* there – made free use of city resources."

"Volunteers often leave shipments at the encampment on the edge of town. Non-perishables, medical supplies…" Gwen nodded. "I've done it myself, on occasion. There are a lot of people in need."

Another short silenced descended over the room.

Flo, as usual, was the one who shattered it. "So, her parents die and she, just… what? Stays out there alone, all this time? In the wild?" She scowled. "I don't buy it. How could someone just slip through the cracks of society, without anyone ever noticing? We live in the age of technology! Constant surveillance!" She shook her head vigorously. "It's not possible. There's got to be another explanation."

I stared again at the little girl in the picture. I wasn't sure I was fully sold on her being the source of Salem's most infamous ghost story, but I *was* sure I disagreed with Florence.

It was absolutely possible to slip through the cracks in society.

People did it all the time.

I'd very nearly done it myself.

Just…

Disappeared.

No one to care. No one to look for me. No one to even know I was missing in the first place.

Before I came to Salem, I moved through life without making much of an impression. More ghost than girl. If my car hadn't broken down… if I'd never walked through the doors of The Gallows… if I'd never stepped foot in The Sea Witch…

I didn't even want to think about where I'd have ended up.

Certainly not in love with a strong, caring, selfless man. Certainly not with a group of crazy, funny, amazing friends.

Certainly not with a steady job in a cool-as-hell coffee-slash-book-slash-occult store. Certainly not with a puppy who was growing so fast, I could hardly keep up. Certainly not in a fixer-upper house in an adorable neighborhood that, with a little bit of TLC, would turn into a home.

"We'll keep digging," Welles said, calling me back to the present. "Not sure we'll find much of anything. But if there's more to find, we'll find it."

"It's a hard pill to swallow," Cade muttered. "All those days of searching, all that effort to catch the fucker who did this... and we've got nothing. No answers. Just a legend. And a forty-year-old paper trail that ends in a puff of smoke." His voice tightened. "The Feds are gone. Left town this morning and took their remaining interest in this case along with them. SPD will continue to search. But if our suspect has really lived out there in the backwoods for her whole life... I have a feeling it's going to be tough to find her. Not if she doesn't want to be found."

"Would it be so bad if you didn't?" I asked.

Everyone looked at me.

I fought the urge to cower under the weight of so many intense stares. "I just mean... She didn't really do anything criminal, or even bad. She was trying to help Rory when he hurt his ankle. Her actions weren't malicious."

"Tell that to Annie Thurman," Flo muttered.

"What happened to Annie..." I shook my head. "I don't know. I think she's mixed up. I think... no one ever tried to help her work through what she saw out there. Her parents abandoned her. They threw money at the problem, thinking that would fix it. And when it didn't, they stuck her in a fancy care facility for two decades."

Everyone was silent, contemplating that.

The meeting fizzled out not long after. The was no big moment of consensus. No satisfying conclusion to reach. We all got up and went our separate ways, each battling with the uneasy realization that this was not a Hollywood ending.

In real life, not every case is tied up neatly with a satin bow. But I figured, at the end of the day, even if we never found out exactly what had happened in those woods, we'd already been given the best possible outcome.

Rory was home.

Safe.

Alive.

Seemingly no worse for wear.

That was more than I'd dared hope for, this same time yesterday. And I planned to take that as a win, no matter how it came.

The Gravewatch men dispersed to their various duties — surveillance, skip-chasing, security, and whatever else badass private investigators did to merit charging such exorbitant hourly fees. Judging by their swanky offices, they weren't hurting for cash flow. The building was located on Pickering Wharf, a busy area of restaurants, shops, and offices crammed onto a narrow, one-way-traffic loop that overlooked the docks. Prime real estate.

The limited parking was its only downside. Since it was pouring rain, Cade went to get the car while I waited under the front awning with Gwen and Florence. He'd parked in an open spot down the block.

Gwen opened her fancy black umbrella with a flourish. "All right, ladies, I'm heading back to the store. I left Agatha and Sally there unsupervised," she said worriedly. When our eyes met, she arched an auburn brow in question. "See you tomorrow, Imogen?"

She wasn't just asking as a boss trying to lock down an employee. She was asking because she was worried that, now that the case was wrapped up and my car was fixed, I was going to high-tail it out of town without leaving a forwarding address. She wanted me to stick around Salem — and not just for a handful of shifts.

"See you tomorrow, boss," I assured her, smiling. "You know,

I'm thinking of redecorating Zelda's space. Making it my own, since I'll be around a while… Getting some personalized appointment cards…"

Her eyes twinkled. "Good."

"I'm heading over to The Sea Witch to check on Gigi, Rory, and Declan," Florence cut in. "You want to come with, Imogen?"

"I do. But can we go later this afternoon? I need to go home for a bit first. Socks is in desperate need of a bath."

"Listen to her! Calling Cade's house *home*." Flo squealed and grabbed my arm. "I love this!"

"Me too!" Gwen squealed.

I couldn't help joining in with a squeal of my own. "Me three!"

"Get in the car, dollface."

We all jolted at the sudden intrusion into our squeal-fest. My head swung sideways and I felt all the blood leave my face. There, standing in the pouring rain, his expensive suit getting wetter and wetter with each passing second, was Adrian.

He was holding a gun.

And he was pointing it straight at me.

Damn and blast.

"Adrian, what the hell?" I snapped, staring at him. My primary emotion probably should've been fear, but all I felt in that moment was annoyance.

"*This* is Adrian?" Flo asked.

"Your asshole ex-boyfriend Adrian?" Gwen added.

"*Idiot* ex-boyfriend Adrien," I corrected. "Based on recent events."

"Shut up!" His hand tightened on my arm and he started dragging me toward the curb, where his Ferrari was idling. It was blocking the flow of traffic down the one-way street. People were beginning to honk as the cars piled up behind it, crowding the busy wharf.

"Where do you think you're going?" Florence cried. "You can't just take Imogen! Are you crazy?"

"I'm leaving," Adrian snapped. "And I'm taking Imogen with me. We have unfinished business."

Normally, I might've formulated a retort. Seeing as there was a cold gun-barrel pressed tight to my temple, I chose to remain silent at this particular juncture.

Florence was less inclined toward silence. "You are one dumb fuck."

Adrian froze solid with one foot on the curb, the other planted in a rapidly deepening puddle. "Excuse me?"

"You heard me! You are," she hissed, annunciating every word so he couldn't fail to understand she meant them sincerely. "*One. Dumb. Fuck*. Seriously. Don't you realize where you are right now?"

Adrian said nothing. His grip on my arm tightened to the point of pain, and I couldn't quite hide my grimace.

Where was Cade when I needed him?

Where were the badass boys in the office?

Gwen bobbed her thumb backward at the glass window, which was etched with the word GRAVEWATCH in super-sleek font. "This is the best private investigation firm in the state," she said flatly, still clutching her fancy umbrella. "I would let her go, unless you want them on your ass."

"I don't fucking care!" Adrian snarled. He started moving again, yanking me backward toward the driver's side of the Ferrari. I didn't fight him. The gun barrel was still pressed hard to my temple.

Adrian released my arm, but only so he could grab the door handle and pull it open.

"Get in," he ordered.

I didn't move.

"Get. In." The gun bit into my skin. "*Now*."

I got in.

I had to scramble over the center console — no easy feat, the Ferrari interior was ultra-compact — to the passenger side. As soon as I was clear, Adrian slid into the driver's seat. I only had a few seconds to glance out the window at Flo and Gwen before we rocketed away from the curb. But my heart lurched inside my chest when I saw the glass door to Gravewatch fly open as Graham, Welles, and Keir flew out of it, into the rain. They looked at our fleeing taillights for approximately three seconds, then started sprinting after us.

Oh boy.

"Fuck, fuck, fuck," Adrian chanted under his breath, eyes on the rearview mirror. He'd seen the legion of badasses, too.

"Adrian, this is a bad idea."

"Shut up!" He screamed at me. "Just shut the fuck up!"

I shut up.

My heart gave another lurch as we swung abruptly off the one-way loop around Pickering Wharf, onto a main road. The second we did, I saw red and blue strobes light up the unmarked black SUV that pulled into traffic behind us.

Cade.

"*FUCK*!" Adrian shouted over the sudden drone of the sirens.

"I told you it was a bad idea."

"And I told you to shut up!"

Suddenly, I didn't feel like shutting up.

Suddenly, I was feeling pretty freaking pissed.

"You know, Adrian, I've had about enough of this."

He glanced over at me like I was nuts.

"I mean... *Really*?" I scoffed without humor. "You're kidnapping me? *Kidnapping me?* It wasn't enough that you beat me? That you used me? That you made me feel like a freak every day we were together? That you forced me to pack up in the middle of the night and *flee the freaking state?*" I shook my head in disbelief. "No.

Apparently not. Because here you are. Fucking up my life, yet again!"

"You're the one who—"

"I am not done," I cut him off. "You are a waste of my time. You are a waste of my energy. You were nothing but an anchor around my ankles, keeping me down. And when I left, I cut you loose."

"Dollface—"

"I came here. And I found people who aren't an anchor. They don't hold me down. They lift me up. They support me. They don't want to use me for money or manipulate me for profit. They've cared about me more in nine freaking *days* than you did in *nine goddamned months.*"

He made a hairpin turn, teeth gritting together as his temper rose. "You can't just—"

"Do you see that cop car behind us?" I cut him off again. "The man I love is behind the wheel. He's coming for me. He will always come for me. Because he's loyal. He's selfless. He's also sweet and he's kind and, I would be remiss not to mention, he's a fucking god in bed. *Way* better than you ever were."

"I'm dynamite in bed!"

"If you could locate the clitoris, or actually cared whether or not your partner finished... I'm sure that might be true. *Maybe.* Alas..."

He took a wild turn and, like the machismo idiot he was, accelerated through it instead of braking. The Ferrari's tires skidded through a deep puddle. We started to fishtail. I screamed, sure we were about to careen out of control. Adrian spun the wheel at the last second, straightening us out before we could fully hydroplane.

"You're going to get us killed!" I screeched at him when we were once again racing down a straightaway on solid asphalt.

"If I go back to A.C. without you, I might as well be dead!" he yelled back. His dark, sultry eyes were wild. Frantic. "Viggo will fucking kill me if I don't square up with him!"

"Not my problem."

"It *is* your problem! You're the one who bailed on the residency!"

Christ.

I was *so* not about to have this fight with him for the umpteenth time. I glanced around, trying to spot Cade through the rear windshield. Three SPD cruisers had joined the pursuit, flanking his dark SUV. Behind them, I thought I spotted Graham's black Ford Bronco, bringing up the rear.

Adrian took another turn — too sharp, too fast. My neck spasmed with whiplash as I was flung bodily across the cab, into the side door. My head cracked against the window, hard enough that I saw stars. When I'd blinked most of them away, I belatedly grabbed my seatbelt and clicked it into place.

"Adrian," I said, trying to breathe through my mounting panic. "Please slow down."

He was beyond listening. "We were good together. You know we were, doll. We can be good again. You'll see. We'll get back home, and I'll fix it. I'll fix everything."

"It's too late."

"Don't say that!" He gripped the wheel tighter and jammed his foot against the gas, accelerating us to twice the legal limit. We were flying down the road, now. Running red lights, weaving through lanes.

If he kept this up, we were going to crash.

Cade and the others had fallen back slightly. Eased their pursuit. Perhaps they realized the close tail was only exacerbating the problem. But it wasn't enough. Even without the sirens breathing down our neck, Adrian was driving with a recklessness that terrified me.

"Adrian…" I tried again. "Slow down. Please."

"It doesn't have to be this way! Don't you get it?"

"Put on your seatbelt at least."

"Don't act like you care about me!" He swerved around a slow-moving car in the left lane, bringing us into oncoming traffic in order to pass. "If you'd just—"

He didn't see the truck.

I saw it, but that didn't do me much good. I wasn't the one holding the wheel. My feet weren't the ones on the pedals.

The box truck turned into traffic, and we struck it directly in the side. Adrian managed to whip the wheel to the right as we collided, which prevented us from being fully crushed under about a dozen wheels, but wasn't enough to save us. We scraped along the flank of the truck with a metallic groan and a shower of sparks, then hurtled toward the side of the road. The Ferrari nearly flipped as we hit the curb and flew up onto the sidewalk.

By the grace of god alone, we came back down on all four wheels before we slammed into a telephone pole. The front of the sports car folded in on itself like an accordion. I felt the seatbelt knife across my chest as the airbag exploded into my face. My head snapped forward on impact, leaving me dazed. When I looked over to see how Adrian was doing…

My stomach dropped straight to the pavement.

His body was crunched up against the steering wheel. His face was battered, blood dripping from his nose. His airbag had deployed, but it was already mostly deflated. I couldn't tell if he was breathing. He was either out cold or…

I didn't want to think about the other possibility.

Before I'd even had a chance to fully recover, the passenger door was being ripped open. Cade was there. He used a pocket knife to deflate my airbag with one smooth jab, then he was crouched beside me, running his hands up and down my extremities to ensure I wasn't seriously injured.

"Are you okay?" he asked, his gorgeous eyes brimming over with worry.

"I think so," I managed to rasp.

"Are you bleeding anywhere? Does anything hurt?"

"No. I'm fine, Cade." I sucked in a breath. "Is Adrian—"

His jaw went tight as his eyes moved behind me. He shook his head. "Not looking great. I called the ambulance on the way, they were trailing me. They're pulling up now. They'll do what they can for him."

My eyes pressed closed.

Damn it to hell.

I hated Adrian.

He was a total asshole.

But that didn't mean I wanted things to end this way.

Cade pulled back to allow the paramedics to examine me. After feeling my neck to make sure I didn't have a spinal injury, they guided me gently out of the car and toward a waiting stretcher. Behind me, two of their colleagues worked to free Adrian. I was relieved when I heard him gasping for air and responding to verbal cues as they loaded him onto a stretcher of his own, his neck stabilized in a stiff brace.

He was alive.

Lucky bastard.

Cade held my hand as they loaded me onto the stretcher. He squeezed tight. I'd never seen him look so serious.

"Cade, honey. Think of it this way. Now you don't have to kill him. You can arrest him for attempted kidnapping instead. Win win."

His lips didn't even twitch.

He was not in a joking mood.

"Honey, I'm *fine,*" I assured him. "Really. I'm okay."

He didn't say anything. Just continued to grip my hand like, if he let go, I'd disappear.

I looked at one of the paramedics. "Um. Hi. Do you think this is going to take very long? Because, at home, my puppy is covered in mud and he really needs a bath if he's going to sleep on my feet tonight."

"Oh." The paramedic shook her head, looking confused. "I'm…

not exactly sure." She glanced at her colleague and lowered her voice a few decibels. "Let's do a neuro exam. Just to be safe."

That made Cade chuckle.

Rude.

They were wheeling me toward a waiting ambulance when I glanced over and saw a small crowd of onlookers had gathered on the sidewalk to watch the drama unfold. At the front of the group, there was a woman around my age, dressed in a mossy green dress. Her hair was plaited into about a zillion braids. Her ears were concealed by pointy prosthetics. And a pair of intricate wings were hooked over her shoulders, fluttering in the damp November breeze.

"Oh my god!" I yelled, delighted to see her. "*Moonbeam!*"

Her eyes shifted from me to the Ferrari and back again. "Girl... You have some *seriously* shitty luck with cars."

I nodded in agreement. "Don't I know it."

EPILOGUE

THREE MONTHS LATER

"I'm just saying," Florence whispered under her breath. "I like him. I think they'd be good together."

"If you push her, she'll never go for it," I whispered back.

We were hiding behind a large house plant, staring surreptitiously across the crowded room at Georgia, who was chatting with one of Desmond's colleagues at the university. He was cute. He'd made her laugh twice in the past ten minutes they'd been talking. He was a professor of economics, a recent divorcee, and (according to Des) one of the nicest men he'd met in his life.

We were hoping like hell he'd ask Gigi out to dinner. If anyone on planet earth deserved a nice guy, it was her.

"What are we talking about?" Gwen interrupted, appearing beside Florence. She was holding three shot glasses of clear liquor. Tequila, judging by the smell wafting off the tops.

"Georgia and Professor Potential over there, flirting up a storm." Flo grinned and snatched one of the shot glasses. "Cheers to love!"

We clinked our glasses against hers. As we did, my eyes

snagged on the shiny, vintage engagement ring resting at the base of her fourth finger. Desmond had popped the question on New Year's Eve. Tonight, all of their closest friends and family had gathered to celebrate the news. (Gwen had volunteered to host at her house, which had recently wrapped up its extensive renovations.)

The happy couple was planning to make it official next summer. I was a bridesmaid, something I'd never been before, but probably would need to get used to, based on the way things were going. I had a feeling Gwen and Graham would be tying the knot within the year. They weren't yet engaged, but the way they looked at one another…

That kind of love was the forever kind.

It was evident in every facet of this house. The house Graham had fixed up, floorboards to ceiling panels, for Gwen. The house Gwen had decorated, with ultimate care and consideration, for Graham. The house they'd together made into a home. The finished product was truly stunning, all traces of renovation tools and painting supplies long gone, all remnants of their efforts tucked out of sight.

I downed my shot, blinking the tears from my eyes as it burned down my throat. I'd barely had a chance to set my empty glass down on the side table when Rory came running up to me, his socks skidding on the shiny hardwood floor.

"Imogen! Did you know there's a room upstairs that looks just like a library?"

I grinned down at him. "Yeah, bub. I did."

"Oh." He looked a little crestfallen.

I dropped into a crouch and ruffled his hair. My voice lowered to a conspiratorial whisper. "Did *you* know there's a deck off the library with a telescope for star-gazing?"

His hazel eyes widened. "Seriously?"

"Seriously." I grinned wider. "Go check it out. You can probably spot Pluto."

I'd hardly stopped speaking before he set off in a blur of motion.

He'd rebounded from the events of the fall remarkably well. No darkness lingered. No traces of trauma, though I knew Georgia still worried. She would likely *always* worry, for the rest of her life.

I didn't blame her. There'd been no real resolution when it came to the case. The so-called Witch of Salem Wood had never been found — not by police, not by Gravewatch, not even by the eager urban-legend chasers and true-crime podcasters who'd poured into town in the aftermath of Rory's rescue, hoping for some thrilling content they could exploit for cash.

If she was still out there somewhere, she had no intentions of being brought back to civilization.

The media fervor would die down eventually. As for the ghost story, though… The whole incident had breathed new life into an old mystery. I had a feeling Salem's youth would be whispering the rhyme about the voice-stealing witch for decades to come.

Initially, we'd all been concerned the rabid public interest would prevent Rory from moving on with his life. But, so far as I could tell, he was fine.

He was resilient.

Just like his mom.

I was unbelievably grateful for that. After seeing what the same experience did to Annie Thurman, I knew things could've ended differently. I'd visited her at Oak Grove several more times over the past few months, but had made little progress in sorting through her chaotic mind-scape. Her doctors were planning to scale back her medications, which I was hopeful might induce more clarity in the future.

Even if it didn't, though, I would keep visiting. Keep trying. Talking to her. Sometimes, just sitting with her. Last week, I'd brought her a piece of Sally's cheesecake and actually gotten a smile in return. One that reached her eyes. Next week, I was going to bring Agatha along with me. (The healing powers of canasta knew no bounds.)

I watched Rory race across the room to catch up with his brother, a happy flutter inside my gut. He and Declan were closer than ever. The incident had brought them together, an unanticipated side effect of the four-day separation. He'd even grown to like living at The Sea Witch, he'd confided to me just last week when I swung by for dinner.

He moved so fast, he collided with Cade, who was standing by the door embroiled in a conversation with Agatha and Sally. Judging by the tightness of his jaw, they were probably inviting him to dance naked beneath the moonlight on Imbolic.

He was a firm *no* on that particular RSVP.

(Me, Gwen, Florence, and Gigi, however, were a definitive *yes*.)

When Rory crashed into Cade, he dropped a hand onto the boy's shoulder to steady him. Leaning down to catch his eyes, he said something that made both of them laugh.

"He'll make a good dad," Florence whispered.

I jolted and glanced back at her. She and Gwen were both watching me with soft, hopeful expressions.

"Yeah," I said, somewhat stiffly. Trying not to panic. "He certainly will."

They traded a glance.

"So, Flo," I hastily changed the subject. "Is your engagement party everything you dreamed of and more?"

"It better be after all the effort I put in," Gwen muttered lowly. "The flowers alone... Who wants fresh orchids in February?"

Flo rolled her eyes. "You're the maid of honor, not the maid of guilt trips. And I offered to reimburse you for the orchids!"

"You know it's not about the money!" Gwen's lips pursed. "It's about the five florists who laughed at me like I was a crazy person when I called."

"I've told you a thousand times, Gwennie, the trick is if you just keep talking, you can wear almost anyone down," Flo said sagely. "Eventually, you break their spirit. They'll do whatever you want."

Gwen heaved a sigh. "Remind me, when I get married, to make Imogen in charge of all florist and food vendor interactions."

"Oh?" Flo snorted. "Are you getting married? Has Graham proposed, and you've failed to tell us?"

Gwen shot her a glare. "Now you're *definitely* not in the wedding party."

"Oooh, tragedy!" She snapped back sarcastically. "How will I live without having to stuff my boobs into an unflattering coral dress?"

"As if I'd ever make you wear coral!" Gwen half-screeched. "With my auburn hair? It would clash like crazy in all the pictures!"

I decided to wade in before their tiff could escalate to a full-blown spat over hypothetical dress colors in a hypothetical wedding.

"Gwen, I meant to tell you earlier this week — the new hires are doing great! I really like them both. I think they're ready to start taking shifts without you there to supervise, if you need a day off."

Just before the holiday season, Gwen had hired on two college students to help out around The Gallows. One, I was happy to discover, was the pimply-faced freshman I'd met on Halloween, who'd dressed up as Han Solo and complimented our witchy costumes. His name was Arthur. He was consistently hilarious. (And consistently five minutes late for his shifts, but no one was perfect.)

The other hire was a quiet girl I'd yet to make crack a smile, despite numerous attempts. Her name was Kenna. Not only was she consistently five minutes *early* for her shifts, she also always stayed late to help with inventory. Kenna was a bit of a mystery, but I knew no one could remain immune to the strange gravity of Salem for long. We'd pull her into the fold at some point.

"They really are great, aren't they?" Gwen grinned. "I'm glad. Graham and I are finally going away on a long-overdue vacation next month. It'll be a relief to know the store is in such great hands." To underscore this point, she reached down, grabbed my gloved fingers, and squeezed.

My heart panged. "Where are you and Graham going?"

"The British Virgin Islands."

"Whatever you do, don't have beach sex," Flo muttered. "You'll wind up with sand in places sand should *never* be. Trust me on that."

Swallowing a laugh, I ignored Flo. "You guys deserve a break in the sunshine. How warm will it be?"

"Warmer than New England, that's for sure. Two weeks of bikinis and blender drinks." Gwen's eyes were brimming with excitement, but a shade of guilt crept in. "Don't worry, though. I'll have my phone with me in case you need me while I'm gone—"

I shook my head. "I won't."

"But—"

"I've got it, Gwen. The store basically runs itself. I can easily handle the inventory orders, plus my client list for a few weeks."

Though, it must be said, my client list was growing bigger and bigger every day. Since I'd arrived in October, I'd built a steady stable of regulars. I was booking months in advance, these days — and raking in enough tips to keep Socks in stuffed squeaky toys for the next decade.

Not that I needed the money.

I didn't even need to work, anymore — not if I didn't want to. The death of my uncle had opened up a whole wide world of financial possibility.

After years of scraping by, living in mildewed motel rooms and scrimping to afford the basic necessities, it was nice not to have to read price labels at the grocery store. No more guilt trips over buying clothes for myself — new clothes, not thrifted ones I had to tailor.

Admittedly, I did still enjoy the occasional afternoon of thrifting. Whenever I hit the local stores, Gwen was an eager shopping partner, helping me find my style. Under her expert tutelage, my half of Cade's closet was now stocked full of new dresses, pants, shoes, shorts, and sweaters.

Cade's closet.

He'd be mad if he heard me calling it that. He was constantly correcting me.

Our closet, beautiful. This is your home, too.

I'd officially agreed to move in after the Adrian kidnapping attempt. It was probably too fast, and probably seemed insane to most people... but to me, there was no point in putting off the inevitable. The fact of the matter was, I loved Cade. I wanted to be with him. Not just temporarily — forever. There was no doubt in my mind we were eventually going to live together. Delaying that move felt arbitrary to both of us.

So, I moved in.

Though, sometimes, I still had sleepovers at The Sea Witch with Gigi, just for old time's sake. Lord knows I wasn't about to drive after indulging in her limoncello. Especially not in my fancy new wheels.

Last month, Puck had set me up with one of his souped-up, special-edition luxury models. It had a zillion features — *zero to sixty in two-point-eight seconds!* — but I didn't really care about that. All I knew was, it was black, it was sleek, it went *fast,* and it never broke down. It was the first big purchase I'd made, after getting access to my bank accounts. A celebration, of sorts, to close out that drawn-out saga.

I would've liked to sort out the mess that was my uncle's estate over the phone, but quickly learned that would not be possible. I had to go to Florida in person, provide several forms of identification, and make multiple sworn statements to the stern bank officers that I was not, in fact, a grifter trying to impersonate one Imogen Warner, and was, in actuality, the real Imogen Warner with the documents to prove it.

I'd flown down to Orlando in late November, just before the Thanksgiving holiday. I hadn't been back to Florida since I left ten years prior. I'd insisted I would be fine going by myself. That it was a long time ago, and I could manage on my own. Still, I'd never been more glad to have Cade Hightower's warm hand laced with mine as that plane touched down on the tarmac.

He spent four days helping me sort through the financial stuff, getting my uncle's gaudy mansion listed for sale with a shark of a realtor, and helping me dig through the storage unit his "contact" had found by snooping through the estate records.

It was at the outskirts of town, in a creepy industrial park I wouldn't have felt safe visiting on my own. Cade snapped the padlock off with a pair of bolt cutters and heaved up the rolling door so we could enter. I hadn't known what to expect.

Dead bodies?

More financial statements of secret accounts?

Thousands of VHS tapes of my *Child Clairvoyant* episodes, recorded for posterity?

Instead, inside I found a time capsule of my life from ages zero to five. My life before my uncle came into the picture. My life with my parents.

It was all there. The pictures — in gilded frames and thick books and paper pharmacy envelopes. In undeveloped rolls of film. In stacks and boxes. Pressed between book pages. Blown up on canvases. So many photos, it would take a lifetime to get through them all.

Mom and Dad, young and in love, on the beach with their toes in the sand.

Mom sitting at the chipped kitchen table, a look of concentration on her face as she flipped tarot cards from a familiar deck.

Dad chopping wood in the backyard, axe in hand.

Mom and Dad on their wedding day.

Mom standing by the window in their first apartment, heavily pregnant.

And me.

So many photos of me.

In their arms, on their shoulders. With pink ribbons in my hair and cake frosting on my fingers. In diner booths eating French fries. At Disney World waiting in line to ride the spinning teacups.

They'd documented everything. And, as I sat on the cold floor of the storage unit flipping through picture after picture, the watercolored shades of my old memories, so faded and weak, filled in with vibrant new life. A riot of new color I'd never, ever forget.

In the unit, there were other things, too. Things I was surprised my uncle had kept. Sentimental items from his own childhood, when he and my father were just boys. I supposed, some part of him had loved his brother, once. Before he was charged with the raising of his niece. Before he was twisted by greed and narcissism.

I'd taken several photo books with me when we finally left. The rest, it would take more than a few days to sort through — physically and emotionally. And, for the time being, I was eager to get back to Salem. Back home. I had clients waiting for me. I had friends. I had a puppy, left in the questionable care of one Florence Lambert.

I was ready to leave Florida behind.

This time, on my terms.

Cade had one final surprise up his sleeve before we hopped on the plane. He'd driven us to Disney World on the last day of our trip. We'd walked around, hand in hand, taking in the sights. Riding rides, snapping photos. Like any ordinary couple. But ordinary fell away the moment he brought me over to the gift shop, where he purchased something that made my eyes sting.

A snow globe.

Inside it sat Cinderella's castle. And when you shook it in your hands… Sparkles fluttered through the water, a starburst of vibrant purple. Just like the one I'd treasured as a child.

It was the most thoughtful gift I'd ever received.

(Besides, perhaps, a faded Baltimore Ravens sweatshirt.)

Now that we were back home, that snow globe sat on my nightstand. I looked at it every night before I fell asleep in Cade's arms, feeling like the luckiest woman who'd ever lived.

"Imogen!" Declan's yell called my gaze toward the stairs, where he and Rory were peering out at me from between the banister rungs. "You've got to come up and try the telescope!"

"Give me a minute, space-invaders!" I called back. "I'll be right there!"

Their footsteps pounded up the stairs, a cacophony. Gigi heard it. Our eyes snagged across the room and she smiled at me. Her eyes were warm. She looked happier than I could ever recall seeing her since we'd met back in the fall. Her gaze left me when the cute professor appeared back at her side, extending out a fresh glass of white wine for her.

"She looks happy," a voice murmured in my ear.

I whipped around, startled to see Cade standing close by. I hadn't even heard him approach. "I think she is. And she deserves to be, after everything she's been through."

He nodded.

Georgia O'Banion had endured a lot, these past few months. Between Rory's disappearance and the brutal divorce battle against Donny that followed, it was more weight than any one woman should've had to bear on her shoulders. But now… she was finally free.

Free and clear.

I knew the feeling.

It was a good one.

"You want them?" Cade asked, out of nowhere.

"Want what?"

"Kids." His chin dipped toward the stairs, where Rory and

Declan had stood only moments before. "Do you want them? We've never really talked about it."

My lips parted as I expelled a large gust of wind. "Um…"

"Breathe, Goldie. No wrong answers, here."

God, this man.

He was so good.

Sometimes, I still caught myself thinking I didn't deserve him. Then again, after everything I'd been through… maybe I did. Maybe a man like Cade Hightower was my reward for all the darkness. The final stop on the Imogen Warner International Tour of Misery.

If he was the end game…

He made all the previous stops worth it.

"I'm not sure," I blurted, cheeks aflame. "I never thought I wanted them. Not because I don't like kids. I just… I never thought I *could* want them. You know? I never thought I'd ever settle down long enough."

His eyes softened. "But you're settled."

"I guess I am."

His pause was careful. He didn't want to push me into anything. "And now that you are?"

I thought about it. I didn't think for long; I didn't have to. The answer was right there, staring me in the face, as I thought about my future.

"Now…" I whispered. "I'm thinking kids would be good."

His eyes flared with emotion. "Yeah?"

I nodded. "Yeah."

"How many?"

How many?

I blinked. "I don't know. How many do you want?"

"As many as you'll give me."

That was a freaking good answer.

A freaking *great* answer.

"Sounds perfect," I whispered, lifting up onto my tiptoes.

He met me halfway, stooping down to claim my lips in a long, lingering kiss. The kind that stole my breath and made my stomach somersault like an Olympic gymnast.

Just the way I liked it.

When the party broke up, Cade and I were two of the last to leave. If I had to guess, Sally and Agatha would be the final stragglers. They knew how to close out a shindig. Gigi had left hours ago with the boys — driven home to The Sea Witch by none other than the handsome professor. (Much to our collective delight.)

Gwen and Graham stood in the doorway, waving goodbye as we all filed down their front steps. Flo and Des lead the way. Agatha and Sally brought up the rear. I was sandwiched somewhere in the middle between Cade and Sawyer, trying not to trip after downing one too many shots of tequila.

We all spotted the moving truck at the same time. It was difficult to miss, parked in front of Gwen's historic center-front Colonial, hazard lights flashing as its contents were unloaded by several burly men.

Scratch that.

It wasn't parked in front of Gwen's. It was actually in front of the stunning Victorian next door. The movers were schlepping boxes down the gangplank, up the walk, into the house. Their muscles strained under the weight. I couldn't help noticing that most of the boxes said BOOKS on the sides in thick black sharpie.

Hmm.

Overseeing the move-in process was a woman around my age, with dark hair swept up into a messy bun atop her head and thick-framed, nerdy glasses perched on the tip of her ski-slope nose. She was toting a box of her own, this one labeled PRIORITY. Her fingers were even more ink stained than Desmond's.

Double hmmm.

"Take the ones marked 'books' into the office, if you don't mind," she told her movers. She had a low, sultry voice made for radio broadcasts. "Sorry they're so heavy... and that there are so many of them..."

With my head averted to the left, I wasn't looking where I was walking. Thus, I nearly fell down on my ass as I bumped straight into the solid wall that was Sawyer. The towering blond had stopped smack in the center of the walk, boots planted on the pavestones. His dreamy blue eyes were fixed on the woman next door, and he looked like—

I didn't know what he looked like.

Frankly, I didn't know him all that well. Like most of the Gravewatch men, he rarely said more than three words at a time. But his expression was intense as it locked on the brunette next door, and it did not shift away. Not even for a second. His eyes were fixed on her like a tractor beam.

What was that all about?

Before I could ask, Sawyer spoke. He only said one word, but the voice he said it in was hoarse with disbelief.

"Skye?"

At the sound of her name, the girl turned. Her eyes swept across the group, moving quickly over Flo, Des, me, Cade, Agatha, and Sally... before she spotted Sawyer.

At which point, she blanched.

Completely.

All the blood drained out of her face in one heartbeat, leaving her pale as a ghost. Her hands went limp with shock. The box slipped out of her grip. It hit the pavestones, exploding on impact. Rolled reams of thick, weathered parchment flew out the top. They looked like charts of some kind.

"Sawyer?"

His frame went tight as she gasped out his name, sounding thready with panic. He took two steps closer to the fence that divided her property from Gwen's and clipped, "What the fuck are you doing here?"

Color hit her cheeks — nearly as red as the frames of her glasses. But she managed to swallow down her mortification as she narrowed her eyes at him.

"I live here," she said stiffly. "What are *you* doing here?"

He just stared at her. He didn't answer her question. Instead, he asked one of his own.

"There a reason why you never fucking called me back?"

Triple hmmm.

The woman's cheeks got even redder.

Sawyer took two more steps, bringing his body straight up to the fence. His voice dropped lower, but I could still make out his words.

"There a reason you snuck out that morning without a fucking word?"

That morning?!

What morning?!

"It's complicated," the girl — Skye — said weakly.

Sawyer, for the record, did not look happy with this answer. But before he could say anything else, she bent down, snatched her fallen maps from where they'd rolled across the walk, and stuffed them back into the top of her PRIORITY box. Then, with a panicked sweep of her eyes across the lot of us, she turned and ran — yes, *ran* — into her new house and shut the door.

We all turned, as a unit, to look at Sawyer.

His jaw was clenched.

"How do you know Skye?" Desmond asked, blithely unaware of the tension.

Sawyer's eyes went flinty as his head swung slowly toward the professor. "How do *you* know her?"

"Oh. Err… She just started working with me at the university." Des shrugged. "She's cool."

Sawyer's eyes went even flintier.

"Of course she's cool," Agatha boomed, loud enough to make us all jump. "She's a Proctor. I knew her grandmother. Cool is in her genetics."

"It's good she's finally moving in," Sally murmured. "We need to keep an eye on her…"

"Seems like someone already is," Flo said, staring at Sawyer.

His teeth ground together in annoyance. With one last, scathing look at the house next door, he stalked down the walk, crossed the street, and disappeared into the night.

Curiouser and curiouser…

A hand hit the small of my back, warm and strong. I looked up at Cade and smiled.

"Take me home, Hero-Hair."

"You got it, Goldie."

We waved one final goodbye to our friends. Then, I slid onto the back of Cade's sleek black motorcycle, wound my arms tight around his middle, and held on as he drove me across town.

Back to Socks, who had doubled in size and now took up the vast majority of our bed at night.

Back to our shingled fixer-upper on Juniper Point.

Back home.

THE END

NEXT UP...

Stay tuned for more details on **WORST LAID PLANS**, Book Three in the Witch City series, an opposites-attract romance starring Sawyer and Skye. (And the whole Salem crew!)

PLAYLIST

1. *Lonely Hearts Club (Stripped)* — Winona Oak
2. *Next Life* — ROSIE
3. *Survive My Own Mind* — Ashley Kutcher
4. *Wrongside* — MisterWives
5. *Chronically Cautious* — Braden Bales
6. *Kill the Sun* — Motherfolk
7. *I Can See You (Taylor's Version)* — Taylor Swift
8. *The Bottom* — Gracie Abrams
9. *Bleeding Out* — Chance Peña
10. *Let Me Go* — Benson Boone
11. *Antichrist* — Holly Humberstone
12. *Piano In The Sky* — Winona Oak
13. *When It Ends* — Avery Lynch (feat. JORDY)
14. *Oat Milk* — Sydney Rose
15. *My Love Mine All Mine* — Mitski
16. *All Of The Girls You Loved Before* — Taylor Swift
17. *Your Bones* — Chelsea Cutler
18. *True Love Will Find You In The End* — Headless Heroes
19. *All Through the Night* — Sleeping At Last

About the Author

JULIE JOHNSON is a New England native and internationally bestselling author. When she's not writing, Julie can most often be found adding stamps to her passport, drinking too much coffee, and avoiding reality by disappearing between the pages of a book.

She published her debut novel on a lark, just before her senior year of college, and she's never looked back. Since, she has published twenty other novels, which have been translated into more than a dozen different languages and appeared on bestseller lists all over the world, including Der Spiegel, AdWeek, Publishers Weekly, USA Today, and more.

You can connect with Julie on her Instagram (@author_julie), in her natural habitat (the bookstore), or on her website (www.juliejohnsonbooks.com).

For major book news and updates, subscribe to subscribe to JJ's newsletter.

Connect with Julie:
www.juliejohnsonbooks.com
juliejohnsonbooks@gmail.com

ALSO BY JULIE JOHNSON

STANDALONE NOVELS:

LIKE GRAVITY

SAY THE WORD

FOREIGN AFFAIRS

UNCHARTED

THE BOSTON LOVE STORIES:

NOT YOU IT'S ME

CROSS THE LINE

ONE GOOD REASON

TAKE YOUR TIME

SO WRONG IT'S RIGHT

THE GIRL DUET:

THE MONDAY GIRL

THE SOMEDAY GIRL

THE FADED DUET:

FADED: PART ONE

FADED: PART TWO

THE FORBIDDEN ROYALS TRILOGY:

SILVER CROWN

GOLDEN THRONE

DIAMOND EMPIRE

THE ANYMORE DUET:

WE DON'T TALK ANYMORE

WE DON'T LIE ANYMORE

THE WITCH CITY SERIES:

BAD LUCK CHARM

AT LAST SIGHT

Made in United States
North Haven, CT
18 May 2024

52674442R00274